P9-CDA-488

**Bruton Memorial Library
Plant City, Florida**

Donated by
Plant City High School
Class of 1954

in memory of

**ANN LUNEBERG
BARBER**

MISS JULIA TAKES THE WHEEL

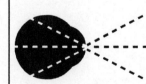

This Large Print Book carries the
Seal of Approval of N.A.V.H.

MISS JULIA
TAKES THE WHEEL

ANN B. ROSS

THORNDIKE PRESS
A part of Gale, a Cengage Company

GALE
A Cengage Company

Farmington Hills, Mich • San Francisco • New York • Waterville, Maine
Meriden, Conn • Mason, Ohio • Chicago

BRUTON MEMORIAL LIBRARY
302 McLendon Street
Plant City, FL 33563

Copyright © 2019 by Ann B. Ross.
Thorndike Press, a part of Gale, a Cengage Company.

ALL RIGHTS RESERVED
This is a work of fiction. Names, characters, places, and incidents either are the product of the author's imagination or are used fictitiously, and any resemblance to actual persons, living or dead, businesses, companies, events, or locales is entirely coincidental.
Thorndike Press® Large Print Core.
The text of this Large Print edition is unabridged.
Other aspects of the book may vary from the original edition.
Set in 16 pt. Plantin.

LIBRARY OF CONGRESS CIP DATA ON FILE.
CATALOGUING IN PUBLICATION FOR THIS BOOK
IS AVAILABLE FROM THE LIBRARY OF CONGRESS

ISBN-13: 978-1-4328-5886-5 (hardcover alk. paper)

Published in 2019 by arrangement with Viking, an imprint of Penguin Publishing Group, a division of Penguin Random House LLC

Printed in Mexico
2 3 4 5 6 7 23 22 21 20 19

As Binkie Enlow-Bates
is always there for Miss Julia, so
Sharon B. Alexander is for me.

Thank you, Sharon. This one is for you.

CHAPTER 1

"Miss Julia," Dr. Bob Hargrove said as he clicked his pen closed and twirled himself around on his little stool, "you are the most boring patient I have. I can't find a thing wrong with you."

"Well, I'm sorry I can't pique your interest with some small malfunction or another." I ran my hand down the front of my blouse, ensuring that all the buttonholes were filled. It's hard enough to undress in a doctor's office, but even more difficult to redress, hurrying as one must to be put back together before he comes waltzing in to announce the verdict of one's yearly examination.

"But," I went on, "I get so tired. I don't have the stamina or the energy I once had. And it's hard to bend over or to get out of a chair. And my joints ache and my neck is stiff and my back hurts all the time — something has to be wrong."

"Nope," he said, coming to his feet with a slight groan — an indication that he might be dealing with some of the same symptoms. "What you're describing is a natural result of aging."

"I suppose," I said, bowing to the obvious, "but I don't like hearing it." My age was a tender subject with me and I didn't like him bringing it up and blaming everything on it. I could still recall the time in my life when every small complaint was laid at the feet of certain internal organs that are exclusive to my gender. Now, however, as those organs have taken themselves into retirement, doctors were blaming everything under the sun on advancing age.

"None of us do," he said, as if all his patients were octogenarians, and I knew for a fact that his practice consisted mostly of young families. Then with a sidewise glance at me, he asked, "So, how's your driving these days?"

"My driving's just fine," I said, stung by the question. How did he know that I'd backed into my boxwood hedge, crushing three of the bushes, gotten mired in the sodden ground cover, and had had to call a wrecker to extricate the car?

"Well, keep in mind that age affects the reflexes, and aging is a fact of life, if life lasts long enough. I'm happy to assure you that yours is lasting quite well."

"And I certainly appreciate hearing that, but I declare, I hate to think of suffering through every day of what's left of it."

He bent his head and stared at me over the top of his glasses. "I can give you something for the aches and pains if you'll take it."

"No, I don't want a row of medicine bottles on the windowsill over my sink, and I don't want to have to keep a schedule of when and how much of each one I should take. I don't want to have to be *medicated* just to be able to get out of bed each morning."

"How much exercise do you get?"

"My word, Dr. Hargrove, I go up and down the stairs a half dozen times a day. I get plenty of exercise."

"But maybe not the right kind," he said, leaning against his desk and crossing one foot over the other. "Why don't you consider some form of regular guided exercise? You might be surprised at how helpful it can be."

"Well, I don't know. I'm not interested in running a marathon for charity or walking ten miles for some disease or another."

"No," he said, straightening up and getting ready to move on to the next patient.

"I'm talking about a low-impact exercise class that you'd do two or three times a week."

"Like what?"

"Like yoga, or Zumba, or some kind of aerobics. Tai chi is an excellent form of exercise. I recommend it."

"Dr. Hargrove, I am a Presbyterian, as you well know, and most of those exercises include some all-encompassing religious view that is most definitely at odds with the Nicene Creed. I don't want anything interfering with my spiritual well-being, thank you very much."

"Well, think about it anyway," he said, closing my chart. Then, as if suddenly remembering something, he said, "I guess Sue told you that we're leaving for Europe next week — Monday, in fact." Sue Hargrove was a friend, a fellow member of the garden club and the book club, and, in my opinion, a most suitable wife for the well-respected physician. She gave lovely parties.

"She told several of us a while back," I said, "but, I declare, I didn't realize that the time is upon us. I must have you both for dinner before you go." After that conventional invitation, it occurred to me that something more important was staring me in the face. "Doctor, if my memory serves me correctly, Sue said something about an extended tour — a matter of months, even. Will you really be gone that long?"

The thought of being without the services of my physician, even though I rarely had need of them, filled me with anxiety. I think he could see the dawning realization of looming abandonment on my face for he stopped and patted me on the shoulder.

"Don't worry, Miss Julia," he said. "I have a locum tenens coming in. He and his family will be staying in our house, and he'll take care of my practice. He's highly qualified, a graduate of McGill in Montreal, in fact, and —"

"He's from Canada? What's he doing way down here?"

"Came to his senses, I expect," Dr. Hargrove said with a wry grin. "His wife's from California, so maybe she drew him south. Anyway, he'll be available just as I've always been. You won't even know I'm gone."

I wasn't so sure of that. First of all, a locum tenens meant that his substitute didn't have a practice of his own, otherwise he would be too busy to take over for someone else. And second of all, what was the reason he didn't have a busy practice of his own?

The substitute would certainly bear keeping an eye on, but all I could do at the present was thank Dr. Hargrove for seeing me, wish him happy travels, and go home, hoping none of us would require medical care while he was traipsing around Europe.

CHAPTER 2

By the time I turned the car into the driveway at home, I felt sure I was coming down with something. My face was cold and clammy, my hands were trembling, and my shoulders were shivering and shaking.

"Wouldn't you know it?" I mumbled, gathering my keys and my purse to go inside. "Here I am — getting sick just as my doctor will be out of the office, out of town, and out of touch."

I entered the house through the backdoor, expecting to find Lillian in the kitchen. She wasn't, so I sank into a chair at the table to unbutton my coat and take my pulse.

Lillian came through from the dining room, stopped short when she saw me, then said, "You're home mighty early. I thought you had things to do."

"I did, but I didn't do them. Lillian, come see if I have a fever."

Lillian frowned, then walked over to the

13

table. "You gettin' sick?" She put her hand on my forehead in the time-honored way of detecting a fever.

"I think I am. See how my hands are trembling? And I'm shaking all over, and I'm about to freeze to death."

"Well," she pronounced as she removed her hand, "don't look like you got a fever. You jus' cold, Miss Julia, an' no wonder. It's February out there, an' the temp'rature jus' barely past the freezing mark. Why don't you go set in the liberry an' I'll bring you some hot tea."

"Well, I'm not *that* sick," I said, getting to my feet. "Obviously. So a cup of coffee would be better." Feeling a little undone that I wasn't exhibiting more symptoms, I took myself to the library, turned up the gas fire in the fireplace, and huddled, still in my coat, on the Chippendale sofa.

I just *knew* I was getting sick. The problem was that it was so slow in declaring itself. If it went the way these things usually did, I'd have a few days of feeling out of sorts, then just as soon as Dr. Hargrove lifted off for foreign lands, it would hit me full force and I'd have to see a doctor who practiced medicine by wandering from pillar to post, filling in for others.

I could just see it. I would wake up

14

Monday morning — Dr. Hargrove's leaving day — covered with a rash, burning with a fever, and coughing my lungs out. There would be nothing for it but to call in that new doctor who didn't stay in one place long enough to be held accountable for any mistakes he might've made.

Feeling immensely sorry for myself, I managed to perk up at the sound of Sam's coming home and speaking with Lillian. Mindful of the fact that no one had good fortune in all aspects of their lives, I was eternally grateful for having bountifully received it in the form of my second husband. Which was only fair, since I'd totally missed out with my first one.

In fact, as I listened to his warm conversation with Lillian, I felt easier facing the possibility of an imminent illness attended by an itinerant physician. If anyone would look after me, it would be Sam. As I would for him.

Not only did we trust each other with life and death decisions, we'd had Binkie, my curly-headed lawyer, draw up medical power-of-attorney documents to make that trust legally binding. The only snag had been in designating to whom that power would descend if either of us was unable to step up to the plate. Meaning of course, if one of us was dead or otherwise incapacitated.

Sam had gone back and forth over his choice, considering both sheriff's deputy sergeant Coleman Bates and J.D. Pickens, PI, as possibilities, but had finally decided on Binkie. He'd said, "I entrusted my law practice to her, and that had been my whole life for many years. Why stop with that? Besides, I expect I'll get the benefit of Coleman's input, too. In personal matters, Binkie has no problem listening to her husband."

I'd had no hesitation in designating Hazel Marie Puckett Pickens as my second in command. LuAnne Conover, my longtime friend and sometime irritant, had been aghast at my selection.

"Julia," she'd said, "I like Hazel Marie, you know I do, but to give her that much authority over your very life, why, how could you? She was Wesley Lloyd Springer's kept woman for years and even had a child by him. How do you know that she wouldn't get rid of you in a minute if she had the chance?"

She was referring to my first husband, unfaithful in life, but now permanently settled in the Good Shepherd Cemetery for these past several years. The child of whom

16

LuAnne spoke was Lloyd Pickens, fairly recently adopted by Hazel Marie's husband, J.D. Pickens, PI, and the light of my life. If ever good fortune had come out of bad, he was it.

"LuAnne," I'd responded after a great sigh, "I would trust Hazel Marie with my life — which obviously I have done by naming her. She's like a mama bear when it comes to protecting her own, and she is the most sincere and openly honest person I know." And, I'd thought to myself, if that hurts your feelings, I can't help it.

"How're you feeling, honey?" Sam said, as he came into the library from the kitchen. He leaned down and kissed me on the cheek. "Lillian says you might be coming down with something."

"Well," I said, smiling just because he was there, "if I am, you could be next."

"No worries," he said, sitting down beside me. "I'll take whatever you have to give."

Then after telling him the results of my annual checkup, I began to bemoan the fact that we would be without our trusted physician for who-knew-how-long and would have to depend on an unknown replacement in the form of a locum tenens.

"I think that's what's making me ill," I

17

said, summing up my feeling of loss even though Dr. Hargrove had yet to go anywhere. "If I have to get sick, I need to do it before he leaves."

"But," Sam said, taking my hand, "who says you have to get sick?"

"Well, nobody, I guess. I'm just thinking ahead because I don't want to be at the mercy of a substitute. Why, Sam, everybody knows that a substitute is somebody who didn't make the first team."

"Not necessarily," Sam said. "For all we know this new doctor was a straight A student, but simply doesn't like being tied down to one place. He may have wanderlust, like somebody else you know."

I smiled at that, for my sweet husband loved to travel, see new places, and learn new things. He'd done a good bit of it during our marriage right by himself, for I was a homebody, preferring my own bed and a regular routine. It worked fine for us.

"That's true," I said, nodding. "And I shouldn't judge him before he even gets here." I would, however, withhold judgment only until an announcement of his temporary appointment appeared in the newspaper. At that time, I would learn where he got his medical education and what kind of clinical experience he had, which would, in turn, tell me all I needed to know as to his qualifications to diagnose, prescribe, and treat both me and mine.

"Sam?" I said, as he picked up the newspaper and flapped out the folds. "I'm thinking I might ask Bob Hargrove for a prescription for some kind of preventive medication before he leaves. Just, you know, to have on hand in case I need it."

"And what," he asked with a cock of his eyebrow, "would that preventive medication prevent?"

"Well, I don't know. But all you see on television these days are ads for every ailment under the sun and for some things that I didn't know even qualified as ailments. And the *names* they give them — the medicines, I mean, not the ailments."

I turned to look at him as another thought occurred to me. "Do you think those big pharmaceutical companies have special divisions just to think up what to call all those new drugs?"

"I wouldn't doubt it," Sam said, folding the paper to a front-page article. "They have special divisions for everything else."

"I can just see it," I said, letting my imagination roam through the possibilities. "A group of very smart young people who've never had a pang of any kind in their lives, sitting around throwing out suggestions for naming the next wonder drug. They'd want something catchy and easy to remember so patients can tell their doctors what they want. Except," I went on, "they're just about scraping the bottom of the barrel by now. Have you heard some of the names they've come up with? And, Sam, you know how things catch on and become part of the culture. I wouldn't be a bit surprised to be introduced some day to Ms. Otezla Jones or Miss Lyrica Smith. Maybe even to Miss Repatha Wright."

Sam laughed. "You may be right."

I knew I was, and I'd not even mentioned the possibility of twin sisters named the Misses Tena and Kyleena Brown.

CHAPTER 3

"You know," Sam said, putting aside the newspaper, "we really should be grateful that Bob Hargrove is bringing in a locum tenens. He could've just as easily — maybe more so — turned his practice over to the hospital during the time he's gone."

"Really? How could the hospital run a private practice?"

"That question," Sam said with a quick glance at me, "just shows how healthy you are, and thank goodness for it. You're out of touch with what's been going on in medicine in the last ten years or so. You ever wonder why I gave up my seat on the hospital board?"

"Well, not really. I just thought you'd had enough. I mean, you've been on every board in town at one time or another, anyway."

"That was part of it," Sam said, nodding. "But it was mostly because I could see the way the wind was blowing — and I didn't like it." Sam shifted in his seat beside me, an indication that he was troubled. "Honey, medicine is not practiced the way it once was. Used to be that one of the reasons young men — and women — put in all the years to become doctors was the opportunity to be on their own, to have their own practices that included personal relationships with their patients. Many of the general practitioners prided themselves on cradle-to-grave care of their patients."

"That's exactly what I expect from Dr. Hargrove," I said with firm approval. "My only concern is that he'll predecease me, and I'll have to look for another doctor. That's why I'm not too upset at his taking so much time off. I want him to get the rest he needs so he'll stay healthy."

"Well, I'm sorry to tell you that it doesn't work that way anymore. See," Sam said, crossing one leg over the other, "it used to be that most of the ones who went to medical school were definitely not the corporate types — they had no desire to work for somebody else. They were independent souls — some, I admit, independent jackasses, but you'll find that kind in any field. Except for a very few — like Hargrove — who're holding on to the old ways, they've now bought into the new way of practicing medicine."

Frowning at the thought of changing something that had worked well for years, I said, "But what's new about it? They still see patients, don't they? And diagnose and treat whatever they have, don't they? I don't understand how else medicine could be practiced."

"Well, it's like this. Somehow or another — and it beats me how quickly and easily it's come about — hospital administrations have jumped into the catbird seat, and with that, you get the whole corporate setup — CEOs, CFOs, business plans, financial projections, and you name it. The practice of medicine as a business — *because,* honey," Sam said, sitting up straight to make sure that I understood the problem, "private equity companies are buying up small hospitals, which means, in turn, that those hospitals are run to make a profit."

"What's a private equity company?"

"One that's owned by stockholders who expect a return on their investment. So, doctors now work for the hospitals — hired by them, sent patients by them, and drawing a salary from them. And not only that, they're often given quotas as to the number of patients they're expected to see per day, and the worst thing is —" Sam stopped, drew a deep breath as if to calm himself "— the worst thing," he went on, "is that when they admit a patient to the hospital, they have to turn the care of that patient over to another group of salaried doctors — hospitalists, they're called."

"What?" I asked, staring at him. "You mean your own doctor doesn't take care of you?"

"That's right. Your own doctor won't even make rounds. They work nine to five in their offices, and the hospitalists are in charge during the hospital stay."

"Well, that doesn't make sense. If your own doctor thinks you need to be admitted, he ought to be the one in charge. How can these hospitalists know your history? Or anything else about you?"

"Beats me, honey," Sam said with a sigh. "And it beats me how those independent-minded doctors could just fold and give in to it. Of course, they get weekends off, and they don't get phone calls at night, and they get regular vacations, as well as regular incomes, and, perhaps the biggest attraction, they don't have all the clerical problems. I mean, the hospitals keep the medical records, apply for insurance, Medicare, and Medicaid payments, do all the billing and collecting, and keep the government happy with tax reports and so on. I can see how appealing that would be. Very few doctors are businessmen, but I can't help but think that they've made a poor bargain — sold their souls, even.

"But," he went on, "I understand some of it. A lot of 'em come out with huge student loans, so to work for a hospital saves them from having to borrow more to set up an office. And with the increase of highly specialized practices that require unbelievably expensive technology, only hospitals can afford them. Still, it seems to me that the changes benefit everybody but the patient. Physicians used to be taught to treat the patient, not the disease. But now hospitalists treat the disease, and the patient is apt to get lost in the process."

"Well," I said, verging on outrage, "just who came up with those bright ideas?"

"I wish I knew, although I can guess. The ones who've come out on top are the hospital administrators who are answerable only to stockholders. They're now the top dogs. After years and years of deferring to their medical staffs, doctors now work for them, rather than the other way around."

"I don't think it ought to be that way, Sam. Why hasn't Dr. Hargrove told us about this?"

"He has, but he's made no changes, so you probably didn't notice. He's one of the few in town who've refused to contract with the hospital." Sam stopped, thought a minute, then said, "I don't think Dr. Harry Holcomb did, either."

"No wonder. He's as old as the hills. Besides," I went on, "I've heard things about him."

Sam smiled without comment, as he often did when I referred to gossip. "Well, anyway, if any of the holdouts admit you to the hospital, they'll continue to care for you while you're there."

"Well, thank goodness for that. I don't want one of those hospitalists around me at all. Why, the very name gives me cold chills. They ought to call them substitute doctors since —" I stopped, suddenly thinking of Dr. Hargrove's replacement.

Sam, who could follow my thinking better than I could most of the time, said, "Not the same, honey. A locum tenens isn't a hospitalist. He'll follow Dr. Hargrove's lead, not the hospital's, in the way he runs the practice. I'm sure Bob wouldn't have hired him otherwise. That's one thing you don't have to worry about. Of course," Sam went on with an indulgent smile, "just stay well and neither of us will have to worry about any of it."

"I certainly intend to, especially since I've now learned how the practice of medicine has been turned upside down and inside out.

"But you know, Sam," I went on, recalling something that Mildred Allen had complained about quite recently. "Maybe that explains those computers that all the doctors haul around with them. Mildred went in not long ago to have a stress test and she had to see a string of doctors. Every one of them, she said, came in pushing a little table on wheels with a computer on it — like it was an appendage or something. And to make it worse, during the whole time the doctors spoke to her, they kept their eyes on the computer screen, tap-tap-tapping away. She said it was disconcerting to have what was supposed to be a one-on-one conversation with one's physician while his eyes stayed glued to that screen."

"Yes," Sam said, nodding, "they have to keep records of everything to send to a central computer in the hospital."

"Sounds like big government to me — keeping tabs on everybody."

Sam smiled. "Pretty close to it, I guess. But of course, doctors have always kept records — handwritten, but later transcribed by a typist. They kept them not only to chart a patient's progress, but also for legal purposes. You know, in case they were sued sometime in the future."

"Yes, Dr. Hargrove always comes in with a pen and a pad, and scribbles down anything I complain of. But Mildred said having that computer between them was like having a robot listening in and taking notes on everything that was said. She didn't like it.

"And furthermore," I went on, "she said the screen was always turned away from her so she couldn't see what was being entered." I stopped and thought for a few minutes, then said, "And, you know, Sam, computers are taking over our whole lives. There's no telling what the things are doing, nosing into our private lives, keeping records until Doomsday — it makes me ill to think of it. And another thing, every child in school has to have a computer nowadays. I'm not sure they even learn what it means to *write.* All they ever do is ENTER."

"Well, we went through the Industrial Age when everything changed."

"Not me," I said to lighten things up. "I'm not that old."

Sam laughed. "Me, either, but we're certainly going through the Electronic Age.

And we'd better get used to it, because everything is changing."

"I can ignore whatever else changes," I said, reaching for his hand, "just as long as you don't."

CHAPTER 4

We both turned as we heard the kitchen door open and close, then Lloyd's greeting to Lillian. After a short conversation with her, he left the kitchen, crossed the hall, and came into the library.

"Hey, Miss Julia, Mr. Sam," he said, walking to the fireplace and warming his hands. "Boy, it's cold out there."

"It sure is," Sam said, smiling at him.

"I hope your coat's warm enough," I said. "I've just come in myself and can testify to how bitter it is. And that reminds me. Has your father gotten home yet?" J.D. Pickens was a private investigator under contract to a major insurance company to investigate suspected fraud and other illegal activities. He was often away from home for days at a time.

"No'm, I think he'll be home this weekend." Lloyd, finally warmed up, began divesting himself of his heavy jacket. "At least I hope he will."

"Well, then," I said, "be sure to remind your mother to let the faucets drip tonight. They're calling for a hard freeze, maybe even dropping into the teens, which could mean frozen water pipes. To say nothing of downed trees and broken power lines."

"Yes'm, I will. But mama says the best money she and J.D. ever spent was buying that self-starting generator. She says that worrying about losing power is a thing of the past now."

"I know what she means," I said, thinking of the comfort of having one ourselves.

"How's school these days?" Sam said, having had enough, I suspected, of weather talk. Lillian and I could discuss it for hours, which we often did.

"Pretty good," he said, sitting on the opposite sofa facing us. "I guess."

"Just pretty good?" Sam asked. "What's going on? You sound a little jaded."

Lloyd shrugged his shoulders. "I don't know about that. I'll have to look up *jaded* before I say either way."

Sam grinned — he often pulled out a word that Lloyd and I had to look up. "World weary," he said.

"Then no, I don't think it's that," Lloyd said, leaning back. "It's more of trying to figure how to get out of doing something I don't want to do without hurting anybody's feelings. It's a dicey situation."

Immediately visions of bullying, cheating, or gang-related problems popped into my head. "Are you in trouble, Lloyd?"

He grimaced. "I'm gonna be if I'm not careful. See, I heard — I mean, somebody told me — that Andrea Mason is going to ask me to the dance the school's having for Sadie Hawkins Day."

"Mason?" I asked, going over the name in my mind to place her family. "If it's the Masons I know, they're very nice."

"Oh, she's nice, but she's tall, too. And I'm not."

Sam frowned. "I thought it was usually the girl who worried about height differences."

"Ordinarily, I don't worry about it — we're pretty good friends. But if they play a lot of slow dances, I have to worry about where my eyes come up to."

Sam immediately got it, but it took me a minute. He tried not to laugh, holding himself in as he nodded in acknowledgment of a truly dicey situation.

"To make it worse," Lloyd went on, "somebody else told me that Janice Mc-Donough is going to ask me, and maybe

Leigh Swanson, too, and they're both kinda short. So, see?" He shrugged his shoulders as if having a plethora of dates in the offing was a burden to be borne. "It's not the height that worries me, it's the number of them, and how I'll have to choose which one I go with."

"Well, Lloyd," I said with a smidgeon of pride, "it sounds as if you're a popular boy."

"No'm, I don't think so. It's mainly because I'm a good dancer so —"

"You *are*?" I asked, surprised.

"Yes'm. J.D. showed me how, and he's real good. He said I'm a natural when it comes to moves, so now all the girls want to go with me."

"Well, I declare," I said, at a loss for anything else to say.

Lloyd frowned, twisted his mouth, then said, "I don't even know why we have to have a Sadie Hawkins Day dance, anyway. I mean, who is Sadie Hawkins, anyway?"

"Why, Lloyd," I said, surprised that he had to ask, "Sadie Hawkins was a character in the *Li'l Abner* comic strip. She was, unfortunately, the homeliest girl in Dogpatch and had no suitors for her hand. In desperation to marry her off, her father declared an official Sadie Hawkins Day on which a footrace was held when the women

33

chased the men. Whoever got caught had to marry the girl who caught him."

"Good grief!" Lloyd said. "And here I've been worried about having to *dance* with somebody."

"Well," I said to ease his consternation, "I could have it wrong. It's been a long time since I've seen that comic strip."

"I think it's been discontinued," Sam said. "Al Capp died some while ago. But he created some memorable characters. Remember Senator Jack S. Phogbound? And Jubilation T. Cornpone?"

"And Joe What's-His-Name?" I said, smiling. "I never could pronounce his name, but the one with a black rain cloud over his head."

"Nobody could," Sam said. "That comic strip became a social commentary during a time of protests, riots, and general unrest, especially on campuses. The genius of Capp could make you laugh and at the same time blow your head off. One thing he came up with could still be used today. Remember S.W.I.N.E.?"

"No, what was that?"

"Students Wildly Indignant about Nearly Everything," Sam said, laughing even as he shook his head. "Just watch the news and see if I'm right."

"Well," Lloyd said, clearly having had enough of our reminiscing, "I guess it's no wonder that the county high school has what they call a Turnaround dance. It's the same as ours — the girls ask the boys — but they don't have to wonder who Sadie Hawkins is.

"Or," he went on, dolefully, "if the boys know what's supposed to happen if they get caught. And I've got *three* girls chasing me."

Sam, who was still trying to keep a straight face, said, "Oh, I don't think you need to worry about anything permanent. In fact, it seems to me that you're already caught. Now it's just a matter of which one you want to end up with at the dance."

"It's worse even than that," Lloyd went on, rolling his eyes. " 'Cause, see, the word's gotten around that I'm getting a car. The girls like that, too."

"A *car*!" I said, sitting up straight. "Why, Lloyd, you aren't old enough to drive. Who's getting you a car?"

"J.D. is, and, yes ma'am, I am. I'm fifteen, and I've taken driver's ed, so I have my beginner's permit. I have to have a licensed driver with me until I'm sixteen, but, see, all the girls like J.D., too, and he'll be with me when I drive."

"They Lord!" I said, wondering what

35

Hazel Marie's swashbuckling husband would think of next and wondering what I could do to nip Mr. Pickens's too-much-too-soon idea in the bud as well.

"But that's a problem, too," Lloyd went on, frowning. "Because, see, the licensed driver has to ride in the front seat, so J.D. will have to sit by me while I drive, and my date, whichever one I take, will have to sit in the backseat by herself. None of 'em would like that, and the whole evening would be shot before we even got there. And the other two'll have their feelings hurt and probably won't ever speak to me again."

"Lloyd," Sam said, pontifically, "I am going to issue a Solomonic solution for you. Tell those young ladies that you couldn't possibly choose one over the others, so you'll take all three of them, or — how about this? They could draw straws to narrow it down. Either way, it would be out of your hands."

Lloyd's face brightened. "That could work, and I wouldn't have to turn anybody down. At least it'd be better than what Mama came up with. She said I had to take the first girl to ask me, and I'd have to sit in the backseat with her and let J.D. drive us. But, see, I want to drive. I mean, what's the use of having a car if you don't get to drive it?"

"That's a very good question," I agreed. And, furthermore, I intended to take that matter up with Mr. Pickens just as soon as I could hem him up.

CHAPTER 5

I dreamed of Lloyd that night. I dreamed
he was running for his very life while a bevy
of wild-eyed, skimpily clad teenage girls,
screaming their heads off, chased after him.

I woke up and lay there, blinking into the
darkness, trying to rid myself of the image.
Then I recalled Amy Randall's tale of woe
at the last circle meeting. Her son, Les, had
covered himself with glory during the
football season, and by so doing had been
twice featured as Player of the Week in the
Abbotsville Times.

"As soon as those pictures came out,"
Amy had said, "his phone started ringing. It
was one girl after another all afternoon,
until I finally had to make him turn it off so
he could eat his supper in peace. It certainly
hadn't been that way in my day." And her
day had not been that long ago.

Several of the other mothers of boys
agreed with her, saying that their sons, too,

had been on the receiving end of full-bore attention from girls.

"It starts in middle school," Ida Monroe announced, speaking from the experience of raising four boys. "As soon as they move up to sixth grade, the girls start noticing boys and they're off and running. And every last one of them has a cell phone."

"If you think phone calls are bad," Lisa Hudson had chimed in, "consider emails and tweets. Instagrams, too, and don't forget YouTube and Facebook. At least you know when a phone rings. There's no way to know what's happening through the silent forms, and the young girls of today know them all."

"Boy crazy!" Jessie Beasley had pronounced with a sniff, but her children were in their fifties, so she'd never had the problem of ever-present cell phones and instant messaging with their ability to reach out and touch someone without their parents knowing a thing about it. "Since when," she'd gone on, "has it been that every child from age five and up has to have a cell phone of his own? I didn't have my own phone till I was twenty-five and it was a Princess phone by my bed. And it couldn't be glued to my hand, either."

I'd seen Margaret Worsham turn her

careworn face away and pretend she'd not heard the conversation. As the vigilant guard of a third daughter's journey through puberty, she had probably fought the good fight as best she could. I had heard her say that the whole world of so-called social media was arrayed against her and every other mother in the land.

But the problem for me was that I'd thought Lloyd would escape such attention, so to suddenly learn that he was in for even more than his fair share of it had shaken me. I had viewed his entry into puberty with equanimity — even after learning that he was the proud owner of an electric razor. I'd been sure that as an undersized, glasses-wearing, nonathletic A student, he would escape the attention and the resulting pitfalls of being attractive to girls of his age. Nothing had surprised me more than to learn how wrong I was.

"Sam?" I whispered, having sensed a change in his breathing. "You awake?"

"Hm-m? Yeah, I guess. Why're you awake?"

"Lloyd."

"Lloyd? Why? What's got you worried about him?"

"Those *girls,* Sam. Why're they after him like that? He's not a sports star or any kind of teen idol or whatever. Of course *I* know he's head and shoulders above most boys his age, even though he's shorter than most, too. I thought he would mature quietly and peacefully until he reached about thirty when he'd be able to choose a nice, sweet girl who would recognize his very real qualities, and they'd live happily ever after."

Sam started laughing, shaking the bed, then he said, "Honey, those very real qualities you're talking about have just been recognized a little earlier than you expected. Lloyd is a catch, didn't you know that? You have to give those girls credit for recognizing what you and I already know."

"But why? What do they see in him? I don't understand it."

"Personality, honey, and he's got it in spades. Self-confidence, too, which is very appealing to women. I mean, I should know, shouldn't I?"

I smiled and elbowed him. "Oh, you."

"Look," Sam went on, "he's not what you and I would've called a dreamboat — and thank goodness for that — but he's outgoing, courteous, and always willing to help. Pickens told me that there's an open-door policy at their house with kids dropping in to get help with math or chemistry or whatever. And remember the tennis tournament last spring? Didn't you notice he had his own cheering section?"

"Well, yes, but I thought that was just school spirit. Or something."

"Oh, and remember this," Sam said, "he's president of his class and of the Latin Club, and he has some kind of office in the Key Club."

"There're only three members in the Latin Club, so that shouldn't count." I wasn't yet willing to concede that Lloyd was any kind of *catch*.

"Okay," Sam said, stifling a yawn, "I'll give you that, but he's always up to his neck in volunteer work of one kind or another. If anybody wants something done, he's the first one they turn to. And one other thing, he's fun to be with. He's both likable and funny — a pretty unbeatable combination."

"Well, shoo," I said. "I thought I was the only one who sees how special he is."

"No, you're not the only one, but if it'll make you feel better, I think those girls are after him because he'll make sure they have a good time. He's considerate, Julia. People like him."

"Well, my word," I said, beginning to see the boy in a new light. "I guess I just haven't noticed the impression he makes on others, but I'll have to say that I've always thought he would go far."

Sam chuckled. "Yep, if he manages to survive high school."

After being reassured by Sam that Lloyd's natural good sense would keep his head on straight in spite of having become the center of female attention, I was able to turn to other matters of concern. To that end I called Sue Hargrove the next morning and asked her and the doctor to dinner the Saturday night before they were to leave.

"Oh, Julia," she'd said, "we'd love to, but I'm afraid we can't. The Crawfords are coming in Friday and staying with us. Don is the doctor who'll be taking over while we're gone, so Bob will be familiarizing him with the practice over the weekend. And," she added with a laugh, "I guess I'll be entertaining his wife and two children while trying to get packed. But it's so nice of you to ask us."

"Well, I apologize for waiting so long to do it. To tell the truth, Sue, the time slipped up on me. I thought it would be another week or so before you left. But I hope you both have a wonderful time. We will certainly miss you." Which was an understatement if there ever was one.

"Thank you," Sue said, "but we'll be back,

maybe sooner than anybody expects. I still can't believe that Bob is willing to leave the practice even for a few days, much less for a couple of months. The only thing that attracts him is a medical meeting of some kind in Stockholm, which he really wants to attend. That's how he rationalizes being gone. But, Julia, I hate to ask you because I know you never need to be asked to do the nice thing, but would you mind having the Crawfords over sometime — or at least introducing Lauren around a little?"

"Why, of course," I said, readily agreeing to sponsor, so to speak, the new couple in town. "It would be my pleasure." And more than that, it would be a way for me to take the measure of the physician in whose care we were being left.

Sometimes, I thought after we'd hung up and I'd been relieved of hosting a last-minute dinner, it's enough to have offered without having to actually follow through. Not that I wouldn't have enjoyed the company of the Hargroves, but I wasn't sure that I could've refrained from expressing my dismay at the loss of my physician's services for a period of months. Which would've been poor manners, to say the least. The man deserved a vacation. Everybody does, but my *doctor*?

The thing to do, I told myself, was to make sure that everybody stayed healthy. I'd have to watch myself as well as Sam and Lloyd and Hazel Marie and her twin toddlers. And then there were Lillian and Latisha, her sprightly great-granddaughter, to watch over and, I guess, Mr. Pickens, too. Although I couldn't imagine him getting sick — no self-respecting germ would be so presumptuous.

"Julia," Sam said after I'd moaned again about being under the care of an unknown quantity — and quality — if any of us got sick, "Bob Hargrove is not going to leave his patients in the hands of an incompetent. Think of what he'd have to come back to if he did — no practice at all. You're worrying over nothing, sweetheart."

It didn't relieve my concerns that the hospital chose that very Sunday to announce in the *Abbotsville Times* the employment of three new doctors. Although I had no intention of making an appointment with any of them, I read their write-ups with interest — and with increasing apprehension. One had graduated from the University of Michigan Medical School and had done a residency in a Boston hospital, both of which sounded impressive enough, although clearly he wasn't a Southerner.

45

Upon closer reading, I realized he wasn't a "he" either — Dr. Sydney Pulaski was a woman.

I had no problem with her gender or her educational background, but I certainly did with the other two. One wasn't even a physician — he was a DO — a doctor of osteopathy. Since Sam was at the Bluebird café with his friends, I went immediately to the dictionary:

Osteopathy: a medical therapy that emphasizes manipulative techniques for correcting somatic abnormalities thought to cause disease and inhibit recovery.

My word! Had they hired a chiropractor to practice medicine? *Manipulative techniques* certainly sounded like it. Why, I could remember when osteopaths were not even considered for hospital privileges. Nor were naturopaths, but now — according to a national hospital's commercials — they, too, were hospital staff members. What would be next — witch doctors? medicine men? acupuncturists? alchemists? Don't get me wrong — anybody can go to whomever they want and receive whatever treatment they want for whatever ails them, and more power to them. The problem I have is with the very recent elevation of these outliers to the same level of authority as fully qualified and accredited physicians.

What had changed? Probably, I told myself with a wry twist of my mouth, the recent effort to be inclusive of everybody and not hurt anybody's feelings or make them uncomfortable by telling them flat-out that they weren't up to the job.

But it wasn't just practitioners who blamed every disease known to man on maladjusted or malaligned bones who presented problems for the unwary patient. There was also a subspecies of practitioner known as certified physician assistants who were permitted to both diagnose and treat patients under the supervision, it was claimed, of a fully qualified physician.

Doris Blanchard had run afoul of one of those assistants when she had gone for her annual checkup. She'd showed up, she told us at the last book club meeting, but her doctor hadn't. "He dumped me off on some young girl who'd had a fraction of his education, and I'll tell you, I was stunned. But what could I do? There I was half naked, waiting to be poked and prodded, and it's hard to show proper outrage with no clothes on."

But, Doris had gone on to tell us, contrary

47

to her expectations, that she'd never had anyone be so interested in the explicit description of every little pain, twitch, or tingle that she'd ever experienced.

"That young woman," Doris said, "now knows me inside and out, and futhermore, she comes to the phone when I call the office. Which is more than I can say for the doctor I've been going to for years — he might return a call at the end of the day, or he might not. He figures if you're really sick, you'll call back. But Marsha is Johnny-on-the-spot — I can always reach her. And you know what? Next year I'm going to make an appointment with her, and if it hurts the doctor's feelings, well, it serves him right."

With that backhanded compliment to another class of nonphysician, Doris had nodded her head firmly and eaten another pineapple and cream cheese sandwich.

As for me, I was appreciating Dr. Hargrove more and more for staying out from under a hospital that had become so open-minded that a medical degree was no longer a requirement to practice medicine.

What was the world coming to? I was even more at a loss for an answer when I read the background of the third hospital employee — he had a medical degree, but it was from some kind of school in Haiti. *Haiti!*

I had to sit down to catch my breath.

What kind of medical school did Haiti have? I had no idea, except I could be fairly sure it didn't come up to the level of Duke or Chapel Hill or Emory or a dozen others I could name that weren't even in the South.

There was only one reason why anyone would go to an osteopathic school or to an offshore medical school — their applications for admission to recognized medical schools had been rejected. In spite of that, however, their applications for positions on the medical staff of the Abbot County Hospital had been accepted. Did the hospital administrator not know the difference? Or was he able to hire them at lower salaries than he would've had to pay traditional physicians, thereby making his end-of-the-year bottom line look better?

And if that's what the administrator of the Abbot County Hospital was doing, then it all boiled down to this: A businessman was in charge of the general health and well-being of every resident in the county. And that was enough to make anybody sick.

CHAPTER 6

On further thought, I realized that the hospital administrator — a man by the name of Stuart Barlow — couldn't be the only one to blame for the current state of affairs. It was, after all, the Abbot *County* Hospital; that is, it belonged to the county, which made it come under the purview of the county commissioners — none of whom had a smidgeon of medical education or experience. All of them, however, knew how to read a financial statement. So, again — medicine being run as a business.

"What's the matter with you?" Lillian asked a few days later, as I sat at the kitchen table wondering if my lethargy was a sign of worse to come in the form of a debilitating illness. "You been doin' nothin' but mumble all day long. Who you talkin' to, anyway?"

"Myself, Lillian. I'm talking to myself. I've been telling myself that this country has the best doctors and the best hospitals in the world, so there's no need to worry about the future of medicine."

She dropped a dishrag into the sink and turned to look at me. "Now, why you got something like that on your mind?"

"Oh, I don't know. Just been watching the news too much, I guess. And being a little antsy because Dr. Hargrove is beyond reach — that's enough to make anybody nervous. But," I went on with an effort to shake off the doldrums, "I promised Sue Hargrove that I'd have the new doctor and his wife over for dinner. If they're free Thursday evening, Lillian, let's try for that. Would Thursday suit you?"

"One's about as good as another for me. What you want me to serve?"

"Let's just do our old standbys — a standing rib roast, asparagus casserole, and oven-browned potatoes. No, wait, let's do that casserole that you make with frozen hash-browns. Of course, that makes two casseroles on the table, but Sam loves potatoes that way, so who's counting? Your yeast rolls, definitely, and for dessert, well, let's see. With the weather so cold, maybe we should do something hot, like a cobbler or something. What do you think?"

"Well," Lillian said, "if you're lookin' for something Mr. Sam likes, you can't beat

51

Biscuit Tortoni. It comes straight out of the freezer, so it's not hot, but it sets light on the stomach after a heavy meal."

"That's perfect, and it can be made ahead of time. Let's do that. Oh, and a salad — maybe tomato aspic to add a dash of tartness. Now," I said, reaching for a notepad, "to decide who else to invite. The new doctor, I understand, is in his late thirties, and his wife is somewhat younger, probably late twenties, and, I declare, Lillian, I hardly know anybody in that age group. I'm about to outgrow anybody to invite for dinner."

Lillian's eyes rolled up in her head. "Don't get started on gettin' old again."

"I'm just making an observation. Oh, and by the way," I said to get us off that subject, "his name is Don Crawford and his wife is Lauren. They have two children, four and six, and I can't imagine the state Sue's house will be in when she gets back. And that reminds me, I must suggest a babysitter when I call Mrs. Crawford. I am not in the mood to entertain children too young to use a knife and fork."

"I hope you soon get out of whatever mood you in. I declare, Miss Julia, if you don't quit worryin' about ev'ry little thing, you gonna worry yourself to death."

"Well, you're right. I know you're right.

But if I don't worry, who will? I just wish I could find something to worry about that I could do something about. I feel a great need to *fix* something. I just can't find anything that's fixable."

"You can fix that babysittin' thing with Janelle," Lillian said, referring to her well-qualified teenage neighbor. "She's lookin' to make some money to buy herself a fancy dress for the senior prom."

"Perfect. Janelle's a nice girl with a level head. I'll recommend her. I'm glad that's settled." I turned to leave the kitchen, then stopped. "In fact, everything's settled except inviting the guests. I guess I'd better do that before we get too far along."

"Yes'm, I guess you better."

I already knew who, besides the Crawfords, I was going to invite — the youngest couples I knew, Hazel Marie and J.D. Pickens, for one, and Binkie and Coleman Bates, for the other. Neither couple was what you'd call *young* — after all, age depended on one's perspective — but both had young children, as did the guests of honor, so an appropriate subject for conversation was at hand.

I had briefly thought of expanding my guest list, but quickly discarded that idea. The new couple could be easily overwhelmed with too many names and faces to remember, and a large group prohibited any kind of meaningful conversation. Much better to have a more manageable guest list, not least because I would have a chance to take the measure of the physician I might have to rely on if circumstances of dire need should arise. It behooves us all to prepare for the worst.

I knew what to look for in the new doctor. I wanted to see a friendly and outgoing — but not too outgoing — personality. No joking, loud laughter, or hyperactivity for me. I like a doctor who is all business with the exception of greeting me politely and with obvious interest in my welfare.

I wanted to see a neat, well-dressed — but not too expensively dressed — professional. I well recalled having been sent by Dr. Hargrove for a bone density test, merely as a preventive measure, and being seen by a doctor whose belt flap hung loose, and, furthermore, his pants had not been properly hemmed. They had been so long that the cuffs were frayed from dragging along the floor as he walked. All I could think of at the time was if he couldn't be bothered to thread a belt through the loops, what else would he be careless about. What, I wondered, did such a slapdash approach to his appearance say about his interest in caring for a patient? A lot, I concluded, and decided to go elsewhere if my test indicated a need for treatment. It didn't, thank goodness.

I also wanted to see, or perhaps feel, from the new doctor an air of competence. I wanted to see someone who was comfortable with himself and his knowledge, cool in emergencies, and sure of himself, but without any hint of arrogance.

A lot to ask? I didn't think so. To my mind, what I was looking for was entirely reasonable to expect of a physician. Actually, when you come right down to it, these matters were entirely reasonable to expect of any professional — be he, or she, lawyer, accountant, insurance agent, or whatever.

Sue Hargrove's phone rang so many times that I was on the verge of hanging up when a soft voice tentatively asked, "Hello?"

"Mrs. Crawford?"

"Yes?"

Deciding that enough questions had been asked, I firmly said, "This is Julia Murdoch. I am a friend of Sue Hargrove, and her husband, as well. We are so glad to have you in town, and I was wondering if you and Dr. Crawford would have dinner with us

Thursday evening."

"Oh, well, I don't know." She paused, and just as I was about to fill the silence, she went on. "I'll have to see what Don thinks. He might have plans. But you're very kind to ask us. May I call you back?"

"Oh, yes, please do." I gave her my phone number, then the information she would need in relaying the request to her husband. "Come about six o'clock, if you will. And I understand that you will need a babysitter. You couldn't do better than Janelle Maybin."

I gave her that number as well, but before I could go on Lauren Crawford said, "Well, I don't know. Don doesn't like leaving the children with strangers. I'll have to ask him."

I hardly knew how to reply to that, but finally said, "Please tell him that Sam and I are eager to meet you both and to introduce you to two couples who could make your stay in Abbotsville most pleasant. They, too, have small children and will be getting babysitters. You're fortunate that Janelle will be available."

"Yes, ma'am, I'll tell him."

"And," I went on more urgently, "let me know as soon as you can." I wanted her to know that I couldn't wait until Thursday afternoon to invite the other guests.

"Yes, ma'am, I will. Thank you so much."

Thanking her in turn, I hung up. Then, shrugging my shoulders at the lukewarm response to an invitation, I chalked it up to being a young wife overwhelmed with two small children, a move to a strange place, and perhaps to having been poorly raised.

"Poor raising" was a catchall category in which we placed anyone who seemed out of step with the way we did things — specifically social things — in Abbotsville. They were subsequently judged on how quickly and eagerly they caught on and began to fit in. After that phone call, I had my doubts about Lauren Crawford's agility.

CHAPTER 7

Still feeling slightly discomposed by Mrs. Crawford's tepid response to my phone call, I found myself going over and over it for the next hour or so. I kept thinking of what I would say if I could take her in hand and instruct her in the niceties of social matters — for her own good, of course. And for her husband's as well, since the wife of a professional man can at times mean the difference between success and failure. Here is what I would tell her:

No matter how difficult your day has been, when someone calls to extend an invitation, your response is always given with great warmth and appreciation. You must sound delighted, even if you're not. By the choice of your words and the tone of your voice, you let the caller know that her invitation has brightened your day even if you would never in a million years accept whatever it is that she's offering. That's only good manners. After all, she didn't have to ask you in the first place, and you should acknowledge your awareness of that.

But you do not hem and haw, and say that you have to ask your husband. That makes you sound like a child instead of a grown woman with a mind of her own. It is permissible, however, to say that you have to *check* with him to be sure he hasn't made plans of which he has yet to tell you. But you do not give the impression that you would much rather the caller had never thought of you at all.

Take Hazel Marie and Binkie as examples. They were both thrilled to be invited to my house for dinner — at least they made me think they were. But even if they had not been actually thrilled — I mean, really, how could they be when dining in my home wasn't exactly a rarity — neither of them had let me know it. They immediately accepted the invitation, thanked me for it, and left me feeling that I had done them a great and unexpected favor by including them.

To sum up, in a well-run household, it is the wife who oversees and directs the social life of the couple — Amy Vanderbilt said so, as had Emily Post before her. The wife doesn't have to ask permission to arrange an evening with friends — she will already know her husband's likes and dislikes, and will be ready with a polite and believable excuse if one is needed. Therefore, when she accepts an invitation, she tells her husband what they will be doing on a certain evening at a particular time, as well as what he should wear, and he, in turn, acquiesces with no more than a minimum of protest.

That was it. That's what I would tell her if she asked my advice — an unlikely occurence, I acknowledged with a sigh. And even more unlikely, since it was the good doctor himself who returned my call and accepted my invitation to dinner.

Ah, well, maybe the new doctor's wife was younger than I'd thought. Maybe she was tired of meeting new people every few months, knowing that no long-term friendships would ensue. Maybe she'd had enough of her husband's wanderlust and expressed it in the passive-aggessive manner I'd detected in her responses. And maybe I'd just caught her at a bad time, and she would prove to be a delightful young woman who would add zest to my circle of friends. And, finally, maybe I didn't know what I was talking about and was reading too much into a simple telephone conversation.

Actually, as I thought of all my good

advice going to waste, I recalled that I had once had an apt pupil who'd taken whatever I'd said to heart and was now a prize graduate. Hazel Marie had come to me as a pitiful example of a young woman who'd never had any training in — nor even an introduction to — gracious living. Why, she hadn't even known the difference between a tea and a coffee, much less the need to reciprocate after accepting an invitation. And, my stars, her clothes and makeup! Not enough of one and too much of the other. But she had listened to what I said and watched what I did, and turned herself into a lovely young woman with excellent manners and an air of refinement. Then when she married Mr. Pickens and I'd thought all my tutoring had been for naught, she had been able to soothe even that savage beast. Filled with confidence by that time and in her own sweet way, she had turned him into the semblance of a gentleman — rough around the edges though he continued to be.

Lillian and I were so accustomed to having guests for dinner that we could probably do it blindfolded, as the saying goes. Although why anyone would want to do it that way, I don't know. While she prepared the food, I set the dining-room table, using my second best china — the Spode, not the Haviland, since this was to be a casual, friendly affair. Also for that reason, the two five-armed candelabra stayed in their usual places on the sideboard while a low arrangement of florist flowers was centered on the table with two single candlesticks spaced on each side.

Binkie and Coleman were the first to arrive on that cold, blustery evening, and I marveled again at the change in Binkie. In her office she was strictly business, but in a social setting, she was as bright and talkative as she could be. She was always a happy addition to any gathering, laughing and mixing easily, as Coleman watched her with indulgent admiration.

Hazel Marie and Mr. Pickens came in along with a gust of wind, which sent him straight to the fireplace, while Hazel Marie asked, as she always did, if she could help.

After shaking hands with the men, then hanging coats and scarves in the hall closet, Sam saw that everyone was seated in the living room, where the conversation, sparked by Binkie, was already lively. Mr. Pickens was his usual impudent self, whispering to me that I looked lovely by candlelight — a remark that needed no response other than a roll of my eyes.

When six-twenty had come and gone with

no word from the Crawfords, I signaled to Lillian to serve the hors d'oeuvres — hot olive cheese puffs — and punch in small stemmed glasses. My friends had long before given up expecting anything livelier in my home, although I was beginning to question what harm there would've been to serve the occasional spirited drink, especially on a wintry evening. But not this evening, and not to a doctor on perpetual call.

Having planned a heavy meal, I had deliberately gone light with the predinner snacks — to my regret, for I distinctly heard Mr. Pickens's stomach grumble at the slim pickings. But what could I do? The guests of honor were missing, inexcusably late without the courtesy of a phone call.

Sam, however, came to the rescue. Standing, he said with an easy smile, "Julia, I think we should feed these hungry people and save some for the Crawfords. He's undoubtedly been held up by an emergency. That's what you get, folks, when you invite a busy doctor to dinner. Let's adjourn to the table."

That was all well and good, I thought as we took our places at the table, but what was holding up Lauren Crawford? I couldn't count the number of times that Sue Hargrove had come alone to everything from a formal dinner party to the cotillion's annual dance at the country club. A doctor's wife either learns to go it alone or resigns herself to a limited social life.

Just as we were all seated, the doorbell rang. Sam sprang to his feet as Lillian, bearing a platter of sliced roast beef, appeared from the kitchen. He hurried to the door, and she backed out of the dining room. We were going to have either a cold entrée or a reheated one.

Excusing myself, I hied to the living room to greet the late-comers, herding them quickly toward the table, as Sam took their coats. Dr. Crawford made a few easy apologies, saying simply that he'd been unavoidably detained and left it at that.

After making introductions, I directed the guests of honor to their places — Lauren Crawford on Sam's right and Dr. Don Crawford on my right. Spreading my napkin in my lap, I nodded to Lillian as she peeped around the swinging door of the kitchen, and the dinner began.

While Lillian served the various dishes, I was eager to put Dr. Crawford at ease. "We are so glad to have you in town, Dr. Crawford —"

"Don, please," he said easily.

I smiled at the expected correction. "Thank you, Don. We hope you'll enjoy your stay in Abbotsville. We don't have big city amenities, but I think you'll find the town has its compensations."

Binkie, seated on my left, laughed as she added, "Golf, and golf, and a little more golf. That's about all the compensations we have, unless you're a hunter, in which case you have to wait for the right seasons."

Mr. Pickens, down on Sam's left, immediately picked up on Binkie's idea of local amenities. "I beg to differ, Ms. Enloe-Bates," he said with a teasing smile. "Why, we have empty streets that're perfect for runners, and we have a miniature golf course for beginners, and don't forget the shuffleboard court. And there's high school football, basketball, and volleyball if you're into spectator sports. And, oh, yes, we have fairly good television reception for three stations, but if you want more than that, you have to get cable."

"Oh, J.D.," Hazel Marie said, "it's not that bad. You'll make them think we live in the sticks. And, really, Lauren," she said, turning to Mrs. Crawford, "there's so much to do here, you'll have to keep a schedule. There's the book club and the garden club, circle meetings, Women of the Church

65

meetings and their projects, and I'm sure the medical wives have a club as well."

The bantering went on like that for several minutes, but as I kept an eye on the table, I'd noticed a brief look of dismay cross Lauren's face as Hazel Marie had listed the numerous activities in town. And as I did, I couldn't help but note the stark contrast between Mrs. and Dr. Crawford. He was a nice-looking, almost handsome man, with dark hair and startlingly blue eyes. He had a compact build with a strong-looking upper body of average height. She, on the other hand, was a Nordic blonde, so blond in fact, that another shade or two lighter would've qualified her as an albino. She wore her hair slicked back and gathered with a narrow black velvet ribbon. Even her eyelashes and brows were blond, with no effort having been made to darken them. Her complexion, too, was so fair and untouched with cosmetics that I knew Hazel Marie would love to get her hands on her. Her only touch of color came when Sam or anyone else directed a question or comment to her. Then her face flushed and she answered without looking away from her plate. Lauren Crawford was a slight young woman who would've been better served dressed in something other than a gray sweater-dress that was so roomy she could've turned around in it without creating a ripple.

While absorbed in my critical, but concerned, assessment of the doctor's wife, the conversation had gone on around me. As I tuned back in, I heard the word *surfing,* but declined to comment because I wasn't sure if they were talking of surfing the waves or the Web.

Since neither was of interest to me, my attention returned to that colorless young woman who certainly needed a helping hand — preferably one holding at least a lipstick. Maybe, I thought, when she notices how attractive Hazel Marie and Binkie are, she'll take the hint.

Her husband, however, elicited no censure from me. He was neatly dressed in a white shirt, subdued tie, and a long-sleeved blue sweater — perfect for a casual dinner on a bitter night. As, indeed, were the outfits of both Coleman and Mr. Pickens, although their sweaters were of different colors. Don Crawford fit right in, both dressing and conducting himself as if he'd been brought up in Abbotsville.

His wife was another matter entirely, and I recalled that handsome men often seemed to choose unattractive wives. Not always, of course, as assuredly Coleman and Mr. Pickens had not, but it happened often enough to be noticed.

Giving Lillian a signal to pick up the plates to clear the table for dessert, I recalled that it was far more common that beautiful women chose unattractive husbands. But in many of those cases, wealth went a long way toward improving a man's looks.

After dinner, we regathered in the living room, where Sam stoked the fire and made sure that everyone was comfortably seated. The conversation continued with Coleman's telling of serving a warrant on a wanted man who had been found hiding in a clothes dryer, and Mr. Pickens telling how Ronnie waited patiently by the door on the days that the little twin girls were in preschool. Several others joined in to tell the Crawfords about Ronnie, the Great Dane, who was boarding with the Pickens family until his owner, Thurlow Jones, regained his health. Then, of course, we had to tell some stories about Thurlow, the town's most outrageous citizen.

It was only a while before I noticed that Lauren Crawford had had little, if anything, to add to the conversation, although her husband's open interest encouraged the telling of more stories of local lore. Sam, too, had noticed her nonparticipation, for, seated next to her, he tried to draw her out or at least to include her. She responded in monosyllables or with a smile, a nod, or a glance at her husband.

Hazel Marie had noticed as well, for she moved across the room to a chair next to Lauren and began asking about her children. Hazel Marie did this in an intimate manner so that the two of them were not the center of attention. Lauren seemed to respond warmly, although I could not hear what was said.

Since it was a weeknight — deliberately chosen by me — it was not a late evening. By eleven o'clock, Sam closed the door on the last of our guests, turned to me and asked, "Well, what did you think?"

CHAPTER 8

"I'm not sure you want to know," I said. Then, turning toward the kitchen, I went on. "Let me check on Lillian. I'll be back in a minute."

As expected, though, the kitchen was both clean and empty. Lillian and I had worked out such matters long before this, so she had gone home when her work was done. I checked the lock on the back door, turned off the lights, and resumed the discussion of the evening with Sam.

"Oh, me," I said tiredly as I sat in the wing chair opposite his, "that poor young woman. You tried valiantly, Sam, to draw her out, but she just wouldn't be drawn. What do you think is wrong with her?"

"Painfully shy," he said with a note of sympathy in his voice. "I felt sorry for her, but the more I tried to interest her, the more uncomfortable she seemed. I think she would've much rather I'd ignored her."

"That's almost pitiful, until I think of how at her age she should've already learned how to at least *act* her part. How old do you think she is, anyway?"

"The only hint I got," Sam said, "was when she said — only in answer to my question, mind you — that she and Don had met when she was a freshman in college and he was an intern. That would mean about an eight or nine year age difference. And they've been married long enough to have two children. In other words, old enough not to be out of her depth around nice, friendly folks like us."

"My feeling exactly. It's interesting, though," I went on in a musing way, "that he is so approachable and at ease among strangers. And entertaining — that medical school story he told was quite funny. In other words, he had no trouble keeping up his end of the conversation — such a stark contrast to his wife. Overall," I added, "I got a good feeling about him. He seemed both confident and competent, so I don't think I'd hesitate to call on him if we needed anything."

Sam nodded. "That's good, but I'm going to worry a little about her."

"I know," I said, nodding back. "She doesn't exactly epitomize what I'd call

71

California glamour."

Sam smiled. "I was thinking along the lines of whether she'll enjoy her stay here. If she doesn't, they could pull out and leave the Hargrove practice in limbo."

That was not a comforting thought to take to bed, so I resigned myself to seeing that Lauren Crawford enjoyed her stay in Abbotsville. Which was exactly where I wanted them to be until my doctor returned.

Midmorning the following day and, as expected, Hazel Marie called to thank me for having them, compliment me on the dinner, and comment on how much she and Mr. Pickens had enjoyed the evening.

After completing her due diligence, she said, "But, Miss Julia, I felt so sorry for Lauren Crawford. What is *wrong* with her?"

"I declare, I don't know," I said. "Sam and I talked a little last night, and he thinks she's just very shy. But it's been my experience that shy people generally outgrow it, or at least learn to compensate for it. I mean, they don't have to turn into blathering chatterboxes. All they have to do is learn to smile occasionally and answer a question with more than 'Yes,' 'No,' or 'I don't know.' "

"That is true, but that's about all I got

when I tried to talk to her. She did show a little interest when I asked about her children, but as soon as I mentioned a playdate with my girls, she began to sink back in her shell. I pushed a little, saying I'd call her and set up a time, but she mumbled something about Don's being very particular about who their children were with."

As I absorbed that, Hazel Marie seemed to have a sudden insight. "You know," she said in an awed tone, "now that I think of it, I think that was an insult."

"Pretty close to it," I agreed. "Although I don't think she has enough gumption to have meant it that way, or to even realize how insulting it actually was. But who knows, Hazel Marie? She's a puzzle, all right, especially in light of how easy and comfortable her husband was."

"I *know,*" Hazel Marie said emphatically. "I feel safer than I did about his taking Dr. Hargrove's place, although we're unlikely to need him. Our little girls are seen by a pediatrician, thank goodness, and she's not planning to go anywhere."

"So what're you going to do?" I asked. "I mean about following up with Lauren Crawford. I wouldn't blame you if you just do nothing." Actually, the more I thought about the woman's response to a playdate with Hazel Marie's children, the hotter I could feel myself getting. After all, shyness is not an excuse for rudeness.

Hazel Marie, however, was not as easily stirred or as quickly angered as I. "I'll probably sleep on it for a while," she said. "Then maybe ask her to come for tea and bring her children to play with the girls. Surely she — or he — wouldn't worry about them if she's in the same house."

It was all very strange, we concluded, but also not a long-term problem. The Crawfords would be gone when Dr. Hargrove returned, and some other town would be dealing with them — or trying to deal with them. For myself, I had done my duty by having them for a meal and introducing them to two attractive young couples. As far as I was concerned, they were now on their own. Especially since by bedtime, Lauren Crawford had not called to thank me or to reciprocate in any way at all.

But long before bedtime, during her lunch hour to be precise, Binkie had called with her thanks and especially with her compliments to Lillian.

"I'll tell you what's a fact," she'd said, "if I can ever learn to cook roast beef without getting it either so rare or so well done it's inedible, I'll be happy. Lillian's is always perfect."

"Well, it almost wasn't," I said, "since the Crawfords were so late. But you know Lillian would be glad to show you or tell you how she does it. I wouldn't know how to begin."

"Speaking of the Crawfords," Binkie said, blithely abandoning the subject of cookery, "I didn't get a chance to speak with Lauren last night, so I called her between clients this morning. I wanted to tell her about St. Mark's preschool program — we have Gracie enrolled there, and it's really excellent. And it's about the only one that'll take children on a short-term basis. But," Binkie said with a sigh, "Lauren wasn't interested. She said her children are homeschooled."

"Uh-oh."

"No," Binkie went on, "that's understandable. It's probably easier on the children than changing schools every few months. It was just the way she put it."

"Why? How did she put it?"

"Well, I may be reading too much into it, but she said — and I'm quoting — 'Don *likes for me* to homeschool them.' I didn't think much of it at the time, but the more I think of it, the stranger it sounds. I mean, it wasn't as if, for whatever reason, they

75

thought it best for the children, but rather the decision was based on what *he* liked. Doesn't that sound odd to you?"

"Well, yes, it does," I said, "but remember whom you were speaking to. Hazel Marie and I have already decided that she's the odd one, and you may've been quoting her, but she may not have been quoting him. Exactly, I mean."

"Hm-m, yes, I guess that's true. Don't repeat this, but Coleman felt a little uneasy about him."

"Really?" That stunned me, for I'd given Don Crawford high marks on my assessment of him. On the other hand, Deputy Sheriff Sergeant Coleman Bates was an able and experienced judge of men, having seen so many at their worst. "What did Coleman say?"

"Oh, he just said that Don was a little off-putting and something about the way he stared at whoever he was talking to."

"My goodness, I didn't notice that at all."

"Well, you know Coleman. His thinking may be a little warped since he deals with so much riffraff." Then Binkie laughed. "Come to think of it, so do I.

"Anyway," she went on, "I just wanted you to know that I've made an effort with Lauren. Since I didn't get anywhere, I'll probably let it go. Not because she wasn't interested in St. Mark's, but because she wasn't interested in much of anything. I know everybody says they don't have time for things, but, Miss Julia, I really don't. Coleman and I are so busy that we have to take Gracie out of school and go out of town just to be together. I really don't have time for someone who has to be courted, and I hope you'll understand."

"That's perfectly all right, Binkie. You don't need to explain anything to me. I understand and I appreciate you making the effort. And to be honest, I had them over last night mainly because Sue Hargrove had asked me to. Of course, I probably would have eventually, anyway. So let's both of us say that we've done as we should toward Lauren, and the next move is up to her."

Binkie laughed again. "We'll probably be waiting awhile for that."

After hanging up, I found myself feeling unsettled, not because none of my young friends had a good impression of Lauren Crawford, but because one of the most trusted of them had questions concerning *Don* Crawford.

Mentally throwing up my hands, one thought kept running through my head —

Oh, won't you come home, Bob Hargrove, won't you come home?

CHAPTER 9

Well aware that I was on the verge of stepping off the edge of a canyon, I visited Hazel Marie the next morning — not, however, without calling first, as one should. She seemed pleased to see me, although with the twins in preschool for half the day, she'd probably looked forward to having a few hours to herself. Yet now, there I was using up her free time.

"Hazel Marie," I said after she'd taken my coat and led me into the living room of the lovely old house that Sam had once owned, "I hope you didn't change any plans for me. This could've waited, although you know how I am — when I get something on my mind, I can't rest until I do something about it."

"Oh, no," she said, "I had nothing planned for the morning, and I'm always glad to see you. Let's go to the dining room and sit at the table. James is bringing in coffee, and

79

I'm tired of balancing a cup and saucer while trying to talk." She laughed easily, knowing that I would recall the incident to which she was referring. We'd both been at the last circle meeting when Elaine Whitmire had leaned over to speak to someone, tilting the saucer she was holding so that a full cup of coffee toppled off into her lap. No lasting damage was done, for Elaine had been talking so much that her coffee had cooled considerably.

James came in from the kitchen, smiling broadly at me as he laid out cups and saucers, a coffeepot, and a plate of cookies. "Been a long time since I seen you, Miss Julia," he said. "How's Miss Lillian doin'?"

"She's doing well," I said. "Still trying to keep up with Latisha."

"An' that's a job," he said, as we laughed at the thought of the little whirlwind that was Lillian's great-granddaughter.

Hazel Marie and I sat at the table, prepared our coffee to our tastes, then she said, "What's going on, Miss Julia? I can tell you have something on your mind. I hope it's not Lloyd you're worried about."

"Oh, no, not Lloyd. As far as I can tell, he's thriving in high school, but since you've brought it up . . . Hazel Marie, is Mr. Pickens really buying that child a car?"

She smiled. "I think we're going to have to stop thinking of him as a child. Though it's so hard for me to do. I can't believe he's old enough to drive, but J.D. says that if he's going to be a safe driver, he needs to be an experienced driver. He wants Lloyd to have a lot of supervised driving time before he's turned loose to drive by himself. And I guess that makes sense, but the thought of Lloyd behind the wheel, well, it just gives me nightmares."

"But does he really need a car of his own at his age? I mean, he's not even sixteen yet."

"I know, but with his beginner's permit, he can drive with a licensed driver in the car with him. So J.D. is planning to buy him an old, used car that he says can be dented and scratched and even crashed while Lloyd is getting experience. He says it'll be a lot cheaper to let him wreck an old, beat-up car than one of ours."

"Lord, Hazel Marie! He's expecting him to have a *wreck*?"

"No, no, that's not what he meant. J.D. says a new driver has to back up about a hundred times before he learns how to do it. And that he'll back into something about ninety-nine times while he's learning — I know I still can't back up straight."

"Me, either," I admitted, as a certain harrowing experience in reverse came to mind. "In fact, I've been known to drive all around the block just to avoid having to back up a few feet."

"Anyway," Hazel Marie went on, "J.D. says it's likely that Lloyd will end up in a ditch a few times, and an old, heavy car that already has dents and scratches on it will be safer and cheaper for him to learn in.

"And think of this, Miss Julia, J.D. will be letting him learn to drive on all kinds of roads, and turning around in empty parking lots, and questioning him on the rules of the road every weekend he's home. So, what finally made me see the wisdom of it was realizing that by the time Lloyd can drive by himself, he'll really know how to do it."

"Well," I conceded with some reluctance, "I guess that makes sense. I just know that I didn't learn to drive till I was twenty-two years old, so fifteen sounds a little young to me."

"Yes'm, I know. I was about the same age as you before I began to drive, but it was because we didn't have a car for anybody to drive."

"Well," I said, holding out my cup for a refill, "that wasn't really what I wanted to talk about. I mean, I intended to talk to you about it eventually, but something else has come up. And I realize that I may be starting something that could be severely damaging to someone, so, Hazel Marie, please don't let this go any further.

"Well, wait," I went on, "it'll have to go one more step, but Mr. Pickens is certainly not a gossip. Not that you are, I didn't mean that. I mean I trust you both not to repeat this, but I need to ease my mind about it. Else I'd keep it to myself, which is probably what I ought to do."

"What in the world?" Hazel Marie said, frowning as she sat straight up in her Queen Anne dining chair.

"All I want to know is this, has Mr. Pickens said anything to you about Dr. Don Crawford? I mean, has he said what he thought of him? Because, see, it's like this. He made a good impression on me — especially in contrast to his wife — and he did on everybody else who was there the other night, except for one person. The problem is that I respect that one person and his — or her — instincts. It's got me befuddled, Hazel Marie, because what if Sam or I fall ill before Dr. Hargrove gets back? I want to know the kind of doctor I'll be dealing with."

She turned her cup around in its saucer,

looked away, then back again. "Well," she said, "I'm like you. I was impressed with him, but J.D. was kinda wishy-washy. But you know he never takes anyone at face value. He withholds judgment, I guess you could say, until he's sure one way or the other. I sometimes think he's too suspicious of people, but he says he's been burned too many times."

I leaned back from the table, absorbing Mr. Pickens's reserved opinion of Don Crawford. Like Coleman Bates, Mr. Pickens often had to deal with the dregs of the earth. Had those experiences given them the ability to recognize certain qualities or traits that would be invisible to others?

"What, exactly," I finally asked, "did Mr. Pickens say about him? If you don't mind repeating it."

"Oh, I don't mind telling you. Actually, it was so silly that I had to laugh. He just said he looked funny."

"Looked *funny*? What does that mean?"

Hazel Marie shrugged. "Just the way he looked, I guess."

"Well, that's interesting because I thought he looked quite nice. He was wearing pretty much what the other men were wearing."

"No, that wasn't what he meant. He meant he *looked* funny."

"That's what I meant. I didn't notice anything unusual."

"No, Miss Julia, J.D. meant the way he looked *at* people. He stared, he said. Without blinking, he said."

"Oh, my goodness, that's pretty much what Coleman said." Then I gasped and leaned my head on my hand in dismay. "Oh, me, now I've just told you who else had reservations. I didn't mean to do that. First thing you know, I'll be accused of starting a smear campaign around town. Forget I told you, Hazel Marie. Forget I even brought it up. I am so sorry."

"Oh, don't worry about it," she said. "I know you're not a gossip. Besides, like I told J.D., the man was just doing what he'd been taught to do. How many times have you and I told Lloyd that he should look people in the eye, especially when speaking to them?"

"Well, yes, that's true. We have done that, and I can remember my mother telling me the same thing. Thank you, Hazel Marie, I feel better about the whole thing now. Dr. Crawford was just doing what he'd been taught. He was being polite."

The whole thing was troubling, though, specifically because of the high esteem in which I held the opinions of Coleman and

Mr. Pickens. If anybody could recognize warning signs, it was those two.

But warning signs of what? That Don Crawford was *too* polite? Ridiculous. I had met people who were too polite — you know the type. They're the people who fawn over you, who're courteous to the point of oiliness, and who make you wonder what they're really after. Don Crawford had done nothing like that, and I, who prided myself on being able to read people, had not noticed the intense gaze that had twitched the antennas of two law enforcement men.

Thinking back on the dinner party, I pictured Dr. Crawford on my right and realized that most of the time his face had been turned toward the rest of the table, only occasionally glancing sideways to include me in his audience. I had had little opportunity to notice what he did with his eyes, nor, I realized, had Sam, who, as a concerned host, had directed most of his attention to Lauren.

Well, it was a conundrum, there was no doubt about it. But was it worth worrying about? No, I answered myself. In fact, if I had to call on the doctor because of ill health, I would *want* him to give his full attention to whatever problem I or Sam had. So stare all you want, Doctor, I thought to myself. Make sure you see everything there is to see. Don't overlook a single thing.

myself. Winke wink, you see. Anything that
is to see. Don't overlook a single thing.

CHAPTER 10

I declare, February is the longest month of the year and usually the coldest. Not only did it seem to never end, I could never warm up. The days were short and drizzly, the evenings long and dreary in spite of my efforts to stay in a cheerful frame of mind.

To fill the never-ending evenings — which started about four in the afternoon and lasted till dawn — I went so far as to set up a card table in the library and get out one of Lloyd's old jigsaw puzzles. Sam was entranced with the seascape puzzle and quickly put the outside pieces together. My interest, however, waned after realizing that there was almost a square yard of unrelieved ocean to fill in. I mean, how many similar-looking pieces do you have to try in order to fill one empty space?

"Sam?" I said one evening while we pored over the puzzle, "aren't you glad we don't live in Sweden or Norway — one of those places where it stays dark all day long for months at a time?"

He glanced up. "Yes, I can truthfully say I am." Then he laughed. "Why're you thinking of that?"

"I'm just tired of winter, that's all. I don't know how people stand to live in semidarkness for most of the year."

"Oh," he said, snapping a puzzle piece in place, "it's probably not that bad. People adjust to whatever climate they live in, and Nordic people compensate by excelling in winter sports. Especially in the Olympics."

"Well, more power to them," I murmured, slightly sarcastically, being unimpressed by athletic prowess cultivated in order to stay warm.

Sam sat back and crossed his arms over his chest, giving me his full attention. "Now what's all this about?"

"Boredom," I quickly said in an effort to shrug off my melancholy. "Which is my own fault. There're plenty of things to do, I just can't bring myself to do them. So I'm blaming my laziness on the weather and the time of year. Just overlook me, Sam. I'll get over it.

"Actually, though," I went on, "I've had the Hargroves on my mind, wondering how they're enjoying Europe in midwinter. I would've picked a better time of the year, if it'd been me."

"Well, you know the main reason they went was so he could attend that meeting in Stockholm. And I expect Sue was just glad that he was willing to take time off at all, so the time of year didn't matter."

"Oh, I know," I said. "And I'm happy for them." Finally finding one puzzle piece that fit, I decided to stop with a win. "I'm through for the night," I said, getting up from the card table. "This thing is making me edgy."

"A little testy, too?" Sam asked, raising his eyebrows.

I smiled. "Yes, but not at you." Then, reaching the fireplace, I turned and said, "Sam, you mentioned the word *Nordic* a while ago. That's the word that came to mind when I first saw Lauren Crawford. Bless her heart, she is so fair that she's just plain washed out. No color at all. Wouldn't it be wonderful to see what she'd look like with a proper makeover?"

"I don't know about that," Sam said, a cautionary note in his voice. "Young women today know all about cosmetics, so if she doesn't use them, she probably doesn't want to."

"But I'm talking about a *professional*

90

makeover — very lightly applied with just a smidgeon of color so that it looks natural. She could be a beauty. And think of this, Sam, wouldn't that help her self-confidence? To know how good she looks? Why, she might blossom out with a perfectly delightful personality."

"Maybe so," Sam said, giving up on the puzzle. "But you could also be opening a can of worms, even damaging what little self-esteem she has. Of course, I don't know what you have in mind, if anything in particular, but . . ."

"Hazel Marie," I said, my mind racing ahead to visualize a makeover to end all makeovers. "I have Hazel Marie in mind."

And right then, my mind went into overdrive as I imagined a beauty session that would include makeup application, hair styling, and the selection of clothing that enhanced the figure rather than smothered it.

"I'd be careful about that," Sam said, "if I were you. To suggest such a thing would make her think she needs help."

"Well, she does."

Sam laughed. "I know, honey, but it could really hurt her feelings. Shame her, even, and I know you don't want to do that."

"No, of course I don't. I'll just have to

think of a way to include her without letting her know it's about her. Maybe invite her to a class with one or two others. That way, she wouldn't feel singled out."

"Maybe," Sam said without enthusiasm. "Still, I'd be very careful, whatever I did."

Assuring both him and myself that I was always careful, especially when there was a possibility that someone's feelings could be hurt, I went to bed feeling energized. I'd told Lillian that I had a great urge to fix something, and what better project could I take on than a young woman who badly needed fixing?

I woke up that Saturday morning with renewed vigor — I had something to sink my teeth into and be helpful to someone else at the same time. I was well aware, however, that I had to step gingerly, move carefully, and use great delicacy if I was to accomplish my plan. In fact, I was so acutely aware of the need for care that I'd even prayed about it.

As Sam had pointed out, there could be some deep, embedded reason that Lauren Crawford avoided cosmetics when they were abundantly available and so easily used. Perhaps she had religious qualms about using them, although I'd gotten no hint that the Crawfords were anything other than members of a mainline church. I mean, she'd not worn an organdy cap or anything like that.

So I decided to let things alone for a while and let them perk along in my mind. If it was meant to be, something would occur to show me how to approach Lauren without either humiliating or enraging her. I would simply bide my time.

Lloyd helped by offering a distraction. He came over that morning to see if Sam wanted to go downtown with him. They often did that on Saturdays — going to the sports store and looking at new fishing rods and equipment, then having lunch at the Bluebird.

Sam and I were still at the breakfast table when Lloyd joined us. Lillian set a cup of coffee at his place, and I had to smile. The boy had always liked coffee, but I had limited his intake when he was younger out of concern that it might stunt his growth. Come to think of it, maybe it had.

After welcoming him, Sam said, "We're all atwitter waiting to hear which girl you're going to take to the dance. Or," he amended with a smile, "which girl you're going to let take you."

"Oh, boy," Lloyd said, almost moaning as he closed his eyes and shook his head. "Looks like I'm not even gonna go. At least as anybody's date."

"Why?" I asked. "What happened?"

"Well," he said, his shoulders slumping, "the word got around that I was gonna have more dates than I could handle and none of the girls wanted to be turned down. So they got together and decided that none of 'em would ask me. So that means," he added with a frown, "that I'll have to go stag or not go at all."

Sam smiled with sympathy. "Oh, the perils of popularity."

Lloyd gave him a sickly smile, and I said, "Oh, Sam, it's not funny. I'm so sorry, Lloyd."

"Oh, I don't really mind," he said. "And I guess Mr. Sam is right. Better to laugh than get strung out about it. I don't mind going stag, except I can't decide whether to ask any of those girls to dance when I get there or just ignore them. Like they're doing to me."

"I think," Sam said, "that those three girls could've handled it better. In fact, I'm surprised that one of them hasn't broken off and snagged you for herself. All's fair, you know. But there's one compensation for going stag, Lloyd — you can drive Pickens to the dance without worrying where your date is sitting."

"That is true," Lloyd said, looking up with his bright smile back in place. "And he'll probably let me drive around for a while before we get there — which I couldn't do if a date was in the backseat."

Sam and Lloyd had just gone on their way when LuAnne Conover called. She was in high spirits, exclaiming as soon as I picked up the phone, "Julia! Guess what! I have the *best* news!"

I am sorry to say that my first thought was that something terrible had happened to Leonard, her longtime cheating husband whom she was in the process of divorcing. I was able to hold my tongue just long enough, though, and thank goodness for that, because her news had nothing to do with him.

"I got the job, Julia! They just called and told me. Isn't it wonderful?"

"Well, yes," I said, somewhat mystified, "if it's what you want. I didn't know you were looking for a job."

"Oh, yes, you did. I told you weeks ago that I needed something that paid a decent wage."

She'd not said one word to me about looking for a job, but you don't argue with Lu-
Anne Conover, so I didn't. And the fact of
the matter was that she'd probably told
everybody she'd seen and had just assumed
I'd been one of them.

"Well," I said, brushing aside who told
who what, "tell me about it. What kind of
job is it?"

"It's perfect, that's what it is, although I
wasn't expecting to hear anything on a
Saturday. But," she went on, "I guess in a
business like theirs, one day is as good as
another."

"What kind of business is it? Did you apply at just the one or at several?"

"A half a dozen, at least," she said with a
touch of exasperation. "I declare, Julia, you
would think that a good receptionist would
be a valued employee. But you know I've
been doing part-time work for a nonprofit,
and the only ones who don't profit are the
people who work for them. I might as well
have volunteered my time for all the salary I
got. But now," she said, taking a deep
breath, "now I have a decent job with
decent wages in a business that knows the
value of having the right person interfacing
with the public."

"Well, tell me," I said again. "What busi-

96

ness is it? Where will you be working?"

"At the Good Shepherd Funeral Home!" she said. "Isn't it wonderful!"

"Um, well," I said, not wanting to commit myself, "it certainly sounds interesting. What will you be doing?"

"I'll be the face of the funeral home — the first person that the public speaks to on the phone or meets when they come in. It's a very important position, Julia, and they chose me for it."

"I am delighted to hear it, LuAnne. It sounds ideal for you. You're always so warm and welcoming, eager to meet people, and never at a loss for words. You're perfect for it. I'm not surprised that they offered it to you."

"Well, it wasn't a given, I assure you. They told me last week when I interviewed that they were looking at two other applicants. So after my interview, I sat in the car and watched who came and went to see who the others were — what my competition was like. I knew right away that one of them didn't have a chance — too young, for one thing. And I ask you, who wants to look down a cleavage when they've come to buy a casket? The other one, though, was my real competition. I didn't know her, but she looked professional — I could tell by the way she walked. But I think what did her in was her frown. She was one of those women who frown even when they smile because the frown is really a wrinkle. So, anyway, the job is mine and I'll start the week after next."

"My sincere congratulations, LuAnne. I am so happy for you."

"Well, I do need your help, Julia. They told me how important a first impression is — especially for grieving families, which are their primary customers. Except, of course, those for whom they're grieving. I have to be friendly, but not bubbly. I mean, who wants a perky little twit trying to sell you an urn for cremains? I've got to be sympathetic, but not so much that I'm not businesslike because they *are* in retail, you know. It's actually a selling job. And I have to dress carefully, too — not so plain that I look like I'm the one in mourning, yet not so flashy that I'm inappropriate for the circumstances. It's a fine line I have to walk."

"My goodness," I said, impressed with the demands of a receptionist's job. "I had no idea how much is involved. I am really pleased for you, but how can I help?"

"You can help by asking Hazel Marie if she'd show me how to get a more natural look — I think sometimes I may have a heavy hand when I contour. And I'd love her to look through my closet to see what I'll need to reach that perfect balance between plain and flashy, and maybe make some suggestions about a more professional hair style. She did work as an Avon Lady at one time, didn't she?"

"A long time ago," I said, my heart lifting at the perfect opportunity for a styling session that more than one stylee could attend. "But you don't need me to ask her. Just give her a call — I'm sure she'd love to do it."

"I know, and I will, but I thought you'd be interested in sitting in. We could all use a little help now and then, you know."

No, I hadn't known and still didn't. And, furthermore, I could do without LuAnne's opinion on what I needed, cosmetically speaking. Stifling a sharp reply, however, I let her get away with it, for I now knew how not to approach Lauren Crawford.

CHAPTER 11

I couldn't decide if LuAnne had hurt my feelings or simply enraged me. What did she think I needed help with — my face, my hair, or my clothes? As far as I was concerned, not a one of the above. But even if I did need help, I certainly wouldn't advertise it by admitting it to her — it would be all over town by nightfall. No, I'd go to Hazel Marie by myself, get the benefit of her expertise, then let the changes, if any, speak for themselves.

So with that, I determined to leave Lauren Crawford alone for good. I would not hurt her feelings as mine had been hurt. After all, it wasn't my business to introduce her to Estée Lauder or to Ann Taylor. I realized now that the minute I even hinted that she could use some help, she'd begin agonizing over every aspect of herself, wondering why she hadn't noticed, as well as wondering who else had.

"Julia," Sam said late Monday afternoon, "I think I'll run over to Barnes and Noble tomorrow. Is there anything you want?"

"I don't think so. The good books don't come out until April or May, and again in the fall. I'll just look through whatever you get."

"Well, we're in for another month or so of bad weather, so I need something to read. Having a stack of unread books around is like having money in the bank to me." Then as he started to turn away, he stopped. "Oh, by the way, I forgot to tell you, but while you were at your circle meeting this morning, Don Crawford called."

"I hope it was to thank us for having them to dinner."

Sam grinned. "He mentioned it, but he was calling to ask me about a good handyman."

"Handyman!" I put down the newspaper I'd been scanning. "Surely they haven't broken something at the Hargrove house?"

"No, nothing like that. Seems the good doctor is into real estate. Instead of investing in the stock market, he buys small houses in the towns where he spends a few months — if he likes the town, that is. And if the houses need updating, he gets that done while he's around to supervise, then rents them out when he moves on. It's a pretty good plan," Sam said, nodding in approval, "and if he's chosen well, they'll gain in value over time. Anyway, he called to ask if I could recommend somebody. Apparently, he doesn't like dealing with a construction company — too many hidden costs, he said. He's had better luck dealing one on one with somebody who can do a little of everything."

"I hope you knew who to recommend, both to him and to us. Just as soon as spring arrives — if it ever does — there're a number of things around here that need repairing."

"You're right, but the only person I could think of was the man who bought the apartment building where Miss Mattie Freeman lived. Remember? He was updating the empty apartments and doing all the work himself. What was his name?"

Ah, yes, I recalled, dredging my memory, he of the well-turned arms. "Mr. Wheeler," I said, "Nate Wheeler, that was his name. But, Sam, if he was well-off enough to buy that whole building, why would he hire out as a handyman?"

102

"I don't know that he would, but I spoke with him a couple of times while you were busy in Miss Mattie's apartment. He showed me one of the kitchens he was working on and said doing that kind of work was beneficial to his mental health." Sam smiled at the memory. "And he had the grace to say it ironically and laugh about it. I liked him."

"I did, too, and so did LuAnne and Helen Stroud. He's a widower, if I remember right."

"Well, then, I may drop by and visit with Mr. Wheeler, see if he minds my passing his name along to the doctor. Maybe if he can't do it or doesn't want to, he'll know someone who will." Sam smiled. "I'll mention that we might be interested, too."

"Couldn't hurt," I said, smiling back at him.

Learning that Don Crawford invested in real estate, as did I, served to elevate him a degree or two more in my estimation. I would be interested in seeing what and where he had bought property for rental purposes. Location is so important, you know, so I wondered if he'd been in town long enough to know where to buy and where not to. And I couldn't help but wonder if his wife shared his interest.

Wouldn't it be a marvel if she turned out to be a flip-or-flop partner like those couples on television? Maybe there was a lot more to her than she'd revealed over a dinner table. I hoped to goodness there was.

But she was no longer my problem — not that she'd ever actually been — but I'd been awfully close to making her my problem. I firmly put all thought of Lauren Crawford out of my mind and focused on how to find out where Don Crawford's new property was. Purely as a matter of personal interest, of course, but if he'd chosen well, there just might be another house for sale in the same area.

Sam came in, back from his trip to the bookstore in Asheville and, smiling, pulled a book from his sack. "Got you the new J. A. Jance."

"Oh, good. I didn't know she had a new one out. What did you get?"

"John Sandford," he said, looking pleased with himself.

"Virgil Flowers? Or Lucas Davenport?"

"It's a Davenport, and I'm reading it first."

I laughed. "Well, hurry up with it. You know I have a crush on Lucas, although Virgil runs a close second. But come on," I said, getting up and taking his arm, "let's go to the kitchen where it's warmer. Lillian is making hot chocolate."

We'd just settled in at the table when Lloyd, looking tired and somewhat woeful, dropped by on his way home from school. He spoke to us as he let his backpack fall to the floor, then he flopped down in a chair at the kitchen table, where Sam and I were enjoying mugs of hot chocolate. It was a perfect afternoon for a hot drink — overcast, damp, and chilly.

Lillian set a steaming mug in front of Lloyd. "You look like you need something to perk you up. That school's wearing you out."

"No'm, it's not school. I guess it's just me. Anyway," he said, looking up at Sam and me, "I just came by to tell you that J.D. bought me a car."

"When?" I said, turning to look out the window. "Where is it?"

"It's getting washed and cleaned up at the dealer's. We'll get it tomorrow after school, and I'm real happy about it."

In spite of that claim, he didn't look at all happy. In fact, he looked as droopy as a basset hound.

"Well, tell us, Lloyd," Sam said. "What kind did you get? We want to be able to recognize you and wave as you drive by."

"Well, see," the boy said, "it's kinda like this. J.D. asked me what kind I wanted, and I had in mind a little two-seater with bucket seats and four on the floor, maybe in a bright color, like red, but not anything fancy or expensive like Mr. Horace Allen's. I was just thinking about something sleek looking that looks like it's moving when it's setting still. I didn't care what make it was, but I made a big mistake."

"Oh?" Sam said, as his eyebrows went up.

"Yessir, I was so excited about getting a car and not wanting to be too picky about it, I just said I'd be happy with whatever he picked out."

Uh-oh, I thought.

"So what did he pick out?" Sam asked.

"It's a, well, a . . ." Lloyd paid special attention to his mug of hot chocolate, carefully stirring the melted marshmallows. "It's a Pontiac Bonneville."

"A Bonneville?" Sam said, his eyebrows going up. "I thought they'd stopped making that model."

Lloyd nodded. "Yessir, they have, but they made this one in 1998, which means it's older than I am. J.D. says that just proves how reliable it is 'cause it's still running. But I'm worried it might be on its last legs. I mean, it's already got four hundred and ten thousand miles on it."

Sam reared back in his chair. "Four hundred and ten *thousand*?"

"Yessir." Lloyd's shoulders sagged.

"Bucket seats?" Sam asked.

"No, sir. Bench."

"No console with gear shift?"

Lloyd shook his head. "Uh-uh, on the steering column."

"But," Sam said, trying for an encouraging word, "that's a big, heavy car that'll give you a comfortable ride."

"Yessir, it's big all right. They use the same wheelbase to make hearses, so I guess it's comfortable, too."

Before any of us could laugh, Lillian leaned over to refill Lloyd's mug. "What color is it? I bet it's something real pretty."

"It's gray."

"Oh, I like gray," she said, dropping in more marshmallows. "That's my favorite car color."

"Well," Sam said, joining Lillian's efforts to help Lloyd see the bright side, "it'll keep you safe, that's for sure. And I think we can say that somebody else has gotten all the kinks out of it by now."

"Yessir," Lloyd said, clearly still seeing only the dark side. "And I really don't mind that it's not a little sports car. It's just that I didn't exactly expect a Sherman tank instead."

Sam made a valiant effort not to laugh, but I could tell how close he was to it. As for me, the more I heard about the car in which Lloyd's life would be put at risk, the better I felt. In fact, I was feeling quite lighthearted at the thought of Lloyd in a car built like an army vehicle.

Lillian came over to the table and put her hand on Lloyd's shoulder. "You wanta eat supper with us, honey?"

"No'm," he said in as mournful a tone as I'd ever heard. "I better not." With a despondent look on his face, he got to his feet and picked up his backpack. "I better go on home and let J.D. know how happy I am."

Well, that did it, for we could hold it in no longer. Sam burst out laughing, then Lillian had to hold on to the counter, she was laughing so hard. And by that time, I was weak from trying to hold it back. And to his credit, Lloyd managed a sheepish grin as Sam jumped up and hugged him.

"Don't worry, Lloyd," he said. "I clearly see a little red coupe in your future. Anybody who has to drive a Sherman tank to school deserves one."

Chapter 12

After supper, an hour or so later when the house was still and quiet, Sam and I were in the library where Sam was yawning over the seascape puzzle. Every once in a while he would try a puzzle piece, then discard it for another one. I had just finished the easier of the two crossword puzzles that the *Abbotsville Times* published every day, leaving the more difficult one for my brilliant husband.

"Sam?"

"Hm-m?"

"Do you realize that you promised Lloyd a little red car?"

"Uh-huh."

"He'll count on that, you know."

"That's all right," Sam said, getting up from the card table. "I hope he will. It'll make driving that ancient Bonneville a lot easier."

"Well, I hope you'll discuss it with Mr.

Pickens and Hazel Marie first — him, especially, since he seems to be the car dealer in the family. I'd hate for a little red car to suddenly show up in their driveway and they not know a thing about it. It could undermine their parental authority."

Sitting down beside me, Sam laughed. "What've you been reading?"

"I didn't have to read anything," I said, slightly on the defensive since, as a matter of fact, I had recently read an article on family dynamics. "It's just common sense not to interfere between children and parents. And Hazel Marie told me that Mr. Pickens intends to make Lloyd an experienced driver before turning him loose to drive alone. That big car he's bought will protect him while he's learning, and it won't matter if he dings it up while he learns. So, see? The man knows what he's doing — at least, in this case."

"Honey, I'm not going to go out tomorrow and buy a red sports car for a boy with a beginner's license. You will notice that I did not promise *when* he'd get it. It could be when he graduates from high school, or maybe after he completes his first year of college, or even on his wedding day. Whenever it is, I will most assuredly talk to his parents first."

"Oh, well, good. I just don't want the boy to be disappointed."

"He won't be. In fact, knowing what's in the future will make him a better driver — he has something to look forward to and work toward. Besides, he may change his mind about what he wants when the time comes."

I smiled and took his hand. "I apologize. I should've known that you'd thought it through. This will teach me not to get between a man and his car."

Sam laughed. "Yeah, we like to think it's the only field that's ours alone. By the way," he said as if he'd just remembered it, "has Lillian said anything to you about that house?"

"What house?"

"It's on Rosewood Lane, two blocks over from hers, but down a little — apparently it's been sold. She asked me about it before you came down for breakfast this morning. I drove by it later, but nothing was going on."

"Is she concerned about it?"

"Oh, no, just the opposite. I think the neighbors are hoping for some upgrading — some improvement of the area, you know. They've seen some people going in and out, that sort of thing."

"Are you thinking it's the house that Don Crawford bought?"

"Just wondering is all. But if it is, I'm also wondering if he's jumped in before knowing the town well enough. Location, location, and so forth, you know."

"Hm-m, yes, I do know. And I'm not sure I'd buy in that area unless I had plans to improve the surrounding houses. Which I doubt that he has, since you said he wants to do the improvements while he's in town so it'll be ready to rent out when he leaves. He'll have time to fix up only one house — even if that much — before the Hargroves get back.

"And," I went on, sitting up straight with a sudden thought, "if he has bought it, don't you wonder if he knew what he was doing? He's hardly been in town a full week."

"More than that," Sam said. "He mentioned to me that he'd been here a few times before Bob left — getting familiar with the practice, you know. He could've been looking around on those visits."

"Considering that house's less than desirable location," I said, speaking from my superior position as an experienced purchaser of real estate, "it seems a snap decision to me, and I hope he doesn't get hurt for making it."

"Well," Sam said, yawning again, "if he has bought it, maybe he sees something that we don't. It is a fact, though, that low-income housing is at a premium in this town. He may just be getting in on the ground floor." He yawned again. "Something to think about anyway."

And I certainly did think about it. Maybe that area was ripe for a farsighted developer, one who lived in town and could oversee improvements on a daily basis, and one who could possibly make a pretty penny by filling the need for rental housing in town.

The more I thought about it, which was for a good hour after going to bed, the better I liked the idea. First, I'd need to research the block on which the key house was located — who were the owners, would they sell, and how much would it cost not only to purchase, but also to refurbish the surrounding houses. And, most important, would the return be worth the expenditure?

I tried to visualize the block in question, but couldn't be sure of the number of houses on it. Either six or eight, minus the one that Dr. Crawford had bought — if, indeed, he had — and possibly, if my memory served, minus another one that had caved in under the weight of a fallen tree and a blanket of ivy.

Of course, there would always be at least one holdout who wouldn't want to sell, but a rent-back offer might change a recalcitrant mind. And would it really matter if one house was left derelict in the middle of a row of new-looking houses? Probably not, though it might spur the owner to want to fit in.

If, therefore, after diligent research and a discussion with Sam, the project seemed worthwhile, I might broach the subject of combining forces with Dr. Crawford and forming a development company. With his good eye in seeing profit where no one else had seen it and my financial backing, there was no telling how far we could go. And, even better, we would be improving an area filled with one eyesore after another, as well as providing decent housing for those in need.

I turned over carefully so as not to disturb Sam, settled into my favorite sleeping position, and smiled to myself. What a way to cure boredom! What a way to fulfill my need to *fix* something!

CHAPTER 13

"Miss Julia?" It was Hazel Marie calling fairly early the next morning. "Would it be all right for me to come by after I drop the girls at preschool? I know it's early and you might be busy, but there's something I'd like to talk over with you."

"Of course," I said, as I immediately began to worry that something was wrong. "Come right on. It'll be nice to see you."

I had gotten up that morning renewed and energized by the possibility of a project that I could get my teeth into and cure the winter blues while I did it. But Hazel Marie's call was a downer, as my thoughts went at once to a possible problem between Mr. Pickens and Lloyd over an outdated and overweight Bonneville. Newer and smaller things than that have created great rifts in families many times before this.

So it was with great relief that I listened to what was exercising Hazel Marie because it had nothing to do with Lloyd's means of transportation. She'd come in the back door, as most of us did, and as she had done when she'd lived with me. It showed that she still felt at home in my house, a fact that pleased me more than I could say.

After she'd greeted both Lillian and me, I took her coat, then asked, "Would you like to sit in the library? There's a fire there, and you're probably freezing."

"Oh, no," Hazel Marie said, "let's stay in the kitchen. It'll be like old times, and I'd like Lillian to hear this, too. She may have some ideas I could use." Turning to her, she asked, "How's Latisha, Lillian? I miss seeing her."

"Rambunctious, as ever," Lillian said, on her way to the freezer for cinnamon rolls to go in the oven. "She's likin' school, but she says it sure cuts down on her playin' time."

Soon, with fresh coffee before the three of us and the kitchen warm and aromatic, we sat at the table and waited to discuss whatever was on Hazel Marie's mind.

"So it's like this," she started, then stopped to pass the cream pitcher to me, handle toward me as it should've been. "LuAnne Conover called yesterday morning, and I've been worrying about it ever since."

"Oh-h, LuAnne," I said with a sigh. "What

116

did she want you to do?" As if I couldn't have guessed.

Hazel Marie smiled because LuAnne was forever on the telephone rounding up volunteers for some project or another, usually for the benefit of something that nobody had ever heard of and wouldn't be interested in if they had. She had recently become entranced with the idea of raising awareness of any need that anyone could possibly have. Her calls all boiled down, however, not to raising awareness, but to raising funds.

"She wants me to help her restyle herself," Hazel Marie said. "From the ground up, she said, so that she's," Hazel Marie stopped and made quotation marks with her fingers, " 'suited to interface with the public in a position of grave responsibility.' "

"She *didn't*!" I said, not knowing whether to laugh or bewail LuAnne's choice of words.

"Yes," Hazel Marie said, smiling even as she frowned, "that's exactly what she said."

"What's wrong with that?" Lillian asked, having gotten up to bring a plate of hot cinnamon rolls to the table.

"What's wrong with it is her new job," I said. "She's the new receptionist at the Good Shepherd *Funeral* Home — you know, a *grave* responsibility."

117

"Oh, my land," Lillian said, her eyes rolling back in her head. "Even I know better'n that. But," she went on, always ready to give anybody the benefit of the doubt, "she's a nice lady, an' I 'spect she jus' didn't think."

"Well, of course," I said, smiling even as I shook my head, "that's always LuAnne's problem. So, Hazel Marie, what did you tell her?"

"Oh, I'll do what I can, if she thinks it'll help. She wants me to come over and look through her closet. She wants to know what she needs in the way of basic pieces. But listen to this," Hazel Marie stopped as if changing gears. Then she said, "Yesterday afternoon I asked Lauren Crawford to come over with her children, and she did. I'd decided to try one more time, and if she'd turned me down, that was going to be it. But she agreed right away — didn't even have to ask her husband. The children played well together, although it was too cold to let them go outside. But Granny Wiggins was there, so she kept them entertained upstairs while Lauren and I visited downstairs. I think she really enjoyed the free time." Hazel Marie picked up a napkin and wiped melted icing from her fingers.

"Anyway," she went on, "her children — Jason and Olivia — were entranced with

Granny. Of course she's great fun with children, anyway, but all Olivia wanted was for Granny to hold her the whole time." Hazel Marie pushed back her hair, then she said, "But I'm off the subject. At one point, I think — notice that I said I only *think* — that Lauren expressed some interest in doing something about herself, or maybe *for* herself."

"What she say?" Lillian asked, thoroughly taken up with the story.

"She said something like 'I wish I always knew what to wear when Don and I are invited somewhere.' Then she mentioned the fact that they moved around a lot, so she never felt that she knew how to dress so she'd fit in. It wasn't much, and she didn't *ask* for help, so I was afraid to offer. But, Miss Julia, she said it so poignantly that it's stayed with me and I wish I had offered."

Hazel Marie was still intent on improving her vocabulary and tried to use a new word at least once a day. With her use of *poignantly,* I knew she'd accomplished her purpose for the day. Lillian, however, was frowning.

"Well," I said for the benefit of both, "that is quite touching, Hazel Marie, and I think you're right. I think it was a plea for help, but she's so repressed that she couldn't come out and say so."

"That's kind of what I thought, too. So I want to know if you think it would hurt her feelings if I called and told her that LuAnne wants help with her wardrobe — you know, how to put things together, what goes with what, and what basics every woman should have — and ask if she'd like to join us. Or something like that."

"I think she's given you the perfect opportunity," I said. "But I'd stress the clothes part of it if I were you, at least at first. Then maybe you could ease into getting her to try a little color on her face."

"Yes," Hazel Marie said, "that would be the way to do it. And it shouldn't be too hard. If I could get her and LuAnne together, wait till she feels comfortable with both of us, then we could talk about makeup. Maybe try a few things on LuAnne and let her watch. You know, go slowly like that."

"That lady," Lillian pronounced, "sure do need some kinda help. She look peaked to me."

"She's just very fair, Lillian," I said, "which, of course, is all the more reason she needs to add some color. Hazel Marie," I said, turning to her, "it's good of you to want to help. And you're so good at makeup and fashion and all of that, it's no wonder that everybody turns to you. We all know that you know what you're doing."

"Well, I don't know about that," she said, as modest as always. "But I do enjoy it, and I'd love to turn Lauren into a showstopper. She's really lovely if you can overlook the paleness, because Lillian is right — she does look sick."

"Oh, my," I said, "you don't suppose she really is, do you?"

"No, I didn't get that feeling at all. She ate two slices of James's pound cake, and Ronnie paid no attention to her."

"Well, then," Lillian said, "there's your proof."

"What?" I asked. "Proof of what?"

"Dogs," Lillian pronounced, "can smell when somebody sick."

"That's right," Hazel Marie said, nodding. "And Ronnie barely raised his head when she walked past. He wasn't interested in her at all."

"Well, I didn't know that." But now that I did, I decided that if I thought I was getting sick while Dr. Hargrove was gone, I could check my condition with Ronnie before calling on the doctor's substitute.

"Well, Hazel Marie," I said, "do keep me up to date with your styling sessions. I'll be interested to see how Lauren responds or, actually, whether she even joins you and Lu-Anne."

"I hoped you'd be interested," Hazel Marie said, "because that was the other thing I wanted to talk to you about. I think it would all be easier, especially if Lauren comes, if you joined us, too. I mean, it would be more like a class, rather than one-on-one sessions. That way, nobody would feel singled out because everybody can use some help at one time or another."

Hearing that, I immediately felt singled out, because I knew LuAnne had put that suggestion in Hazel Marie's head. I took immediate umbrage and started to let Hazel Marie know that I wasn't "everybody."

On second thought, though, maybe Lu-Anne hadn't and it was Hazel Marie's own opinion. With that thought, my spurt of anger deflated in a hurry. Maybe I really did need some help. Maybe my morning beauty routine had come to the end of its usefulness. Maybe there were new products on the market that would transform me, and this suggestion was the way my closest friends were telling me that I was in dire need of transformation. It was certainly true that my daily routine — done the same way with the same products every morning for years — had become so habitual that I could run through it in my sleep. And contrary to the evenings when I prepared for a party, there had been mornings when I had done it, at least partially, in my sleep.

"That's very true, Hazel Marie," I said, in a humble state of mind, "so I'd be happy to join you. Everybody can, indeed, use some help now and then."

CHAPTER 14

After Hazel Marie left, I went upstairs to do some soul searching and, while I was at it, a little mirror searching as well. Upon a close and careful examination of my face, I couldn't see that any more products from the Clinique counter would help matters. I didn't use a lot of makeup — just a light foundation, a brush of rouge, and, when I thought of it, some light color on my lips. I had occasionally, for special occasions, played around with an eyeliner, but had usually ended up looking like a raccoon. Or else getting most of it *in,* rather than around, my eyes.

But the hard truth of the matter was that I most certainly could use some help. The even harder truth was that it would take a plastic surgeon's knife to remedy matters. And I wasn't about to do that. No, I'd seen the results of recent plastic surgery on others, which, I readily admit, effected a radical change of a face — if you like that kind of change. For myself, though — no, thank you.

My hair, though, was a different kettle of fish. If Hazel Marie could do something with it, I would be eternally grateful. I would accept any criticism — any suggestions — she had to do something different with it. Velma at the Cut 'n Curl had kept it trimmed for lo, these many years, and had finally talked me into what she called highlighted streaks that had to be done more and more often. By this time, I may actually have been spending more time each week in her salon than I was spending in church. Which, to my shame, says something about my priorities.

After a frowning glance in the full-length mirror, I walked to my closet, opened the door, and looked over the hanging clothes. With a sigh, I conceded that the closet needed a good cleaning and throwing out. There were things in there that I hadn't worn in five years, and more of the same in the hall closet. Why is it so hard to get rid of unused clothing? I well knew that others were in need and would welcome a nice Neiman Marcus suit that had been off its hanger only twice in the past three or four years. Now and then I would get it out, look it over, and reject it, but not to give away. I'd hang it back up, thinking that one day I might need that very suit.

Meanwhile, fashions changed and huge shoulder pads went the way of broomstick skirts. And that was the problem — fashions *did* change, leaving us with closets full of no-longer-wearable clothing and, in order to be even halfway fashionable, sending us on shopping trips to Saks or Neiman Marcus, to say nothing of Target or Talbots.

But let me just say this: How anybody in the world could or would wear what I had been seeing in the high fashion magazines that Velma kept in her salon was beyond me. The last issue of *Vogue* that I'd flipped through featured the most outlandish outfits I'd ever seen. You wouldn't catch me wearing any of them, although I readily admit that they weren't designed for my age group in the first place. But have you ever seen such a conglomeration of plaids, polka dots, paisleys, checks, and stripes in your life — and I mean put together on one model? And some with a few leopard spots thrown in, as well as over-the-knee boots with tassels? Not a one was suitable for a Women of the Church meeting, much less for a Sunday service. They were clown costumes more suited for a circus spotlight than for your

126

normal lunch at the Tête-à-Tête Tearoom.

Nonetheless, I resigned myself to joining the small group of hopeful makeover candidates who were putting themselves in Hazel Marie's hands. But only with this caveat, which I would keep to myself: My presence would really be to help LuAnne and Lauren — if she came — because I was reasonably satisfied with my own way of dressing and my own way of doing my face and hair. If, however, Hazel Marie had a small and carefully worded suggestion to make, I would happily consider it, but I would keep firmly in mind that I was present mainly to give encouragement to those who needed help much more than I did.

After asking Lillian if she wanted anything from the grocery store and getting a frowning look in return, I explained that I was going out for a while and could pick up a few items for her. I had overlooked the fact that she took it as a criticism of her planning if I offered to grocery shop.

"I'm going to look for magazines," I said, "and I know the grocery store carries them."

"What you wantin' to read about movie stars for?" she demanded, giving me a disbelieving stare.

"Not those, Lillian. I'm interested in

something like *Vogue* and *Elle* that show new fashions. This is all to help LuAnne in her quest for grave clothing."

"Oh, well," she said, "I guess that's all right, then. I hear Mr. Conover say one time he bought *Playboy* magazine 'cause it's got real good writin' in it."

That stopped me in my tracks, but on second thought, decided that I didn't need to know anything further on that subject.

So I dropped by the grocery store and I visited the Rite Aid drugstore next door as well. Armed with several glossy magazines, I went back to the car and started on my real reason for being out and about on such a cold day.

Driving slowly along several residential streets on the south side of town, I tried to look as if I had a definite destination. What I was really doing, though, was keeping a sharp eye out for such things as parked service trucks or vans, workmen going and coming, and FOR SALE signs with a banner reading UNDER CONTRACT across them.

Yes, I was looking for the house that Dr. Crawford had bought. I had the impression that I would find it in a less than desirable area, maybe because I might've looked in the same area if I'd been buying a house for rental purposes. And also because Lillian had said that her neighbors had hopes for a block renewal, which was what I was interested in.

Oh, and yes, because the words "low-income housing" had been mentioned. You wouldn't find that in a gated community or up on the mountain where scenic views added thousands to the price of a house.

Noticing a panel van parked at the curb in front of a small house on Rosewood Lane, I slowed as I drove past, figuring that I had found Dr. Crawford's choice. Why else would a termite company be calling on what appeared to be a decrepit residence, unoccupied for obvious reasons? But of course I was less interested in Dr. Crawford's specific purchase than I was in the surrounding houses, where I was thinking of jumping in and getting in on the ground floor.

I circled the block only once, not wanting to draw attention to myself, but taking note of the state of the various houses. They could all use some help — two most definitely needed new roofs, all of them had peeling paint, and I shuddered to think of how many windows needed replacing with double panes just to keep out the wind.

Obviously, this would be a major undertaking even after purchasing one or two of them — if I was able to do that. People become attached to their homes, regardless of their state of disrepair, especially after spending most of their lives paying for them. There were no FOR SALE signs in front of any of them, which told me that whoever owned them intended to keep them — unless, of course, they were made an offer they couldn't refuse.

And that brought up another thought. The people who lived in the houses might not own them. They may already be renters who would be thrilled at the possibility of having their homes refurbished. The behind-the-scenes owners, however, might not want to sell — the renters they had were willing to put up with less than desirable housing because they couldn't afford anything else.

What I needed to do was to sit down and do some figuring. Would it be cost effective to purchase, say, two houses, completely refurbish them, then rent them back to the previous occupants? Clearly, I could not raise the rent above the amount they were already paying — whether as rent or as payments on their mortgages — else they wouldn't be able to afford them. From the condition of the houses, the owners were pushed to their financial limits already. Unless, of course, the owners were essentially slum landlords who would continue to collect rent until the houses fell in on themselves.

With a sigh, I resigned myself to the need of research at a county office to find the true owners. The whole idea was ballooning out of control, and I was beginning to count the cost and decide that I might be getting in over my head. But, then, I had a sudden solution — government subsidies or grants, about which I knew nothing. Yet from what I'd heard, that was how developers descended on the county, buying up huge tracts of farmland, then presenting the county commissioners with architect-drawn plans to build ninety or more houses, including single homes, duplexes, and multiplexes, as well as adorning the whole area with winding roads, play areas, and walking trails.

And all the county had to do in return was give them a break on property taxes, run water and sewer lines and electicity to the area, widen all roads leading to it, and, oh, yes, put in a few traffic lights to manage the increased number of vehicles. And, looking to the future, start planning for a new school in the area. The icing on the cake, however, plus a tug at the heartstrings of the commissioners, was the promise that the new development would be *low-income housing* only, or to use the new euphemism, affordable housing.

Now, just tell me how developers can afford to do that? Developers do not develop unless they can get a return on their investment. And who could blame them? Not I, that's for sure. Only a very few, like the Microsoft founder, can afford to give away millions. The question is, therefore, where does that return on investment come from? Not from low-income renters by any stretch of the imagination.

So the answer was help from the government in the form of subsidies and/or grants. I was not in the least inclined toward something as ambitious as a major development. All I was interested in was the upgrading of a few small homes to give a face-lift to an in-town area and provide decent living space to lifelong town residents. But I couldn't afford to do it out of the goodness of my heart — it had to be cost effective, and I'd have to have a return on my investment.

I needed to talk to Sam. And maybe to Binkie, my Johnny-on-the-spot lawyer, and perhaps to Dr. Don Crawford to see if he wanted to be a part of my grand scheme.

CHAPTER 15

That evening after supper, I told Sam about my vision for renovating a block — perhaps on Rosewood Lane — that badly needed it, and doing it one house, or possibly two, at a time. I laid out the plans for researching the owners (hoping that he would volunteer for that chore), getting a bank loan (or a government subsidy), and describing the spurt of general upgrading of the surrounding area that I hoped it would inspire.

"That whole south end of town could become a showplace," I said, "and it could all start with one little house."

"Dr. Crawford's rental house?"

"Um, well, I guess I was thinking of mine, but of course you're right. That's where I got the idea. What do you think?"

Sam rubbed his hand across his face and got that faraway look that meant he was giving something a lot of thought.

"I think it's a fine idea," he finally said.

"The area could certainly use some updating. Many of those houses aren't fit to live in, and I'm surprised they haven't been condemned before this. If you're looking for a project, it would be a worthwhile one to take on. The first thing to do, though, would be to count the cost."

"Why, Sam, that's what I've been doing all afternoon. I know what I'd be getting into. And I have a legal pad almost full of notes and numbers and estimates to prove it."

"I don't doubt it, honey. You're very good at that sort of thing."

I preened at his compliment — it's always pleasing to have one's abilities recognized.

"But," he went on, "what I'm talking about is counting the emotional cost of dealing with real estate agents, loan officers, servicemen who say they'll come but don't, unforeseen snags that are part of every project, and running the risk of having your houses ready for the market just as the economy has a downturn. These are all obvious pitfalls which I'm sure you've taken into account. But you're a worrier, so I know you'll take them to heart and drive yourself crazy when what's expected doesn't come to pass and something unexpected does. But, again, you know all of this and I know you'll be prepared to deal with whatever pops up."

"Prepared for every *foreseeable* problem, at least," I conceded modestly. "I guess there'll always be some things that you can't prepare for." I didn't mention it, but I was recalling all the problems Mildred Allen and I had faced some while before when we'd remodeled a house together — the worst problem being a near loss of friendship when she'd wanted to add some Victorian architectural features to what I was convinced was your basic Craftsman-style house.

"Of course," I went on, "it wouldn't be as if I've never done anything like this before. But, you know, Sam, even after taking into account every possible contingency, there'll be something that you absolutely haven't prepared for. I mean, an inspector will tell you that the wiring looks fine — and it does, until you tear out some walls. Same thing with the plumbing and the heating systems. And a contractor will tell you that of course you can take down some walls to create an open concept, until you get into it and suddenly you have to have a sixteen-foot steel beam to hold up the roof. And those things cost thousands of dollars."

"True," Sam said, nodding.

"And then there's possibly a termite problem — I got a hint of that this morning — and a mold problem, and maybe a crack in the foundation. It could go on and on, couldn't it?"

Sam, frowning, nodded in agreement. "It can get to be overwhelming."

"Yes, it'd almost be better to build something from the ground up, wouldn't it?"

"Something to consider, anyway."

I sat up straight, looked wide-eyed at Sam as if I'd seen into the future. "You know what would be the smart thing to do?"

"No, what?"

"Hold off and see how Don Crawford's house goes. It's got to be the same age as the others. It's certainly in the same state of disrepair with possible termite infestation, too. It might be better to just sit back and see what kinds of problems he runs into, then make a decision as to what to do."

"Honey," Sam said, "that is a wise course of action. I declare, you are a marvel — a smart businesswoman and good-looking along with it. I'm a lucky man."

I beamed, of course, and soon we were on our way upstairs to bed, both of us smiling — me, because my husband appreciated my talents, and Sam, well, I wasn't sure why he was.

■ ■ ■ ■

"Oh, my goodness," I said just as Sam and I sat down for breakfast the next morning, "I just thought of this, but wasn't Lloyd supposed to come by in his new car yesterday?" I had completely forgotten about the big reveal that he'd promised, having been so taken up with real estate and construction questions the entire day.

"Yes'm, he was," Lillian said, straightening up from the oven with a pan of biscuits in her hand. "What if he didn't get it? What if he wadn't happy enough for Mr. Pickens?"

"Oh, I can't believe Mr. Pickens would go back on his word," I said, although I was never quite sure what the man was capable of.

"Has to be some other reason," Sam said, agreeing with my assessment of Mr. Pickens. "Why don't you call Hazel Marie later this morning and see what happened?"

And so I did, learning from her that Lloyd had had a less than joyous afternoon the day before in spite of taking possession of his car.

"As soon as he got home from school,"

she told me, "J.D. and I took him to the dealer's — we both had to go because J.D. would be riding back with Lloyd. So if he drove there, he would've had to leave his car at the dealer's, and I would've had to take him back to get it. I tell you, Miss Julia, it's like musical chairs trying to figure out which car goes where. Anyway, we came straight home because J.D. wanted Lloyd to change a tire before he started really driving."

"You mean," I said, "it already had a flat tire and you'd just gotten it?"

"No, it was fine. J.D. just wanted to be sure that Lloyd could take off a tire and put it back on. Just in case, you know."

And here I'd been thinking that a flat tire was the reason for having a cell phone, but I didn't say anything.

"Then," Hazel Marie went on, "just as Lloyd got the tire back on — and by the way, he knew exactly what a lug wrench was. I was so proud of him. But anyway, about that time J.D. got a phone call and had to leave just as I was starting to feed the little girls. They were fussing and crying because they wanted to go somewhere in Lloyd's car. Well, it just went from bad to worse, because by the time we were ready to come by and see you, it was dark and, of course, J.D. wasn't back. So Lloyd got to drive only from the dealer's back here to the house."

"Well, that's too bad, but maybe he'll come by this afternoon."

"I'm not sure," Hazel Marie said. "J.D. still isn't back. I was the licensed driver this morning so Lloyd could drive to school."

"That was good of you, Hazel Marie."

"Well, I had to go out anyway — the little girls had to go to preschool. We started out early, though, because it took us almost an hour to move two car seats from my car to his and get them locked in place. Anyway, all three of us rode with Lloyd in his car, and I took the wheel when we got to the high school. Or rather a block from it. Lloyd wanted to get out before we got there."

"Oh, my," I said, feeling bad for the boy. "It might be old, but a boy's first car should be special to him, and I'd hoped he'd be proud to drive up in his very own."

"Oh, the problem wasn't with the car — I think he's reconciled to that and understands J.D.'s thinking on it. No, the real problem was his sisters in the two car seats in the back that were sitting up higher than he was. He said having a family car was okay, but he wasn't ready to have a whole family in it."

"Oh, my," I said again, suppressing an urge to laugh. "That doesn't sound like him. He loves his sisters."

"I know he does, and he's already told me that when he gets his real license, he'll take the girls to school for me. No, I think it was first-day jitters, not wanting any of his friends to laugh at him for looking like a family man. The cushion that J.D. told him to sit on didn't help, either. But at least he can see over the wheel when he's on it."

CHAPTER 16

In the midst of all that, Hazel Marie told me that she would be going to LuAnne's condo the following morning to assess her wardrobe.

"Can you meet us there?" she asked. "I've already called Lauren, and I think she's coming. She had to think about it until I told her she could leave her children here with Granny Wiggins and my girls. So she said she'd try."

"She didn't have to ask her husband?"

"I guess not, although I expect she will." Hazel Marie paused for a second, then she said, "You know, I just can't imagine asking J.D. for permission to do something with my friends. Or to ask permission to do anything, for that matter — other than to buy something really expensive, maybe. He'd think I was crazy."

"I know. So would Sam if I did it. But I hope she'll be there. It would show that she's willing to at least listen to a few suggestions."

"I think so, too. But I'm not going to get into makeup tomorrow unless LuAnne insists. There're some people, you know, who have a moral, or maybe a spiritual, problem with cosmetics. I don't know what they have against them, but I wouldn't want to put Lauren on the spot if she's one of them."

"No, I wouldn't, either. I don't know if you knew Faye Cantrell or not — this was years ago, but she never wore a smidgeon of makeup and I never knew why. I mean, she went to First Baptist, so it couldn't have been a religious reason."

"I knew a Dr. Cantrell," Hazel Marie said. "He saw me when I thought I'd broken my arm when I fell off the monkey bars at school."

"That was her husband and it's interesting that now we know two doctors' wives who don't — or didn't — use makeup. Anyway, I remember somebody commenting that Faye was a beautiful woman without it, but she'd be stunning with it. Of course, Faye had more natural coloring than Lauren does, so she didn't look washed out."

"Well," Hazel Marie said, "I'm just going to stick with clothes tomorrow — what goes with what, and what LuAnne needs to fill out her wardrobe. You be thinking about it, too. You know, like what you'd expect to see if you had to go to a funeral home."

"My goodness, Hazel Marie, I've never even thought of something like that. I don't know that I'd be expecting anything in particular. But," I said, turning it over in my mind, "I guess that shows that most people have other things on their minds when they visit a mortuary."

"I'm sure they do, but if the receptionist happened to be dressed in something outlandish, they would notice. The fact that they don't shows she was correctly dressed. Don't you think?"

"Yes, I guess so," I said, "if you put it that way. So the trick for LuAnne is not to be *un*noticed, exactly, but rather to blend in so well that she doesn't divert a visitor's attention from the purpose at hand — sad, though it may be."

"Yes, that's what I'm thinking."

"Then you may have a problem. LuAnne is always well-turned out — whatever the event happens to be. But she has as many red suits in her closet as Nancy Reagan."

"I guess that's my fault," Hazel Marie said. "You remember several years ago when she asked me to do her colors? Well, we never got around to doing them, probably because she knew her favorite color was not her best color. She's a warm tone, if there ever was one."

I didn't know what she was talking about, but I said, "Why don't you bring your scarves with you? You can do LuAnne's colors and maybe Lauren's, too — at least enough to show her what a little color would do for her."

"That's a good idea. So we'll see you at LuAnne's tomorrow about ten?"

"I wouldn't miss it."

A car turned into the driveway that afternoon and parked by the back porch.

"Lloyd's here!" Lillian called from the kitchen, and Sam and I hurried to see our little boy all grown up behind a wheel.

The three of us rushed outside, taking in the huge gray machine filled with Hazel Marie, the twin girls in their car seats, and Lloyd, looking too small and too young to handle all that horsepower.

He grinned as we approached, and it seemed to me that it was a prideful, yet self-effacing, grin — trying to appear suitably grown-up yet being as thrilled as a child at Christmas.

"Come see my car, Mr. Sam," he called as

he opened his door so we could see inside. "Look, it's got a radio and a disc player — J.D. put that in for me. They weren't standard from the factory back in the old days."

The "old days" to us, of course, were just yesterday, but to Lloyd they were part of a vast cloud of events that may or may not have occurred before he was born.

As Sam leaned over to look at the dashboard, Lloyd unlatched his seat belt and slid off the air-cooled mesh cushion he'd been sitting on. "Get in, Mr. Sam, see what you think of it," he urged.

Sam did, and the two of them began talking horsepower and tachometers and air pressure and the like while I walked around to Hazel Marie's window to speak to her and the little girls.

Leaning over, I whispered, "How's his driving, Hazel Marie? Do you feel safe with the girls in the car?"

"As safe as can be," she said. "He's an excellent driver." Then with a smile, she whispered, "He hasn't gone over fifteen miles an hour yet."

Sam and I did our part in admiring the ancient vehicle, and so did Lillian. She told Lloyd that if he ever wanted to trade up, she'd be open to letting her car go.

Of course we invited them all in — it was

too cold to linger outside — but they had to get home for supper. The three of us stood watching as Lloyd got back in, adjusted his cushion and his seat belt, then cranked it up, smiling broadly as the engine responded with a satisfying roar. Then with an arm across the back of the seat and his head turned sharply, he slowly began to drive in reverse, zigzagging only once on his way out of the driveway. I held my breath, but he adroitly missed my boxwood hedge by inches, only to bounce across the curb onto the street.

Grinning with success, he waved to us, then shifted into drive and took off at a sedate speed.

"My goodness," Lillian said as we returned to the kitchen, "it's cold out there! But don't Lloyd look all growed up, settin' there behind the wheel like he been doin' it all his life. I declare, seem like jus' yesterday he was hoppin' on a bicycle, an' now here he is, drivin' a great big car."

"Uh, Lillian," I said, smiling at her, "it *was* just yesterday that he was hopping on a bicycle."

Then, turning to Sam, I asked, "What did you think?"

"I think Pickens did good," he said, nodding for emphasis. "He risked disappointing the boy, but he's put him in something that will protect him as well as anything but a Mack truck. But," Sam went on, barely suppressing a smile, "Lloyd is not completely reconciled. He told me that he still hasn't driven up to the school — he said he really didn't mind driving his sisters around, but he doesn't want his friends to see him sitting on a cushion. He said it makes him look like a little ole family man with hemorrhoids."

"Oh, for goodness' sake," I said, laughing. Then on further thought, I said, "It seems to me that you and Mr. Pickens could figure out how to jack that seat up so he won't have to sit on a cushion."

Sam nodded. "Maybe so. I'll see."

But I wasn't through. "Did Lloyd say anything about all those girls and the school dance?"

"Not a word and, to tell the truth, I didn't think to ask. He'll come up with something sooner or later."

CHAPTER 17

I parked the next morning in a visitor's slot near Helen's condo that was now leased to LuAnne. The Arboretum was well named for it was a small cluster of aging condominiums in the midst of mature trees that provided protection from street noise and neighbors collecting for some worthy cause. Hardly anyone knew the condos were there, or maybe they had been there so long that they'd been forgotten about. There were no gates and no gatekeepers, but the place had been ideal for Helen Stroud — it was quiet, out of the way, and affordable. Which also made it ideal for LuAnne — both of them had shed husbands who had deeply disappointed them by their way of living and/or their ability to provide.

Helen had recently come up in the world by contracting with Thurlow Jones when he fell off the roof of his house and banged himself up. None of us could help but wonder just what that contract involved. I mean, when a woman moves into a man's house, takes over refurbishing said house, and takes control of his checkbook, what is one to think? The worst, in my opinion, except for the fact that Thurlow, with two broken legs and a misaligned hip, could no longer walk, much less run after a woman. Whatever the arrangement between them was, it seemed to work for both of them — Helen was given a free hand in updating an aging mansion and Thurlow got a nurse, a manager, a housekeeper, and an interior designer all in one. Although he probably hadn't bargained for quite so much, the alternative would've been long-term care in a sparsely staffed nursing home.

So when Helen moved out of her condo, there it was for LuAnne to lease — the perfect answer to her dilemma of what to do about her husband of thirty years who'd been having an affair for twenty of them — unbeknownst to her or to anybody. Who, I ask you, could conceive of such a bland nonentity like Leonard Conover being able to conduct an undercover assignation as he had done for so long? It's the quiet ones you have to watch — you never know what's going on in their heads.

LuAnne met me at the door, welcomed

me in, and started talking. "I saw you drive up. Come on in the bedroom. Hazel Marie is already pulling things out of the closet, and I've just started the coffee and put a coffee cake in the oven." LuAnne was going a mile a minute, and before I could reply, she went on, whispering this time. "Lauren Crawford came with Hazel Marie, and she seems so nice. But, Julia, she's the one who really needs help. Have you ever seen anyone — that age, I mean — who looks so behind the times? I could do wonders for her if she'd just let me, and I hope she learns something from all of us today. How does she expect to hold on to her husband — and him a *doctor* — when there're all these sexy-looking women around? That girl needs to *do* something."

I nodded in agreement and, in a warning whisper, said, "I think so, too, but don't say anything to her. Hazel Marie wants to ease her into trying some makeup without making a big deal of it." Then, handing my coat to LuAnne, I said in a normal tone, "I've been looking forward to this, especially after looking through my own closet yesterday. It's full of things I hardly ever wear."

"Tell me about it," LuAnne said. "I know how that is, because when I moved here, it was the perfect time to get rid of a lot of things. I just hope I don't regret that second trip I made to Goodwill."

"Well, you know what they say: You should move every five years just to clear things out."

At LuAnne's invitation, I walked into her bedroom, where Hazel Marie was sliding coat hangers along the rod in the closet and Lauren Crawford was watching from an oversized chair in a corner. I am not being critical when I say that LuAnne's furniture overwhelmed the two-bedroom, one-and-a-half-bath condominium that was now her home. I would've had the same problem if I'd been reduced to a smaller place with smaller rooms and had had to fill them with the furniture I already owned. But I have to say that a mahogany breakfront in a dinette looks slightly out of place, as does a canopy bed that touches the ceiling. I felt I should walk sideways just to get through the rooms, but LuAnne had the things she loved around her, as I would have had as well. You don't just throw out a Sheraton sideboard with fruitwood inlay because you don't have the perfect place for it.

"Oh, Miss Julia," Hazel Marie said, sticking her head out of the closet as I entered, "I'm glad to see you. I'm pulling everything out and sorting them by color."

"What can I do to help?" I said, then turning to Lauren in the corner, I said, "It's so good to see you again. How are you this morning?"

Lauren smiled and murmured something that sounded like "Just fine," but I wasn't sure. Hazel Marie responded to my question by saying, "You can go through that pile of dark colors. I may have put some navy in with the blacks."

LuAnne bustled back in, announcing that coffee was served at the dinette table, and we all moved back out of the bedroom. Nothing had gotten done except the emptying of LuAnne's closet, but the serving of food and drink was always a part of any meeting of friends or committee members.

As we sat around the table, Hazel Marie kept us on point by suggesting that we all look at the veins on the insides of our wrists. "That will tell you if you have warm or cool undertones," she said. "If they're blue, then you're a cool tone, but if they're green, that means you're a warm tone."

"Green veins?" I asked, startled.

"Yes, well, at least greenish because the undertone of your skin will be peachy or golden. Look at LuAnne. She's definitely a warm tone with that auburn hair and the warm, golden color of her complexion."

Hm-m, I thought, how much did Velma have to do with that auburn hair? But then I conceded that LuAnne was merely keeping the same hair color she'd always had, just as many of us were doing.

"Miss Julia," Hazel Marie said, as she turned my hand over to look at the prominently blue veins, "you're a cool tone. See how the pink undertone of your skin comes out next to LuAnne's golden tone?" She put down my hand and reached for Lauren's. "Now, Lauren is also a cool tone, although her undertone isn't as pink as yours." She placed Lauren's hand next to mine, and sure enough, my skin was noticeably pinker than hers — from my Scotch-Irish forebears, I supposed. "Lauren," Hazel Marie went on, "seems to have more of a blue undertone, which is great — you're all different, so we'll be able to see how different colors affect the different skin tones."

Lauren certainly needed some different colors, for she practically blended in with LuAnne's cream-colored walls. Her clothes did not help because she was wearing a bulky sweater with pants, both in shades of ivory and cream, some of which matched the color of her hair.

Sitting next to her, I could see that her eyelashes were quite long, although they

153

were so white that they looked more like fuzz than lashes. That was something so easy to fix that I wondered again why she didn't do it, if indeed she had some religious reason for failing to do so. I had a great urge to snatch up a mascara brush and at least start on her face.

"Lauren," I said, hoping for an answer to my wonderings, "I meant to say something to you the other night, and I apologize for failing to mention it. But we would love for you and the doctor to visit the First Presbyterian Church while you're here. There's a very active young adult Sunday school class that you might enjoy."

"Oh," she said, blushing, "well, I don't know. It's so hard to try new churches as much as we move around."

"Perfectly understandable," I assured her. "But if you ever want to try it, I'll be happy to introduce you."

That was probably the wrong thing to say, for it seemed the last thing Lauren wanted to do was to be the focus of new people.

Hazel Marie jumped in to help me. "My girls love their Sunday school class, Lauren. We'll be glad to pick up your children if they want to go. I'll make sure they get to the right class."

Lauren nodded, then said, "Thank you.

I'll see what Don says."

And that was the end of that.

When we finally got down to business, Hazel Marie went through LuAnne's wardrobe like Sherman through Georgia. She flipped through the piles of clothes, discarding some, sorting others, and quickly putting together work-suitable outfits.

"LuAnne," she finally said as she brushed a lock of hair from her face, "you could use two new white or cream blouses — not shirts, but blouses. Maybe one with ruffles or lace, and the other a plain silk one. I would also suggest a brown skirt and matching cardigan."

"Brown!" LuAnne cried. "I never wear brown."

Hazel Marie smiled. "I noticed. But brown is a good basic color for you, and you could use a nice brown suit for the days when the funeral home has a viewing of a notable person. I'd also suggest some yellows and oranges — nothing real bright, though. You could dress up, say, a cream sweater or blouse with a scarf in those colors. As for these red suits, most of them are too bright for you. This one here, though," she said, holding up one of LuAnne's favorites, "is a warm red, which works well for you, but I'd stay away from red entirely when you're working. It just wouldn't look right to grieving families. For spring and summer, I'd recommend a few things in ivory — that would look great on you — and in green, but a yellow-green, not anything deeper or brighter. Think earth tones, and you won't go wrong.

"Also," she went on, "I'd recommend that you not wear these high heels — they're practically stilettos."

"But I'm so short," LuAnne almost wailed. "I need the height."

"LuAnne," I said, intervening with my opinion, "you don't want to be on your feet all day long in those spiked heels. Get something comfortable."

"But what?" she said. "I don't want granny shoes."

Hazel Marie smiled. "No, you don't want old lady shoes, but wide, stacked heels are back in now, so if you look for some no more than one and a half or two inches high, they should be comfortable enough to wear all day. And look fashionable, too."

"Well, okay," LuAnne said, sighing, "I guess you're right. But this is all going to cost a fortune."

"Not really," Hazel Marie said, snatching up a black skirt and a green-and-black-plaid jacket with a cream sweater underneath to show her. "You have some lovely pieces here already, so just a few more things in the right colors will give you a lot of options."

"Well," LuAnne said only half graciously, "I guess you're right. But what about my makeup? Do I need to make any changes?"

"Yes, maybe a few." Hazel Marie smiled, knowing she was treading on dangerous ground. "First thing, for your look at work, I'd not wear eye shadow. Save that for evenings or weekends. And I'd encourage you to use a soft brown eyeliner with a very light hand, and a coral blush. And you might try a lipstick with a brown tone, rather than pink."

"Oh, my goodness," LuAnne said, "I've been doing everything wrong!"

"No, not really," Hazel Marie said in a comforting tone. "We can all wear exactly what we want to, but remember that you have to appear a certain way in your new job — so my suggestions come with that in mind."

"You're right," LuAnne conceded, much more quickly than I'd expected. "I understand what you're saying, and why. But would you show me how to do it? And tell me what to buy, because I don't have any beauty products in the colors you recommend. Do me first, then Julia and Lauren if they want to. I can't wait to see what you do with each of us."

They Lord, I thought, as Lauren looked startled. Leave it to LuAnne to say exactly what she'd been told not to say. Nonetheless, she often said exactly what everybody thought, but who were more able to keep it to themselves than she was.

CHAPTER 18

Hazel Marie had brought her large cosmetic case that seemed to contain every color, shade, tint, and hue of facial enhancements known to cosmeticians and fashion editors alike.

She had LuAnne sit in front of a large mirror, then quickly redid her face in the correct colors, and even I could see the difference they made. LuAnne practically glowed not only from the applications, themselves, but also from her pleasure in the result.

"Oh, Hazel Marie, you are a genius!" she said, admiring herself in the large mirror and in the handheld one. "This looks great! *I* look great! How did you learn to do all this?"

"Oh, just fiddling around with various products and reading a little here and there," Hazel Marie said in her modest way. "I love doing it."

"Well, you certainly know what you're doing," LuAnne said, popping up off the chair. "Let me write down everything so I'll know exactly what to buy. Here, Lauren," she said, taking Lauren's arm, "sit right here and let the expert go to work on you."

I almost gasped aloud for fear that Lauren would be offended, but she docilely and only slightly hesitantly sat down in front of the mirror.

"I used to wear a little makeup," she almost whispered, "but then the children, well, you know, they take up so much time. I guess I've just let it go."

"Oh," Hazel Marie said in an offhand way, "that's so easy to do, isn't it? But I think we owe it to our husbands to take care of ourselves, don't you?"

"I guess," Lauren mumbled, "but Don doesn't like too much makeup on a woman. He says it cheapens her."

"Well," Hazel Marie said, as if Don's opinion was of little concern, "we'll just do it so light and natural looking that he won't even notice. Except to think that you look especially nice."

Then she proceeded to sponge a light foundation on Lauren's face, along with a tinge of pink blush on her cheeks. With a remarkably sure hand, Hazel Marie filled in Lauren's eyebrows with a light pencil and made a very fine gray line around her eyes. Then, as a finishing touch, she brushed mascara on Lauren's lashes.

"Now, look," she said, stepping back. "See how that brings out the gray in your eyes? And watch this." Hazel Marie draped around Lauren's neck a succession of colored scarves, one after the other, some in jewel tones and some in pastels. And I'll tell you what's a fact — the woman was a raving beauty — and her hair hadn't even been done.

"My gracious, Lauren," LuAnne said, almost but not quite speechless as she expressed her admiration. "You are lovely. I mean, I'm sure you always were, but now, well, now. . . . Hazel Marie, tell me what you've been reading so I can learn how to do that."

Lauren, it seemed, was as taken with her new look as we were. She kept looking in the mirror, turning her head from side to side, and smiling with pleasure. Her eyes sparkled, she sat up straight, and she spoke with less diffidence than she usually did.

"Oh, thank you, Hazel Marie," she said. "I didn't realize what a difference it would make. You've made me look so nice. I just wish I could do it myself."

"You can," Hazel Marie assured her.

"Soon it'll become second nature. But on your real busy days, if you'll just do your eyebrows and lashes, and dab on a little blush, you'll be more than ready to face the world. But don't forget to always moisturize first."

I had watched all this in silence, but I, too, had been stunned by the remarkable transformation. Hazel Marie had changed a washed-out, sickly looking woman into a vibrant, glowing model of health and beauty.

"And now," LuAnne exclaimed, "let's do hair. I need a new hairdo, Hazel Marie, something professional looking, but easy to maintain and that I can do myself."

Hazel Marie laughed as she replaced cosmetic jars and tubes in her case. "Sorry, LuAnne, we'll have to do hair another time. I've got to pick up the girls at preschool, and I'm about to be late."

So we quickly got into our coats and, bidding LuAnne good-bye with our thanks, we went our separate ways.

All afternoon I marveled at what Hazel Marie had wrought with a few carefully chosen beauty products and wondered why Lauren hadn't discovered them herself. Especially since she'd admitted to having worn makeup in her younger days. Girls, it seemed to me, began to experiment with cosmetics in high school (or sooner if their parents were lax), so that they gradually became expert in the selection and application of what looked best on them. Somewhere along the line, Lauren had hit a bump in the road and failed to continue learning how to make the best of herself. It was as if she'd eschewed any enhancement of her natural blessings and had deliberately chosen to blend into the woodwork.

A lot of young women let themselves go once they're married and have children underfoot. They seemed to see no reason to go to the trouble of fixing their hair in an attractive way or of doing anything to their faces. And, of course, adding a few more pounds and wearing loose clothing occasionally accompanied the loss of interest in their appearance. I knew, because I'd seen them in grocery stores or on the sidewalk downtown, usually trailed by stair steps of little children.

But it didn't seem to me that Lauren was in that category, or at least she didn't have to be. Her husband certainly made a good living — she could've had help with the children and with her house if she'd wanted it. She could've easily bought the necessary cosmetics — drugstores were full of reasonably priced items. In other words, she had the time and the means to keep herself attractive. In fact, if Hazel Marie had done Lauren's hair and dressed her in clothes that fit both her frame and her coloring, she would have been even more striking. And because of Hazel Marie's magical touches, we had also caught a brief sight of a warm personality.

So I didn't understand where the extreme diffidence about her looks and her manner had come from. I wondered just why Lauren appeared to make every effort to look unattractive — why in the world would anyone do that? But, of course, it was not my problem. Far be it from me to interfere with someone else's choices, whether it be the shade of lipstick or the clothes or the entire manner of life one chose. Every woman for herself, I always say, although if my opinion was ever sought I'd be more than happy to give it.

A day or so later, LuAnne called to say that she'd like to drop by for a few minutes.

"Of course," I said. "Come on by. I'm doing nothing but wondering if spring will ever come."

When she got to my house, I led her to the library, where a fire was burning in the fireplace. She plopped down on one of the facing Chippendale sofas and blew out her breath as if she'd run a mile.

"Whew," she said, "I've been buying cosmetics, and I'll tell you the truth, there's so much to choose from I don't know if I'm coming or going."

"I thought you'd written down what Hazel Marie recommended."

"I did! But just the shades, not the manufacturers. Julia, there's Estée Lauder and Lancôme and Bobbi Brown and Elizabeth Arden, and that's just in the department stores. You go to a drugstore and there's Maybelline and Revlon and L'Oreal and a dozen others that I've never heard of. But," LuAnne said with a wave of her hand, "that's not what I want to talk about. Now, Julia, you know I love Hazel Marie to death and I value her advice more than I can say. But I went by to see her yesterday to ask her a little more about the *kinds* of clothes I should wear."

"Oh," I said, "I thought that was pretty well decided. I mean, you want to look professional, which to me means classic styles like skirts and jackets with blouses or sweaters. You can't go wrong with that kind of look."

"Yes, you're talking about what we used

165

to call the preppy look. That was back in our college days, and as far as I can tell it went out years ago." Then leaning forward, LuAnne said, "Let me ask you something, Julia. What news channel do you watch?"

"News channel?" I frowned at the seeming switch of subject, then rose to take a tray of hot spiced tea and sugar cookies that Lillian brought in. "Thank you, Lillian. It smells wonderful."

After speaking to LuAnne, Lillian left us to continue a conversation that seemed to be heading in a strange direction.

Taking the mug of hot tea I offered her, LuAnne said, "Well, tell me. What do you watch most of the time?"

"I guess it would be Fox News. Sam turns it on, so I get caught up in it for the rest of the day. Unless I turn it off until six o'clock."

"Exactly!" LuAnne said. "That's what I watch, too. Now, don't tell me that you haven't noticed the way those women dress. Even the ones who're anchors and have their own programs. Julia, have you ever seen so many tight dresses or so much exposed skin? Half of them wear those cut-out dresses that show shoulders and upper chests, and the other half wear dresses that're cut so low that they reveal a definite cleavage. In other words, traditional, classic clothes are O-U-T, out."

"But, LuAnne . . ."

"I know, I know," she interrupted. "Hazel Marie doesn't recommend that kind, but maybe she hasn't kept up with the times, either. Now I know that those Fox women are younger than I am and slimmer, too. But I'm not entirely over the hill, and it seems to me that, being in the front office as I will be, that I ought to wear the current styles."

"Well, LuAnne, an office in a funeral home is not exactly like being on national television. Besides, those women are probably dressed by a professional wardrobe mistress or some such, and what they wear may be decided by higher-ups. They may not have any choice at all."

"That's my point," LuAnne said, sitting primly upright. "I do have a choice, and I think I should follow the current styles, which include cut-outs, tight skirts, and deep decolletage. Just watch the other channels, and you'll see they're all doing it — it's the *in* thing these days."

"I don't know, LuAnne. Haven't you noticed the irony of sexily clad women bemoaning some man's inappropriate behavior? Now, wait," I said, holding up my hand as she started to reply, "I know that doesn't excuse the men who paw at every woman within reach, and I know it sounds as if I'm saying that the women 'ask for it,' but it looks strange to me for a woman with her bosom practically hanging out to act like she's shocked — actually, *hurt* — when a man takes it as a come-on."

"I think you have it all wrong, Julia," Lu-Anne said, somewhat defensively. "You just haven't kept up with things."

"Maybe not, and I may well have it wrong. Maybe the day will soon be here when women can wear bikinis to work and men won't even notice. But I'll tell you this, Lu-Anne. The only person you have to please on your new job is the one who hired you. Do you think that he — or she — would be pleased to have a Playboy Bunny in the front office of a funeral home?"

She hopped up and, putting her mug on the tray, said, "You are so far out of the mainstream, Julia, you don't even know that Playboy Bunnies are a thing of the past. I've got to go home."

And she went, mad at me for not agreeing with another of her wild fancies. Which, to tell the truth, wasn't all that unusual, so I went back in to have another mug of hot spiced tea by myself.

CHAPTER 19

I declare, LuAnne was the hardest woman I knew to get along with — something that I should've been used to by this time. And I guess I was, for it didn't bother me half as much as it once had when she'd leave in a huff. It made no sense that she kept asking my opinion about anything. I always told her what I thought, but if it didn't agree with her take on the subject, she'd get mad, leaving me to feel that I'd let down a friend.

But as I've said, it didn't worry me so much anymore. She always came back around acting as if we were always in full agreement. She'd taught me that you have to take your friends as they are and that all of them have their quirks. As I do myself, although not as many strange ones as some people I know.

With the house quiet and the room warming nicely, I put my head back and dropped off for a few minutes. I heard the telephone ring, but it wasn't until Lillian touched me on the shoulder that I came fully awake.

"Telephone, Miss Julia," she said in a low, but urgent voice. "I wouldna woke you, but it's a man."

With the conversation with LuAnne still on my mind, I couldn't help but laugh. We all — and I'm talking about us women — hopped to when a man wanted us.

"Well, my gracious, Lillian. I'd better answer it, hadn't I?"

"Mrs. Murdoch?" the man said when I answered the phone. "This is Nate Wheeler. You remember me?"

"Indeed I do, Mr. Wheeler. We met at Miss Mattie Freeman's apartment the day she passed. How are you these days?"

"Doing well, thank you. I hope you don't mind my calling out of the blue, but I happened to run into your husband at Lowe's, and he mentioned that you might be interested in buying a house on Rosewood Lane."

"Just thinking about it because, as far as I know, none are for sale."

"Well, that's why I'm calling," Mr. Wheeler said. "Dr. Don Crawford has closed on number eighteen Rosewood, but he was also looking at number sixteen next door — from the same owner. Neither has been on

170

the market yet, but Dr. Crawford asked about them at just the right time. I thought that you might like to know that number sixteen may be available. If you're interested, that is."

"I just may be," I said, running numbers and questions through my mind. "Do you know what kind of condition it's in? I mean, did you inspect both for Dr. Crawford?"

With a low chuckle, Mr. Wheeler said, "They're both in pretty bad shape — I won't mislead you on that. But if you're prepared for some extensive remodeling, you'd have a nice, in-town rental property."

"Hm-m," I said, still thinking over the possibilities. "I expect that Dr. Crawford chose the one in better condition. I would've if it'd been me."

He laughed again. "It'd be a toss-up. I'm sure you've noticed that they're essentially the same house — just with opposite floor plans. But you should know that we're talking new wiring, plumbing, roof, and heating and cooling systems before we even get to redoing kitchen and bathroom. The good thing is that they're quite small — two bedrooms, one bath — so we're not talking a huge outlay."

"Then tell me this, Mr. Wheeler," I said, "will you be doing that work for Dr. Crawford and, if so, would you take on the other house for me?"

"Actually, that's the reason I'm calling. I don't mean to be pushy, but you and the doctor could get some savings if, say, when I contract with a roofer, it could be for both houses at the same time. Same way with the electrician, the plumber, and so on."

"I certainly don't think you're being pushy. I think you're making good sense. So," I went on, "you'll be Dr. Crawford's contractor, is that right?"

"Yes, I've agreed to oversee the subcontractors, then do the carpentry work myself. I can do the same for you, especially by negotiating with subcontractors for two side-by-side houses instead of one at a time. Then if you want to bring in a different carpentry team, that'd be fine, too."

"That is thoughtful of you, Mr. Wheeler, and quite tempting. Would you give me a couple of days to talk to a real estate agent and to make an offer on the house? If I decide to, that is."

"Yes, ma'am, on one condition — you call me Nate. If we're to do business together, it should be on a less formal basis."

I smiled, though not entirely agreeing with him. I've found that doing business with someone quite often called for more formality rather than less. But I said, "Then we'll also dispense with Mrs. Murdoch. I shall be in touch with you in a day or so, as soon as I decide if purchasing number sixteen is feasible. Thank you so much for calling, Nate."

I put down the phone and began considering Mr. Wheeler's, I mean, Nate's, offer. It could be a sound business opportunity, or it could be an out-of-work man's way of drumming up business for himself. Yes, I was being my normal skeptical self and looking a gift horse in the mouth. However, even if lining up a job for himself was Nate's real purpose, it didn't lessen the benefit to me of what he had proposed.

I immediately called Nell Hudson, the real estate agent with whom I'd lately done business, and asked about number sixteen Rosewood Lane.

"Well," she said, surprise evident in her voice, "that's suddenly become a popular area. Our office just sold a house on Rosewood. Is there anything going on that I need to know about?"

"Not that I know of," I assured her, wanting to put any rumors of a land grab to rest. "I'm just looking for a small rental possibility. And something to keep me occupied while I wait for spring to get here. If you have any suggestions of something in an-other area, I'm not averse to considering them."

"Well," she said again, "since we just handled the sale of number eighteen, I happen to know that the owner might listen to an offer on number sixteen. Would you like to make one?"

"Not," I said firmly, "before even looking at it, Nell. Are you free this afternoon? Can you meet me there about two o'clock? No, wait," I said, a wonderful idea just occurring to me, "what about four — is that too late for you?"

"Uh, no, I guess not. And we still have a key, having just shown it a couple of weeks ago. Although I must caution you, Miss Julia, the house isn't officially on the market."

Which meant, I took her to be saying, that it would take an attractive offer to tempt the owner.

"I understand," I shot back at her, "that number eighteen wasn't, either. Nonetheless, it was sold. How much did it sell for?"

"Oh, well," she said, hedging, "I'm not sure I can find that out at this time."

"Nell," I said, about tired of a Realtor's sleight-of-hand, "let's not play around. The sale price is a matter of public record, or will be when it's recorded. You can let me know when we meet at four."

I declare, I thought as we hung up, as much business as I'd given Nell Hudson, you would think that she wouldn't play around with me. I had heard good things about another broker, a Mr. Blair, who was open and aboveboard with his clients, often telling them what they didn't want to hear but what they needed to hear. Nell Hudson would have to come to understand that she wasn't the only Realtor in town.

Hoping, though, that I had not outsmarted myself by making such a late appointment — darkness came so early this time of year — I picked up the phone and punched in Hazel Marie's number.

"Hazel Marie," I said when she answered, "I want to show my support and encouragement to Lloyd, although I want to be sure that it's all right with you and Mr. Pickens before doing so. When will he be home from school?"

"J.D. or Lloyd?"

"Oh, Lloyd, of course. He's the one who needs practice driving. I'm meeting Nell Hudson over near where Lillian lives about four, and I thought it would be a good time to let Lloyd drive me there. Unless, of course, he can only drive with a parent with him."

"Oh, no, any licensed driver who's over eighteen is okay with parental consent. Which, of course, you have. And he'd be thrilled that you trust him to drive you. I'm picking him up about three-thirty and letting him drive home, so come on by if you don't mind riding with two empty baby seats in the back."

I laughed. "Not at all. Just happy that they'll be empty. I don't think I could watch Lloyd's driving and the twins, too."

CHAPTER 20

A little before four that afternoon, I drove to Hazel Marie's house and parked at the curb. Feeling slightly foolish for driving four blocks only to park and transfer to another car, I reminded myself that Lloyd could not drive the four blocks to my house to pick me up. Or if he did, his mother and sisters would have had to come with him, then they'd have to be driven back to their house after I got in. Musical chairs, indeed.

Seeing Lloyd sitting behind the wheel of the gray Bonneville with the motor running, I walked across the yard toward him. He smiled proudly and waved as I approached.

"Hey, Miss Julia," he said as I opened the passenger door and slid in beside him. "I heated up the car for you."

"That's very thoughtful," I said, wondering how long he'd been running the motor — probably since the moment he'd gotten home from school. But I well recalled the thrill of being able to drive and smiled to myself. "Do you know where we're going?"

"Yes'm, Mama told me. I'm pretty sure I know how to get there. It's over by Miss Lillian's house, and I've been there on my bicycle."

"That's right. I'll show you which one when we get there, but, Lloyd, there's another reason I wanted you to go with me. Besides just wanting to ride with you, I mean. I'm thinking of buying a small house as an investment, and I'd like your opinion on the merits of this one." I often took opportunities as they occurred to include Lloyd in investment decisions, knowing that he would eventually be responsible for the inheritance from his father — his biological one, that is, the one who had ignored marital vows and rested now in the Good Shepherd cemetery. It's never too early to instruct children in the art of financial management.

Lloyd drove down the driveway, stopped and looked both ways — twice — then pulled out onto the street. Proceeding slowly and deliberately toward Rosewood Lane, he glanced at me, noticing my grip on the door beside me.

"Uh, Miss Julia," he said, grinning, "if you feel safer holding on to something, use the armrest, not the door handle."

"Oh, my goodness," I said, quickly un-handing the handle. "I didn't realize what I was doing." And felt some shame for so obviously revealing my discomfort at riding with an inexperienced driver.

"That's all right," he said. "I'd be nervous, too, but I don't want to lose you if the door comes open."

After pointing out the house at number sixteen Rosewood, I withheld any comment as Lloyd pulled to the curb, scraping the tires against it as he did so. Having done the same on several occasions myself, I pretended not to have noticed.

"This is it?" he asked, looking skeptically at the little house with its peeling paint, its swaybacked roof, and its tilted porch.

"Doesn't look like much, does it? But it's in a good location, so I want your honest opinion. I'm really not convinced myself." Then as a car pulled in behind us, I said, "Here's Nell Hudson now. Let's go in and have a look."

And so we did and, to tell the truth, I was not overly impressed. The interior was in no better shape than the outside, and I wondered about tearing it down and starting from scratch. The lot itself was a nice size, though not extensive, but there was a lovely magnolia tree in the backyard and a few crepe myrtles in the front. The number of lard cans with withered plants left in the kitchen meant that someone had once loved the place.

After listening to Nell extol the virtues of the decrepit house, I headed outside, having seen enough. As we stepped out onto the porch and waited for Nell to lock the door behind us, I saw a woman, bundled up in a heavy coat with a woolen scarf over her head, leave a car and scurry across the yard next door. Hesitating, I took a minute to be sure who it was, then called to her.

"Lauren," I called, waving to her. "How are you?"

Lauren Crawford hesitated at the steps to number eighteen, then waved back, barely looking my way. I took a few steps toward her, but had no intention of lingering in the cold, wanting only to be friendly to a possible next-door home owner.

"Oh, Miss Julia," she said as I approached, almost cowering in the upturned collar of her coat. "What . . . ? I mean, I, well, I guess I wasn't expecting to see you here."

"That's no wonder. I'm rarely in this part of town, but I'm giving Lloyd some driving time and also looking at the house next door. Has Dr. Don started on this one yet?"

"Uh, no, I'm not sure when. . . . He just asked me to come look at it, so I better do it and get on home." She'd climbed the two steps to the porch by then, and, her face hunched down into the folds of her coat collar and scarf, she began to inch toward the door.

Feeling as uncomfortable as she was behaving, I quickly said, "And I, too. So nice to see you, Lauren." And I took myself back across the yard and got into the Bonneville. But not before telling Nell Hudson that I would let her know if I decided to proceed.

She, however, with a Realtor's instinct of knowing when someone is in a buying mood, pointed to the house next door and said, "I didn't handle the sale of that one, but an agent in our office did. So if you're interested, the buyer is also looking at some county property."

What she meant was that if I was following in the footsteps of someone more knowledgeable of property values than I, she could keep me abreast of what he was doing and where he was doing it.

"Interesting," I said, "but I'm not interested in county properties. I know nothing about them."

"Neither does he," Nell said, laughing a

little. "He's that new doctor in town."

Wondering what she would pass along about me, I quickly thanked her again and slid into the car.

"Sorry, Lloyd," I said as he cranked the engine and turned up the heater. "I should've called you over and introduced you to the new doctor's wife. But, I declare, she obviously had something other than the social graces on her mind."

It was not a habit of mine to judge people, but that uncomfortable meeting with Lauren Crawford proved to me that she was, indeed, a strange one. Then it struck me that the face I had glimpsed inside a thick scarf had not revealed one tinge of color on it. Obviously, she was not following Hazel Marie's instructions for bringing out her eyes or anything else. Perhaps as she'd mentioned, her husband had not approved and, if so, it meant to me that he, too, was a strange one.

"You want to go anywhere else?" Lloyd asked. "This is a free taxi service."

I laughed, knowing that he wanted to keep driving. So dismissing both Lauren and Nell from my thoughts, I came up with another reason to keep driving. "Let's go to that little drive-through coffee shack right off

Main Street. I think they have hot chocolate, too."

However, as we approached the narrow drive that led to the serving window, I had some sudden second thoughts. What if Lloyd pulled in as close as he had to the curb and scraped the side of the building? We could have hot coffee all over us, as well as a sizable bill for repair and restoration of a local business. I closed my eyes and clamped down onto something on the door — handle or armrest, it didn't matter.

"Hot chocolate or coffee?" Lloyd asked, and I opened my eyes to see us parked quite decorously beside the serving window and a young woman waiting patiently for our order.

Lloyd passed a cup of hot chocolate to me, then placed his in a cupholder. "I'll drink mine when we get home," he said, relieving me of the additional worry of his handling the wheel while sipping from a cup. "I guess we'd better go on back anyway. Mama worries. But, Miss Julia, about that house. I think it could be fixed up to look real nice. And it sure needs it, because if somebody doesn't do something soon, it's going to fall down. And that'll make a blight on a street that's close to Miss Lillian's house. So I'm kinda inclined to go for it.

Besides, it'd be fun to see what we could make of it. If," he went on, making me proud of his acuity, "you can get it at a good price."

"I'll think about it and let you know," I said, preparing to change cars as we neared his house, "but thank you for going with me. I value your advice, and I commend you on your driving skills. You didn't frighten me once."

He laughed. "But you're probably glad to be back in one piece, right?"

Silently agreeing, I laughed with him.

"I declare," I said to Lillian as I disencumbered myself of coat, gloves, and scarf at home, "I simply do not understand some people."

"Who you talkin' about?"

"That new doctor's wife — the one filling in for Dr. Hargrove," I said. Then, not wanting to be misunderstood, I went on. "It's the doctor who's doing the filling in, not his wife, except she's the one I'm talking about. Lauren Crawford. I just saw her over on Rosewood Lane, and I do believe she would've walked right past me if I hadn't spoken to her."

"What you doin' over on Rosewood Lane?" Lillian asked. "You don't know anybody over there 'cept me, an' I'm right here."

Hanging my coat in the pantry, I said, "I know, and that's why I need your advice. Do you know the houses at numbers sixteen and eighteen over there? Dr. Crawford has bought one, and I'm thinking of buying the other one, fixing it up, and renting it, as he plans to do. What do you think of that?"

She took a minute to consider the question. "I don't think I think too much of it," she finally said. "If they the ones I'm thinking about, they about to fall in."

"That's what Lloyd said."

"He's right, then. Though it'd be a blessin' for somebody to do something to that block. Ole Mr. Clabe Hammond pro'bly who owns 'em, since he owns 'bout everything else on that street."

"Hm-m," I said. "That's good to know. He's a regular slum landlord from what I hear."

"Me, too. Though I hear he got in big an' heavy with that fancy hotel they wanted to build next door to Miss Hazel Marie. He could be hurtin' for money."

"That's even better to know," I said, perking up at the thought of doing business with someone with a cash-flow problem. "Listen out for me, Lillian, and let me know if you

185

hear anything else. And let me know what your neighbors think."

"I already know what they think. They be real happy to see somebody do something to that block, 'cause we all work hard to keep up our places. An'," she went on, bearing down on her words, " 'specially 'cause ole Mr. Hammond always comin' 'round lettin' us know he wants to buy if we want to sell."

"*Really?* That doesn't sound as if he needs to sell anything. Although he's apparently already sold one to Dr. Crawford."

"Well, but," she said, knowingly, "he's not been around lookin' to buy anything here lately, either."

CHAPTER 21

I had about decided against buying — or offering to buy — the little house on Rosewood Lane until I settled on the sofa in the library and began to mull it over. Strangely, my mulling centered only on the pluses, even though the many minuses were looming in the background. Also looming in the background was Nell's hint that Dr. Don might be buying property out in the county — why would he be doing that? But undeveloped property was beyond my range of interest, so I stuck firmly to considering the little house on Rosewood, realizing that I might just be looking for the good and ignoring the bad.

The first good thing to come to mind was the fact that the interior walls were composed of shiplap — the poor man's alternative to plaster, but now wildly popular due to a certain television designer. Only a few years ago, I would've consigned those walls to the trash heap. Now, though, they were a valuable asset.

And another good thing was the suggestion of hardwood floors under the peeling linoleum. And the third was that with Lloyd's sudden interest in dating who knew who and driving who knew where, he needed something else to occupy his mind and fill his time.

"Sam," I said as he came into the library and headed for the fireplace to warm his hands, "what do project managers do?"

His eyebrows went up at the question. "Well, they manage the various projects on a job — making sure the right workmen show up on schedule, overseeing whatever they're working on, checking that the jobs are done right — that sort of thing. They're overseers essentially, ensuring that everything is to code and correctly done. Why?"

"I was just thinking," I said, deciding that project manager wasn't the right slot for Lloyd. I would have to think of something else. Maybe he could be the project manager trainee on the Rosewood Lane job, which meant I'd need a project manager in chief. Perhaps Nate Wheeler? If, of course, he could combine that with being the contractor. He had, after all, proposed to contract all the projects on both houses, which to me meant that he could manage them as well.

"Well," Sam said, "tell me more. What're you just thinking about?"

"Oh," I said, as if it were of little concern, "that little house. Lloyd likes it, especially because it's close to Lillian and could affect the value of her house. I was thinking it wouldn't hurt for him to learn some of the basic manly skills of construction and so forth."

"That's not a bad idea," he said, then, sitting beside me, he cocked one eye in my direction. "But when do you think he'll have time to learn such manly skills? He's in school most of the day, and the afternoons are full of meetings, practices, and I don't know what all. He's rarely home before dark, and tennis starts in a few weeks. Maybe he'd have some free time this summer — if he doesn't volunteer to work at the tennis courts again."

"Oh, well. Of course you're right. To be honest, Sam, I was trying to think of ways to keep him occupied, now that he'll soon have the freedom of the road. And to get him interested in something more than a gaggle of young girls fussing over who's going to dance with him."

"Honey," Sam said, laughing as he put his

arm along the back of the sofa, "you're fighting a losing battle. And you're jumping the gun as well. It'll be almost a year before he's sixteen and can get a real driver's license. In the meantime, I don't think you need worry about that gaggle of girls with Pickens or Hazel Marie along for the ride.

"Still," he went on, "it's not a bad idea for him to do some sweaty work — as soon as it gets warm enough to sweat, that is. He could work on Saturdays now, doing the demolition on your little house — clearing it out and getting it down to studs. I expect Nate Wheeler will soon start on Dr. Don's house, so Lloyd can see how it's done."

"Yes, that could work," I said, then on further thought, subsided. "Of course, Lloyd may not even be interested. I declare, Sam, I am getting bad about thinking up things for other people to do. But I don't want him growing up with a sense of privilege, and having a car handed to him and having a bunch of girls running after him could warp his character. He needs to know what it means to have to work for something — work hard, I mean."

"I don't disagree with you," Sam said. "But here's a thought — why don't you let Lloyd buy the house and you be the project manager until he can take over when school is out?"

I sat straight up, my eyes wide. "What a wonderful idea! I never thought of that. But that way, *he* could make the decision of whether or not to buy it, and *he* could make the purchase offer, and *he* would be the owner of record. If all that wouldn't occupy his mind, I don't know what would. I'll talk to Binkie tomorrow to see if he can afford it."

"Oh, he can afford it, but it should be Lloyd who talks to Binkie."

"Oh, of course. Yes, you're right. But I should run it by Mr. Pickens and Hazel Marie before saying a word to Lloyd, shouldn't I?"

"Yes, I would. And also be prepared for Lloyd himself not being interested. He has a lot of new things to contend with as it is."

"That's exactly why I want to fill his mind with something different. But, Sam," I said, frowning, "tell me again what a project manager does. I may not be up to that."

"Don't worry," he said, smiling, "I'll help you. And if I know Pickens, he will, too."

"Oh, me," I said, moaning because I could see it already, "I don't know that I can work with him. In spite of my best efforts, we always seem to cross swords and disagree with each other."

Sam laughed. "He just likes to tease you."

A few days later, Hazel Marie called, saying that she only had a minute because she had to drive Lloyd's car to school so he could drive home.

"Thank goodness Granny Wiggins is here," she said, "so I can leave the girls at home. It's too cold for them to be out, and it's about to rain, or maybe sleet. But listen, something's worrying me and I want to ask you about it."

"My goodness, Hazel Marie, what is it?" And even as I asked it, all sorts of dreadful visions began to pop up in my mind.

"Well, it's Lauren Crawford," she said, relieving me of my immediate concern over dire problems closer to home. "I may be reading too much into it," Hazel Marie went on worriedly, "but it feels like she's just dropped me. I've tried to tempt her to come for lunch or to go out for lunch, and she's been busy — doing what, I don't know. And just now, I called to ask her children over for playtime tomorrow, and she gave me another weak excuse.

"And when I mentioned it to Granny, she told me that the little Crawford girl, Olivia, doesn't play much anyway. All she wants to do is sit in Granny's lap — I've already told you about that, but it doesn't sound right for a five-year-old."

"What about the little boy?"

"Jason's only three, so he's entranced with the girls' toys — they're all new to him. But I don't know, Miss Julia. I wonder if I've offended Lauren in some way. She sounded so distant when I called, and I had the feeling that she'd rather I just left her alone."

"Well, that's interesting," I said, then proceeded to tell her of my seeing Lauren on Rosewood Lane. "I had the same feeling. She would've walked right past me if I hadn't called to her, and even then she barely stopped to speak. Maybe she was embarrassed because she wasn't wearing any makeup, but it was still strange. I don't know about you, Hazel Marie, but when somebody acts as if they don't want to have anything to do with me, I let them have their way. I can't imagine you've done anything to offend her. In fact, just the opposite — you've welcomed her to town, offered to introduce her around, invited her to church, and had her over with her children several times. And you had Granny Wiggins babysit for her when we all went to LuAnne's. I don't know what else you could've done to befriend her."

"Well, wait a minute," Hazel Marie said, "I've just realized something. She wasn't all that warm and friendly before we went to LuAnne's, but since then, she's been downright frigid. The very next morning I called to ask if she'd like to go with me to my book club. It's a lot of fun because we don't read anything real serious, and we were meeting that night. Well, let me tell you, she couldn't get off the phone quickly enough. She was barely polite, so I thought maybe I'd just called at a bad time. But now, I don't know. It's obvious that I've done something, but I don't know what it could be. Unless I was *too* friendly, and it put her off."

"No, you haven't done anything — it's *her,* Hazel Marie. Some people just don't want anybody close to them. She may have emotional problems, who knows? Maybe it's all that moving around that her husband does, so she's afraid of having a real friendship because she knows it won't last. That's her loss, and you shouldn't let it worry you. You tried, and that's all anybody can do.

"But here's another thing," I went on, recalling that strange meeting on Rosewood Lane, "she told me that her husband wanted her to look at that little house, and Nell Hudson told me that he's also looking at some county property. It may be that he has her doing what he should be doing, but is too busy in the office to do it. Doctors are bad about that — their work always comes first, and everybody else has to take up the slack for them."

"Why in the world would he be interested in county property?" Hazel Marie asked.

"I have no idea, and it may not even be true. Now, tell me what those sweet babies of yours are up to."

We talked about the twins for a few minutes, then hung up, but I wasn't sure that I'd eased her concern about Lauren Crawford. Hazel Marie always thought, if anything went wrong or anybody was unhappy, that it must be her fault in some way. It never was, of course, but she took the world's problems on her own shoulders.

I, on the other hand, never felt I was to blame for anybody else's strange ways and quickly struck them off my dance card. So to speak. It was, however, interesting that Lauren Crawford's sudden U-turn occurred right after our makeover session at Lu-Anne's when several of us were together.

Now, there was a thought. Hazel Marie hadn't been the only one there, so maybe it'd been somebody else who'd turned Lauren off. LuAnne, for instance, had been known to mortally offend someone without any intention of doing so.

But, oh, my word — what if it had been me?

CHAPTER 22

Well, if it had been me, and if Lauren was that sensitive, then so be it, because I couldn't dredge up any memory of having said or done anything to offend her. In fact, I recalled thinking, as we left, how compatible we'd all been. It had been a delightful morning, one that I hadn't especially wanted to attend, but was glad, when it was over, that I had.

Looking back now, though, that seemingly pleasant morning had produced a couple of decidedly unpleasant consequences. First, there was LuAnne, who, discounting all of Hazel Marie's advice, was wanting to publicly flaunt her shoulders, chest, and bosom — thighs, too, probably — in the most unlikely workplace you could imagine. And now I'd learned that, dating from that same morning, Lauren was exhibiting a markedly cooling-off of friendliness toward Hazel Marie. And for the life of me, I could think of no reason for either abrupt change.

There certainly had been none as we'd left LuAnne's condo. In fact, both LuAnne and Lauren had hugged Hazel Marie and thanked her over and over for her help. But something had to have happened — people don't just turn from one extreme to the other without a reason.

On second thought, though, LuAnne certainly did. She darted from one enthusiasm to the other like a hummingbird sampling every flower in the garden. She jumped around for no apparent rhyme or reason — in fact, most people described her as good-hearted but flighty. So I fully expected her to get cold feet before showing up for work at the Good Shepherd Funeral Home in a partially exposed state. She'd think twice and change her mind again, especially since it was still February.

Lauren, however, was another matter. I didn't know her well enough to account in any reasonable way for her sudden about-face. But how anyone could cold-shoulder Hazel Marie was beyond my understanding. If anyone had had reason to do so, it would have been me. After all, if a strange woman showed up at your door with a child bearing your own husband's name and likeness, would you want to befriend her? I didn't, and at the time it had galled me to no end that I had kept being thrown into her company.

But that's how we live and learn and change our attitudes. There was now a special place in my heart for Hazel Marie, all because of the basic sweetness of her nature. She would never knowingly hurt anyone, and besides the estate and the child he'd left, she was the only other good thing that had come from Wesley Lloyd Springer. The old goat.

Well, maybe, I mused as my thoughts flitted here and there, learning what made Lauren Crawford tick the way she did was another reason to buy the little house next to the one her husband had bought. That would be a minor reason, granted, so the next question to myself was this: Was I interested in her enough to want to know more? And the answer was no.

Still, if I could be of help to her, I would certainly do so, regardless of any personal interest in her welfare. Even more important was putting Hazel Marie's mind at rest, fearing as she did that she herself had done or said something that had turned Lauren against her.

For my own part, if people liked me, then well and good. But if they didn't, I didn't much care. There were a lot of people I could do without quite easily. I think that as we grow older, we stop worrying over what people think of us. We don't have the time to waste on what can't be helped.

Hazel Marie, though, would suffer over what she might have done to offend Lauren. And all my telling her that she'd done nothing wouldn't ease her mind. So with Hazel Marie's welfare my main concern, I decided to keep my eye on Lauren Crawford and find out just what that young woman's problem was.

For the time being, however, I had more pressing matters to handle. I needed to talk with Hazel Marie and Mr. Pickens about the house on Rosewood Lane. Even though I felt a strong responsibility for Lloyd — not only because he and I shared Wesley Lloyd's considerable estate, but also because I cared so much for the boy — I knew better than to overstep and impinge on the rights of his parents.

With that in mind, I called Hazel Marie and asked when Mr. Pickens would be home. A little surprised that I was interested in his whereabouts, Hazel Marie told me he'd be home that evening for a few days.

"Well," I said, "I'd like all of us to have a

little talk. Could you both come over in the morning, or would you prefer I come over there?"

"Oh, my goodness," she said, "that sounds serious, Miss Julia. What's going on? Is anything wrong?"

"Not one thing is wrong. I'd just like your permission to do something with Lloyd."

"*Do* something with him? Why? What's happened that he needs something done to him?"

That was Hazel Marie to a T, always thinking the worst, jumping to conclusions, and worrying over the least little thing.

"It's something good, Hazel Marie," I assured her. "It's just too complicated to talk about over the phone. Besides, I want Mr. Pickens to hear it, too. Actually, I want your approval for something I have in mind for Lloyd."

"He's too young and inexperienced for a sports car, Miss Julia. J.D. doesn't want him to have one yet."

I laughed. "I'm not in the market for a car, don't worry about that. I think the one he has is perfect for him. I want to ask about something entirely different."

"Well, okay, why don't we come over about ten tomorrow, if that's all right? But I'm going to worry about it all night."

"Hazel Marie," I said, "believe me, it's not something to worry about. I just have an idea of how Lloyd could spend a constructive summer, that's all." And there, I'd given her a hint without going into details, which ought to keep the worrying down to a minimum.

"You want to do *what*?" Mr. Pickens put his coffee cup down and swiveled his black eyes at me. He and Hazel Marie were sitting with me at the kitchen table and, at his tone, Lillian scrunched up her shoulders and leaned over the sink.

So I told him again. "But see, it was Sam's idea, and I should've waited to let him present it to you. But he had a semiemergency dental problem this morning, and the dentist told him to come on in. Look," I said, including Hazel Marie in my glance, "Lloyd is at the age when he needs to be kept busy, and it seems to me, he also needs to learn how to take care of his assets. What better way to do both than to buy, remodel, and either rent or resell a little house?"

"I can think of a few," Mr. Pickens said, leaning back in his chair. "He could cut grass, deliver newspapers, bag groceries, babysit his sisters, and that's just a start. What does he know about buying and selling houses? Or remodeling them?"

"Well, that's the thing — he can learn. But it'd be more than learning how to demolish and remodel. He'd learn about investing and turning a profit." I swallowed hard. "I hope."

Hazel Marie, looking at her husband, said, "That would be good for him to know, don't you think?"

Mr. Pickens hunched forward, his sweater-clad forearms on the table, as he looked from one to the other of us. "You're both forgetting that he's underage. He can't legally get a loan, sign an offer to purchase, or become the owner of record."

"Wel-l," I said, not exactly meeting his eyes, "you're his legal guardian, so I thought . . ."

"But," Hazel Marie said, "Sam and Binkie are the guardians of his estate. Why would he need to get a bank loan?"

"Exactly!" I said, pleased that she'd gone right to the point. "He wouldn't, except for the opportunity for him to learn how banks work. And the loan would be small enough that if things didn't work out, he wouldn't get hurt. But, of course," I went on, avoiding Mr. Pickens's eyes, "he'll need an adult to stand in for him, to take responsibility. I would do it, and so would Sam, but not without your approval."

Hazel Marie looked at her husband, waiting for his response. Her husband, frowning, studied his coffee cup.

"No," he finally said, and my heart sank. "Nope," he said again, shaking his head, "if anybody's going to have his back, it'll be me." Then he turned that swarthy face toward me, a small smile curling his mouth. "If you don't mind turning your idea over to Pickens and Son, I pretty much know my way around a construction site."

CHAPTER 23

So there it was. It couldn't have worked better if I'd planned it that way. By the time we finished that morning, Mr. Pickens had taken to the idea as if it had been his own, saying that he and Lloyd would be equal partners in the enterprise.

"I'll speak with Binkie," he said, "and let her know what we're doing. If she and Sam think it's a good deal for Lloyd, we'll let his estate buy his half of the purchase price."

As I opened my mouth to protest, he put up his hand and said, "I know what you're going to say, but he can learn about banking when we get a construction loan. We'll have the house — or rather, the lot, if the house is as bad as you say — for collateral. Which means we'll be lucky to get enough to replace the roof. We'll have to count our pennies and be careful how much we spend to get the house in salable condition. More than that, though, he'll learn he has to risk money to make money, which means he'll have a say in every decision that's made. He'll learn how to compare prices, how to buy smart to stay within budget, and how to drive a few nails. How does that sound?" He was almost daring me to find something to complain about, but I didn't have a quibble.

"It sounds just fine to me," I said, sitting back and basking in what I had wrought.

"Well," Hazel Marie said, "it all sounds good to me, too. But what if Lloyd isn't interested?"

Mr. Pickens's eyebrows went straight up. "Why wouldn't he be? What boy wouldn't want to fix up a house and sell it for a profit?"

"Oh, I don't know," she said. "It just seems that a lot of plans are being made for him, instead of with him."

"He'll love it," Mr. Pickens said, putting an end to that line of thinking.

"Lillian," I said, changing the topic, "who did you say owns that little house?"

She turned quickly from the sink, as if she'd just heard what we'd been talking about. "Prob'bly ole Mr. Clabe Hammond, since he owns just about ev'rything that's fallin' down. He don't fix nothin' up."

"Tell Mr. Pickens what you told me about

his cash-flow problem."

She frowned. "I don't know 'bout his cash, but I heard he lost his shirt tryin' to buy a hotel that never got built."

"That'd do it, all right," Mr. Pickens said with a smile that verged on the self-congratulatory. And well it should've, for it was due to his efforts and a few of mine that the plug had been pulled on an ill-planned boutique hotel right next door to his house.

"All right," Mr. Pickens said, standing up. "I've got my marching orders, so I'm ready to have at it. Miss Julia, I'll let you and Sam know our plans as soon as we have any. First order of business, though, is to tell Lloyd what we'll be doing."

"Well, I think *ask*ing . . ."

"Don't worry about it. He'll love it." Mr. Pickens slipped on his coat, helped Hazel Marie with hers, told Lillian that she was as beautiful as ever, and started for the door.

"One little thing," I said, stopping him. "Before Sam had this bright idea, I'd planned to take on that house myself. Pursuant to that, I'd spoken to Mr. Nate Wheeler, who's remodeling Dr. Crawford's house next door. I had sort of made arrangements with him to help with contracting and so forth, and I thought . . ." I trailed off as he stared at me.

"You pay him anything?"

I shook my head. "It didn't get that far."

"Then don't worry about it." And out he went, his arm around Hazel Marie as he hurried her through the cold wind to their car.

"I declare, Lillian," I said as the door closed behind them, "that man unsettles me."

"Yes'm, that's prob'bly what he mean to do."

I made a quick turn toward her. "Why, I think you're absolutely right. He does it on purpose, doesn't he?"

"It jus' the way he is. He's a teasin' man."

"Yes," I said, nodding, "that's what Sam said, too. Well, anyway," I went on, picking up our cups and saucers from the table, "I hope he knows enough about construction for Lloyd to learn something."

"Oh, I 'spect he do. They's no tellin' what all Mr. Pickens knows."

"That," I said firmly, "is the unmitigated truth."

Sam returned from his visit to the dentist, grinning crookedly from the Novocain, and said, "Sorry, honey, to miss being here, but I'm glad to have that filling replaced. How did it go?"

"Better than I thought it would," I said. Then, "Almost too well, in fact. I think I presented it so attractively that I talked myself out of a job. There I was, planning to have something to do myself, and by the time they left, Mr. Pickens had taken it over entirely. I don't quite know how it happened, except he immediately jumped on the idea of doing it with Lloyd. And the next thing I knew, it was Pickens and Son about to go into business."

"Don't you think that's a good idea?"

"Well, yes, I do. I just thought I might have a little part in it somewhere."

"I expect," Sam said, as if seeing into the future, "there'll be times when he and Lloyd will be glad to have you help out. What's Pickens going to do when he has to go out of town? Who's going to be there to accept a load of lumber and Lloyd is in school? Who's going to tell those two that orange isn't a good color for a kitchen?"

I laughed. "You're right. All I have to do is be available, and I'll have plenty to do."

Sam headed upstairs, and as I passed the phone on my way to the library, it rang and I answered it.

"Julia?" A whisper.

"Yes?"

"Can you talk?"

"Who is this?"

"Sh-h-h, it's me."

"LuAnne? What's wrong? Why're you whispering?"

"Because," she said in a normal tone, "I don't want every Tom, Dick, and Harry to hear me, and I have something to tell you."

"Where are you?"

"I'm at work," LuAnne said. "Where do you think I am? It's my second day on the job and you won't believe what's happening."

"What?"

Her voice dropped again. "Old Dr. Holcomb — remember him? Well, he passed last night, and we've got him. And we've also got his wife and his *girlfriend*!"

"What! Are they dead, too?"

"Oh, for goodness' sake, *no*. Wake up, Julia, and listen. They're here *grieving*."

"*Both* of them?"

"Yes! It's a madhouse around here. We have them in different slumber rooms — one's in the Lilac room and the other in the Camellia room. You know, to keep them apart because everything's supposed to stay calm and quiet. Serene, even. But I tell you, Julia, every salacious thing we've ever heard about him over the years is absolutely true.

But don't tell anybody. Uh-oh, I have to go. Talk to you later." And she hung up.

Well, well, so all the whispered stories about Dr. Harry Holcomb were true. I'd heard them for years, but had given them little credence because the man was otherwise highly thought of. He'd been one of those doctors who were always available, not only to their own patients, but to other physicians when they needed help. He was around for school activities when children could get hurt, and first responders knew he was always on call for highway accidents. In fact, he'd been instrumental in organizing the first emergency medical team in the county.

On the other hand, however, LuAnne had once told me about the time she and Leonard had gone to see *Out of Africa*. As they went in after the film had started, they'd left in the middle, and as they walked up the aisle they passed Dr. Holcomb and a young woman sitting together. LuAnne said that she'd not been paying attention and wouldn't even have noticed them except the young woman had suddenly flung a coat over her head.

"I certainly looked then," LuAnne had said. "I mean, there was Dr. Holcomb staring straight ahead at the movie while his girlfriend sat there covered with a coat. That sort of thing gets your attention, don't you think?"

The remarkable thing about all the stories was the fact that Dr. Holcomb apparently didn't play around. He was faithful to one girlfriend for years and years — even bought her a condo, I'd heard — and it was a mystery to me why Eileen Holcomb put up with it. Or for that matter, why the girlfriend did, either.

Of course, I was dying to know who she was. I'd heard it was a nurse at the hospital, but that had been pure guesswork. Someone else said she was a real estate agent, but then a rumor went around that he was involved with a friend of his wife. Nobody seemed to know for sure — just that it was somebody who had held on to his heart for decades, as apparently had his wife.

I couldn't help but wonder if he ever got them mixed up.

Well, live and let live, I always say, except what you've tried to keep secret is likely to come out when you die. At least that's what happened to Wesley Lloyd Springer, and now it was happening to Dr. Holcomb. Be assured, then, that one's secrets — no matter how well kept — will eventually out. So my advice is to live accordingly.

CHAPTER 24

The following week was quite busy for Pickens and Son, but not for me. They did let me know that they'd made an offer on the little house, after Binkie and Sam had okayed Lloyd's use of funds, but old man Hammond, thinking that he had a live one, had put an unconscionable price on the house. You'd have thought it had an ocean view and a tiki bar. Lloyd, eager to get started, had been all for paying it, which just goes to show how much he had to learn. Mr. Pickens had laughed in Mr. Hammond's face and walked away, saying there was more than one decrepit house in town. And he proceeded to put it out that he was looking at several others. A few days later, Mr. Hammond made a fairly reasonable counteroffer, and they went from there until Mr. Pickens was satisfied.

Hazel Marie let me know that a roofer had been lined up for the following week, and

Mr. Pickens had employed a couple of carpenters who didn't mind heights to repair the rotten rafters.

"And," she'd said, "J.D. and Lloyd have spent a couple of afternoons and early evenings tearing out the interior walls. They're planning to work all weekend, too. Even missing church to get in a full day on Sunday, and I don't know how I feel about that."

"Oh, surely," I said, with a touch of dismay, "they can spare an hour for church."

"You would think," Hazel Marie responded with asperity. "But J.D. said it was more like all morning by the time it took to dress, go to church, then undress and redress, eat lunch, get their tools together, and get started. He said that I should just consider that their ox was in a ditch and not worry about it."

"My goodness," I murmured, slightly impressed by Mr. Pickens's knowledge of Scripture. He could come up with an answer for everything. "Well, what can you do? At least, it won't last forever and they'll be back in church every Sunday."

Hazel Marie sighed. "Well, Lloyd will at least."

I left that alone, for it's unbecoming to

criticize a woman's husband. To her face, at least.

The following week slipped us into March with little letup of cold, windy weather. I drove past numbers sixteen and eighteen Rosewood Lane a couple of times but, not wanting to overstep, didn't stop. The roofers came to both the Crawford and the Pickens houses, quickly putting on new roofs that looked like fancy hats on bag ladies. Nate Wheeler's white pickup was parked out front of number eighteen every day — every weekday, that is — and once I recognized Lauren Crawford's large SUV parked behind it. From that, I assumed that she was her husband's project manager or at least assigned by him to make sure Nate was working when he was supposed to.

The second Sunday that Mr. Pickens and Lloyd eschewed church in favor of demolishing the interior, Sam and I drove over and went in. We did it in the afternoon, not during church hours, although I'm not sure that Mr. Pickens took note of the fact. I well knew that the point one is trying to make often goes right over the head of the one at whom you've aimed.

Both of them, Mr. Pickens and Lloyd, were filthy, their faces covered with masks and everywhere else covered with dust and dirt from ripping out cabinets, ceilings, and wallboard. Debris was everywhere, although they were just beginning to haul trash to the large container in the front yard. We had brought cookies and hot chocolate, which were well received, even though I had to look away from their dirty hands and faces as they ate.

"Lloyd," I said, wishing there was a place to sit since my back rebelled against standing too long, "what's the latest word on the Sadie Hawkins dance? Are you still going alone?"

"Oh, gosh, don't remind me," he said, rolling his eyes. "It just gets worse and worse. Now, I've heard that Debbie Morse is going to ask me and I have to sneak around at school so she won't hem me up."

"You don't want to go with her?"

"It's not that — she's all right. It's just that I can't handle three of 'em, much less four."

"But," I said, "if the first three are still boycotting you, wouldn't you rather have a date than not? A bird in the hand is worth three in the bush, you know."

Mr. Pickens was listening to this, his black eyes dancing in his head. I had a feeling that he was quite proud of his son's appeal

216

to the fairer sex — probably thinking that Lloyd was following in his footsteps.

"Well," Lloyd said, "I don't know what I'm gonna do. Actually, nothing, I guess, 'cause I'm not supposed to ask anybody myself. I have to wait to *be* asked, but so far all I've heard are rumors that *some*body will. I just wish somebody — just about anybody — would. It's getting down to the wire — the dance is next weekend."

Before I could respond, Sam, who'd been wandering around among the studs, turned to Mr. Pickens and asked, "What's your plan for the interior? Will you put walls back where the studs are?"

"We're thinking open concept — that's all the rage right now." Mr. Pickens discarded his Styrofoam cup and pointed out what he and Lloyd were planning. "Lloyd thinks we should make this entire half of the house into a kitchen, dining, and living room. Then do two bedrooms and a bath in the other half." He took out his tape measure and wandered away with Sam to show him the placement of the rooms. "It'll be tight, since it's a small house to start with. But if we make one room out of half the building, we'll have to have a supporting beam right here where this wall will come out."

Sam nodded, knowingly. "Probably be

worth it, though. One big room will feel more spacious than two small ones."

When they walked off, discussing the best place for a washing machine and dryer, as well as where the new furnace would go, I asked Lloyd how he was liking the construction business.

"I like it fine," he said. "I just wish we had whole days to work on it. By the time we get here after school, it's almost dark, so we don't get much done."

"But you're in no hurry, are you? School will be out in a few months and you'll have all summer to work on it."

"Yes'm," he said, "but Mr. Wheeler is really going to town on the house next door, and I know we're not in a race, but I'd like to sorta keep up with him."

"But you really don't need to. My understanding is that Dr. Crawford plans to rent out his house, and you're planning to put yours on the market, aren't you? So there'll be no competition involved — renting and buying draw different groups of people."

"Uh-huh, I know," he said, nodding. "It's just that I like to get things done, and not let 'em drag out forever."

I certainly understood that attitude — I had it myself. Then, very carefully, not wanting to give away my own competitive feelings, I asked, "Do you see much of Dr. Crawford? Does he check on the progress over there?"

"No'm, I've not seen him at all. But Mrs. Crawford comes by every now and then. At least, I guess that's who it is, or," he said, laughing, "it's Mr. Wheeler's girlfriend."

"Oh, I wouldn't think so. Mr. Wheeler is much too professional to have a girlfriend at a work site."

"Well," he said, "I guess being in my situation, I just have girlfriends on the brain."

We laughed at that while I took pride in his ability to laugh at himself. "Mrs. Crawford drives a dark blue SUV," I said, "so now you'll know when she comes."

"Then that's who it is. She finally waved at me the other day when I was taking out a load of trash. Before that, she'd not even looked this way."

"Well, just be friendly, as I know you will be. From what I've seen, she's one of those people who blow hot and cold. Friendly one day, and doesn't even recognize you the next."

"Yes'm, I heard Mama say the same thing. And I sure see it happening at school — all the girls like me one day and won't have anything to do with me the next."

■ ■ ■ ■

The following afternoon, Sam and I dressed in funereal clothing — he in a dark gray suit and subdued tie, and I in a light gray suit and black sweater. Plus overcoats, for the weather was still bitterly cold. Ordinarily we would have been preparing to attend the viewing of the recently deceased, but not this time. LuAnne had called to tell me that the Holcomb family's plans did not include a public viewing.

"It'll be in the obituary in tomorrow's paper," she'd said. "The viewing was limited to family only — they had an open casket. When the family got through, we closed the casket and that's the last time anybody'll ever see him. His oldest son gave us explicit orders — no one else is to be allowed access." LuAnne had paused to catch her breath. "You know what that means, don't you? They're keeping that Sheila woman away from him."

"Sheila who?"

"I'm trying my best to find out, but no one seems to know. She's not all that attractive, Julia. I got a glimpse of her yesterday when Mr. Thompson — he's the owner here, you know. Anyway he was herding her into the Lilac room because Eileen was just coming in, and he knew to keep them apart. Here's a secret, Julia, I think Dr. Holcomb died at his girlfriend's condo — wouldn't that be awful? I bet they won't put that in his obituary, don't you?"

I agreed that they wouldn't, then listened as she explained that the family was having a celebration of life in the activities room of the First Lutheran Church and it would be open to the public.

"He won't be there, though," LuAnne assured me. "It's going to be on the afternoon after the funeral, which will be private, too. Family only. And I heard that the two sons will be at the door to make sure his girlfriend doesn't sneak in, either at the funeral or at the celebration of his life. Wouldn't that be awful? I mean, for her and Eileen to come face-to-face, both of them crying their eyes out over a man who couldn't be faithful to either one of them."

Now, with Dr. Holcomb already safely interred, Sam and I parked at the Lutheran Church Activities Center and went in to offer our condolences. LuAnne, I noticed, had been right, for both Holcomb sons were greeting guests at the door, carefully scanning faces like airport guards. They welcomed us and pointed us toward their

221

mother, who was seated in a large chair, as a receiving line curved around her. We extended our sympathy, remarked on how Dr. Holcomb would be missed by the entire community, ate a couple of finger sandwiches, and went home.

"Sam," I said, as he drove us away, "if you ever get a girlfriend, she can bury you. I'm not going to fight over the privilege like Eileen and that Sheila woman are doing. It's unbecoming of both of them. Downright tacky, in my opinion."

Sam laughed. "Eileen's just asserting her authority as the official widow. It's important to her."

"A little late, don't you think? I'd be more likely to assert my authority as the official *wife.*"

"You are certainly that," he said, taking my hand and bringing it to his mouth for a quick kiss. "And I wouldn't have it any other way."

I smiled. "Me, either."

CHAPTER 25

"Sam," I said as the six o'clock news ended, "have you ever noticed how attractive doctors are to women?"

"No," he said, his eyebrows going up at my line of questioning, "I can't say that I have."

"That's because you've never watched *General Hospital.*"

He nodded judiciously. "Probably. Except," he went on, "I'm not convinced that they're more attractive to women than any other group."

"Well, take it from me," I assured him, "they are. And I'm wondering why. I mean, what's the underlying reason since you can't say they're any better looking as a whole than any other group of men. Well, Dr. Crawford is certainly a handsome man, but, as much as I like and admire Bob Hargrove, I wouldn't put him in that category."

Sam rubbed his fingers across his mouth

and gave the question considerable thought. "I'd say that it only *appears* that doctors are more likely to fool around because you know more doctors than, say, accountants."

My eyebrows went up at that. "You mean accountants fool around, too?"

He laughed. "I have no idea. I'm just saying that doctors are the subjects of gossip more than most groups because people know them. Or know *of* them."

"Maybe so."

"I know so. How many accountants do you know?"

"One. Ours."

"And how many doctors?"

"All of them, I guess. But I still think there's something about doctors that draws attention, although I readily admit that many of them may be falsely accused. But that just proves my point — what is it that makes physicians vulnerable to suspicion and gossip?"

"Competence, Julia. That's a very attractive attribute, especially to patients who need their help. Haven't you ever felt a special bond between you and your doctor?"

"To Bob Hargrove? I should say not." Sam was getting much too close for comfort, making me view Dr. Hargrove in a different light. "Besides, he's much too young for me."

"Not that young," Sam said, his eyes twinkling as he teased me. "And speaking of him, I wonder how he and Sue are enjoying their vacation."

"I do, too. Maybe we'll get a card from them soon. But you know, Sam, I'm wondering how Dr. Crawford is doing with the practice. Have you heard anything? And by the way, he's a lot younger than Dr. Hargrove."

"As far as I know, he's doing fine. Staying busy, I expect, with all the flu that's going around. Too busy for fooling around, anyway. You're not implying that he is, are you?"

"No, not at all," I said, holding up my hand. "Not one word, in fact, either way. I'd say that you're right and he's much too busy even to look after his own affairs. He has his wife overseeing the work on the house he bought and probably some county property, too. I told you about that, didn't I?"

Well, no, apparently I hadn't, so I passed along what Nell Hudson had told me, which made Sam wonder, as Hazel Marie and I had, what Dr. Don could want with a parcel of undeveloped land.

"And here," Sam said, shaking his head,

"I'd admired his plans for rental property."

"Well, anyway," I went on, "now that I think of all the doctors in town, maybe I've had him in mind all along. It was LuAnne who made me think of him."

"Why am I not surprised?"

"Oh, she means well, Sam, and she made the point to me that doctors are constantly around attractive women, some of whom may be only too willing to tempt or to be tempted. She just may be right to be concerned. I think I might be, too."

"About *him*?"

"No, more about his wife. Sam, that young woman just seems to make herself *un*attractive. I mean, that severe hair style — all slicked back in a ponytail and not a smidgeon of makeup. And you have to admit that Don Crawford is a handsome man with a warm personality, and she's such a nonentity in both looks and personality. I told you how striking she was when Hazel Marie fixed her face, and you could almost see her come alive. Yet now she's cut us all off as if we were leading her down the primrose path. Or something." I stopped and picked a piece of lint off my sweater. "I can't help but think that she's vastly unhappy, and what makes a wife most unhappy? A wandering husband, that's what."

"Oh, I doubt he's a wandering husband. With a busy practice and an interest in real estate, he has enough on his mind without adding a girlfriend or two. Besides," Sam went on, "I'd think a suspicious wife would be trying to make herself more attractive, not less."

Not sure that he understood women as much as he thought he did, I said, "You might be surprised. Some women could be so devastated at losing what was supposed to be theirs that any effort is simply beyond them. They just give up, feeling that crumbs are all they deserve, especially if children are involved. You know, they may feel they have to keep the family together at all costs."

"Well, that's pretty sad," Sam said, "but noble in a way." Then he turned to look at me as the idea dawned on him. "You think something like that is going on with the Crawfords?"

"No, not really. For one thing, Dr. Crawford hasn't been here long enough to start anything, and if he has someone in another town, why would he keep moving around? No, I don't think he's the problem at all. It's her, but if she can't get herself straightened out, he could *start* looking around. At least, that's what LuAnne thinks, and I wouldn't be surprised if Hazel Marie thinks the same."

"You may not be giving us husbands enough credit, honey," Sam said, taking my hand. "Not all of us are vulnerable to temptation even when a marriage isn't the best."

"I know, but not all husbands are as trustworthy as you, and I thank the Lord for you every day of my life. Although," I went on, smiling as I cut my eyes at him, "that doesn't make me less thankful that you're not a doctor."

"Miss Julia! Mr. Sam!" Lloyd called as he came through the kitchen door. "Anybody home?"

"In here, Lloyd," Sam said, getting up and beckoning him into the library. "Come on in and get warm."

"Where's Miss Lillian?" the boy asked as he dumped his backpack in the hall.

"She's grocery shopping," I said, getting to my feet. "Are you hungry? I can fix you something."

"No, thanks," he said, plopping down on the facing sofa. "I had a power bar when school let out. To give me strength for the walk, you know." He grinned.

Sam said, "I thought you were a man with wheels. What're you doing walking home?"

"Mama had to take the girls to the pediatrician — just a checkup — and J.D. is off somewhere investigating something. So," he said with a shrug of his shoulders, "I'm afoot again."

Sam laughed at what I assumed was a literary allusion that he understood and I didn't. "Well, we're glad you broke your long walk with a stopover here. How's the house coming along?"

"Pretty good," he said, sitting up with sudden interest. "Just wish we had more time to work on it, but Mama's going to let me drive over to check on things as soon as she gets back. Electricians were supposed to be there today, and I need to see how far they got. J.D. will call tonight to find out."

"Sounds as if you have things under control," Sam said.

"I think I have. I *hope* I have, but that's why I came by. I'm going to the Sadie Hawkins dance after all." Lloyd treated us to a pleased smile. "Debbie Morse went for a football player, thank goodness."

"Why, that's wonderful," I said. "Which one of the others asked you?"

"Not which *one*," he said, grinning broadly. "All three of 'em."

"What!" I said, "But doesn't that put you back into having to choose one?"

"No'm," he said, unable to stop smiling. "Not at all. I'm taking all three, only I had to promise that none of them would have to sit out any dances. So it's like this. I've gotta take turns dancing with one of 'em every third song, and I've gotta make sure the other two have partners. They said if any of 'em have to sit out a dance, I'll regret it to my dying day." He laughed. "But that's not a problem. I've already lined up some buddies who're going stag and they owe me. It's gonna work out fine, because J.D. will ride with us so I can drive, and the girls said they don't mind riding together in the back. So it's all settled and nobody's mad at me anymore. Although," he said somewhat mournfully, "I'll prob'bly be worn to a nub with all that dancing."

Sam and I laughed.

"You'll be fine," Sam said. "Any boy who can manage three women at a time is bound for great things."

"It was you who gave me the idea," Lloyd said. "You said I ought to take all three, so I just kinda mentioned it a couple of times — not to them, but to others because that's the way to get something out that you don't want to say directly. And it worked, 'cause they think it was their idea. So don't tell on me."

Sam gave him a conspiratorial smile. "I wouldn't dream of it. We men have to stick together."

CHAPTER 26

I shot straight up out of a sound sleep, the night blaring with sirens and the dark room strobing with red and blue lights.

"Sam!" I cried, shaking him. "Wake up! Wake up, something's going on!"

I threw off the covers and grabbed a robe against the chill and ran to the front windows. Sam was close behind as we peered down at the street, seeing nothing but flashes of colored lights reflecting off rain-streaked vehicles.

Quicker than I was, now that he was awake, Sam hurried to the side window and opened the curtains. "It's the Allens," he said, speaking of Mildred and Horace. "There's half a dozen cars, trucks, and vans in the driveway. EMTs, firemen, cops, you-name-it. Throw something on, Julia, we need to get over there."

We both threw something on, and soon were hurrying across our side yard onto the

Allen grounds, then, swerving around a fire truck and an emergency van, we gained the front porch. The double doors were wide open with uniformed men and women going in and out, some carrying medical paraphernalia, others talking on phones, and a few standing around waiting to be told what to do.

"We're neighbors, the Murdochs," Sam said to an officer who was writing on a chart. "What happened?"

The officer peered closely at us, and I wished I had put on more than a tatty bathrobe — like a fur coat, if I'd had one. The night was as cold as the North Pole, and I was about to freeze.

"You know these people?" the officer asked.

"Yes, of course," Sam said. "Been neighbors for years. What happened? Can we help?"

Glancing at me, the officer said, "You know the lady of the house?"

My heart dropped as we moved out of the way of a stretcher being carried in. Was it Mildred who would be carried out?

"Yes," I said, "we're close friends. Is she all right? Can I help?"

"Ah, well, yes, maybe so." The officer looked around, perhaps for some senior advice, but then he decided on his own. "Mrs. Allen is, well, pretty upset. Maybe you could sit with her, calm her down a little?"

"Of course," I said, relieved by the assumption that Mildred was not the patient. "Is Ida Lee with her?"

"Who?"

"Her housekeeper," I said, then remembered that Ida Lee was away for two weeks visiting her family in Chicago — a strange place to visit in the dead of winter, but the only time Mildred felt she could do without her. "Oh, my goodness, she's not here. Yes, officer, I think Mrs. Allen needs us. We won't get in the way."

"Slip through here, then," he said, pointing at the door. "She's in the kitchen, being seen to."

What did that mean? First of all, why did she have to be seen to? And second of all, why was she in the kitchen? The times Mildred had been in her kitchen could probably be counted on one hand — a fact that did not bode well.

And then I heard why. A cry of anguish that gradually increased in volume before dying away issued from the back of the house.

"Hurry," the officer said, urging us inside.

So we did, edging through the crowd at the door, we entered the grand foyer of the house, then went through the dining room by veering around the table that easily sat twelve and often did, and through the swinging doors of the butler's pantry, and on into the huge kitchen, where I expected to find Mildred being administered to by a covey of medical personnel.

There were only two young women, one in a dark uniform with EMT printed in yellow on the back of her jacket and the other in a police officer's uniform. One held Mildred's hand, and the other patted her back, neither of which was stemming the flow of tears or moans.

"Mildred!" I cried, kneeling as best as I could beside her. "What's wrong? Are you hurt?" Looking up at the two women, I went on. "Is she hurt? What happened?"

Before they could answer, Mildred suddenly flung her arms around me, crying, "Oh, Julia! It was awful, thank goodness you've come. What am I going to do? I can't stand it! Somebody needs to do something! What're they doing? Why won't you tell me anything?"

Assuming that wasn't addressed to me since I didn't know anything to tell her, I did a little patting of my own, trying to soothe her anguish. "Tell me, Mildred. What happened?"

"Horace," she said, her face contorted and streaked with tears. "Oh, Julia, I think I've killed him."

"Oh, no! No, Mildred, surely not." But I was recalling the time that she almost *had* killed him, the time that she raked his bedroom with a snipe-shooting shotgun that she kept under her bed. She hadn't been aiming at him then — we'd thought it was a burglar climbing in the window. But maybe she'd aimed this time.

Sam, with his legal caution and an eye on the two officials taking note of everything that was said, quickly stepped in. "You're upset, Mildred. Let's find out what happened before you say any more. Officer," he said, addressing the policewoman, "could you get us an update? I'm assuming with all the help around here that the injured party is just that, and not deceased at all. I'm sure it would help Mrs. Allen to know where things stand."

The policewoman nodded, somewhat grudgingly, I thought, and left the kitchen. She was back almost immediately.

"They're taking him out now," she said. "Going to the emergency room."

Mildred threw her head back and that

236

anguished wail began again. I wanted to clamp my hand over her mouth, but Mildred was a large woman who could scream if she wanted to. So I waited until it died out.

"Come on, Mildred," I said, getting to my feet with difficulty, "let's go upstairs and get you dressed, then Sam and I will drive you to the hospital. We'll be only a few minutes behind them, and they'll tell you something there." But all I could think of was Horace with a hole in his chest or, worse, scatter shot all over his chest and face. Everywhere else, too.

Surprisingly, Mildred hauled herself to her feet, clinging to a cashmere blanket that had served to cover a satin gown. She sniffed wetly, then turned to the young EMT. "Have some coffee, dear. I'm sure you get tired of hand-holding."

Give Mildred credit, I thought. She was always concerned with the comfort of her guests.

Sam took me aside, saying, "While you help her get dressed, I'll run across and get some clothes on. Then while you get dressed, I'll drive her to the hospital and stay with her until you get there. Will that work?"

"Perfectly," I said, appreciating his logical

mind, "but if she can't dress herself, we're in trouble."

Walking with Mildred toward the foyer, I hoped that she could get up the stairs without help. There was no way that I could either get her up them or stop her falling from them.

Actually, she made it to the upstairs hall with little effort, then, with a gasp of pain, turned toward her bedroom on the right at the top of the stairs.

"That's where I found him, Julia," Mildred said, pointing behind us as she wiped away tears with the edge of the cashmere blanket. "Lying right out there on the floor. There's no telling how long he'd been there, suffering, in pain and agony, and I knew nothing of it. He was on his way back, you know."

No, I didn't know, but I could guess. Mildred and Horace had separate bedrooms. The rooms weren't even adjoining. They faced each other at each end of the wide, upstairs hall. Mildred had once laughed as she told me that they almost had to buy a ticket to visit each other. I had concluded from that information that their visits were few and far between.

In her silk-swathed bedroom, Mildred calmly proceeded to gather the clothes, under and outer, that she wanted to wear, and all I had to do was help her with the buttons.

Just as we started back downstairs, I saw the headlights of Sam's car as he drove up to the porch. I was glad to know he was there, for the large house, after the comings and goings of so many first responders, was now eerily quiet.

"Let's get you in the car," I said, guiding Mildred toward the door. "Sam will take you to the hospital and wait with you till I get there, and I won't be long."

"Wait," she said, stopping abruptly, then erupting in a surge of tears. "Our *doctor,* Julia!" she wailed. "Dr. Hargrove's not here! I've never really needed him, but now that I do, he's not here!"

"Oh, but Dr. Crawford is, Mildred. He'll be there, doing exactly what Dr. Hargrove would do. Horace is in good hands, you don't need to worry about that."

As it turned out, she did.

Sam and Mildred were in the waiting area of the emergency room when I got to the hospital. He rose to meet me as I entered, then said that the young woman in a glassed-in nook had told them to take a seat, that someone would soon come to take Mildred, but probably not Sam, to Horace.

That meant, to me, that Horace was still among the living and that the next woman to see him wouldn't be LuAnne Conover at the Good Shepherd Funeral Home.

We walked over to the row of chairs, where Mildred was anxiously waiting. "Someone will come for you in a minute," Sam assured her. "I didn't know this, but apparently they let family members stay in the emergency room while they're doing whatever it is they do. I think that means he's awake and aware of what's going on, and that's good news."

Mildred gave Sam a plaintive look and said, "Is that new doctor here? Is he taking care of my precious?"

"Uh, well, I don't know. I gave them his name, told them he was holding the fort for Bob Hargrove, so I assume he's back there." Sam smiled at her. "Doctors have their own entrance, you know, so he probably came in that way."

It was only a second or two later that a nurse or a nurse's helper came out of some electronically operated doors and walked straight to Mildred. "Mrs. Allen? If you'll come with me, I'll take you to your husband."

Mildred sprang from her chair in a spritely manner, surprising me since she'd been leaning on my shoulder as if she could barely stay upright. "Is he all right? How is he?"

"We'll let the doctors tell you," the nurse said, kindly enough. "The cardiologist wants to bring you up to speed."

"Wait for me, Julia," Mildred pleaded. "Will you? I can't face this alone."

"Of course," I said. "Sam and I will be here until we hear from you. And praying for you both."

We watched the two of them disappear as the doors whooshed closed behind them. With the thought of prayer in my mind, I recalled that Mildred's Episcopal church occasionally held healing services, so I turned to Sam. "Should we call her priest? I don't know him, but surely he'll come if he knows he's needed."

"Let's wait awhile — it's barely four o'clock. Let's hope we'll learn a little something soon."

Suddenly my hand clamped down on Sam's arm. "Sam!" I whispered. "Did that nurse say *cardiologist*?"

Sam frowned, then nodded. "She did."

"Then Mildred couldn't have shot Horace. If she'd hit his heart, he wouldn't be needing a cardiologist, would he?"

With a quizzical look, Sam said, "I seriously doubt it. Why do you think she shot him?"

"Because," I said, lowering my voice, "don't you remember? She shot at him once before. And that was the first thing I thought of when she said she'd killed him."

"Well," Sam said, "I suggest that we conveniently forget we heard that, although there were two other witnesses. Right now, I'm concerned about something else."

"What?"

"When I went home to put on some clothes, I called Don Crawford to meet us over here — the same as I would've done if it'd been Bob."

"And?"

"He said he doesn't see emergency cases — they're taken care of by staff hospitalists. He said if Horace is admitted, he'll drop by the hospital tomorrow and see how he's doing."

"Well!" I said, on the point of outrage. "That's a poor way of doing things. I thought he was running the practice the way Dr. Hargrove does, and *he* certainly would've been here."

"I know," Sam said, agreeing with a nod. "But, then, we're friends. Maybe with all the changes in the way medicine is practiced now, he would've bowed to the emergency room staff, too."

"But Mildred and Horace are his patients, Sam. Forget friendship! They're *patients,* and Bob would've been here!"

Sam nodded agreement. "He would've, yes. But Bob would've called in specialists — the cardiologists and so on — if they were needed. We really can't blame Dr. Crawford for not coming out to see someone he doesn't even know."

Well, *I* could, and proceeded to do just that. Dr. Hargrove's friends should receive the special treatment to which they were accustomed to having from him, and I was surprised and dismayed that Dr. Crawford had chosen to relinquish Horace's care to a group of strangers with unknown pedigrees.

Chapter 27

We waited and waited, sitting in the lounge until the windows began to lighten with dawn. Sam had brought cup after cup of coffee, and I'd dozed in between trips to the ladies' room.

"What can be taking so long?" I asked, knowing that Sam knew no more than I did, but asking anyway.

"No telling," he said, trying not to yawn. "They're probably doing electrocardiograms among many other tests. And monitoring him before either admitting him or sending him home."

"After all this? Surely they won't send him home. What would Mildred do without Ida Lee?" I could visualize Mildred constantly calling on Sam and me to help with nursing care.

"She'll hire registered nurses round the clock. Don't worry about it — Mildred has the constitution of a horse, honey. When the going gets tough, she gets tougher."

"Well, you're right about that," I said, nodding. "It's just that she has to go through some kind of helpless act until she decides to take hold." I squirmed in the hard chair, then went on. "But, Sam, I'm sitting here getting more and more furious with Dr. Crawford. The idea of his just turning over and going back to sleep when Bob Hargrove's close friend may be back there dying just does me in. I don't think either Bob or Sue would approve of that."

"No, they wouldn't. But remember, Bob would've called in the specialists, just as they're doing without either him or Dr. Crawford. Horace is getting the same level of care he would've gotten anyway."

"That's not the point," I said. "It's the principle of the thing that gets to me. I don't think Dr. Crawford is living up to his contract, which surely calls for him to get out of bed and see to his patients."

Sam smiled and patted my knee. "I expect so, but there's not much we can do about it."

I subsided, knowing he was right. But, I thought with a flash of righteous anger, I am surely going to tell on him when Bob Hargrove gets home.

■ ■ ■ ■

About nine o'clock that morning, Horace Allen was moved from the emergency room and admitted to the intensive care unit. Then it was strongly yet gently suggested that his wife go home and get some rest. From the way it was worded by one of the ER nurses, it appeared that Mildred had required as much attention as had her husband.

So Sam and I drove her home, then at her pleading, I accompanied her inside. Walking up the stairs with her, I suggested that she go straight to bed since she'd been up most of the night.

"That's what *I* intend to do," I said, my eyes so heavy I could hardly see. "And Sam, too, I expect."

"I doubt I can sleep," Mildred said, piteously, as we entered her bedroom. "I'm much too worried about what happened, what could've happened, and what might yet happen. I'll probably never sleep the same again."

Then she began to rummage through a lingerie drawer, pulling out a lace-enhanced nightgown. "I'll also never wear that gown I had on again. Horace loves it, which was what instigated his heart attack in the first place."

She was telling me much more than I wanted to know, so I busied myself with hanging up the dress that she'd flung on a chair.

Then, in her underclothes, she suddenly collapsed in a velvet chair and the tears began again. "Oh, Julia, if you could've seen him — tubes and wires all over the place, and people coming and going, and machines moving in and out — it was horrible. And my poor Horace looking so pale and helpless, and all the while I was sitting there watching and praying and thinking that it was our love . . . Well," she said with a mournful sigh, "it can't be helped, but I guess that's the end of that."

Thinking that there had apparently not been much of *that* to begin with, I chose my words carefully. "Maybe not, Mildred. We both know people who've had heart attacks and gone on to lead normal lives."

"Ah," she said, "but what do we really know about what goes on or *doesn't* go on in their lives?"

"That's true," I said, too tired to do anything but agree with her. "Did the doctor tell you he shouldn't . . . you know?"

"No, but I know he will. I guess he figures

he has plenty of time to get into that. Horace is in no shape now to even think of exerting himself.

"See, Julia," Mildred went on, "I have to *protect* him from everything that will put a strain on his poor, damaged heart. And that means from *me* as well. I just didn't realize the depth and intensity of his feelings. I mean, my mind can roam over a dozen things while his focuses entirely on what he's doing, and that's not healthy. Obviously."

By an act of will I closed off the mental image her words evoked. I had no desire to know what went on in somebody else's bedroom.

But by this time Mildred had undressed and redressed in the fresh gown while I smoothed out her bed with my back turned. I think that she was so accustomed to being dressed with Ida Lee's help that it didn't occur to her that I would be discomfited at the sight of such a vast expanse of flesh. Well, even at a small expanse, truth be told.

I pretended to a nonchalance that I didn't feel.

Then, just as Mildred began to crawl into bed, she jumped back and let out a shriek. *"Julia!"*

"What! What is it?"

"Ida Lee! I have to call her and tell her to come home. What was I thinking? I should've called last night, so she would already be on her way. Oh, what will I do? It could be tomorrow by the time she gets here."

"Oh, Mildred, I wouldn't do that. She's supposed to be back this weekend anyway, isn't she? Why don't you let her have her full time away? They'll keep Horace in ICU for several days, so you won't need help till he gets home."

"I'm not talking about for *him,*" she said. "I need her for *me.* And, besides, she'd *want* to be here if she knew how badly I need her."

I wasn't too sure of that. I knew that Ida Lee was more than well paid — she had to be, considering that she stayed in the job in spite of what was asked of her. But I also knew that Mildred was a demanding employer and expected constant attendance. But if Ida Lee decided to take her full vacation, we could have another Allen in the hospital.

"Well," I said, soothingly, "I'm just suggesting that you won't really need her until Horace gets home, and by that time she'll have had the full two weeks with her family — which she certainly deserves." The last thing I wanted to have happen was Ida Lee not returning at all.

Mildred seemed to consider that, but then she said, "I know what I'll do — I'll get her a Gucci handbag as a thank-you gift for dispensing with a few more days off. Because I'll tell you the truth, Julia, I need Ida Lee more than I need Horace. Not that I don't love Horace, but he's not as helpful or as handy as she is."

I had no reply to that, so I firmly took my leave, telling Mildred to get some sleep for Horace's sake. But walking across her lawn to my house, I couldn't help but wonder at that marriage. It was certainly one for the books — if anyone was interested enough to research it, which certainly wasn't me.

I'd just walked through the kitchen door with my mouth open to speak to Lillian when the phone rang. Lillian gave me a questioning look as she answered it, then handed it to me.

"It's Mrs. Allen," she said,

My word, I'd barely gotten home and already she was calling.

Taking the phone, I said, "Mildred? What's wrong? You ought to be asleep."

"I know," she said, "and I will be just as soon as I tell you this and get your opinion about it. See, Julia, I'm thinking that I ought to get Horace a new car. What do you think?"

I could scarcely believe she was lying awake after watching Horace being brought back from near-death and was now thinking of a new car. Why, the man might never recover at all. Why did she have cars on her mind?

"I haven't thought about it at all, Mildred," I said, somewhat testily, which was the way I felt. "Why are you thinking of such a thing?"

"Well, because," she said as if it was obvious, "Julia, you know he drives that little foreign sports car that he just had to have, and he loves it. But it's hard to drive. Why, Julia, that thing has a six-speed dual clutch manual transmission, so he has to shift gears all up and down the gearshift every time he slows down, speeds up, or comes to a stop, and that's such a strain. I'm not sure he'll be able to manage that after a heart attack. And it's also very low to the ground — you have to go through contortions to get in and out of it. I won't ride in it myself. I like a big, comfortable, easy to drive car, and I think I ought to have one like that waiting for him when he's able to get out and around again."

"Well, that's thoughtful of you," I said, wondering what in the world she'd think of next. "But I'm not sure I'd trade in a car he loves, even if he can't drive it, without mentioning it to him first. The shock might set him back."

"Hm-m," she said, "I hadn't thought of that. Maybe I'd better discuss it with someone who knows something about cars. Somebody who'd know how much of a shock it'd be to find, say, a Mercedes S-Class in the garage rather than a Porsche Boxster."

"Good idea," I said, then, almost asleep on my feet, I went on. "And I know just the someone you need to talk to. J.D. Pickens is an expert on cars that meet the needs of each particular driver."

CHAPTER 28

The next day or so brought a hint of spring — the temperature rose into the fifties, then we were in for more raw and rainy conditions. The weather was the least of my concerns, though, for I was beginning to think that I'd found a home in a hospital waiting room. Mildred not only wanted, but expected, a companion on her daily visits to the ICU. I realized that I was wanting Ida Lee home more than Mildred was, but a spring snowstorm was delaying departures from Chicago.

Niggling around in my mind, however, was that flame of righteous anger at Dr. Don Crawford, who, to my mind, was not fulfilling his obligations either to Bob Hargrove or his patients. Oh, he'd come by to look in on Horace, all right, but that was all he'd done. He had apparently taken no interest in looking over his chart, checking his medications, or noting the results of the tests that had been performed on Horace. He had made no more than a drop-in visit, the likes of which any acquaintance might make.

Horace, however, seemed to continue to improve, although he had no memory of what had put him in the hospital in the first place. He hardly had time to worry about that, though, for after three days of intensive care, he was abruptly moved out.

Getting everything secondhand from Mildred, I gathered that Medicare would pay for only three days and, despite the fact that the Allens could afford a longer stay, out he went. And ended up in rehab — a term that brought visions of celebrities' addiction problems, which, being neither a movie nor a rock star, Horace most assuredly did not have.

Come to find out that rehab simply meant a place of physical rehabilitation — like a gym or something — after a stroke or a heart attack, for which Horace certainly did qualify. He was admitted to The Safe Harbor to begin a fairly rigorous regimen of physical therapy for twenty-one days, no more and no less — Medicare requirements again.

"My word, Sam," I said one evening as we discussed what was going on, "it's not just hospital administrators who're running the practice of medicine. It's also the government. Somebody, somewhere has decided how long a patient needs to recover from a heart attack, and it seems that one size fits all."

"So it does," he said, nodding agreement.

"Well, I don't like it. Horace is still under the care of a group of hospitalists and specialists, but he has no personal physician — certainly not Dr. Crawford, who hasn't shown his face since that first day. What has he been doing, I'd like to know."

"Well," Sam said, "where Horace is now isn't conducive to daily visits by a busy practitioner. The Safe Harbor is way out in the sticks, or haven't you noticed?"

"I certainly have. It's almost a forty-five-minute drive out in the county and forty-five minutes back. And I ought to know since I've driven it every day since Horace has been there. I've thought of letting Lloyd drive us since Mildred wants to go only in the afternoons when he'd be out of school anyway. You know, to give him more experience and to keep me company while Mildred goes in to see Horace. But, Sam, once you get out of town, that road has almost no shoulders and there's a weed-filled ditch on both sides. So if Mildred thinks she's too nervous and upset to drive herself, I'd hate to think how she'd feel with Lloyd at the wheel."

"Why isn't Ida Lee driving her? She's back, isn't she?"

"Yes, but Mildred claims that Ida Lee is too busy, so that leaves me who has to take her."

"I know, honey, but you're being a good friend. Let's just be thankful that Ida Lee is back. You could be spending nights with Mildred instead of with me."

I smiled. "I'd draw the line at that."

It was a fact that Mildred tended to put her own needs before those of anyone else. Perhaps we all do, but not to the extent that she did. Yet she was a dear and close friend, and of all the women I knew, the most like me in what and how I thought about things. It was only her tendency to expect constant attendance during one of her stressful times that began to rub me the wrong way.

I mean, I had my own obligations and my own needs to deal with. I couldn't dance to her tune day in and day out, yet that was what she expected. Of course, different people respond in different ways to stress. I, for instance, tend to withdraw into myself to suffer alone and in silence. But not

Mildred. She needed an audience, someone to listen and to sympathize with her expressions of agony.

Take the day that Horace had been in rehab only a few days. That morning, Mildred called early while I was still in the bathroom, only half dressed.

"Julia," she said, a pitiful note in her voice, "I've just been lying here thinking about what you said. Does that husband of Hazel Marie's really know how to match a man with the exact car he needs?"

"Mildred, for heaven's sake, it's not yet seven o'clock. What're you doing awake and thinking of such a thing?"

"Well," she said, "with Horace away, I'm not sleeping well these nights."

That, of course, was understandable. I knew she was concerned about her husband, but I also knew that she was rarely out of bed before noon even when Horace was in health. She could make up for hours of sleeplessness by staying in bed all morning, and often did.

"Anyway," she went on, "I'd like to speak with Mr. Pickens, but you know him better than I do. Would you bring him over maybe late this afternoon when we get back from seeing Horace? I want to hear what he'd suggest for Horace, and I want you to be here, too, if you will. I'll want to talk it over with you afterward."

"Mildred —" I began, my patience wearing thin. Then I gave up. "I'll see if he's free and let you know."

"She wants *what*?" Mr. Pickens let his tape measure snap closed as he stared at me as if I were crazy.

Knowing that he and Lloyd would be working late at the house on Rosewood, I had dropped by to propose a consultation with Mildred about vehicle appropriateness vis-à-vis a special-needs driver.

"Well-l," I said, hedging a little, "I know it sounds odd, but Mildred wants to reduce any extra strain on Horace's heart. It's already damaged, you know, and she worries that all that gear-shifting will cause another attack. Or maybe she's thinking that the excitement of driving a Grand Prix race car will be too much for his heart. I know that the sound of that huge engine revving up is enough to stop mine."

"If he's that bad off, he shouldn't be driving at all." Mr. Pickens wiped his sweaty face with a filthy rag, creating strange shadows on the exposed studs of the wall. Lloyd had stopped whatever he'd been doing and now leaned against a sawhorse to listen to us.

"I can't disagree with that," I said, in an attempt to mollify his reaction. "But until a doctor tells him he can't drive, you know he will. And she wants to be prepared before the thrill of driving that souped-up car — and shifting all its gears — strains him too much. She wants to replace it with something more sedate."

Lloyd straightened up and, giving Mr. Pickens a teasing look, said, "I know where there's a real sedate car she might like."

"You wish," Mr. Pickens said, glancing at him with a grin. Then he turned to me. "Sure, I'll talk to her, but only in general terms. I'm not about to choose a car for Horace — that's up to him in my book."

"Well, you know Mildred," I said and left it at that because we both knew who held the purse strings in that marriage.

Mr. Pickens grunted in reply, then extended his tape measure and made a pencil mark on a board. "Can't do it till sometime over the weekend, if she's in that much of a hurry. Pickens and Son have their hands full here."

Agreeing to meet him at Mildred's whenever he had time for her, I turned to leave. Already, though, dark had fallen and Mr.

259

Pickens, holding a flashlight, insisted on walking me to the car.

Looking across the narrow yards at number eighteen Rosewood, which also had lights burning, I said, "Looks as if Nate Wheeler is working late, too."

"No, he knocks off about five-thirty, but he gets in a full day — not like us who're more hit or miss. That's Don Crawford checking on things. See, there's his car." Mr. Pickens nodded toward the shiny Lexus parked under a streetlight at the curb. I recognized the luxury car only because Sam had considered buying one the last time he'd had new car fever.

I sniffed. "Ever since he left Horace Allen to strange doctors, I've just had no use for him."

Mr. Pickens's white teeth flashed in a quick grin. "But Horace is getting better, isn't he? Maybe that's why."

That was one way of looking at it and, as I considered his comment, Mr. Pickens opened the door of my car. "Here we go," he said.

Recalling Nell Hudson's passing along of inappropriate information, I hesitated before getting in. "Have you heard that Dr. Crawford is looking at some county property? Why would he do that if his main interest is rental houses?"

"No idea," Mr. Pickens said with a glance at the lighted windows of the house next to his. "And I hadn't heard that he's looking at anything else. Long-term holding, maybe, thinking it'll increase in value. And he may be right."

"Huh," I said, sliding behind the wheel, "that'd be the only thing he's gotten right."

Chapter 29

That following Saturday morning, I kept waiting to hear from somebody — Lloyd, definitely, but Hazel Marie would've done.

When eleven o'clock came and went, I could wait no longer.

"Hazel Marie?" I said when she answered the phone. "How did it go last night? Did Lloyd have a good time?"

"He must've," Hazel Marie said with a laugh. "He was still in bed at eight o'clock this morning, and J.D. had to roust him out to go work on the house."

"Oh, that's too bad. The boy needs his sleep."

"They're putting up drywall today — which is hard work — so he'll probably be in bed by sundown. You know he's not used to staying up late, and he and J.D. didn't get home till well after midnight last night."

"My goodness," I said. "I didn't know a school dance would last that long — a prom, maybe, but not a Sadie Hawkins dance."

"Oh, it didn't. It was over at eleven-thirty, but then they went to the IHOP and J.D. treated them all to breakfast. He said he sat at a table by himself so Lloyd and his three dates could have some privacy in a booth. He said they had a grand time discussing who had come with who, what they were wearing, and who had been the best dancers. J.D. said it sounded like a debriefing after a hazardous mission."

"So Lloyd had a good time?"

"Oh, my land, yes," Hazel Marie said. "Although he's paying for it this morning. I took them some coffee and doughnuts about an hour ago, and he almost went to sleep sitting straight up."

I made a successful effort not to remind her of the dangers to the boy's health that lack of sleep could cause. Instead, I told her that Sam and I were eager to hear about the dance from Lloyd himself.

"We want to know how the triple date went," I said, laughing. "That was Sam's idea, you know." Still smiling as we hung up, I felt a surge of pride for our boy who had handled a dicey situation so well.

You could tell that spring was trying its best

to overtake winter — fruit trees were budding, boxwoods were bright with new growth, dandelions dotted the front lawn, and daylight lasted a few minutes longer each day. Yet there was a freeze warning for that night.

By late Sunday afternoon the clouds had rolled in and the temperature began to drop again, but that's when Lloyd came over to visit.

Sam and I were sitting in the library by the open fire, both near asleep after reading the paper and having a light supper, when Lloyd rang the back doorbell. Sam had spent a couple of hours helping Pickens and Son that afternoon, so he was in a deeper doze than I was. With the kitchen empty on a Sunday when Lillian was off, we usually kept the doors locked, so I let Lloyd in.

"I thought you'd still be working on the house," I said as we walked to the library. "I mean, since you usually work long hours on Sundays."

"No'm," Lloyd said, divesting himself of a car coat. "We put in a couple of hours today, and Mr. Sam really helped out. But I think J.D. was getting tired, so we quit early today. He said he needed to spend some time with the little girls but he was asleep in his chair when I left." Lloyd grinned at the thought.

"I'll tell you," Lloyd went on, "putting up drywall is not an easy job. That stuff's heavy and hard to handle, but we're moving along on it. If," he said with a grin, "J.D. doesn't give out."

"Hm-m, well," I said. Hearing that Mr. Pickens was running out of steam, I thought he might welcome the services of an experienced designer. I was still looking for something to do.

"I thought you were going to use the old walls — that so-called shiplap. It's so old-fashioned that it's modern again."

"No'm," he said, plopping down on the sofa across from us. "Most of it was in bad shape, but we saved some of it. J.D. thinks we can use it as an accent wall in the bedrooms."

An accent wall? Who would've thought that a private investigator would even know what that was? I sighed, accepting the fact that I had arranged myself out of a job.

"Well, come on, Lloyd," Sam said, fully awake by now, "tell us about the dance and how you managed three dates."

Lloyd leaned back against the sofa, grinning with self-satisfaction. "It went great. I had a great time. But," he said, sitting up, "I'll tell you this. I was about wore out by the time we got there. See, I had to park the car, get out and walk up to *three* front doors. Then meet and talk to three sets of parents, have my picture taken three times, then walk a girl back to the car three times and get each one settled in the backseat. Then I had to dance every dance with one or the other of three girls, then walk each one back to the door when we took them home. I was beat."

Sam grinned at him, then said, "No good-night kisses, Lloyd?"

Lloyd laughed, knowing that he was being teased. "With J.D. watching from the front seat? No, *sir*!"

It was beginning to get dark, but still not that late, when I slipped on a heavy coat to go over to Mildred's. Lloyd had left a few minutes before, having given us a blow-by-blow account of the perils of triple dating.

"Sam," I said as I buttoned my coat, "you sure you don't want to go with me?"

"I'm sure," Sam said, and grimaced as he turned to look at me. "But before you go, do you know where the heating pad is?"

"Heating pad? Why? What's wrong?" I started unbuttoning my coat.

"Oh, it's nothing. I must've pulled a muscle in my back today." Sam gave me a wry grin. "That'll teach me to leave drywall alone."

"Have you taken anything? You want some aspirin? Advil? Tylenol?"

"No, just the heating pad, if you don't mind." He was sitting, somewhat crookedly, in the chair and made no effort to rise. It was so unlike Sam to ask someone else for something that I was immediately concerned.

"Of course I don't mind. And I know exactly where it is, along with an extension cord. Don't move, I'll get it." And so I did, although I almost tripped going up the stairs.

Back in the library, I plugged it in, adjusted the setting, and helped Sam sit up so I could put it against his lower back.

"Don't you want to go to bed?" I asked. "Let me help you before I go. In fact, I won't go. Mildred doesn't need me to hear Mr. Pickens hold forth on the virtues of one car after another."

"No, no, you go on. It's too early for bed, and with a little heat, I'll be all right. Go on, honey, then come back and entertain me with what happened. Besides," he went on, "if you don't, you know Mildred will be on the phone telling you all about it."

He was right, so, slightly concerned about

leaving him in pain, I told myself that I had a good excuse not to linger at Mildred's. Even if she wanted to go over Mr. Pickens's recommendations a dozen times.

Mr. Pickens was already ensconced in Mildred's living room when Ida Lee welcomed me, took my coat, and led me to them. A plate of sliced pound cake and a coffee service was on a tea table in front of a damask-covered sofa. Mr. Pickens was already sampling the cake, although he got to his feet when I entered.

"Come in, Julia," Mildred said, as she motioned me to a chair beside her. "Forgive me for not rising, but I'm so emotionally drained from worrying about Horace that . . . well, you understand, I know.

"Here," she said, offering the cake plate to me. "I've been urging Mr. Pickens to have a drink, but he keeps turning me down. Says he honors Sundays by refraining from spirits on the Lord's day." She laughed appreciatively. "I think he's been around you too long."

"That's probably it," Mr. Pickens said, his black eyes glinting.

"So," I said, taking the chair beside Mildred, "have you two decided anything?" Worried about Sam's back, I was ready to

268

move things along and get back home.

"Oh, we've just been visiting," Mildred said, clearly enjoying Mr. Pickens's presence and in no hurry to conclude, or even begin, our business.

Since I thought that business of little moment and nothing more than time away from my ailing husband, I was in no mood for a couple of hours of chitchat.

So, after mentioning that Sam wasn't feeling well, I pushed things along by saying, "Mr. Pickens, do you have any suggestions about the best car for Horace when, and if, he can drive again?"

He hunched forward, his forearms on his knees, which were spraddled out in a typically masculine position, and said, "It's obvious enough that any of the luxury sedans will be roomier and easier to drive than his Boxster, although, I warn you, he may not think so. That car's a jewel, and I don't know a man alive who'd give it up easily. But if you're going to buy something, you should look at the high-end sedans that have the new electric steering system. It'll probably be an option, but if you get it Horace will be able to turn the steering wheel with one finger. Mercedes offers it, I know, so the others probably do, too."

"One finger?" Mildred asked, clearly

impressed. "That's exactly what Horace needs."

"And," Mr. Pickens went on, "they all come equipped now with a camera for reversing, and be sure to get the blind spot assist, which is probably standard, but might not be. With that, you don't have to twist your neck around to see if anybody's coming up on the left. I'd definitely get that on any new car I bought."

"Well," Mildred said, "that sounds good, too. But what about those cars that drive themselves? I've been thinking that's what Horace needs. He could just sit behind the wheel and *feel* like he's driving, but he wouldn't be at all."

Mr. Pickens almost laughed, but quickly straightened up and said, "I wouldn't recommend that — too experimental. Besides, they're not available to consumers yet and, from the results I've heard, it'll be some time before they are."

"That's too bad," Mildred said. "I was hoping that I could get a driverless car and he'd never have to strain himself again."

Having had enough of Mildred's fanciful ideas and wanting to get back to Sam, I said, "You can accomplish that easily enough, Mildred. Just get him a roomy car and hire a driver."

"I've been thinking of that, too," she said, any hint of sarcasm drifting past without recognition.

"Well, I'd be careful," Mr. Pickens said, "if I were you and not do anything rash."

"Like what?" Mildred asked.

"Like getting rid of that Porsche. Buy him another car if you want to, but let that one sit in the garage. I know if it was mine, and it suddenly went missing, I'd have a heart attack on the spot. A man and his car are not easily parted."

CHAPTER 30

Mr. Pickens was thoughtful enough to walk me home in the dark, so I did the conventional thing and invited him in.

"Thanks, but no," he said. "It's been a long day, and I need to get home. Tell Sam we sure appreciated his help on the house today. You need to come by and see what we're doing. Things are moving right along."

"I'm glad to hear it, but, Mr. Pickens, I'd appreciate it if you'd keep Sam from doing any heavy work. He's thrown his back out as it is."

"Oh? Sorry about that. A heating pad and a couple of aspirin ought to put him right."

I knew that, so I thanked him again and went inside.

Sam was already in bed, but not asleep. He had the extension cord of the heating pad strung across the room to an outlet.

"Don't trip on that cord," he cautioned as

I entered the bedroom.

"I see it, but how're you feeling?"

"I'm okay." He smiled, then grimaced as he tried to turn over. "Can't seem to get comfortable, though, and I think this cord is wrapped around me a couple of times."

I went straight to the bathroom and brought back two aspirins and a glass of water. "Here, take these, then get yourself settled, and I'll fix the heating pad for you."

He could barely sit up to take the medicine, and I wished we had something stronger in the house.

"How in the world," I asked, "did you get up the stairs to bed? You can hardly move without pain."

"Well, you would've laughed to see me, but I crawled up the stairs, then crawled into bed, thinking it would ease off if I could lie down. It hasn't."

"Oh, Sam," I said, wondering aloud if I should call the doctor.

"No," he said. "It's just a pulled muscle, and a few hours of rest will do the trick."

He didn't have a comfortable night, nor did I. He moaned and groaned at each movement, so I was up before dawn. Something had to be done and, whether Sam liked it or not, he was going to see the doctor.

Calling Dr. Hargrove's office as soon as it opened, I spoke with Libbie, his longtime receptionist, telling her that Sam needed to be seen as soon as possible.

"He's in severe pain, Libbie, and I know Dr. Hargrove would have him come in. So I'm sure that Dr. Crawford will want to see him, too. What's a good time?"

"Well," she said, "Dr. Crawford likes his appointments to stay on schedule, so he wants walk-ins to come about five."

"No, that won't do. Sam's in a bad way, and he needs to be seen right away."

"I tell you what," Libbie said, "y'all come on, and I'll work him in. We don't want Mr. Sam to be in pain."

"Oh, thank you, Libbie. We'll be there just as soon as he can get out of bed. But will you get in trouble?"

"Probably," she said airily, "but I can't be fired — at least not till Dr. Hargrove gets back."

"And certainly not then, either," I said, determined, just as soon as Bob Hargrove got home, to speak to him about the arrogance of putting off emergency cases till late afternoon and the resultant lowering of office morale, as well. And I intended to mention a few other things, too.

It turned into a production to get Sam to

the doctor's office. Every movement created such agony that just getting him dressed was a trial, even though Sam tried to hide it. Lillian and I helped him downstairs and into the car, but he was sweating by the time he was seated for the ride.

We waited almost an hour before Sam was called in to see Dr. Crawford — an hour of pain for Sam and of agitation for me. I stayed in the waiting room, waiting for Dr. Crawford to call me in, as Dr. Hargrove would have, to tell me what was wrong with Sam and what would be done for him.

Instead, Sam, still unable to straighten up, was helped by a nurse back to the waiting room. "He has a prescription," the nurse said. "I'd get it filled right away, and get him started on it."

Half insulted by not being told this by the doctor himself, I got Sam in the car and headed for the drugstore. "What did the doctor say?" I asked.

"A pulled muscle," Sam said, "just as I thought. That'll teach an old man not to do a young man's job."

"Oh, shoo," I said, "LuAnne Conover pulled her back out just by leaning over to make up a bed. It's just the way it happens." I drove into the lot at the drugstore and parked. "You stay here, and I'll get the

275

prescription filled. Just think, in about fifteen minutes, you're going to have relief."

Sam bravely smiled. "If I can stand it that long."

Carrying the prescription, I walked through the drugstore to the pharmacy in the back and handed it in. They knew us there, and I was greeted with warmth by Dave Daniels, the pharmacist.

"I'll wait," I said. "We need it filled right away, if you can."

"For you, Miss Julia, that's right now." And it was after only a few minutes that I was handed an amber vial of white tablets. "Uh, now," Dave said, leaning over the counter, "this is strong stuff, so I'd dole it out carefully."

Turning the vial around, I read *Oxycodone* on the label and underneath it the words, "Take one caplet every 3 to 4 hours for pain."

"Oxycodone?" I asked, holding the vial at a distance, as I recalled hearing a lot about this particular medication, and none of it good. "How many did you give us?"

"Dr. Crawford ordered sixty."

"*Sixty?* I've yet to meet a pulled muscle that lasted that long."

"Well," Dave said, lowering his voice, "I'd try giving Sam only half a tablet at a time.

Then switch to something over the counter as soon as he gets relief."

"Good advice," I said, and headed out in high dudgeon. Even I knew that sixty tablets or caplets or doses of that fearsome drug handed out like candy was a recipe for disaster. In this case, the cure was most certainly worse than the disease.

As soon as we got home, I sliced a caplet in half and gave one of the halves to Sam. Almost in minutes, he was able to straighten up and move around without pain. For the rest of the day, he rested, napping occasionally, until about four o'clock, when he began to show signs of discomfort again.

I gave him — although hesitantly — the other half, then at bedtime I suggested he take some Tylenol. He slept well all night and the next morning, he was virtually without pain. Another dose of Tylenol had him on his feet and back to normal.

"Lillian," I said as we discussed it in the kitchen, "I don't know what to think about that new doctor. The idea of giving Sam so much of such a strong drug makes me question his judgment. I mean, what if he took every one of these tablets? Why, by the end of the week, he could've been a drug addict."

Holding up the offending vial, I went on.

"I'm going to hide these things and hold on to them a few days, just to be sure that Sam won't need them. Then I'm getting them out of the house."

"Yes, ma'am, I would, too," Lillian said. "An' we better not tell a soul they in here. Bad people be breakin' in to steal 'em."

I hadn't even thought of that, but it was a real possibility, so that was another thing to tell Bob Hargrove. In the meantime, though, every month or so the sheriff held a Drop Off Your Unused Drugs Day, and I would drop off the remaining fifty-nine tablets, relieved to have them out of the house. To tell the truth, as long as those tablets were on hand, even up high and in the back of a cabinet, they seemed to emit an alluring call to come get them and just try a few.

So there was another great black mark against Dr. Crawford. Why had he been so generous with a drug that had caused so much suffering? Had he not read the literature or listened to the news? What if he had turned my beloved Sam into a shambling addict who roamed the streets looking for what he could no longer live without?

I shuddered to think that I could've had a hand in it by blindly following the doctor's orders to dole them out for the least little twinge.

CHAPTER 31

There was, however, no doubt about it — we were living in a drug-taking culture, and I'm not talking about what was bought on the street. Just listen to the television advertisements, all aimed at your average hard-working, stressed-out person resting on a sofa after supper. Every other ad on the screen pushed some wonder drug — possibly made from *jellyfish,* of all things — that would turn you into a new and vibrant person. Just start on some pills or drink some high-powered potion every day or rub something on your skin and all of a sudden your golf putt would drop into the hole, you'd ace your tennis opponent, or you'd blossom into the life of the party. All you had to do was talk your doctor into prescribing this wonder drug that would change your life.

Did people really fall for that? Obviously they did or drug companies wouldn't spend millions on advertising their wares. One advertisement that really disturbed me was the one that made a rational case by saying something like, "You take something for your heart, and you take something for your joints, why not take something for your brain?" If anyone fell for that, I'd think he really did need something for his brain. I'd recommend a heavy dose of Scripture every morning rather than a slug of some mind-altering drug concocted in a laboratory and tested on a rodent.

Well, I sighed, as these thoughts flitted through my unmedicated brain, maybe that's why doctors were so free with their prescriptions — it would be futile to argue with self-diagnosed patients. I expect patients came in already knowing what they needed for their complaints, already fully prepped by television advertisements. Maybe busy physicians had given up trying to explain that a decent diet, a full night's sleep, and reasonable exercise would be better than a prescription for some synthetic remedy. Even though some of those patients were people who wouldn't put a synthetic thread on their bodies.

And maybe ordering sixty tablets for what was cured by two halves of one was the result of doctors' having been awakened too often in the middle of the night by someone else who couldn't sleep.

I didn't know the answer. All I knew was that I would from now on question whatever Dr. Crawford prescribed either for me or for mine. And that was a crying shame, because I had always put my wholehearted trust in every physician under whose care any of us had ever been. But from now on, I would look askance at whatever any of them recommended, suggested, or prescribed.

But, then, given my natural skepticism, that's pretty much what I did with everyone I knew. Except Sam, of course.

He came to the breakfast table the next morning looking like a new man. Gone was the frown, the look of pain, the stiff back, and the careful movements.

"Julia," he said as I poured coffee into his cup, "I don't know what Dr. Crawford prescribed, but it's worked a miracle. He certainly knows his business."

"So it appears," I said, keeping my concerns about pill-peddling doctors to myself. "Just don't get too rambunctious or you'll pull that muscle again."

"That's right, Mr. Sam," Lillian said, putting a plate of biscuits on the table. "You got to be careful how you walk, an' how you set down, an' you can't be doin' no heavy liftin'. Least till you know it's all healed up. An' even then," she went on with a laugh, "you got a good excuse to get outta doin' anything you don't want to do."

"Good thinking, Lillian," Sam said as we laughed.

We all turned in surprise as Lloyd walked in, closing the back door behind him.

"You're not in school?" I asked.

"Spring break."

"You're not driving alone, are you?" Sam said. "I didn't hear a car turn in."

"No, sir," Lloyd said, taking his usual place at the table as Lillian fixed a plate for him. "I'm back on two wheels. Temporarily, I hope. Both my sisters have real bad colds, and Mama feels like she's getting one, and Miss Granny didn't come in because she's sick, and James is sneezing his head off, so I thought I'd better get out while the getting was good.

"And all that," he went on, "means that Mama can't ride with me 'cause she doesn't want to take the girls out, and J.D. is gone for a few days, so I've got time on my hands."

"Maybe," I said, "you can work on your house."

"No'm, we're waiting on the drywall crew. J.D. decided that it's too big a job for us to try to tape, mud, and sand all those seams. Especially since neither of us knows how to do it. So we're at a standstill." He buttered a biscuit, took a bite, then said, "But I'm on my way over there now to unlock for the drywall men. I'll probably sweep and straighten up a little while I wait, but J.D. said I didn't have to stand around all day while they work.

"Actually, I'm kinda glad to have a few days off, except I sure do miss getting to drive. I might get rusty while I wait for somebody to ride with me."

"Well," I said, hoping that I wasn't offering what I couldn't deliver, "how would you like to drive my car?"

"*Your* car?" Lloyd's eyes got big. "Oh, wow, you mean it?"

"If your mother says it's okay, then, yes, I mean it. It seems I'm committed to driving Mrs. Allen out in the countryside every afternoon to visit Mr. Horace. And I'm bored to tears with the same old thing every day. I figure you'll give us something else to think about."

"Uh-huh," Lillian said, half under her breath, "I 'spect he will."

"The only thing, though, Lloyd," I said,

"is that those roads are very curvy and narrow — only two lanes, you know. And there're ditches on both sides and no shoulders to speak of. Still, it's worth having experience with all kinds of road conditions."

Lloyd's eyes were shining with the possibilities, but then he seemed to rethink them. "And we'd have Miss Mildred with us?"

"Yes, that's the only reason I'll be going. She says she's too nervous to drive herself." I tried not to let any skepticism creep into my words, but it was hard.

"She might not want to ride with me," Lloyd said. "I mean, I might really make her nervous."

"We'll put her in the backseat where she can't watch you. But," I went on, "we have to have your mother's permission. I just wanted to be sure you'd like to do it before asking her."

"Man, yes! I just hope I don't hurt your car. And," he said, then stopped. "I've never driven a car like yours — what if I can't drive it?"

"If you can drive your big car, you can certainly drive mine. They're about the same size, only mine's a little newer."

"Yes'm," he said, laughing, "about a

284

decade or so."

"Well, if your mother says it's okay, be ready to go about three-thirty today. And we won't say anything to Miss Mildred. We'll just surprise her."

Lillian's eyes rolled back in her head, and Sam's eyebrows were up around his hairline. But I was tired of having my afternoons taken up with chauffeuring Mildred to visit her husband and waiting alone in the car while she did it. Besides, while waiting I'd already read everything worth reading, and she was fully capable of driving herself.

"Absolutely not!" Hazel Marie had said. "No way are you going to drive Miss Julia's fine car until you're more experienced. And maybe not even then."

Lloyd reported her decision to me as I took note of his disappointment. Actually, it didn't really surprise me, and in one sense I was relieved. I wasn't all that eager to turn over an expensive vehicle to a novice driver, although it was nice to have the credit of having offered it.

"That's all right, Lloyd. You can drive it just as soon as you get your real license. But for now," I went on, "I would still like to have your company and I want to help you get the experience you need. Would you mind driving Miss Mildred and me in your car?"

"*My* car? Really?"

"Yes. I'll buy the gas."

"What about Miss Mildred? She might not like riding in a car like mine."

"If she wants to be driven, which she does, she'll have to like whatever arrives."

"Well," he said, grinning, "okay, then."

CHAPTER 32

Since Lloyd could not drive alone — not even the four blocks to my house to pick me up — it took some doing to get us both in the same car. I had to drive my car to his house, park it out front, transfer myself to his car, then oversee his driving the same four blocks to pick up Mildred.

Half expecting Mildred to cringe at having an inexperienced driver, to say nothing of being relegated to the backseat of an ancient Bonneville, I directed Lloyd up her drive and to a stop at the front steps. But it was Ida Lee's eyes that widened at the sight of a pumpkin instead of my fine coach. Mildred didn't turn a hair. With Ida Lee's help, as well as a little of mine, Mildred settled herself on the backseat and buckled her seat belt, then she looked around the interior.

"Well," she said, as if she rode in an aging chariot every day, "how nice to have a chauffeur. Thank you, Lloyd, for being so kind. Now, Julia," she went on as I slipped into the front seat and refastened my seat belt, "I'm still torn as to what to do about Horace. They tell me he'll be discharged in a couple of weeks, so I need to make some decisions."

And she listed some possibilities having to do with employing a gentleman's gentleman versus round-the-clock nurses, then switched to considering the merits of a Mercedes E Class versus a Cadillac Escalade. As her monologue didn't seem to require a response, I kept my attention on Lloyd's driving.

To tell the truth, I was wondering if I'd outsmarted myself by entrusting three lives to a driver with limited time behind a wheel. I was beginning to feel — now that we were committed — just a little anxious about Lloyd's level of skill. But of course that was one of my purposes — to provide an opportunity for him to gain more of the skills required of a good driver. Another purpose was to encourage Mildred to begin driving herself again.

And another one was to divert her from the subject of Horace and his needs, about which I'd heard a gracious plenty. I was concerned about him and I sympathized with her, but when you've heard the same complaints and the same rhetorical questions over and over for days on end, you're more than ready to change the subject.

Lloyd had easily navigated the wide streets of downtown Abbotsville, so I leaned back, feeling more confident in his driving. At my direction, he'd turned onto Staton Mill Road, which took us southwest of town and out into the county. Traffic had thinned considerably, and so had the road — with hardly any shoulders, it was as narrow as a ribbon. I sat up and began to take an active interest in how Lloyd was managing the change of conditions. He had both hands on the wheel and a frown on his face as he stared straight ahead.

"Lloyd," Mildred sang out from the backseat, "I like your car. It's quite roomy and comfortable."

"Yes, ma'am," he said without shifting his eyes from the road in front of us. "Thank you."

As a panel truck zoomed past in the opposite lane, I lowered my voice. "Stay as far to the right as you can, Lloyd, but don't run off the road."

"Yes'm, I'm trying."

"You're doing fine," I assured him. "It's just that some people don't know what the yellow line means."

"Lloyd," Mildred called again from the backseat, "this may be the most comfortable car I've ever ridden in, but I do wish you'd gotten leather seats. You can't move around very well on this fabric upholstery. I mean, you can move, but your clothes don't."

"Yes, ma'am," he said, leaning forward as his eyes stayed peeled on the road. "I'll remember that."

I murmured, "Just watch for oncoming traffic and stay over. You're doing fine."

"Okay," he said, nodding, then with a heart-stopping yelp, he jerked the wheel to the right as a horn-blowing farm truck loaded with firewood pulled out behind us. Streaking up beside us, leaves and bits of bark swirling in the air, the truck filled the opposite lane and swerved perilously close. I grabbed the armrest and stiffened as Lloyd jerked the wheel too far, running two wheels along the weed-filled shoulder.

"Keep going!" I yelled, straining against my seat belt, as the truck raced along beside us, then, with a puff of diesel smoke, zoomed on ahead. "Stay on the shoulder, Lloyd! Keep going straight! It's all right. Now ease back. Don't jerk the wheel, just ease back onto the road."

He did, and he couldn't have done it better. Unnerved, I leaned back, shaken but relieved that we'd avoided a roll into the ditch or, even worse, a crash into oncoming traffic.

"Oh, man," Lloyd gasped, "I didn't see him!"

"He came up behind us, and he was speeding," I said, but my heart was racing, and I had trouble keeping my voice steady. "Just stay at the speed limit and on your side. You'll be fine."

And still, Mildred talked on, not at all unsettled by the truck's passing. I turned and glanced through the back window, seeing a file of cars and pickups lined up behind us. Then I looked ahead and saw a series of curves before us. Both spelled trouble, but Lloyd was hunched over the wheel, gripping it tightly, and chugging along at the posted thirty-five-mile-an-hour speed limit. Apparently, though, anyone familiar with the road — which seemed to be every last driver behind us — was unwilling to curtail their speed. One vehicle after another began pulling out and passing us — and on the curves, too! But, then, I'd heard more than one native-born western North Carolinian say, "Curves is the onliest place you can pick up any speed."

I wanted to close my eyes, but I dared not. After a long, additional half hour of driving past unrelieved fields and clumps of scrubby pines, I saw The Safe Harbor sitting on a well-landscaped knoll a little way in front of us. A welcoming sign was posted out front along with a sign forbidding smoking on the grounds — a dueling message, if you ask me. Some were welcome, some were not.

"Up there on the left, Lloyd," I said. "Turn in at the sign."

"Yes'm," he said, barely moving his mouth. "If I can."

"Turn on your blinker," I said, speaking in a low voice with hardly a quiver, "and wait till the lane clears out. If anybody's behind us, they can just wait."

"Just ten cars and a 'mater truck," he said, and I had an urge to laugh at his remembering the punch line of a silly joke.

Finally, the road was clear enough for him to turn into the driveway, and I directed him to pull up under the porte cochere by the front door. Mildred, with a short struggle during which she thanked Lloyd profusely and worried aloud about Horace, climbed out. "I won't be long," she said.

"Let's find a place to park," I said. "She won't be ready to go for half an hour at least. But we'll have time to drive around a little more if you'd like to."

"No'm," Lloyd said, as he eased the car into an empty space, "if it's all the same to you, I think I'd rather rest awhile."

He turned off the motor, leaned back, and heaved a great sigh. "That wasn't as much fun as I thought it'd be."

"More traffic than I'd thought, too. We must've hit it just as people were going home from work, although where they all live, I don't know. It should be cleared out by the time we go back."

He didn't reply and, to tell the truth, he did look wiped out, making me wonder if I'd given him more responsibility than he was ready for. "I can drive back if you'd like," I said.

"Oh, no'm," he said, sitting up straight. "I want to. Unless I scared you or something."

"Well, not really," I hedged, then, as our eyes met, we started laughing.

"Whew," he said, relieved or pretending to be. "I was afraid you might never ride with me again."

"You didn't cause it," I assured him, "but you handled it quite well. I might've had us bounding across the fields. Or upside down in a ditch." Then after a few minutes of silence, I decided one more small driving lesson was in order. "You know, Lloyd, the natural reaction to running off onto the shoulder is to swerve the car back on the road — and jerk it too hard or too far. Overcorrecting probably causes more wrecks than we know because we do it without thinking. You're to be commended for not doing it."

"Maybe," he said, "but I sure wanted to."

I'd gotten my nerves under control enough that I was able to smile and give his shoulder a pat. We sat for a while, our windows cracked, and listened to the silence of the wide fields on each side of The Safe Harbor.

After several minutes, Lloyd said, "This lot would be a good place to practice parallel parking. The spaces are marked, and nobody has driven in since we've been here."

"You want to try it?"

He shook his head. "Next time, maybe. I'm just thinking ahead."

A few more minutes passed as I began to wonder what was keeping Mildred. I put my head back and closed my eyes. Lloyd, however, squirmed in his seat, wiped his face with his hand, and sighed again. I thought he might be reliving our close call, and wondered what else I could say to encourage him.

"Miss Julia?" he said, lowering his voice although no one else was around.

"Um-m?"

"If you saw something you shouldn't have seen, what would you do about it?"

Hearing the change in his voice, I came fully awake and considered my words carefully. "Well, I guess it depends. Were you where you shouldn't have been when you saw it?"

"No'm. I was minding my own business, and they just . . . well, it just happened right in front of my eyes, and I couldn't help but see it."

Not wanting to push, I immediately thought that he had seen something untoward at school. School was where he spent the majority of his waking hours, so I assumed he'd seen somebody cheating or smoking or skipping class or engaged in some other nefarious activity.

"Well, Lloyd," I said, "you know that some people will do whatever they think they can get away with, and if you just happened to see it, you're put in an awkward position. You don't want to be a tattletale, and yet you know they're breaking the rules. Maybe just talking to the culprit yourself would help. Warning of the trouble they could be in."

He twisted his mouth, drummed his fingers on the steering wheel, then said, "I don't think —"

"Yoo-hoo, I'm back!" Mildred opened the back door and hefted herself inside. "Sorry to take so long, but Horace was in therapy and I had to wait. He looks so much better — he even walked by himself back to the room. Tired out, of course. I wonder if they're making him do too much. I must schedule a conference with the therapist and find out.

"Well, Lloyd," she went on, jumping from one subject to the next without taking a breath, "I'm ready to enjoy a nice ride back. You're an excellent driver, and I may put you on the payroll this summer."

"Thanks, Miss Mildred," Lloyd said, as he turned on the ignition and shifted into reverse. "I'll try to chauffeur you in style."

That, of course, was the end of any private discussion. If Lloyd was hesitant to tell me the details, he certainly wouldn't divulge them to a third party. I was left alone, therefore, to cogitate on the various kinds of worrisome activities that he might have observed. The topic kept my mind occupied and off any and all driving hazards the whole way home.

CHAPTER 33

We let Mildred out at her front steps where we'd picked her up, and after thanking Lloyd and me several times, she made her way inside. Lloyd drove the two of us on to his mother's house where I'd left my car.

Thinking that he would continue what he'd started, now that we were alone again, I waited to hear what Lloyd had seen that was weighing so heavily on his mind. And while I waited, other possibilities flitted through my mind. The spring months almost always lent themselves to pranks, scuffles, threats, and other means of mischief at the schools as students longed to be free for the summer. It almost never failed that as the sap rose in the trees, so did it in long-enclosed students.

Girls, I thought. He'd only recently gotten himself out of a tangle with three of them, and done it quite deftly, too. Maybe some one of the three had captured his heart, and he was suffering from an unrequited adolescent crush.

But, no, I told myself, that couldn't be it. If he was having girl trouble, he'd talk to his father or to Sam, not to me.

Maybe something to do with the house on Rosewood? He might well talk to me about that since he knew my interest in it. But what could have put such a worried look on his face? Was Mr. Pickens cutting corners by using lower-grade materials? I mentally shook my head. Mr. Pickens was a thorn in my side, that was for sure, but he was an honest thorn. Besides, Lloyd didn't know enough to make a knowledgable judgment about anything having to do with construction — regardless of the grade.

"Here we are," Lloyd said as he pulled into the driveway at his mother's house. "Thanks for letting me drive, Miss Julia. Maybe next time I'll do better." He opened the door and began to step out.

"Already?" I asked, realizing that while I'd been mulling over springtime mayhem on school grounds and other possibilities, he'd had a change of heart about confiding in me at all. Not wanting to pry, I climbed out and started toward my car parked at the curb.

"You keep doing as well as you did today,

Lloyd," I said, "and we'll have you driving my car soon. Sam's, too, I expect. And Lloyd," I said, stopping on the front lawn, "anytime you want to talk . . ."

"Yes'm, I know." He turned away, keeping to himself whatever was on his mind. "It's okay. Thanks again, Miss Julia."

He went up the porch steps toward the front door, and I got into my car and went home. Of course my curiosity was aroused, but my concern was far more than simply wanting to know what he'd seen. He was troubled by it, whatever it had been, and when Lloyd was troubled, so, too, was I.

On the other hand, teenagers were prone to emotional ups and downs. They were known to be moody and standoffish one day, then be perfectly normal the next. I recalled how worried he'd been about the Sadie Hawkins dance, yet that had worked out fine. So, even though Lloyd had decided to keep his concern to himself, I had to trust that his great good sense would keep him on an even keel, and that this, too — whatever it was — would pass.

As I walked into the kitchen at home, Lillian looked up from what she was stirring on the stove. "Well, I'm glad to see you walkin' on your own two feet, an' not comin' in on a stretcher or something. How'd Lloyd do?"

"He did fine. He scared me only once, and it wasn't his fault." I sat down at the table, ready to talk to somebody. "I don't know, Lillian. I may have expected too much too soon from him — we were almost run off the road, but he handled it well. Mildred, now, she was oblivious. That woman can surely talk when something's on her mind. She's ready to hire him this summer to chauffeur her around."

"I thought he already have a summer job, messin' with that house with Mr. Pickens."

"He does. She'll have forgotten about it by the time school's out." I looked around, then started to rise. "Where's Sam? How's his back?"

"Upstairs in the sunroom. An' he say his back's as good as new. He'll be down in a minute 'cause he's watchin' for your car an' I'm about ready to put something on the table."

"Then I'll just sit here and wait," I said, settling back and unbuttoning my jacket. "I declare, taking these drives with Mildred just wears me out. It's past time for her to start driving herself."

"Uh-huh, I 'spect it is." Lillian busied herself with removing pans from the oven

300

and the stovetop, then she turned to me. "Um, Miss Julia, I think I better ast you something 'cause word's gettin' out 'round town."

"Oh, my word, what is it?" My first thought was that others had seen the same thing that Lloyd had seen, and that, if it was this widespread, it had to be something truly serious.

"Well, I don't really b'lieve this 'cause Miz Allen, she a real nice lady, but I hear from two different people that she the one that jus' about kill Mr. Allen."

"Oh, Lillian," I said, leaning my head on my hand, not knowing whether to laugh or to cry. "That is so farfetched. Who in the world would start such a rumor? No, he had a heart attack, plain and simple. Although," I went on somewhat hesitantly, "and this is just between you and me, he apparently had it after a particularly intense and active marital interlude."

Lillian frowned. "A what?"

Hearing Sam's footsteps on the stairs, I leaned over and whispered, "In the *bed,* Lillian, and it was Mildred herself who started that rumor. She thought she'd killed him because of it."

Lillian's mouth had fallen open, but she quickly regained her equilibrium and nodded solemnly at the news. "Uh-huh, I hear that happen more'n people think. They jus' don't tell nobody 'cause they shamed at carryin' on like that. I mean, at they age since it's usually ole people it happens to. But any time you hear 'bout a heart attack an' it's some ole somebody, you can't help but think about it."

"Well, no, I never have," I said, thinking now of a few acquaintances who'd been diagnosed with heart trouble. "But from now on, I guess I will."

Sam came in then, walking upright with no sign of an excruciating pain in his back. He smiled a greeting to both Lillian and me and walked over to stand close to my chair. He put a hand on my shoulder.

"How was your trip to the country?" he asked. "Lloyd do all right?"

"Yes," I said and proceeded to give a few details, ending with the declaration that I was just about through running a taxi service, as well as having had enough of being a driving instructor. Our close call with a farm truck loaded with firewood had replayed in my mind and left me shaken by images of what could've happened.

"I don't think," I said, "that I'm suited to teaching someone how to drive."

"That's all right," he said, moving his

hand across my shoulders. "You suit me just fine."

Have you ever noticed how a simple touch of the hand by someone you love can calm and reassure an unsettled mind? Just the nearness of Sam could put the world right for me. And he was never stingy with hand-holding, back pats, and soft touches, or merely standing close enough to feel him breathe. Wesley Lloyd Springer, my late, unlamented first husband, on the other hand, had revealed how little he thought of me by his body language — he ignored me in public and kept his distance in private.

I leaned my head against Sam as he stood by my chair. "I'm so glad you're feeling better. Are you being careful? Not lifting anything or bending over?"

"I'm being careful. I don't want another episode like the one I had. But," he went on, "I don't worry about it because I still have those wonder pills that Dr. Crawford prescribed."

No, you don't, I thought, because I had that little vial hidden away until I could safely dispose of it. And if Sam had another episode, he would most certainly get taken to another physician.

CHAPTER 34

"Julia?" LuAnne Conover asked when I answered the telephone the following morning.

"Yes, how are you, LuAnne? How's the new job going?"

"It's slow right now, which is why I have time to call. It's either feast or famine around here — there're times when bodies are lined up in the back hall and other times when everybody sits around waiting for somebody to die. It gives me the heebie-jeebies. But they're all in the break room now, drinking coffee and eating cookies. And of course I have to stay at the front desk and answer the phone."

"Well," I said, hoping to divert her from further complaints, "I'm glad you have time to call. Maybe somebody will bring you a cookie."

"Not likely."

"Anyway," I went on, "I've missed having

lunch with you, but I probably wouldn't have had time to go out myself. I tell you, LuAnne, I have made that trip to visit Horace so many times that I don't want to leave the house for anything else."

"How's Horace doing?"

"Apparently quite well. He's getting physical therapy, so he's up and walking around. Mildred, of course, is still deeply concerned. She's making plans for his care when he gets home, but I don't know how much she's told him about them."

"Um-m, well, Mildred sort of does what she wants to do anyway. But, listen, that wasn't why I called. I've just witnessed the strangest thing."

"Oh?" I said. "What was it?"

"Did you ever know Cornelia McMurray? I think she was known as Connie, but I never met her. Just heard a lot about her."

"Everybody's heard about her," I said, laughing a little, "but I can't say that I know her. We were introduced years ago at some charity function — can't remember now exactly what it was. She looked normal enough, as I recall, but of course I'd heard the stories. Why? Has she passed?"

"Not that I know of, and I guess I'd know if she had. But, Julia, what is wrong with that woman?"

"Crazy as a loon from all I hear. Why? What've you heard?"

"It's not what I've heard, it's what I've *seen.* Did you know *Dr.* McMurray, her husband?"

"Knew of him, but I was never sure if he was a real doctor or not. He did something with feet, didn't he?"

"Yes, podiatry, which means he wasn't a real doctor. I mean, he hadn't gone to medical school. Just to foot school, I guess, although I've heard that he had a certificate on his office wall that claimed he'd earned a degree in podiatry. That doesn't really count, does it?"

"*I* wouldn't count it, but it seems that everybody and his brother are allowed to practice medicine these days, so who knows?"

"But he went to Harvard, didn't he?" LuAnne asked. "That's the one thing I remember everybody saying anytime his name came up."

"Ha! That's the one thing that Connie made sure everybody knew. Why, LuAnne, I remember people calling him *Dr. Harvard* behind his back, because somebody finally found out that he hadn't gone to school there at all. He'd just grown up in Harvard, Nebraska, and that's where she'd gotten it.

306

Nobody ever called her on it, though, because she really wasn't responsible. People just smiled and let her ramble on."

"But why in the world would he let her mislead people — patients, especially? You'd think any kind of doctor would be concerned about that."

"Well," I said, "I'm not sure that he gave much thought to what his patients thought. I remember hearing that he was as rough as a cob, and that if you had foot trouble, you'd be better off going barefoot than going to him."

"I *know*," LuAnne said. "Miss Mattie Freeman told me one time that she'd gone to him about a toenail fungus that she couldn't get rid of. She said he took one look, and said, 'Oh, we'll fix that right now,' and took a forceps and ripped that toenail off. She said she nearly died right there, and would've gotten up and walked out if she'd been able to walk."

Squinching up my toes, I shuddered at the thought. "Yes, I've heard that he didn't have much of a bedside manner or much of a practice, either. Maybe that's why." I paused, thinking of some of the tales I'd heard about *Dr.* McMurray. "Isn't he dead? I thought he died years ago. Why're you thinking of him?"

"Because *she* comes every year on the anniversary of his passing to sit alone in the Lilac room. In remembrance, I guess. And she was here yesterday."

"I've never heard of such a thing."

"Me, either. But I'll tell you one thing, you'll never catch me doing something like that for Leonard. I'd like to forget him."

"I know what you mean," I said, but LuAnne had just put an image in my mind of Connie McMurray's sitting alone year after year communing with her long-dead husband, and it was something I could've done without. Then she proceeded to add something, in its own way, just as worrisome.

"Well, that reminds me," LuAnne said, apropos of nothing, which was the way LuAnne's mind worked. One topic led to another in a perfectly logical way that she understood, but nobody else did. "Have you seen Lauren Crawford lately?"

"Why, no, I haven't. Why?"

"Oh, I just thought that you were sort of looking after her — you know, introducing her around, taking her under your wing — that sort of thing."

"Sue asked me to have them for dinner, so I did. And introduced them to Binkie and Coleman, and the Pickenses, but that's all. It was Hazel Marie's idea to invite her to your fashion class or whatever it was. I thought then that Lauren might finally be coming out of her shell, but she's not been very responsive to Hazel Marie since then. I can't figure her out, LuAnne. She's a beautiful woman. Or at least she could be. Why?" I asked again. "Have you seen her?"

"Well, yes, I have, but I can't tell you, Julia, because we're not supposed to talk about *anything* that goes on here at the funeral home. Especially what goes on in the director's office — that's highly confidential. So don't ask me. I could lose my job."

Well, I didn't want that to happen, but of course LuAnne had just revealed that not only had she recently seen Lauren, but that she'd seen her there at the funeral home. All of which raised a number of questions in my mind — had there been a death in Lauren's family? If so, I should ask Lillian to prepare a meal to take to the Crawfords. But perhaps Lauren had been there to make arrangements for some future event. Could someone be ill?

At that thought, I was overcome with regret that I had not kept in closer touch. Of course, I had something against Dr. Crawford, he of the reckless dispensing of habit-forming drugs, which made me less than eager to nurture stronger ties. But sickness, ill health, impending loss could easily account for a slip of the pen when writing a prescription. There could be little worse than to have a loved one — or one's own self — with a mortal illness in a strange town, far from family and friends.

"Tell me this, then," I said, "if you can. Is she all right?"

"As far as I know," LuAnne said, "she's fine." But it was said in such a carefully worded way that I knew LuAnne might not know, but, if pushed, she could make a fairly good guess.

I didn't push, deciding instead to try harder to befriend Lauren Crawford in case she was in serious need. Or maybe I'd just ask Hazel Marie if she knew why that young woman had made a visit to a funeral home.

Later that day after an uneventful trip to The Safe Harbor during which I monitored Lloyd's driving and listened to Mildred's monologue, we dropped her off at her doorstep.

As Lloyd waited at the end of her drive for two cars to pass, he said, "I know it's late, but I sure would like a caramel cappuccino from McDonald's. How's that sound to you?"

"Actually," I said, knowing that he wanted to drive a little longer, "pretty good. Let's go ruin our supper."

He grinned, then drove toward South Main, where the popular fast-food emporium catered to the town. Traffic had thinned out, so Lloyd turned easily into the parking lot, then eased the big car into the drive-thru lane behind a shiny new car. He stopped beside the menu board and lowered his window as a scratchy voice said, "Take your order?" Lloyd gave it, then followed instructions to drive to the first window.

"I've only done this once before when J.D. was with me," he said, holding the money I'd given him out the window. "It was real crowded and I really messed up. I didn't get close enough and had to get out of the car to pay."

"Well," I said, watching the car in front stop at the pickup window, "better that than getting too close."

He held his arm out the window, waiting for change, then turned, laughing, to give it to me. I don't know what happened — maybe his foot slipped off the brake — but the Bonneville suddenly spurted forward, then banged into the car ahead of us. That car jerked forward from the impact as a sound of anguish issued from Lloyd's throat.

"Oh, no!" he groaned, almost sobbed.

"It's all right," I said, although it was hardly that. "What happened? Are you okay?"

Draping his arms over the steering wheel, Lloyd leaned his head on them and moaned. "Oh, me. I've hit somebody."

The somebody got out of the car, strode purposefully back to Lloyd's open window, stooped over, and looked in at us.

"We're so sorry," I quickly said, wanting to forestall an angry scene that would sear Lloyd's soul. Then, seeing the face, I gasped, "Dr. Crawford! Oh, we are so sorry. It was my fault. I distracted him. Are you hurt? Is your car badly damaged? We'll take care of it, don't worry about that."

Dr. Crawford's intense blue gaze went slowly from one to the other of us, taking us in. I cringed with embarrassment, even as I ached for Lloyd, wanting to shield him from any belittling words.

But then Dr. Crawford smiled. "It can't be too bad," he said. "You weren't going that fast. Come on, son, let's pull out of the lane, then we'll see what's what."

That done, we all got out and I made the introductions, reminding the doctor that he'd met Lloyd's parents at my house. The three of us stood between the cars and surveyed the two crumpled bumpers. The one on Lloyd's car was barely noticeable — it blended with several other dents — but the one on Dr. Crawford's silver Lexus was crushed to a fare-thee-well. I'd always heard that they don't build cars the way they used to, and here was the proof.

Lloyd's face went as white as a sheet when he saw the damage. "I'm so sorry," he mumbled. "I didn't mean to do it."

Deciding to move things along — people driving by were craning to see what had happened — I said, "Dr. Crawford, you may want to call the police and get an accident report, but that's only if you want our insurance companies involved. If you'd rather not, we will certainly take care of this. In fact, if you'll take it to Tillman's Body Shop — they're the best in town — they'll fix it like new and send me the bill. And while it's in the shop, they'll arrange a rental car for you, which we'll also take care of. We don't want you inconvenienced in any way at all."

"Oh," Don Crawford said with a wave of his hand, "don't worry about it. Nobody was hurt and that's the main thing." Then, glancing at the sick-looking expression on Lloyd's face, he went on. "I don't think we need to involve the police for a little bump like this. The damage isn't that bad, and there's no need to put an accident on the boy's record."

With great relief and a rush of gratitude, I said, "Thank you, thank you. Rest assured that we will make it right. Lloyd, did you hear that? Dr. Crawford doesn't want to make a report, so your license is safe."

Still looking as if he were about to throw up, Lloyd thanked the doctor, shook his hand, and slunk back to the Bonneville. He got in on the passenger side.

Before joining him, I turned to Dr. Crawford. "I expect you know that he's just learning to drive, and this has about done him in. You have every right to be angry, yet you've been nothing but kind and understanding. I appreciate it more than I can say."

"No problem," Don Crawford said. "We all have fender benders now and then, so there's no reason to get bent out of shape about them. Besides, he's young and his dignity should be preserved." Dr. Crawford shrugged his shoulders, smiled, and said, "What's a crushed bumper in the grand scheme of things?"

My estimation of Dr. Don Crawford soared as I walked back to the passenger side of the Bonneville.

Looking in at Lloyd, I said, "You're in my seat."

He shook his head. "I'm letting you drive home."

"Oh, no, you're not. I don't want to drive." I opened the door and motioned for him to get out. "It's all a part of learning, Lloyd. I don't know a soul who's never had an accident. Just be thankful that you chose a nice person to run into. Now, come on and get back on this horse."

He gave me a sickly grin, climbed out, and went around the car to slide behind the wheel again.

"I may never go to a McDonald's drive-thru again," he said.

"Well, I hope you will. We never did get our caramel cappuccinos."

Lloyd managed a smile as he drove slowly and carefully to his house while I contended with a mixture of feelings toward Dr. Crawford with gratitude winning out.

Yet in spite of the doctor's more than decent reaction to the accident, I could not entirely discount his seemingly careless treatment of both Sam and Horace in their times of need. How in the world do you account for a man like that?

CHAPTER 35

Thursday evening Sam and I met Hazel Marie and Mr. Pickens at the country club for dinner, something that we tried to do about once a month. It was a way to catch up with one another and to stay in touch, especially where Lloyd was concerned since we each had a hand in raising him. Sam and I enjoyed the occasional evening out in place of our usual routine of reading the newspaper and bemoaning the state of affairs. Hazel Marie said that a peaceful dinner in quiet surroundings with adult conversation was a welcome change from wiping up spills at the table. Mr. Pickens said he liked the rib-eye steak.

Considering their busy schedules, I was grateful that they made time for us and seemed to enjoy it. As we studied the menu, I pushed the Crawfords to the back of my mind — this was neither the time nor the place to bring up my concerns about either or both of them. I had, in fact, resisted the impulse to call Hazel Marie earlier and share what I'd learned from LuAnne. But actually I had learned very little, just enough to worry me and more than enough to upset Hazel Marie.

So while Sam began describing his back spasm episode, praising Dr. Crawford's wonder tablets to the skies, I kept my silence. Sooner or later, I would have to tell Sam of my reservations about the way the doctor doled out a generous dose of a prescription drug. But for now, it seemed that Sam's back was behaving itself specifically because he knew he had something on hand that would stop the pain if it came back. That's called the placebo effect, I think.

After commiserating with Sam, the Pickenses quickly caught us up with their news — the little girls' colds had about run their course, James was still complaining of feeling run down, Granny Wiggins was back on the job, and Lloyd was spending most of his spring break working on an essay of some kind.

"He's up in his room practically all day every day," Hazel Marie said. "But now that the weather has warmed up, he needs to be out more. Apparently it's a research paper he's working on, and he says he'd rather get it done now instead of waiting till the last minute. Which, I guess, is a good thing."

"Well," Mr. Pickens said, "it better be. He's falling down on the Rosewood house."

"Oh, surely not," I said, disturbed that Lloyd might not be pulling his weight. "He was thrilled about working on that house with you. And he told me that you were at a stopping place — something about waiting for the drywall crew."

Mr. Pickens nodded. "That's right, but he was supposed to check at least once a day to see how they're coming along. I'm not sure he's been over there since Monday at all."

"Oh," Hazel Marie said, quickly coming to her boy's defense, "I expect it's because he's not been able to drive, don't you? I mean, with you gone and my having to stay in with the girls."

Sam smiled. "It's hard to go back to a bicycle once you get your hands on a car. And he may feel he's in the way, what with men on stilts mudding the ceilings."

"Maybe," Mr. Pickens conceded. "I just don't want him starting something he's unwilling to finish. Besides, he needs to make some money to pay for that run-in he had with a Lexus."

I made no comment to that, knowing already that Mr. Pickens and I had some differences in how to raise a boy. I knew, in a way, that he was right, but I didn't like it.

So I sat listening to the discussion, feeling deeply concerned about what was after all most likely a typical teenage reaction. But reaction to what? Was he simply tired of construction work? Had he lost the thrill of being a partner in Pickens and Son? Had the accident at McDonald's crushed his spirit or damaged his dignity? Or was his inattention to the little house related to whatever he'd seen that he'd almost told me about?

While these thoughts raced through my mind, I felt some discomfort for not having asked Lloyd to drive Mildred and me the past few days. For that reason, he could be thinking, after our close call with a farm truck and an even closer one with a Lexus bumper, that I didn't want to ride with him again. But the fact of the matter was that Mildred had wanted to make a few extra stops, stretching our two-hour daily outing to three or four hours, and I had thought to spare him the bother. It had taken all my patience to run Mildred's many errands as it was.

"But you know," I said, feeling the need

to mount a defense, "that he's given up some of his afternoons to drive Mildred to visit Horace, which is a good deed in itself. And," I said, turning to Mr. Pickens, "I expect he'll come around now that you're back. The fun of it for him would be working with you, not standing around checking on the work of strangers. Besides," I went on, dredging up a possibility, "the drywall crew may have made him feel in the way. Or something."

"Maybe," Mr. Pickens said again. "But I don't want him feeling sorry for himself because he has to ride his bike when we can't drop everything to let him drive."

"Oh, I don't think that's it," I said. "He comes to see us on his bike all the time." But had he lately? What with being at Mildred's beck and call, I couldn't be sure.

Our dinners were served then, and the conversation turned to other matters. I, however, continued to fret over Lloyd's apparent disinterest in the house on Rosewood Lane.

The following morning I sat down alone, held my new smart phone that had replaced my much-easier-to-use fliptop, and devoted twenty minutes to sending a text to Lloyd. This was to accomplish two things: to get

320

Lloyd out of the house and to practice the art of texting. After using the delete key more often than any other, I managed to type and send a message:

WOuld u like to drIVe Mrs. A & me this afernoon?

The answer came back before I put the phone down:

Yes! What time?

Feeling exhilarated by his enthusiasm and what I assumed was his eagerness to have a chance to drive, I replied:

See u about 3,

then worried about ruining his ability to spell correctly.

So, a little before three, I drove to the Pickens house, parked at the curb, walked over to the driveway where the aging Bonneville was idling in place with Lloyd behind the wheel.

"I'm so glad you're able to go," I said as I slid into the passenger seat. "I was afraid your father would have you working at the house or that you'd be too engrossed in schoolwork."

"No'm, I'm happy to go. I just hope we don't meet any farm trucks this time, and I'm not going to suggest McDonald's again, either."

"You'll be fine," I said, realizing that I had overworked that adjective, but using it anyway.

We picked up Mildred, who, again, had trouble sliding on the upholstered backseat. Her dress got twisted up around her hips as she tried to slide, but couldn't. Eventually, with Ida Lee's help, she got her dress tail smoothed out beneath her, and we set out on another trip to visit Horace.

"Well, I'm delighted," Mildred said as soon as she was settled. "Lloyd, I'll tell you, as much as I appreciate Julia's help, I much prefer a man to be driving. A man just gives one confidence, don't you think?"

Lloyd glanced in the rearview mirror, a little smile on his face, and said, "Yes, ma'am, I hope so."

"Julia," Mildred went on with scarcely a pause, "I've decided what car to get for Horace, and at first I was going to wait till he gets home. But now I'm thinking that it ought to be in the garage waiting for him. That way, he won't have an excuse to put off buying it and, in the meantime, think he can get away with driving that Boxster car again. Don't you think that's the way to handle it?"

"Well, maybe so," I said, then pointing ahead, said, "Turn right at the sign, Lloyd."

He nodded, made the turn, and took us onto Staton Mill Road, which after numerous twists and curves would lead us to The Safe Harbor.

"What kind did you decide on?" I asked, giving Mildred a quick look.

"I decided to buy American, so I'm getting a Lincoln Town Car. You can't beat them for comfort and room to stretch out in. And they must be easy to drive, because why else would every private agency use them?" She paused, then went on. "Of course, I've never driven one, but I've ridden in the backseat many times, so if Horace needs a driver, this is the perfect car for him. I've ordered a black one."

"Lincolns are lovely cars," I said, "but I've never driven one, either. You might should give it a test run before you commit to it, Mildred. You know, to see how easy it is to steer for one thing. Horace will probably be limited to in-town driving for a while at least, so he'll be turning a lot of corners."

"That's a good idea," Mildred said. "I'll let Ida Lee do a test drive. I declare, I've gotten so used to being driven that I don't even want to get behind a wheel again. Now," she said after a deep sigh, "if I could only get Horace to feel the same way. He just goes crazy when he gets in the driver's seat. I won't ride with him anymore. Of course," she continued, laughing, "I can't squeeze into the Boxster's passenger seat in the first place." She stopped, then, as if she'd just thought of it, asked, "You don't suppose that's the reason he loves that car so much, do you?"

"Oh, I wouldn't think so," I assured her. "I think some men prefer little sports cars for their power and speed and, I guess, their sleek looks. It must give them a sense of control." I stopped, fearing that I'd come too close to the state of the Allens' marriage, then added, "Or something."

"We're here," Lloyd said, flipping on the blinker to make a left turn into the rehab facility.

"Oh, how nice," Mildred said. "You're such a good driver, Lloyd. I hardly minded the drive at all. I won't be but thirty minutes, not a minute more. All Horace does is moan about the food, and that's as long as I can put up with hearing it."

Lloyd pulled up beside the front door, jumped out to open Mildred's door, and waited for her to struggle out. I was pleased with his gentlemanly conduct, although he hadn't opened the door for Mildred the first time we'd come. But who could've blamed him then? We were both recovering from a close call and, to tell the truth, I'd been so shaken that I hadn't even noticed that he'd remained in the car. As if to make up for his lapse, he not only opened the car door for her this time, he walked her to the door of the building.

As he resumed his place behind the wheel, he asked, "You mind if we drive a little more?"

"Not at all," I said, pleased that he was eager to improve his skills. "Where do you want to go?"

"Oh, I thought we could drive maybe another five miles or so, then turn around and come back. I've never been any farther on this road, and I'm thinking I ought to know the county better than I do. Now that I'm driving, I mean."

"I think so, too. Actually, it's been years since I've been this far out in the county, so I don't recall much of it."

I stopped, remembering the little cross-roads community not much farther on where Hazel Marie had grown up and might still have distant kin living there. Did Lloyd know that? Should I mention it? I had no idea how much he knew or even how much he remembered of his young years when his real father visited him once a week on Thursday nights. All I knew was that it wasn't my place to enlighten him.

Unless, of course, he asked. So as he turned back onto the road and headed deeper into the county, I tried to prepare myself for any questions he might ask.

"There's a little convenience store with a couple of gas pumps not too far from here," I said. "At least, there used to be. We can turn in there and get something to drink if you'd like. It's a good place to turn around, too."

"Okay," he said. Then driving with more confidence as the road opened out with little traffic before us, he went on. "It sure is pretty out here. Lots of fields and undeveloped areas this side of the mountains, but not many houses."

"Farming country."

"Uh-huh, I see a few houses way off in clumps of trees." He laughed a little. "I guess people don't much like having neighbors."

"Not close ones, anyway."

He suddenly looked up in the rearview mirror, braked a little, then resumed speed. "Did you see that?"

"No," I said, turning to look back. "All I see is the back of a car heading toward town."

"He was waiting at that little dirt road for traffic to clear before pulling out."

"I didn't see him. Who was it?"

"Well, I didn't get a good look," Lloyd said, "but I'm pretty sure it was Dr. Crawford. It was his car, anyway. Not that many silver Lexus SUVs in town. If it was him, they sure fixed that bumper in a hurry."

CHAPTER 36

"Doctors get special treatment, honey," I said, straining to turn around for a better look. The car was just disappearing around a curve. "But what in the world would Dr. Crawford be doing way out here?

"Although," I went on, "I did hear that he was looking for some undeveloped property, and he'd certainly find it out here. But what would he do with it, I'd like to know."

"Maybe sell the timber on it?" Lloyd suggested. "There were trees on both sides of that dirt road he was coming out of."

"Who knows?" I said lightly, with a wave of my hand. "I admit to following his lead with the house on Rosewood, but I'm not interested in buying a forest."

Lloyd laughed at that. "Maybe he was seeing a patient who couldn't get to the office."

"Not likely," I said with just a tiny edge of sharpness. "If he couldn't see Mr. Allen in the emergency room, he surely wouldn't make a house call."

Lloyd turned into the graveled lot of Jimmy's Gas & Groceries and stopped short of the gas pumps.

"You want something to drink?" he asked.

"No, but you run in if you want something."

"No'm, I'd as soon go on back. Maybe practice parallel parking, if Miss Mildred's not ready."

So he turned the car around and headed back toward The Safe Harbor. I noticed that Lloyd was driving with more confidence — he even took one hand off the steering wheel for a few minutes.

"Right there," he said, pointing to a dirt road on our right as we passed. "That's where that car was coming from."

"Uh-huh," I said, seeing nothing of note except a thick growth of scraggly pines on both sides of the dirt lane and a tilted mailbox with faded numbers, but no name, on it.

Lloyd eased into the fairly sharp curve not far past the lane, and soon The Safe Harbor loomed before us on its well-manicured knoll. Lloyd slowed, then turned in.

As he manuevered up the driveway, he said with some hesitation, "Uh, Miss Julia, I really didn't see who was driving that car. It might not've been Dr. Crawford."

"I know, honey," I said with a reassuring smile, "but don't worry. I'm not going to spread the word around. It's really none of our business who it was or what he was doing out here."

"Yes'm, but that car's the only . . . , well, what I'm thinking is it could've been *Mrs.* Crawford. I mean, I guess it could've. I didn't get a good look, but she drives it sometimes when she comes to check on their little house.

"Oh, look," he said, as we drew closer to the porte cochere, "there's Miss Mildred. She's waiting for us."

So that was the end not only of our speculation about an unusual car, but of our conversation in general. And, I realized with disappointment, the end of my hope that the boy would reveal what had so concerned him on our earlier drive.

But maybe it no longer concerned him. Maybe after sleeping on it, whatever he'd seen had receded in importance to him. That would be fairly typical of teenage behavior, or so I had come to understand. If that was the case, then far be it from me to bring it to the forefront again.

On the other hand, his apparent loss of

interest in the little house on Rosewood continued to disturb me. It wasn't like Lloyd to flit from one thing to another, leaving some undone and others only partially done. He had always had an even temperament that seemed to have grown stronger as he matured. So it bothered me that in this one area, he was beginning to show signs of indifference and inconsistency toward the work that he'd begun with such anticipation.

Even worse was the thought that he'd turned sulky when his parents couldn't drop everything whenever he wanted to drive. That was unattractive to even contemplate, and it saddened me to think of our boy sinking into a sullen resentment when he didn't get his way. In fact, though, such an attitude was so foreign to Lloyd's nature that I could scarcely credit it. I couldn't believe that he could so quickly begin to think that riding a bicycle was beneath him.

The trip back to town passed without incident, but not without a constant flow of words from Mildred. After dropping her off at her front porch, I knew I had only a few minutes to ease into the subject of Lloyd's loss of interest in construction work.

"So," I began as he drove out of Mildred's

driveway, "how's the little house coming along?"

"It's looking great," he said with enough enthusiasm to ease my concerns. "J.D. went over with me this morning and the drywall looks really good. We're going to start priming the walls tomorrow — at least that's the plan. Seems like J.D. gets called away an awful lot, and I don't like to start something by myself." He gave a little laugh. "Afraid I'll do something wrong and have to do it over. Or ruin something."

"Oh, I doubt you'd do that," I said.

"Well, I just feel better when J.D. is there, too. But," he went on, "you should come by and see it, Miss Julia. We'll be putting in kitchen and bathroom cabinets next week."

"I might just do that. You'll be working all weekend?"

"I hope so. But if you don't see the Bonneville or J.D.'s car, don't bother stopping. We won't be there."

"What about your bike?" Then before he could answer, I went on. "Don't you occasionally ride it over there?"

"I have," he said with a shrug, "but, you know, I'd rather not. Too much rain here lately."

Not that much, I thought to myself. But it would take getting caught in only one downpour to keep me home fairly permanently, so I didn't push it.

I walked to my car with a lighter step after Lloyd pulled into the Pickenses' driveway. I had pinpointed Lloyd's problem with the little house, and it was something that need cause no worries about his attitude toward work. He simply liked working with his father rather than, for fear of doing something wrong, by himself. Mr. Pickens should appreciate that and be pleased by it.

"There you are," Lillian said as I walked into the kitchen. "I tole Mrs. Allen you be back real soon, so you better go ahead an' call her. She say she really need to talk to you."

"Well, for goodness' sake," I said, "talk to me is all she's done for the past hour. What does she want now?"

That was a rhetorical question, but Lillian answered it anyway. "She don't tell me what she want, but she call two times already. I got supper waitin' on you, an' Mr. Sam settin' in there waitin' on you, too. Go on ahead an' call her back so you can eat in peace."

Fearing that Horace had had a relapse, I used the kitchen phone to return her calls. "Mildred? Is everything all right? What did

333

you want to talk to me about?"

"Oh, Julia, I'm so glad you called. I have just had the most wonderful idea, and I want to know what you think."

"Okay," I said, exercising great patience as I watched Lillian put a bowl of beef stew and a plate of cornbread on the table. "What is it?"

"Well!" Mildred said as if with a roll of drums. "You recall your Mr. Pickens praising Horace's Boxster car? He just went on and on about what a fine car it is, expressing, it seemed to me, a great desire to own one himself. So, here's what I'm thinking — he could buy that very car! What do you think of that?

"See," she went on before I could answer, "I could sell it to him and have it out of the garage before Horace gets home and gets tempted to drive it again. And he'd know that Mr. Pickens would give it a good home. Don't you think that a Lincoln Town Car would be much more appealing if that little sports car wasn't sitting right next to it?"

"I don't know, Mildred," I said, as Sam came in from the library with a welcoming smile. "But I'm not sure that Horace would be happy about losing his car."

Then I thought of how thrilled Lloyd would be to have a little red sports car in their garage. And I had no doubt that Mr. Pickens would be equally so, but of course I could not speak for him. But even if Sam wanted to fulfill his promise to Lloyd by buying the car, that Porsche was too much car for a fifteen-year-old, as well as for a private investigator who didn't need to draw attention to himself.

"Well, of course Horace won't be happy about it," Mildred said, "but I have to do what is best for him. Once a man has a heart attack, there're any number of things he has to learn to do without. And shifting through all six gears — well, I guess it's only five, because one would be reverse — that's just one of them and might not even be the worst."

"Well, that's true. But, Mildred, I don't know what Mr. Pickens would do about your offer. You'll have to talk to him yourself. I just think that Horace would be devastated to find his beloved car gone and a huge sedate Lincoln parked in its place. You really should talk to him about it before you do anything."

"Well," Mildred said, disappointment obvious in her voice, "I don't need to talk to him because I already know what he'll say. But, see, I was kind of hoping that if Mr. Pickens didn't want it, you'd buy that car for Lloyd. I'll give you a good price, and it'd be perfect for him."

"It's crossed my mind," I admitted, "but it's too much too soon. Besides, Hazel Marie and Mr. Pickens wouldn't want him to have such an expensive car. Talk to Mr. Pickens if you want to, but not about getting it for Lloyd. They want to keep his feet on the ground."

"Well," she said with a sigh, "you know what I always say: Spend it if you have it, and enjoy what you get with it. And, Julia, I know I've told you this before, but you are undoubtedly the tightest wealthy woman I know."

I laughed, because, compared to her, she was right.

CHAPTER 37

LuAnne called early Saturday morning, suggesting that we go out to lunch. "I feel like I haven't seen you in ages," she said, "and with me working every day, I only have weekends free. Tell Sam that Saturdays are the only time we can stay in touch."

"Saturdays are fine with me," I said, although our friends rarely made social plans on that day. But with Sam up and out early to meet his buddies at the Bluebird café for breakfast, I didn't hesitate. "I've missed you, LuAnne, and I'd love to have lunch. Where do you want to go?"

We met at 11:30 at the Tête-à-Tête Tea-room, and with no fanfare at all, LuAnne ordered iced tea — sweetened with lemon — instead of a glass of wine. I made no comment, although I was pleased that she wasn't drowning her sorrows. Perhaps, I thought, she no longer had sorrows to drown, now that she held an important position at the Good Shepherd Funeral Home.

"This was such a good idea," I said, as the waitress left with our orders. "Tell me how things are going with you. You still like the condo?"

"I love it," LuAnne said. "My only problem is worrying about Helen wanting it back. Have you seen her lately? How's she getting along with Thurlow?"

"No, I haven't seen or heard from her, and that's to my shame. So many things have happened lately that I've hardly kept up with myself." And I proceeded to tell her about the little house on Rosewood, the work that Pickens and Son were doing on it, Sam's painful back episode, Horace Allen's recovery, and my daily drives with Mildred. Oh, and also about Lloyd's new used car and my nagging worry that he was too young to drive.

LuAnne laughed. "Get used to it, Julia. He's growing up. That's what you want them to do, but it's hard when they actually do it."

"Well, but tell me about you. How's the job? You still like it?"

"I do, I really do. Everybody's real nice, and I'm finally learning the ropes. But I'll tell you, Julia, I'm learning more than that." LuAnne leaned closer and lowered her voice. "You wouldn't believe what some people do when they bury somebody close to them."

"You mean the way they grieve?"

She straightened up as the waitress placed our plates before us. We thanked her, passed each other the salt and pepper shakers, then picked up our forks.

"I guess," she said. "But some are so obviously grieving that it touches me, and I find that I'm grieving, too — when I don't even know the deceased."

"That's because you're a caring and sensitive person, LuAnne," I said.

"Well, I try. Um, this is good," she said, sampling her salad. "But some people have strange ideas of what to do when they bury somebody. You'd be surprised at what they bring in to bury with their loved ones — letters, books, pictures of children, and mementos of all kinds — as if they'd be interested in having those things with them."

"I've always thought that was sweet — loving, even. Although it never occurred to me to bury anything with Wesley Lloyd."

"Not even his wedding band?"

"He never wore it anyway. I found it among his tie tacks a couple of weeks later."

"Well, you knew why by then, didn't you?"

"Yes, but the funny thing about it was that I'd never noticed that he wasn't wearing it. I guess that's a commentary on the state of our marriage in the first place."

"Wedding bands, engagement rings, and jewelry in general can really create problems, though," LuAnne said. "Why, we had one elderly lady in our care who was wearing beautiful rings. Now, what we do, Julia, in case you don't know, is to leave their rings and bracelets, and watches — whatever they're wearing when they come in — we leave them on for the visitation. Then right before the casket is closed, we remove the jewelry and give it to the chief mourner — husband, child, whoever. But this one time, the woman's daughter gave us explicit directions to leave her mother's wedding band and engagement ring on. She said her mother had never taken them off, and she wanted them left on for eternity. Well, that was all well and good, except the other daughter came in right behind her with power of attorney and demanded the rings. We had to give them to her, but you can't help but wonder about that family."

"Oh, my," I said. "I hope the first daughter never found out what her sister had done, which means the sister can never wear them. Which kind of takes the joy out of having good jewelry."

"Well, you remember me telling you about Connie McMurray and her husband? Well, there's somebody even weirder than her. Do you know Dr. Dooley?"

"Who?"

"Dooley, Dawley, something like that."

"You mean Dalbee?" I asked. "He's not a doctor. He's a chiropractor. Wesley Lloyd used to go to him for a crick in his neck. And that tells you something about both of them."

"Well, whatever," LuAnne said. "Anyway, one of the morticians told me that when his wife died — the doctor's wife, I mean, not the mortician's — he didn't call any of the funeral homes. He just wrapped her up in a blanket and put her in the back of his old beat-up station wagon and drove her to Chapel Hill."

"For heaven's sake, what for? Why take her two hundred miles to another hospital if she was already dead?"

"Not to the hospital, Julia — to the medical school. He donated her to the anatomy lab."

"Oh, my word, LuAnne, surely not."

"Surely, he did. Can you imagine what she looked like after those medical students got through with her?"

Feeling slightly ill, I put down my fork. "No, and I don't want to. But to top it off, he probably felt proud of himself for donating to a good cause instead of giving her a decent burial. Think of the money he saved! I declare, LuAnne, I don't know what to think about some people."

"Me, either," LuAnne said, "but I'll tell you this. My eyes have certainly been opened since I've been working in that place. And one thing I'm going to do is to write out exactly what I want done when I pass over, and I mean all the way down to the color of flowers that go on my casket. It'll be on file right there in the office so that things will be done just as I want them to be. And, Julia, in case you don't know it, we provide that service for everybody, and you should take advantage of it, too. It's call preplanning."

That sounded a little redundant to me, but both planning and preplanning a funeral service, especially my own, was the last thing I was in the mood for, so I thanked LuAnne for the advice and told her I'd think about it.

"Well," she said, "don't think too long. You never know when you might need it."

With those words lingering in my mind, I

was finally able to make tentative plans for lunch the following Saturday, then to take my leave. I had been happy for LuAnne when she'd gotten the job at one of the most respected businesses in Abbotsville, but now it seemed to have cast a funereal pall across her mind. I didn't enjoy visiting with her quite as much as I once had.

I had deliberately not brought Lauren Crawford up to LuAnne during lunch, not wanting to stir her interest by showing too much myself. But Lauren was on my mind as I walked to my car, and I determined to ask Hazel Marie if she knew of any problems the Crawfords might be having. I felt sure that if LuAnne had known anything further about Lauren's visit to the mortuary, she would've mentioned it. But with what she'd already told me, coupled with the possibility that it might have been Lauren whom Lloyd had seen driving out of an unpaved lane in the forested hinterlands of the county, I felt justified in my concern for that young woman. Even if she hadn't bothered to return my dinner invitation.

CHAPTER 38

After the Sunday service, I went along with the congregation as we followed the choir out through the narthex and began to disperse along the sidewalks. Wanting to speak to Hazel Marie, I stood to the side to wait for her. She'd been sitting with the twins a few rows over from us, but I'd been unable to catch her eye — she'd been too busy keeping the little girls quietly entertained during the service. I gave her high marks for even being there, as I did any mother of small children.

Actually, I gave myself high marks for being there as well. Having deeply disapproved of the church's support of an illegally located nonprofit in town, I had taken a sabbatical from regular attendance for several months. At one point, I had explained to our new pastor that I wasn't against doing good works, just against doing them at a place that damaged others. Unfortunately, the new pastor was so progressive that he'd already helped a number of members progress right off the church rolls. When I'd suggested that he limit his sermon topics to the basics of our faith, rather than focusing on cultural fads like sensitivity training, complete with a safe room in the church basement for any poor soul who couldn't cope with the nerve-wracking pace of life in Abbotsville, he'd had the nerve to smile condescendingly and say, "Well, you do know, don't you, that faith without works is dead?" "Yes," I'd snapped back, so hot that I could barely speak, "I'm familiar with the Epistle of James, and I also know that works without faith is just another government agency."

I was still thinking of moving my letter. I just couldn't figure out where to move it *to*.

While standing around waiting, I spoke to several members of the congregation as they passed on their way to parked cars, and finally saw Hazel Marie emerge from the church. I waved to her, then walked over to greet the little girls and to ask Hazel Marie if she had time to talk that afternoon.

"Why don't you come over?" she asked. "The girls will go down for their naps right after lunch — a perfect time if it works for you."

"That'll be fine. Unless," I said, "you want

to take a nap, too."

Hazel Marie smiled and shook her head. "No, a nap just keeps me awake at night. Come on over when you finish lunch. I'd love to see you."

Then, as if she'd suddenly recognized a reason for my visiting, she said, "Oh, I hope it's nothing really important. I mean, we could talk right now if it is. Is it about Lloyd? Is Mr. Sam's back acting up again?"

"No, no, nothing like that. Really, Hazel Marie, it's nothing to worry about. I just want to discuss something with you. Maybe get your advice."

She smiled at that. "Well, I *hope* it's not important, because my advice isn't worth much."

"It is to me," I said, then leaned close to whisper, "Lauren Crawford."

Her eyes widened and her eyebrows went up. "Come on over as soon as you can." Then taking the hands of the little girls, she said, "Let's go, girls. Come on, hold my hand. Can you tell Miss Julia bye-bye?"

With waves of their tiny hands, the little girls were led off by their mother, and I, too, turned to go home, hoping that Sam would have started to warm up whatever leftovers were in the refrigerator. He had left the church by way of the back entrance, having decided that he didn't want to stand around outside while I waited for Hazel Marie. Fearing that his back was beginning to act up again, I hurried down the sidewalk, crossed Polk Street, and went into the house.

"Honey," I called, "I'm home."

I heard him laugh as I walked down the hall and into the kitchen.

"About time," he said, pulling out a chair from the table. "Come sit down. I'm about to starve."

"Um-m, a cold lunch," I said, surveying the dishes he'd put on the table. "I thought there might be some beef stew left."

"Nope, just ham and potato salad, but plenty of both. Did you catch Hazel Marie?"

"Yes, and unless you have plans, I'm going over to talk with her in a little while. But, Sam, I need to talk to you first. I'm afraid that just by asking about somebody I might be starting something — you know how talk gets around in this town. Here," I said, reaching for the mayonnaise, "let me fix your sandwich." Which I then proceeded to do for both of us.

"Lettuce and tomatoes? Onion?"

"All the way," he said, nodding. "So talk to me. What's going on?"

I handed the plate garnished with potato chips and pickles to him, and said, "Lauren Crawford. I may be reading too much into a couple of things I've heard, but you've expressed some concern about her, so I'd like to know what you think."

I went on to tell him about Lauren's visit to the Good Shepherd Funeral Home for reasons probably known by LuAnne but left undisclosed. Then I told him about the possible sighting of Lauren driving her husband's car in an area where I could think of no reason she should've been.

"Of course," I concluded, "it was most likely Dr. Crawford since he's apparently looking to buy some undeveloped property. Still, Lloyd wasn't sure who it was."

"I hope he was keeping his eyes on the road," Sam said, cocking his at me.

"Oh, he was. That's why he didn't get a good look. Anyway," I went on, "I want to ask Hazel Marie if she's had any contact with Lauren lately. I'm especially concerned about the funeral home visit. I keep wondering if there's been a death in Lauren's family — they're all in California, you know. So she could've been asking about receiving a body from somewhere else so they could have a service here. But wait," I said, my eyes widening, "that doesn't make sense.

Why would she bury somebody here when she, herself, will be moving away in a couple of months?

"I declare, I don't know what to think," I said with a sigh, "but if something has happened, we need to help if we can. Or offer to help. We owe that much at least to the Hargroves."

"Well," Sam said, "you're right about that, but except for coming right out and asking them, I'm not sure what we can do. So talk to Hazel Marie if you want, but I wouldn't get too involved with somebody else's problems. It could be misinterpreted and resented." Sam stopped to let that sink in, then he said, "I'll tell you this, though, that is a sad young woman."

"Sad?" I asked, surprised. "I've thought her strange, but now that you say it, sad may be the better word. Which ties in with something going on with her family. Oh, Sam, that *is* sad."

"You think Hazel Marie may know what it is?"

"Not really, because she'd have mentioned it if she did. Still, she's had more recent contact with Lauren than I've had, and may have picked up some indication of a problem.

"Because if there is one," I said, "we could

offer to keep the children if Lauren needs to fly home. Or take some food to them, or help with any plans she needs to make. It's just so sad to think of her, filled with grief or anxiety, essentially alone in a strange town. And her husband is so busy, I doubt he's much help."

"Well, you run on to Hazel Marie's. I'll clear up here, then I'm going to the little house and see what Pickens and Son are up to."

"Sam," I said, immediately on my guard, "you do not need to be doing any carpentry work. Your back could go out again at any time, and I mean just by leaning over to pick up a nail. I wish you wouldn't go over there and be tempted to help out."

"I promise," he said, putting his hand over his heart, "not to help out at all. I'll just observe and give my studied opinion and expert advice about any and everything they're doing."

"Then take a folding chair so you won't have to stand while giving that advice. You do have to be careful, Sam. Once your back has had one seizure, it's prone to have another one."

"Oh, but," he said, lightly, "I now have Dr. Crawford's wonder pills to put me right."

"No," I said, outwardly teasing, but inwardly giving warning, "if your back goes out again, I'm taking you to the emergency room so one of those hospitalists can see you."

"Fair warning," he said as we both laughed. "I'll be extra careful."

I should've walked to Hazel Marie's house — I needed the exercise — but it was clouding up to rain, so I drove. Mr. Pickens's car was in the driveway, but not the Bonneville, so I knew that Lloyd was getting to drive again. It would be parked on Rosewood Lane as work proceeded on the little house.

Hazel Marie welcomed me in and, fearing to wake the little girls, I tiptoed behind her into the living room.

"James is off," she said, "but the coffee's ready to plug in. Let's sit in the kitchen where our voices won't carry upstairs."

"Oh, good," I said, following her. "I love that huge kitchen."

We settled in at the table in a corner beside a large window that looked out over the side yard. The day had darkened considerably as clouds gathered overhead. I would have to talk fast so I could leave before the rains came.

"So what's going on with Lauren?" Hazel

Marie asked as she propped her elbows on the table and looked expectantly at me.

"That's what I wanted to ask you," I said, and continued on to tell her what LuAnne had told me about Lauren's visit to the Good Shepherd Funeral Home.

"The *funeral* home?" Hazel Marie exclaimed. *"Why?"*

"That's what I want to know. All I can think of is some problem with her family — I mean her extended family. I think we'd know if it was her husband or children. Or," I said, as another thought bloomed, "Dr. Crawford's family, but they'd be in Canada, wouldn't they?"

"I really don't know." Hazel Marie straightened and leaned back against her chair. "Oh, I hate to think what they must be going through — and in a strange town, too. Because, Miss Julia, I don't think they've made any friends, other than us. And we're certainly not close because they don't seem to want us to be, I guess. I mean, I've tried, but when you try and try and get nowhere, you soon become a pest. And I didn't want that to happen. So I admit that I've stopped trying, and now I just feel terrible."

"Well, don't do that," I said. "Of us all, you've made the most effort and should be commended for it. But let's think about this. It seems that Lauren didn't go to the funeral home for a visitation, because Lu-Anne said none had been scheduled that day. So what I want to know is this: Can you think of any reason why she would go in to talk with somebody at the funeral home — and I mean in the director's office?"

"No, I can't think of a one — other than what you've said. If it has to do with her faraway family, I can see that she might go in to ask how to deal with a funeral home in another state, or something like that." Hazel Marie drummed her fingers lightly on the table, then she said, "I'll call her. I'll just call and ask how she's doing. Maybe ask her and the children over again for a playdate — although she's turned me down twice in the past couple of weeks. She says that Don keeps her busy overseeing his real estate — busy enough that he's apparently let her hire some help with the children."

"Then that may answer another question," I said and went on to tell her of Lloyd's possible sighting of Lauren on a county road, miles from town.

A rumble of thunder bestirred me and I rose from the table, thanking Hazel Marie for letting me disrupt her Sunday afternoon.

She walked me to the front door, but stopped there.

"Miss Julia," she said, a frown on her face, "you remember us talking about how Lloyd may be losing interest in the little house? Well, it may be getting worse. He's supposed to go over there after school tomorrow and be sure that all the cabinets got delivered — you know, check the item numbers against the bill, then cut open the boxes and check for damage. J.D. will be gone, so I was going to pick up Lloyd from school in his car, let him drive to Rosewood, then leave him there and come on home. But he's already told me that he'll ride his bike to school because he has to stay late — something to do with the Key Club project. So he can't go to the little house, and he's not at all concerned about it."

"Well," I said, "that's a little surprising, but then again, his school work and the activities he's involved in have to take precedence. He's just putting first things first. I wouldn't worry about it, Hazel Marie, if I were you."

But I wasn't Hazel Marie, so I did worry about it. It wasn't like Lloyd to slough off something his father had asked him to do, and it was inconceivable that he'd turn down a chance to drive his car in favor of riding his bike, especially with a week of rain predicted.

I left soon after that, hoping that Hazel Marie would have a few minutes of peace and quiet before the little girls woke from their naps. I'd barely gotten my seat belt fastened when the heavens opened and rain came down in torrents. I waited it out, not wanting to risk the poor visibility, and as I waited, I went over what I knew about Lauren Crawford.

Not much, I concluded, which raised the question of why worry about her? There's always a fine line between true concern and active meddling, between offering help and actual interference. The difference, I suppose, is in the eye of the beholder. How would Lauren view it?

From what I could tell, she wanted to be left alone. And to be honest, that was what I was inclined to do — just turn the page and go on about my own business. On the other hand, to look the other way when someone seemed troubled didn't sit comfortably with me.

Nor did Lloyd's seeming loss of interest in construction work. Then I began to wonder if his little accident was still preying on his mind, recalling how I'd wanted to hide my head after having caused a few dings myself.

Well, I had no answers, but if it wasn't one thing to worry about, it was two more. But nothing had to be decided or done right away, so I was able to put Lauren Crawford temporarily out of mind. Lloyd, however, was another matter entirely.

CHAPTER 39

The following morning, Monday, I had nothing pressing jotted on my calendar, so I decided to put the day to better use than brooding over what I could do little about. It would, in fact, be a good day to begin putting away winter clothes, holding back a few cardigans and light jackets for the odd chilly day. It wasn't a chore that I particularly enjoyed, but I did it in anticipation of the virtuous feeling I would have when it was done.

All day to myself, I thought, for Mildred had been told that she could bring Horace home and Ida Lee would be driving, so she could help pack his things. That daily afternoon trip had ruled my days for more than two weeks, and although I was happy to help out my friend — even though she was perfectly capable of driving herself — I admit that I was even happier to have the day free.

A phone call early that morning changed everything, although it eased at least one worry that had nagged at the back of my mind. It made me, in fact, recalibrate a lot of my preconceived notions.

"Miss Julia?" the caller asked. "This is Libbie in Dr. Hargrove's, I mean, Dr. Crawford's office. How are you this morning?"

"Why, I'm fine, Libbie," I said, wondering with a stab of concern why she would be calling. "What can I do for you? Is it about Sam? He's getting along quite well."

"No, nothing like that. Well, it's a little about Mr. Sam. Dr. Crawford wanted me to ask how he's doing and if he's had to take many of the oxycodone tablets prescribed for him."

I laughed a little and said with a slight edge in my voice, "Interesting that you should ask, Libbie. No, Sam needed only two halves, so there're fifty-nine left over. And to tell the truth, I've been worried about having so many still around."

"Oh, good," she said. "Dr. Crawford wants to know if you'll donate them to his drive to collect unused medications to send to a mission field. And he said if Mr. Sam needs more later on, he'll give him another prescription."

"Why, that'd be wonderful," I said, immediately regretting the hard feelings I'd had toward an overprescribing physician. "I'd planned to turn them in as soon as the sheriff has another drug-collection day anyway. But I think they'd just be destroyed and be of no use to anybody. How much better to send them where they're truly needed. I'll drop them by the office sometime today."

"Oh, good," Libbie said again, as if relieved that Sam hadn't taken them all. "Everybody's been wonderfully helpful — bringing in all kinds of analgesics from over-the-counter to narcotics. Our patients are eager to turn them in for a good cause, and we have a basket almost full already. It's amazing what we keep in our medicine cabinets, isn't it?"

"It surely is. And, Libbie," I went on, "Dr. Crawford is to be commended for this, and I hope you'll tell him so."

After hanging up, it occurred to me that this was an instance of having wasted a lot of time and energy aiming hard feelings toward someone who did not deserve them. What a thoughtful thing to do — collect unused drugs and send them to people in dire need of them. To say nothing of the kindness he'd shown Lloyd when a lot of people would've claimed a whiplash injury and called a lawyer.

To now view Dr. Don Crawford in an even more charitable light lifted my spirits considerably, and I chastised myself for having been so quick to judge him. But bless his heart, while thinking of the needs of others, he was also having to deal with a problem in his own home. As I thought of that strange, sad woman who was his wife, my heart went out to him, and I wished for pardon for every angry thought I'd ever had about him.

I'd barely put the phone down when it rang again. This time it was LuAnne, who immediately launched into a torrent of words.

"Julia? Would you believe that I have to work on weekends now? I know they mentioned it when I interviewed, but they didn't fully explain it, and I was so eager to make a good impression that I didn't ask any questions. But now my weekend to work is coming up and I have to take today and tomorrow off. Can you imagine having Monday and Tuesday for your weekend instead of Saturday and Sunday? But apparently we have to take turns giving up our weekends and now it's my turn. I don't know what to do with myself today, trying to pretend that Monday is a Saturday."

"How often do you have to do it, Lu-Anne?"

"About every six weeks, we all take turns, but I've already told you that, haven't I?"

"Well, just think," I said, "didn't you just have this past weekend off? That means you have four days off in a row every six weeks. That's almost a vacation."

She was silent for a minute, thinking it over. "I guess so, but think of this. I'll have to work this coming weekend and I won't have a day off until the following one. That's an awful long time to have to get up early every morning."

"But you like the job and want to keep it. You may enjoy being at work on weekends — just try it and see. Besides, weekends are usually quieter than weekdays — you may even need to take a book to read. There probably won't be as many people coming and going."

"Julia," she said sternly with a hint of exasperation, "a lot of people don't just *come* on weekends, they *go.* You wouldn't believe how many people leave this vale of tears between three and four o'clock on Friday and Saturday nights. There've even been studies done on it. So don't tell me to take a book to read. I'll be lucky to get to eat a sandwich. Which reminds me," she said, pausing to regroup, "I have some errands to run, but can you meet me for a late lunch? I mean, if it's my Saturday, maybe it can be yours, too."

"Well, I guess . . . I mean, yes, I'd love to. Twelve-thirty? At the tearoom?"

She confirmed the time and place, and I hung up, mentally rearranging my day. Which did little good, for Mildred called immediately afterward with the news that Horace would not be coming home any time soon.

"They don't like the way his heart is acting," Mildred said, "so they want to keep him another week. They want me to meet with the cardiologist and the physical therapist today, Julia, and I'm worried sick about what they'll tell me. My nerves are just about shot."

"Oh, my, I'm sorry to hear that. Will Ida Lee be taking you? You probably shouldn't be driving."

"No, she's not feeling well, so that's why I'm calling. I told them I could not be there until four because that's been our regular time. Now, Julia, you have been wonderful, driving me every day and I don't want to take advantage. So what I'm thinking is that Lloyd could drive me after school today, and surely Ida Lee will feel better tomorrow. And," she went on, "I am a licensed driver, so Lloyd will be perfectly legal."

Legal, maybe, I thought, but will he be safe? Mildred would start talking and her mind would be a million miles away, and I would no more let Lloyd drive her alone than I would pick up and fly.

"Don't give it another thought, Mildred," I said. "I'll be happy to go with you and Lloyd will, too. It'll give him a chance to get more experience while we wait for you."

So there went my day — completely filled up with a long lunch with LuAnne and another road trip with Mildred.

Except, I suddenly realized, Lloyd would be busy that afternoon with a school activity, which meant I'd have to sit and wait alone for an hour or two for Mildred to finish. So on the off-chance that Lloyd's plans might have changed, I called Hazel Marie and presented the problem to her. I'm glad I did, for his Key Club meeting had been moved to another day, and she was sure that he would love to drive us. "He's supposed to check the kitchen cabinets at the little house," she said, "but he can do that when you get back. Why don't you drop him off there when you get back to town, and I'll pick him up later."

Except, I thought as I hung up the phone, I could be aiding and abetting by giving Lloyd an excuse to put off doing what his father had asked him to do. With my heart sinking at the thought, it occurred to me that Lloyd was doing everything he could to avoid working at that house, at least when his father wasn't around to see that he did. I almost called Hazel Marie back to cancel Lloyd's participation in Mildred's daily trip. Being asked to drive again was another good excuse not to do what he'd been told to do, as had been a now-canceled school activity — just one excuse after another.

Something was going on with that boy, and that afternoon would be a good time to find out what it was.

CHAPTER 40

After dropping the little bottle of oxycodone tablets in the basket at Dr. Crawford's office, I arrived at the Tête-à-Tête Tearoom right on time, only to find LuAnne there before me. She sat at a table by the front window, nursing a glass of wine. I pretended not to notice, but I certainly did and had to restrain myself from pointing out the danger of drinking alone, which she'd obviously been doing.

We quickly ordered the tearoom's famous chicken salad plate, complete with slices of canteloupe and served with yeast rolls.

"Can you remember," LuAnne asked, "when canteloupe was available only in late summer?"

"Unfortunately, I can. But now you can get them almost any time of the year — if you can eat something that's as hard as a rock."

We laughed together, then I asked, "But

how are you, LuAnne? I'm still getting used to your being at work all day. I can't tell you how often I pick up the phone, then remember that you're not at home." That was not entirely true, but it was close enough to let her know that I missed the contact.

"Oh, I'm fine. But you know I was hardly ever at home even when I wasn't working. I stayed busy with committee meetings and fund-raisers and first one thing and another."

"You certainly did."

"But now," she said, after swallowing a sip of wine, "the difference is that I *have* to be at work, whereas when I was volunteering, I could beg off if I wanted to. Of course, I never did, but still."

"Don't forget the other difference," I said. "Now you're getting paid."

"That is true," she agreed, looking somewhat smug at the thought. "And getting that check every other Friday is a great morale booster. But how are you, Julia? Anything going on with you?"

"No, not really. I've been driving Mildred to see Horace every day — or at least riding with her while Lloyd drives. We'll be going again this afternoon so Mildred can meet with the cardiologist. She thought Horace would be coming home, but there seems to be a problem and they're keeping him another week."

"You're awfully good to take her every day — that would get old in a hurry for me." LuAnne chewed thoughtfully for a few seconds, then went on. "Mildred has a good helpless act, but when you get down to it, she's more than capable."

"Oh, I know, but I think she needs the company — the companionship or something. Horace's heart attack has really shaken her, although she seems to be dealing with it fairly well. Except it comes out in some strange ways."

"Like how?"

"Oh, like worrying over what kind of car he should be driving, when right now he can't drive any kind. I think that sort of thing keeps her mind off the possibility of something worse."

"Well," LuAnne said, "if the worst happens, she can be assured that the Good Shepherd Funeral Home will treat him with the utmost respect — as we do all our clients."

"Somehow, LuAnne," I said, somewhat drily, "I don't think that would be very comforting."

"Well, you never know, and I'm just saying. But, listen, I heard that the house Dr. Crawford is remodeling will be listed for sale in the next week or so. Have you seen it? What does it look like? Because, see, I might be interested, and I'm thinking that if I get in soon enough I might get a better deal. You know, for a quick sale."

"Oh, I don't think so, LuAnne. It's my understanding that he intends to rent it. That's what I've heard — that he buys rental property in every town he practices in and gets long-term renters in before he leaves. That's his investment strategy, rather than the stock market." Laying my knife and fork crosswise on my plate to indicate I had finished, I said, "Where did you hear it would be for sale anyway?"

"I don't know. It just seems to be common knowledge."

"Well, I'd be surprised if it was true. And no, I've not seen inside it. All I know is that Nate Wheeler is doing the work, and he's good. But, LuAnne, can you really . . . I mean, are you really thinking of *buying* a house? *That* house in particular, which is surrounded by houses in poor repair?"

"But that's the beauty of it, Julia," Lu-Anne said, leaning forward. "See, you and J.D. Pickens are redoing the house next door, which means that others will soon do the same. If I could buy now, I'd be in on the ground floor, because gradually all those houses will increase in value." She sat back with an air of triumph as if she were the only one to have seen the possibilities. "So what about your house?" she asked. "Are you going to sell it or rent it?"

"Well, first of all, it isn't mine. It belongs to Pickens and Son. I have nothing to do with it, but as far as I know they intend to put it on the market."

"Hm-m," LuAnne said, a faraway look on her face. "I might drop by and look at both of them. Just in case, you know. Although I've always heard that it's not good to do business with friends — if something doesn't work out, you're left with hard feelings."

Uncomfortable with the way the conversation was going, I changed direction. "Speaking of friends, have you heard from Helen Stroud lately?"

"I talked with her last week, and, Julia, that woman is spending money like crazy — *Thurlow's* money, I mean. Because now that he's supposed to be up and walking on crutches every day, she's redoing the library downstairs so his bedroom can be down there. Which also means redoing the bathroom next to it with a huge walk-in shower.

And apparently they're fighting like cats and dogs because Thurlow wants that gigantic dog of his back in the house, and you know how Helen feels about that."

"Oh, my," I said, feeling my spirits drop because that gigantic dog — Ronnie, by name — was well and truly ensconced with the Pickens family. They would hate having to give him back to his true owner, and Ronnie, I felt, would hate leaving his place of honor as the active protector of children to return to a lazy life at the feet of his master.

"Anyway," LuAnne went on, "Helen seems to be ruling the roost over there. I just hope she doesn't spend him into the poor house, because if she does, she'll want her condo back, and where would that leave me? That's why I'm thinking I'd be better off *owning* something, rather than being at the whim of somebody else."

"Well," I conceded, "that's true, but don't overlook the fact that when you own something you're responsible for taxes, for insurance, and for fixing anything that doesn't work. As a renter, you can just call the owner if something needs repairing."

"I know that, Julia," she said with a hint of snippiness. "You forget that I paid all the bills when I was with Leonard, so I know what I'm doing. So don't tell me that you think I need an intervention to teach me how to handle money."

"Not at all!" I said, aghast at the thought and, before I could help myself, going on the offense. "And don't bring up that subject to me ever again. I still get cold chills when I think of how we hurt Helen, interfering in her business as we did. And if you want to get personal, how a few busybodies did the same to me."

"You're right," LuAnne quickly said. "You're absolutely right. Let's forget all that, and talk about something else. You want dessert? I'm having the cheesecake."

"Fine," I said, nodding, "I will, too."

And over two slices of cheesecake, we got over a disagreeable hump and were soon chatting away about other less touchy subjects.

"So," LuAnne said, "how's Lloyd liking his car? I saw him driving it with his mother the other day on my way home from work. Hazel Marie waved at me, but he had his eyes on the road."

I laughed. "I'm glad to hear it. He's being very careful these days. And I think he's liking it fine, although he would've much preferred a sportier-looking car."

"Who wouldn't? That thing is a monster.

I don't know how he manages it."

"Well, don't tell him that. His father picked it out for all the right reasons — number one being Lloyd's safety. And when you're riding in it, you feel as safe as if you were in a tank. And it's very comfortable — even Mildred likes riding in it."

"*Mildred?* You mean she's ridden in it?"

"I certainly do. Lloyd drives her to see Horace most every day. Of course, I go along, too. He still has to have a licensed driver with him, and . . . ," I said, laughing, "even though Mildred qualifies legally, she doesn't with me. Have you ever ridden with her?"

"Good grief, yes, and, believe me, it wasn't an easy ride. She looks everywhere but at the road, talking constantly. She's as bad as Miss Mattie Freeman ever was. You remember her, don't you?"

"I sure do, and I'd drive way out of my way just to avoid being on the same street with her."

"Well," LuAnne said, leaning forward and lowering her voice, "speaking of that, Lauren Crawford almost caused a wreck the other day."

"Oh, no. What happened?"

"She ran a stop sign — just went straight through it without slowing down or looking either way. If I hadn't slammed on my brakes, I would've hit that new Lexus broadside. Scared me to death, let me tell you. But she just went right on like she had the right of way. I don't think she even saw me."

"Oh, I hate to hear that. I'm afraid that she has some heavy problem, something bad going on in her life. I mean, after what you told me about her coming to the funeral home —"

"Don't say that. I didn't tell you anything. I just said I saw her. I can't tell you anything else, I could lose my job."

"No, no, that's what I meant. I have no idea why she was there, but let's face it, nobody goes to a funeral home for entertainment —"

"You can say that again."

"Well," I said, "I mean I'm concerned about her, and hearing that she's driving carelessly worries me even more. Next time, let's ask her to have lunch with us."

"Sure, we can do that. Just don't ask me why she was at the funeral home. . . ."

"I won't."

"I *mean,*" LuAnne said, putting her napkin on the table and gathering her purse, "people are all the time coming in to pre-plan their funerals, and they don't want everybody and his brother knowing their business."

At that, LuAnne gasped and turned an ashen face toward me. We stared at each other — she with a stricken look, and I with a horrified one.

Snatching up the check and turning to leave, she said, "I'll get this, but, Julia, you didn't hear a word. Understand? You didn't hear a word I said."

Partially recovering, I nodded. "Thanks for lunch, LuAnne. I'll leave the tip. And thanks for bearing with me — I think I need to have my hearing checked. I hear only half of what anybody says these days."

CHAPTER 41

Oh, my word! My word! By the time I'd walked to the car, I was shaking all over. I fastened the seat belt, then leaned my head on the steering wheel while a deep anxiety over Lauren's apparently precarious mental state brought me to tears. And thinking of those poor, motherless children, which I immediately did, I began to bawl in earnest.

Snatching up a Kleenex, I mopped my eyes and blew my nose. Then, straightening up, I told myself that going to pieces was no way to deal with anything. But deal with it, I would, one way or the other.

In fact, I'd already started by trying to ease LuAnne's horror at revealing Lauren's business at the funeral home by pretending partial deafness. But of course I had heard, and all I could think of was that Lauren was a woman on the edge of a cliff.

Driving very carefully toward home, I began putting things together. Here was a young woman with no fixed address, required to pick up and move every few months, dealing with small children and a busy husband, burdened with a load of sadness that could've been congenital for all I knew, having no support from friends or relatives, making no effort to tend to herself, and now in the process of planning a funeral.

Her own funeral? That was the question, and the answer seemed as clear as a bell. Should I call a suicide hot line? Did Abbotsville even have one? I didn't know, but I did know to whom I'd turn — someone who'd know what to do.

"Sam!" I called as soon as I walked through the kitchen door. Turning to Lillian at the sink, I asked, "Where is Sam? Is he home?"

"Right in yonder, payin' bills," Lillian said, gesturing toward the library. "Why? What's wrong?"

"I don't know, Lillian, but I need help." I dropped my pocketbook on the counter as I passed and kept on going. "I mean, I need help for somebody else from somebody, *anybody*. I'll tell you later."

Rushing into the library, I hurried up to the desk, my hands still shaking and my breath coming in gasps. "Sam," I said, reaching for him, "sorry to interrupt, but I am worried sick. Tell me what to do, because somebody needs to do something before something terrible happens."

"Slow down, honey," Sam said, pushing aside the checkbook and beginning to rise. "What happened? Are you all right?"

"I'm fine. It's not me, Sam, it's Lauren Crawford. I am so concerned about her." I put my hands on his shoulders and leaned against him, grateful again for the comfort of his strength and great good sense. If anybody knew what to do in a crisis, it was Sam Murdoch.

"Well, come on and sit down," he said, leading me to the sofa. "Now tell me why you're so upset about Lauren."

So I did. I told him — or rather, I reminded him since I'd already told him — of her visit to the Good Shepherd Funeral Home and of the possible sighting of her on a country road. And then I told him of her rejection of every invitation from Hazel Marie, of her near collision after running a stop sign, and then put it all together with his own recognition of her intense sadness.

"And to top it off," I concluded, "LuAnne let slip today that Lauren was at the funeral home to plan or *pre*plan — whatever the difference is — *her own funeral.* Sam, we have to do something. I don't know what, but we can't just sit idly by with these clear signs of imminent disaster everywhere we look."

Sam was silent for several minutes, cogitating as he tapped his fingers against his mouth. "Well, honey, this puts us between a rock and a hard place. My first impulse is to talk with her husband, but he has to be aware of her state of mind. I mean, he *is* a physician, and he could take offense at what could be seen as meddling. Unfortunately," Sam said, leaning over to rest his forearms on his knees, "the one I'd really like to talk to is not around."

"Who?"

"Bob Hargrove."

"Of *course*! He would be the perfect one. Call him, Sam. Just call and lay it all out for him. I'm sure Libbie in his office will know how to reach him."

"No," Sam said, shaking his head, "I can't do that." As soon as he said it I, too, knew it was a bad idea. What could Dr. Hargrove do when he was half the world away? Yes, he knew Lauren, or at least he'd met her, but as good a physician as he was, he couldn't diagnose and treat an emotional crisis on a long-distance line.

"Telling him would do nothing," Sam

went on, "but disrupt his time off, which he badly needs. It would be just like him to pack up and come home. He may even be hoping for an excuse to get back to work, and," Sam said with a smile, "Sue would never speak to me again."

"You're right, though. He would be perfect if he was here. But he's not, so what else can we do?"

"Try to get close to her for one thing. Go to see her, invite her out, call her, let her know you care. Just keep her busy, I guess, so she doesn't have a lot of time alone with whatever problem she has."

"But Hazel Marie has tried that, and Lauren always has an excuse to turn her down. I don't know why her husband hasn't done something. He's so attuned to the feelings of others, you'd think he'd see the state she's in."

"Well," Sam said, "there's not much we can do since we're not close enough to ask her or him directly. Just be available in case she gives you or Hazel Marie or anybody an opening. Then you can urge her to get professional help. Which is what she needs."

"That's true." Then with a glance at my watch, I jumped up. "Oh, my goodness, I've got to go. Lloyd will be sitting there, running his car out of gas waiting for me, and

Mildred will think we've forgotten her. But, thanks, Sam, for listening. And if you can think of anything else . . . well, I'll be thinking of ways to get close to Lauren."

With that, I retraced my steps through the kitchen — grabbing my purse and speaking to Lillian on my way — and flew out the back door, afraid I'd made Mildred late for her appointment with Horace's cardiologist.

I hadn't, but it was a close call. By the time I'd driven to the Pickens house, gotten in the Bonneville, which, if the weather had been freezing, would've been all warmed up, Lloyd was wondering if I'd forgotten. Mildred was openly anxious about being late when we picked her up, so I apologized profusely.

"It was my fault," I said. "I let the time get away from me. But we're all right, so, Lloyd, you don't need to hurry. Driving the speed limit will get us there on the dot."

This was said because Mildred was already urging Lloyd to step on the gas. But there'd be no heavy foot on the pedal while I was in the front seat.

Lloyd drove his usual sedate speed, managing the curves with admirable ease. Mildred and I chatted — she from the backseat and I, keeping my eyes on the road, stiff and upright from the front. But my mind was roiling with concern for the Crawford family — those poor little children, that hardworking husband whose heart went out to suffering humanity both near and far, and especially that beautiful young woman who was at the end of her rope.

Well, a rope wasn't the most salubrious item to dwell on, so I made an effort to concentrate on Mildred's concern about the state of Horace's heart.

"I know you're disappointed that Horace won't be coming home today," I said to her. "I thought he'd been improving."

"He has been," she said, "but apparently not enough. The heart attack left a small amount of damage, but I don't know what that means. They have him up and walking around, doing exercises and so forth, all of which is more than he normally does. So I don't know if that means his heart is improving or if it means he's better off now that it's damaged."

"Hm-m," I said, "that's a good question."

"Well, here's another one," Mildred went on, "does a heart attack affect the memory? Because, I'll tell you, Horace hardly knows one day from the next. He keeps asking why he's in that place and not home in his own bed. I finally got tired of telling him he'd had a heart attack and just told him I'd decided it was for his own good."

"And that satisfied him?"

"It sure did, because I've always been the one to decide what was good for him and what wasn't. It made him feel right at home."

Lloyd slowed the car and flipped on the turn signal. "Here we are," he said, turning onto the drive up to The Safe Harbor.

Stopping in front of the entrance, Lloyd put the car in Park, then got out to open the back door for Mildred. Halfway through her exit, she turned back to me.

"Julia, I'll be a little longer than usual today — the cardiologist wants to go over everything with me, and the physical therapist wants to show me Horace's exercise routines so we can continue them at home. I hope you don't mind, but I expect it'll take an hour or so."

Too late to mind now, I thought, but assured her that Lloyd and I could use the extra time to increase his driving proficiency and bolster his confidence.

As the double doors of The Safe Harbor slid closed behind Mildred, Lloyd slid behind the wheel. "Where to?" he asked.

"Anywhere's fine with me. Why don't we

go on toward that little gas station? I might like something to drink this time, then, depending on the time, we might drive a little farther on. I'm trying to remember where Staton Mill Road comes out — we may end up on Brevard Road."

"Actually," Lloyd said, "it may even be the old Brevard Road. I tried to find it on a county map, but there're a lot of little roads that wiggle around and merge into others. Most of 'em don't seem to go anywhere."

He turned west at the end of the drive, and we began to retrace our route to Jimmy's Gas & Groceries. A mile or so along, I glanced to the left as we passed the entrance to the dirt lane with the leaning mailbox, wondering again what business one or the other of the Crawfords could've had there. But it was none of mine, so I made no mention of it.

Although I was slightly put out with Mildred for springing the inconvenience of a longer wait time on us, I couldn't help but think that I should seize the moment. This, I thought, is the time to get to the bottom of whatever was troubling Lloyd.

CHAPTER 42

"Let's fill up," I said, as Jimmy's gas pumps came into view. "You know how to do it?"

"Yes'm," Lloyd said, veering toward the little station. "J.D. showed me how a long time ago. I always do the pumping when he's along. Rain, sleet, or snow, I'm the pump man." Lloyd grinned. "J.D. says women and children stay in the car, but men get out in the weather. He says I'm right in the middle — I can be a kid and stay in, or I can be a man."

"Well, I declare," I said, because I could think of nothing else to say. I had never thought J.D. Pickens a model of child-raising expertise, but considering a few things like tire-changing and gas-pumping lessons, I might have to think again.

As he pulled the Bonneville to a stop beside the two pumps, I rummaged in my pocketbook for a credit card and a few dollars.

"Get us something to drink," I said, "or whatever you want. I'd like a Coke. It's getting awfully muggy, and I'm about to perish of thirst. I declare, you never know what a March day will bring in the way of weather. Just look at those storm clouds over the mountain."

Lloyd lowered the windows, then left the car, which immediately began to heat up. I found last Sunday's church bulletin in my pocketbook and began fanning my face with it. It is a fact that springtime in the mountains will freeze you to death one day and burn you up the next — unless, as appeared to be happening lately, it floods you out of house and home with rainstorms.

"Here you go," Lloyd said, coming back to my window. "They only had Pepsi."

"My word, Lloyd," I said, as he handed me a cold bottle. "I can't drink a quart of Pepsi."

"Liters are all they have," he said with a grin. "We call 'em bellywashers. I brought you a straw — that'll help."

Well, it was refreshing and I sipped away while Lloyd, licking an orange popsicle as he watched the gallons go in, filled the gas tank.

When we were back on the road, still heading west, he asked, "How's the time?

How much further should we go before turning back?"

"About five or ten more minutes, then we'll look for a place to turn around. Are you all right driving? Not getting tired, are you?"

"No'm, I could drive all day. I just don't want Miss Mildred to have to wait for us."

"That's thoughtful, Lloyd, because she never expects to be inconvenienced." Smiling to lessen the bite of my words, I said, "Mildred is accustomed to people dancing to her tune, which you might've noticed when she mentions Mr. Allen." I stopped, thought for a minute, then went on. "You're at just the age to begin noticing how different some marriages can be — the relationships of the couples, I mean. The Allens, for instance, have a unique relationship."

"I figured," Lloyd said with a smile. "I mean, they're not like Mama and J.D."

"No, Mildred rules the roost in that marriage. It does seem to work for them, though I wouldn't recommend it to anyone else. But now's the time when you should be looking around and noticing what makes a good marriage. That way, you'll know the kind of marriage you want. Then eventually, you'll find a nice young woman who wants the same kind." I let that sink in for a minute. "Of course, you have a lot of time before getting to that point."

"Yes'm, I already know there're some kinds of marriages I don't want. But what I don't understand is how or why they keep on going."

"Well, they don't, always. Lots of divorces these days — not like it used to be when people stayed together, no matter what." I sat up straight and pointed to a clearing on the side of the road ahead. "Let's turn around up there."

Lloyd looked both ways, flipped on the blinker, and eased off the road onto the clearing. From the remnants of a fruit stand at the back, it must have been the site of a roadside commercial enterprise at some point.

When we were back on the highway, heading the way we'd come, Lloyd shifted in his seat and said, "Uh, Miss Julia? Would . . . I mean, why would somebody stay married if they liked somebody else? I mean, well, if you happened to *know* they liked somebody else."

"Lots of reasons, honey. Some people, unfortunately, just get carried away and want the thrill of something new, with no intention of ending the old. Mostly, though, an unhappy marriage is behind it. And some people stay in an unhappy marriage because of children or a lack of money or for social reasons. It's a sad life, though, which is why you should never marry until you're absolutely sure you've picked the right one."

He didn't respond, so I reflected on the explanation I'd given him, pleased that I might've helped him understand some of the dangers of a rash marriage. But as the silence lengthened, it suddenly occurred to me that he had something specific in mind. He wasn't interested in generalities, he was concerned about a particular marriage. My heart contracted at the thought — which marriage was he thinking of? My own with Wesley Lloyd Springer, his father with a different woman? Oh, Lord, I didn't want to talk about that.

Or, heaven help me, was it some problem between his mother and J.D. Pickens, that skirt-chasing ladies' man whom I'd always only half trusted? Oh, please, Lord, don't let it be that.

Mentally writhing with distress, wanting both to change the subject and to answer his concerns, I searched for something to say. Still searching, I noted the familiar dirt lane we were passing and the approaching curve.

"Lloyd," I said, increasingly uncomfort-

able with the silence, "if you know . . ."
Then as we passed the mailbox and entered
the curve, I shrieked. "Stop! Stop!"

He slammed on the brakes, the heavy car
rocking on its chassis. "Good grief!" he
cried, as something — several somethings
— white and feathery banged against the
windshield, flapping and squawking, then
flew or fell off onto the hood and the road.

Crates — shattered and otherwise — were
strewn across the highway, and a huge,
once-tottering chicken truck lay broken on
its side, blocking both lanes of the highway.
A swarm of escaped chickens flew, ran, stag-
gered, flapped, and cackled as they turned
the road, the ditch, and the adjoining field
into a giant poultry yard. One lone highway
patrolman, his arms spread wide, was trying
vainly to shoo them together. His patrol car
was parked in the middle of the road beyond
the truck, doors open and lights flashing.
We could see someone in the passenger seat,
likely the truck driver, and hear in the
distance the sound of sirens approaching.

"Oh, my goodness!" Lloyd said, putting
the car in park and reaching for the door
handle. "We'd better help."

"No, wait," I said, looking behind us.
"Turn on your lights — everything, blinker
and all. We don't want somebody barreling

around the curve and hitting us."

He did, then opened his door to get out. The patrolman ran toward us, holding up his hand. "Stay in the car," he yelled, "and get off the road. Help's on the way."

"Well," Lloyd said with some chagrin as he obeyed, "I guess we wouldn't know what to do with 'em, if we caught any, anyway."

With a jittery laugh, I agreed, then said, "There's not much of a shoulder, but pull on over. I'm still afraid somebody'll plow into us from behind."

After a little to-ing and fro-ing, Lloyd managed to get the big car partially onto the shoulder of the road. Then we watched as a fire truck, an EMT truck, and a fire marshal's car came screeching to a stop on the highway beyond the stricken chicken truck. Doors opened and people spilled out.

"Plenty of help now," Lloyd said, "but looks like we'll be here awhile. They'll have to get that truck upright before they can move it — need a wrecker with a winch, I guess."

"Oh, my," I said, "we have to let Mildred know. Can you call her? Or rather, call The Safe Harbor? She's like me. She never carries a phone."

Lloyd, his eyes wide, stared at me. "You don't have your phone?"

"No, don't you?"

"Mine's in my backpack on the kitchen table. I *never* go anywhere without it, and now I have." He mopped his face with his hand. "Oh, me!"

"Well, let's think a minute," I said. "For all we know, it could be an hour or more before they get that truck out of the way. So far, though, there's nobody behind us. We could turn around and go back to Jimmy's and use his phone. Or," I went on, realizing that I had been writhing uncomfortably for more than one reason, "we're not far from that dirt road where you saw one of the Crawfords. There's a mailbox there, so there could be a house with a phone." And, I thought but didn't say, a bathroom.

CHAPTER 43

One of the uniformed officers on the scene passed us at a trot, heading for the top of the curve to stop traffic. At least I could stop worrying about being rear-ended, so I took the opportunity to direct Lloyd in making a three-point turn. It ended up being closer to a five-pointer, but he soon had us headed back the way we'd come. Beyond the overturned truck, traffic had already begun to pile up in the opposite lane, so we'd gotten out just in time.

After a half mile or so, Lloyd slowed as we neared the lane. "You sure you want to turn in here? We could be at Jimmy's in ten or fifteen minutes."

Ten or fifteen minutes was an eternity with almost a liter of Pepsi inside, so I said, "Let's try it. Surely somebody lives a little way in, or, who knows, the lane could twist around and come out behind The Safe Harbor." I held myself as still as I could, my hand clasping the armrest with a grip of steel in the hope that the action would carry over to other body parts. "Lloyd," I said through tight lips as the car bounced from the paved road onto the dirt lane, "I hate to be . . . well, graphic, but I have to find a ladies' room."

His head jerked toward me, then quickly back. "Out *here*?"

"Well," I said, wiping my face with my hand, "any port in a storm, you know. Surely there's a house in here somewhere with both a ladies' room and a telephone. Actually," I went on, trying to take my mind off the most pressing problem, "I'd thought this was more or less a driveway, but it looks fairly well used and kept up. There may even be several houses along the way."

There weren't, or none that we saw, anyway. There were a few clearings — if you didn't count tall weeds and the occasional scraggly bush among the scrub pines — that may at one time have led to residences. One, though, about a quarter of a mile in, showed signs of recent use by flattened weeds, and I wondered if we were on a lovers' lane of sorts.

We finally found a tin-roofed house that sat alone and forlorn where the lane ended in a circle of packed dirt. No larger than a cabin, the unpainted house had an abandoned feel about it — no cars or children's toys in the yard, no chairs on the sagging porch, and no panes in two of the windows. A still heat, broken by the occasional rumble of thunder, seemed to bear down on the place, as a sense of loneliness emanated from the surrounding trees. But no matter, I had to get out.

"We called it wrong, Miss Julia," Lloyd said. "Nobody lives around here."

Opening the car door, I said, "Then I'm going around back — maybe there's a shed I can use."

"No," he said, "just go to the back, but don't go inside anything. Could be snakes."

That almost cured my problem, right there. But I got out, carrying my pocketbook for the wad of Kleenex in it, and hurried around the side of the house until I was well out of sight of the car. And, there, beside the few cement blocks that led to a back porch, I released the floodgates.

Feeling like a new woman, I hurried back to the car — only to find it empty.

"Lloyd?" I called, looking around and feeling the emptiness of the place. Clouds heavy with rain were boiling up over the treetops and a few sprinkles began to spatter on the car.

"Over here," he said from the front porch as he closed the door of the house. Then he hurried down the steps to the car and slid behind the wheel. "Let's go."

"Gladly." I, too, slid in on my side, closed the door, and fastened my seat belt. "You went inside? It wasn't locked?"

"No, it wasn't locked." He turned on the ignition, turned the car around, then drove onto the lane a little faster than the careful pace in which he'd driven to the house. "We'll go to Jimmy's. Miss Mildred knows we're late by now, and I expect she knows why. Everybody at The Safe Harbor will know what's happened."

"Was there a bathroom?"

"What?" Lloyd asked. "I mean, ma'am?"

"That house," I said. "When you went inside, what did it look like? Did it have a bathroom?"

"Oh. Well, it looked empty, which is why I went in. But it had some dirty cots and pallets on the floor, so somebody's been bunking there. And it had a bathroom, but you wouldn't want to use it."

"Okay, good. I'd hate to think I'd gone public with something that I hadn't needed to." I laughed and, after a second, he did, too.

By the time we got back to the main road,

traffic had backed up far enough to block our way. There was no room for even a generous driver to let us in, so Lloyd put the car in park and left it running for the air-conditioning and the windshield wiper. Rain was pelting down by then.

"We're really stuck now," Lloyd said.

"Well, there's nothing we can do about it, so we might as well settle in. I hope you don't have a lot of homework."

"No'm, not too much." He twiddled his fingers on the steering wheel and looked away. "Actually," he said, clearing his throat, "I was supposed to go by the Rosewood house today and check on the cabinets. They got delivered this morning — at least, I hope they did." With a glance at me, he went on. "I was kinda thinking that we might swing by there after we take Miss Mildred home. Before you go home, I mean."

"Sure, we can do that, but it'll be late with all this going on." I waved my hand at the line of cars blocking us in. "Wouldn't you rather wait till after school tomorrow when you'll have more time?"

"No'm, I'd rather get it done when . . ." He stopped and bit his lip.

"When what?"

"When you can go," he said in a rush. "I

mean, it's been a long time since you've seen what we've done, and I thought maybe you'd like to. Besides," he said after a pause, "J.D. wanted me to check the cabinets today — in case, you know, any of 'em got damaged. He's going to call tonight."

"Why, Lloyd, you didn't have to drive Mildred today — I could've done that. You could've spent the afternoon doing what your father wanted you to do."

"Yes'm," he said, looking down at his hands, "I know. I just didn't want to."

"Oh, really now," I said, perturbed at his admission. "I can't imagine that having a chance to drive a few miles is that important to you."

"No'm," he said, shaking his head. "It's not that. It's, well, I don't much like going over there by myself."

That didn't make sense. He'd had no qualms about going into a spooky, old house that very afternoon and wandering around in it long enough to see a filthy bathroom. Why in the world would he be reluctant to go into a house with neighbors all around? And only recently reluctant, at that, for he'd been working at the Rosewood house for several weeks by now.

"Hey," he said, "look, they're moving."

And sure enough, the line of cars that was

blocking us had slowly begun to move forward. Lloyd shifted from Park to Drive and inched forward, hoping that someone would let us in.

"No cars coming from the other way," I said, unable to refrain from stating the obvious. "They probably have only one lane open, so just ease on in as soon as somebody waves to you."

And soon a kindhearted soul did wave to us, and Lloyd joined the line of cars inching forward on the wet highway. As we approached the toppled chicken truck, we saw that it had been towed to one side so that traffic could resume, although resume on only one lane. A number of people were trudging around the open field, gathering up sodden chickens and putting them in a closed truck. I wondered how many had escaped into freedom through the woods, possibly to end up as somebody's unexpected supper.

"Here," Lloyd said, reaching over and dropping something in my lap. "You better take this. I'm not sure what to do with it." He steered the car back into the correct lane after passing the chicken truck and headed for The Safe Harbor at a normal rate of speed.

"What is it?" I asked, although I could

plainly see that it was an amber plastic vial with a white cap and a scratched and blurred prescription label glued to it. Shaking it, I confirmed that it was empty.

"Where did you get this?"

"On the floor of that house."

"Why, Lloyd, it could've had somebody's medicine in it. He might need a refill or something. You think we ought to take it back?"

"No, ma'am, I do not," he said, staring straight ahead as he gripped the steering wheel with both hands. "I think we ought to get as far away from that place as we can and *stay* away from it. Miss Julia," he said with a frowning glance at me, "that was a drug house."

CHAPTER 44

A drug house? What did that mean, for heaven's sake? I wasn't exactly sure, but I could imagine enough to send a tingle rippling down my back. People who fiddled with drugs in empty cabins deep in the woods weren't the most welcoming when visitors dropped by, no matter how urgently a rest stop was needed.

"You really think so?" I asked, wanting to look over my shoulder to see if we were being followed, which was ridiculous, in that there really was a long line of cars following us.

He nodded. "Yes'm, it had all the signs — empty house, no neighbors, off the beaten path, tire treads in the dirt, and a few empty prescription bottles. Somebody could be selling from it, or it could just be a safe place for people to take drugs, then sleep it off. You know, without being afraid the cops'll bust in."

"Hm-m, well, you seem to know a lot about it, Lloyd. I don't think I would've thought of such a thing."

He shrugged. "You hear things at school. I mean, teachers talk to us, and there're all these videos they show us. You know, to warn us about dirty needles and taking stuff when you don't know what it is. Things like that."

"Seems to me they'd warn you about taking something even — maybe *especially* — when you do know what it is."

"Oh, they do. Anyway, I'm just glad nobody was there. We could've really been in hot water if we'd come tooling up when a sale was going on."

"Well, there'll be no more sales going on now," I said, dropping the vial in my purse for safekeeping. "I'm going to report this to Coleman." Coleman Bates, my special friend in the sheriff's department, was now a sergeant but, with the recent election over, expecting to be promoted. To take down an active drug house could easily boost him to a captaincy. "But what about this, Lloyd? What in the world could one of the Crawfords have been doing there?"

"I've been thinking about that," he said, slowing as the line of cars bunched up. "Whichever one it was could've been looking at property, like you heard. Or they could've taken a wrong turn, like we did."

"That's true," I said, but something else had occurred to me that I was unwilling to even think about, much less mention. "We'll let Coleman figure it out."

Lloyd was silent for a few minutes, then he said, "I don't know, Miss Julia. Word could get around that I'm an informer or something. I mean, I'm all for law and order and all that, but I've got enough to worry about already."

Before I could bore into that, he flipped on the blinker and turned onto the drive to The Safe Harbor. "We're here," he said. "And, uh, maybe we should just tell Miss Mildred about the chicken truck. Not about the house."

"I agree. The fewer who know, the better. And as for being an informer, don't you worry about that. I don't mind informing on drug dealers one iota. I'll tell Coleman and, of course, Sam. Lillian, too, because I tell her everything anyway. And I guess your father, as well — he's in the business of law enforcement, too. But nobody else. Mildred can keep a secret, but with all she has on her mind now, well, there's no telling what she might let slip. We'll just forget about it and let the experts deal with it. But one thing, Lloyd." I stopped and sat up to look for Mildred. "Pull up under the porte cochere where she can see us."

He did, but Mildred didn't come out.

"What did you want to tell me?" he asked, watching the double doors.

"What? Oh, well, speaking of who not to tell, let me tell you that you should never, ever share anything with Miss LuAnne unless you want the whole town to know. That woman — and she's one of my best friends — is an informer of the first order. She can't keep anything to herself. And I don't mean to talk about my friends behind their backs — I've told her the same thing a million times. So don't tell her."

"No'm, I won't."

Then we both started laughing — a little nervously, I admit, but laughing at the thought of Lloyd's sharing a secret with, of all people, LuAnne Conover. It was ludicrous of me to have even brought it up, but that just shows how shaken I was at the thought of our having ended up at a drug house in the wilds of Abbot County. And, even worse, at the thought that Lloyd could be thought a confidential informant and, consequently, appear on somebody's hit list.

"You just forget about it, honey," I said, my laughter suddenly gone as a roll of thunder warned of another imminent downpour. "Don't tell any of your friends — don't confide in anyone, except maybe your father. I expect Coleman will want us to keep quiet about it anyway while he organizes whatever he has to organize. But I don't want word of your involvement getting around school. Just leave everything to me."

We finally got Mildred home, but, I declare, that woman talked the whole way. We heard all the details of Horace's progress — slow but steady, it seemed. We heard about his physical therapy routine, his memory lapses, his diet, his medications, his restless leg syndrome, even his daily constitutionals. She stopped enumerating the items on Horace's rehabilitation routine long enough to commiserate with us about the perils of sharing a road with top-heavy trucks, as well as with tandem trucks, box trucks, and noisy smoke-spewing trucks, then tacked on pickup trucks for good measure. We heard about her plans to employ a gentleman's gentleman to care for Horace when he came home, as well as her intention to have a physical therapist make thrice-weekly visits to her home to increase Horace's muscle tone.

Silence reigned when she finally climbed out of the car at her front veranda and the door closed behind her, closing off a paean of praise and gratitude for our having driven her.

"Whew," I said as Lloyd drove back onto Polk Street. "The more worried she is, the more she talks. But she is a good person, Lloyd, with the kindest of hearts." I looked with longing at my own house as we passed it on our way to Rosewood Lane. "I just hope she remembers to call Lillian and let her know why we're running late. And Sam, too, of course, but he'll be engrossed in the news and may not even have noticed the time. And your mother, too. She'll be worried about you. I tell you, Lloyd, this has taught me a lesson — I am going to start taking my phone everywhere I go. Even if it is as heavy as lead, and I have to empty my pocketbook down to the lint in the bottom in order to find it when I need it."

"Me, too," he said. "But I sure do thank you for coming to the house with me. It'll be dark pretty soon, and it's already raining again, so I'll hurry and check the cabinets."

He pulled to the curb in front of number sixteen Rosewood and turned off the ignition. "It won't take long," he said. "I hope."

"I see Mr. Wheeler's truck's still here," I

said, noting the pickup parked in front of number eighteen as we disembarked and hurried to the porch. "So you wouldn't have been alone after all. But, then, he doesn't work late very often, does he?"

"No'm," Lloyd said as he inserted the house key in the front door. "He starts real early, though." He looked up as another car pulled to the curb behind Mr. Wheeler's truck. "Come on, Miss Julia," he said, pushing the door open and entering. "I need to get started on this."

As I began to follow him inside, I looked back and saw Lauren Crawford getting out of the car. Thinking of Sam's advice to befriend her, I turned back to greet her and, hopefully, to engage her in conversation.

"Come on," Lloyd said again, taking my arm and pulling me inside. "I need to get this done and get home. Mama will be worried." He closed the door behind us, picked up a box cutter, and began to open one of the several cabinet-size cartons in the middle of the room.

"Well," I said, frowning, "I just thought I'd speak to Mrs. Crawford while you do this. I mean, I'll help if you'll tell me what to do, but there's only one box cutter."

"You can look over the cabinets when I get 'em open. Look for scratches in the paint and cracks in the wood — things like that. Things that might've happened during shipment. Anyway," he went on after a brief pause, "she won't stay long with my car parked out front."

That went right past me while I was running my hand over a white upper cabinet, feeling for signs of damage. Then I straightened up and looked at him. "What does your car have to do with Mrs. Crawford?"

"Well," he mumbled as he slit open another carton, "it lets them know somebody's over here."

"What does that have to do with anything? Lloyd," I said, quite firmly, "what is going on? What're you acting so funny about?"

He sighed and put down the box cutter. "Come on," he said, and without looking at me, turned and went into what would eventually be the back bedroom. I followed him into the darkening room, saw him point at a rain-spattered side window, and looked over his shoulder to see a matching window, blazing with light, in the house next door.

"I saw them," he mumbled, his head turned away. "I didn't mean to. I mean, I wasn't looking or anything. I just couldn't help but see them . . . kissing."

"*Who* kissing?" I demanded. Then with a sudden clearing of the mind, I said, "You

407

mean . . . *Mrs. Crawford*?"

"Yes'm," he said, plainly miserable, "and Mr. Nate."

"Oh, my Lord," I said, and would've sat down if there'd been a chair.

"Miss Julia, I wouldn't have looked if I'd known. I just walked back here to get my jacket to go home, and there they were right in front of the window. They didn't know I was here because I hadn't turned on any lights. And I don't want 'em to know."

"No, of course not, but didn't they notice your . . . ? Oh," I said, the light finally dawning, "you'd come on your bike, hadn't you?"

He nodded. "It was up against the porch. I guess they didn't see it."

"Oh, Lloyd," I said, putting my hand on his shoulder. "I'm so sorry that happened, but you know it's not your problem."

"Yes'm, I know, but it kinda feels like it is."

CHAPTER 45

Now, isn't that just the way it goes? Guilt by association, I guess, even when the association is as slight as having glanced through a window. I could feel a spark of indignation light up at the carelessness of the truly guilty parties. How dare they carry on like that where they could be seen? And be seen by an innocent who wouldn't know what to make of it?

Yet even though I was hardly an innocent, I didn't know what to make of it, either. How was I to help Lloyd lift the burden of feeling himself a peeping Tom or an informant or, heaven help us, somebody who was aiding and abetting by keeping silent? Or, if we turn it around, feeling that he was a tattletale or a gossipmonger if he told what he'd seen?

One of the things — well, one of the many things — I've learned about teenagers is that they have strong feelings about fairness. They recognize injustice as soon as they hear or see it. And they have difficulty just shrugging it off or accepting the fact that life, in general, is not fair. As somebody famous once said.

So I tried to ease Lloyd's sense of being an unwitting witness to a wrongful act by telling him that these things have a way of working themselves out, that he should try to put it out of mind, that some adults get in over their heads before they know it, and that it wasn't his problem to solve.

All of which were inadequate responses to his very real question of how he should handle what he had seen.

"Here's the thing, Lloyd," I said as we walked out of the back room and I immediately ran into a cabinet still sitting in the middle of the floor. Rubbing my thigh and limping a little, I went on. "There's nothing you can or should do. You're certainly not going to run tell Dr. Crawford, are you? And you're not going to go talk man to man with Mr. Nate, are you? And as for Mrs. Crawford, I'll tell you that she may already be suffering the pangs of guilt. The whole thing may be in the process of resolving itself, so all you have to do is to keep reminding yourself that it's not your business. You had nothing to do with starting it nor do you have anything to do with ending it."

"Yes'm, I guess so," he said. "But I feel better with somebody else knowing besides just me."

I could take some comfort in that, but of course the onus was now on me. What should I do about an extramarital affair between two people I knew? Taking the advice I'd just given to Lloyd, I reminded myself that it was none of my business. Not by any means, though, did that mean I approved of it.

In addition to knowing some things that Lloyd didn't — the main one being Lauren Crawford's questionable state of mind — I felt downright sick at heart. Being involved extramaritally would be enough to unsettle anybody — except, I reminded myself, somebody who felt above the law like Wesley Lloyd Springer, my late first husband. As far as I knew, he'd never had a qualm about breaking vows and carrying on in unseemly ways. Lauren Crawford, on the other hand, seemed to be having more qualms than she could easily handle.

If that was the case, it would certainly explain some, if not all, of her odd behavior. Which raised her in my estimation, for it showed that she was uneasy in the role of unfaithful wife.

But uneasy enough to plan her own funeral? My word, I could think of better ways to get out of an uncomfortable situation than to start specifying hymns and coffin covers! Of course, there are people — and I've known some — who are so particular that they plan all their social functions down to the type of script on the monogrammed paper towels in their guest bathrooms.

In other cases, though, the social functions of some slapdash women I've known seemed to have been thrown together at the last minute without forethought or writing out a dozen lists of things to do. Most socially minded women, however, and I admit to being one of them, make detailed plans far ahead of time — polish the silver and order floral arrangements the week before, write out a specific menu and a grocery list at the same time, arrange early for a thorough house cleaning, not forgetting the front porch and walkway, set the table the day before, and above all, discuss the details with Lillian a dozen times to be sure we weren't forgetting anything.

Now, I don't think that's being too particular when you entertain a group of critical and sharp-eyed women who will certainly talk about you if your silver is tarnished.

But I draw the line at being so detail-oriented as to make specific personal funeral arrangements, even though it would be your last social function. Making a good impression is important, I admit, but why should I care which hymns are sung — I won't hear them. So LuAnne could recommend pre-planning all she wanted to, I just wasn't that picky.

I couldn't, however, pass judgment on Lauren's attitude about entertaining guests, because as far as I knew, she hadn't entertained any, at least not in Abbotsville. So getting an unexpected glimpse of her personal life didn't help me understand her any better, although I could now see why she had been distracted enough to drive through a stop sign.

I made a mental note to remind Lloyd to be extra cautious if he found himself driving on the same street as she was.

All of these thoughts had been pinging around in my head as Lloyd and I locked the house, got in the Bonneville, and drove to his house, where I just sat for a minute watching sprinkles of rain dance on the windshield.

Lloyd turned off the engine, then, half under his breath, he said, "You think I ought to tell Mama?"

I thought for a minute. "No, not yet, anyway. Your mother is trying to be Mrs. Crawford's friend. She may have already invited her over for tea sometime in the next few days. Your mother would be very uncomfortable, knowing something like that, while trying to pretend that she didn't."

Lloyd managed a tiny smile. "My mother," he said, "doesn't like thinking anything bad about anybody."

"I know she doesn't. And that makes her one of the kindest of all the people I know. I think, for the time being at least, that the best thing for us to do is exactly what you've been doing — staying away from that house unless you have a car to park out front. Those two have been very careless, Lloyd. Who knows? You may not have been the only one to have seen them."

I opened the car door, started to swing my feet out, then turned back. "You know, after thinking it over, I'm going to change my mind about telling anyone. I think that as soon as your father comes home, you should tell him what you saw. He needs to know why you don't like being there by yourself, and, believe me, your father will understand. He is a man of the world and, as such, knows how to handle such matters."

Lloyd was silent for a minute, then he said, "I sure am glad you said that. I'd feel a whole lot better if he knew why I've been so slack."

"He'll understand," I said, repeating myself, but confident that if anybody would, it'd be J.D. Pickens. "But don't tell anybody else about it. Your mother, though, needs to know why we're so late, so tell her about the chicken truck and how we took a wrong turn, but I wouldn't mention the drug house — she'd just worry." I reached over and patted his arm. "It'll work out, Lloyd. I'll let you know what Coleman says, but now I've got to get home before Sam calls out the rescue squad. Sleep well tonight, honey. You've certainly had a day of it."

He walked me to my car in spite of the rain, where I waited until he got inside the house before pulling away from the curb. I'd urged Lloyd to tell no one but his father, but that didn't apply to me. I couldn't wait to get home so I could unload the events of the day on my patient Sam. And maybe on Lillian, too.

Not, I assure you, just to be the bearer of astonishing news, but to have help in knowing what to do about that news. If it had been about anybody but someone whom I already knew had problems, I would've perhaps shared it with Sam, who would've just shaken his head, then forgotten it. But Lauren Crawford was a different kettle of fish. Somehow, and I don't know how or why, Sam and I seemed to feel some responsibility for the young woman who was so obviously in deep trouble.

CHAPTER 46

"I was just before calling out the rescue squad," Sam said as soon as I walked into the kitchen at home. He was sitting at the table while Lillian dipped up supper at the stove.

"We was about to eat without you," she said, whacking a spoon against a pot. "You been worryin' us to death."

"Didn't Mildred call to tell you I'd be late?" I asked, quickly taking my place at the table. "I'm sorry, but Lloyd was anxious to do what his father told him to do, so we went to the Rosewood house. And on top of that, we'd already had a day of it. Here, Sam," I said, passing a basket to him, "have a biscuit."

"Long day, then?" Sam asked.

"I'd call it an interesting and surprising day, even a shocking one. A little scary, too." In fact, the day had been all that and more, and as I sat there staring at a full plate

417

before me, I didn't think I could eat a bite.

"Tell me," Sam said, putting his hand over mine.

So I did, prefacing my recitation with "Don't either of you breathe a word of this." Even though I'd already told Sam some of it, I started with the lunch I'd had with Lu-Anne, where she'd let slip what Lauren had been doing at the Good Shepherd Funeral Home. Then I launched into Mildred's announcement that she'd be more than twice as long at The Safe Harbor than usual, which left Lloyd and me nothing to do but drive around.

"And that's all I intended to do," I said, "but one thing led to another." I told them about being not only delayed, but blocked, by the overturned chicken truck, complete with a description of chicken feathers flying everywhere with some still stuck in various crevices of the Bonneville. I told them about our discovery of an abandoned house in the woods that offered the relief of one problem, but may have presented a more pressing one, which I planned to pass along to Coleman. Then I told them about Lloyd's admission that he wanted company while he uncrated kitchen cabinets at the Rosewood house, and while there, he'd revealed the reason that he hadn't wanted to be at the house alone in the first place.

"Something scare him over there?" Lillian asked with a worried frown. "That house been empty a long time, an' no tellin' who else been in it."

"Not that kind of scared, Lillian," I said, leaning my face on my hand. "Bless his heart, I hate to tell this, but he'd seen Mrs. Crawford and Mr. Wheeler when they thought no one else was around."

"Uh-oh," Sam said.

Lillian stopped and stared at me with her mouth open.

"That's why," I explained, "he didn't want to be there without a car parked out front — so they'd know someone was around. I declare, Sam, I didn't know what to say to him. I think I relieved his concern a little by encouraging him to tell his father, but not Hazel Marie since she'll be around Lauren and would feel uncomfortable with her. I hope that was the right thing to do.

"But," I went on before he could respond, "if Lauren's involved with Mr. Wheeler, that would certainly explain some of her strange behavior, like turning down invitations and driving like a wild woman and walking past without speaking and so on. But it doesn't explain planning a funeral."

"Unless," Sam said soberly, "it's all become too much for her and she sees only one way out."

"But those *children,* Sam," I said, near tears at the thought. "How could a mother . . . ?"

Sam took my hand. "She's fragile, honey. We don't know how long she's been under such a strain."

"Not all that long," Lillian said firmly. "They not been here more'n a few weeks. That's pretty quick to find somebody to fool around with."

Sam nodded. "That's true, but we don't know how much baggage she brought with her. Stress piled on top of stress can take you to the breaking point. But I guess I'm more surprised at Nate Wheeler. He doesn't strike me as the kind of man who'd interfere in a marriage."

"Huh," Lillian said, half under her breath. "That be any kind of man at all, you ast me. If he have half a chance."

"Well," I said, sitting back as I drew a deep breath, "we may be overlooking something. For all we know, what Lloyd saw was a onetime thing. Both of them may now be wallowing in shame because of that one lapse, and I wish I'd thought to tell Lloyd that. These things do happen, I guess, and it's up to the moral character of each one as to whether it progresses any further on the downward slope toward total chaos. And we don't know either of them well enough to be able to predict what, if anything, will be forthcoming, especially in the way of some climactic and very public denouement."

"Miss Julia," Lillian said, her hands on her hips, "I don't understand a word you say."

"Oh, well. All I meant is that we don't know how much has already happened or how much *will* happen. It could be all over or it could be just beginning. And I don't know that we can do a thing about it, whichever it is."

"Yes'm, an' that's the Lord's truth."

We left it at that because we had to. There was nothing we could do, and, as a result, my sympathy swung back and forth between a stressed and burdened young wife and her busy but oblivious husband. And I'll be fully truthful about this — my sympathy tended toward the husband, because I had once been the busy, oblivious, and totally blind party in another triangle.

I tried not to let that influence the way I felt, but it's hard not to draw parallels when you've been in a similar situation. But then there was Mr. Nate Wheeler to deal with.

None of us knew him well — just that he was a widower, fairly new to Abbotsville, unafraid of manual labor in spite of being well-off financially, handsome in the way that some men age well, for I would guess him in his early forties. Hm-m, Lauren's husband was some years her senior as well. Maybe she was attracted to older men.

But here was another thing — what if Dr. Don found out about his wife's new interest? What kind of explosion would ensue? How would he handle having been cuckolded — to use a Shakespearean word? Would he storm out of house, home, and medical practice? I couldn't answer that, either, but one thing was certain — Bob Hargrove's patients could be left holding the bag. Or up a tree, or in hot water, or something else equally perilous.

For the next day or so, my mind was so filled with what Lloyd had witnessed that almost everything else was pushed aside. I worried about him first of all, wondering if I had come across as too understanding of infidelity — offering excuses for inexcusable behavior. Maybe I should have expressed my disapproval of it in no uncertain terms. Teenagers, after all, tend to see things in black and white: This is right; that is wrong.

Yet as we age, hair is not the only thing that begins to fade into gray areas, and we find reasons and excuses for activities that we would have once condemned. "Thou shalt not" turns into "Under certain circumstances, maybe thou canst."

I found myself feeling comforted for having urged Lloyd to confide in his father, and that was as much of a surprise to me as anything else that had happened. Maybe Mr. Pickens was growing on me, but here's the thing — if anyone knew about adultery — whether as perpetrator or perpetratee — he was the one. Any man who was on his third — or was it his fourth? — wife had to be well schooled on the subject. Although let me quickly add that I had no reason, not even a tiny suspicion, that he was anything but totally committed to Hazel Marie. Maybe he'd aged out of fooling around, or maybe he'd finally grown up.

Be that as it may, my mind was easy for having sent Lloyd to him. It never hurts to hear from someone who knows whereof he speaks.

Besides, there were other things that I had allowed to lapse while worrying about things I could do nothing about. And the main one was that little amber vial that I rediscovered in the bottom of my pocketbook a couple of days later. How in the world had I overlooked doing something about that and the cabin in which it was found?

I took it out, held it up, and turned it around in the bright lights of the bathroom and tried to read the patient's name, the physician's name, or, barring both since they were unreadable, the name of the pharmacy where the prescription had once been filled. The label was scratched, torn, and smeared, and I would've thrown it away without another thought if Lloyd had not said that it was only one of several cast aside in the old house. And, of course, if he had not identified that house as a place of drug transactions.

So, with a worried glance at another mass of threatening clouds overhead, I took myself to the sheriff's office downtown on the other side of Main Street to put the vial in the hands of Sergeant Coleman Bates. That, at least, would be one thing I could do and have off my mind.

It didn't quite work out that way, for when I asked for Sergeant Bates at the front desk, I was told that he was in Washington, D.C., taking an advanced course in antiterrorism tactics with the F.B.I.

"Well," I said, impressed but somewhat

nonplused, "what about Lieutenant Peavey? May I speak with him?"

The officer at the desk pushed aside a stack of papers and said, "He retired a few years ago. Can I help you?"

"Well," I said again, not knowing quite what to do, "I hope you can." I held up the vial, then launched into telling him how and where it was found and, leaving Lloyd out of it entirely, how I was sure that I had stumbled upon a so-called drug house. "So," I concluded after describing its location, "I'm sure you'll want to watch the place and raid it just as soon as possible."

The officer, substantial in height and girth, stood up, took the vial from me, and turned it round and round as I had done, frowning thoughtfully as he did so.

"It's unreadable," I said. "I've already tried. Except I think the pharmacy is in South Carolina, so what it's doing up here, I don't know."

"Um-m," he said, squinching up his mouth. "We'll take your report under advisement. Thank you for coming in, Mrs. . . . ?"

"Murdoch," I said. "Mrs. Sam Murdoch, and you're quite welcome. I believe in supporting law and order."

"And we thank you for it," he said, an

indulgent smile playing across his face. "You can leave this with me and not worry about it one minute longer."

"And you'll take care of it?"

"Oh, yes, ma'am," he said. "Forthwith."

I turned away and left, feeling at first quite virtuous for doing my duty as a citizen. The memory of that smile, however, coupled with his "there, there" tone of voice stayed with me and, while waiting at a red light as a sprinkle of rain dotted the windshield, it suddenly hit me that I had been very kindly, but very thoroughly, patted on the head and sent on my way.

CHAPTER 47

Rain came down in buckets the rest of the day and all the next day and into the one that followed. Every evening during the local news, we learned the number of inches that had fallen, setting records all over the western end of the state. We heard reports of fallen trees, power outages, and, scariest of all, mud slides down mountainsides that blocked roads, even interstates, and flattened houses, cars, and trucks.

In between the downpours, the sun peeked out for a few minutes now and then, giving us a promise of better weather someday. It took a while, though, as the ground became soggier and soggier, and we began to think in terms of monsoon conditions. Lillian worried about the little stream that ran behind her house and through a couple of culverts before emptying into one of the tributaries of Little Mud Creek.

"That thing already up over the bank

now," she told me. "No tellin' when it come sloshing over everything."

"Stay over here anytime, Lillian," I said. "You shouldn't ever drive through water that's covering a street."

One good thing about the weather finally occurred to me — it was so miserable that surely a number of trysts would be put on hold. I mean, who wants to meet one's inamorato with dank, stringy hair?

Each morning I placed a call to Coleman, hoping that he had returned to duty. My intention was to hold that desk officer's feet to the fire, but Coleman remained in Washington. To get the whole matter off my mind, I even called Binkie to ask her to tell Coleman when she spoke to him, but she was in court, seemingly from sunup till sundown, so I was stymied every way I turned. And the image of that little amber vial — evidence in my mind of local drug activity — kept nudging me to do something.

Sam tried soothing me with a reminder that the wheels of justice were notoriously slow, but that didn't help. Plus, he had something to look forward to and I didn't. He and Mr. Pickens were planning a day trip to Charlotte to visit a large wholesale warehouse, where they intended to buy at cut-rate prices all the appliances and fixtures needed for the Rosewood house. And to save on outrageous shipping charges to load them into a rented truck and bring them home.

But I, kept in by the rain, resorted to fiddling with the jigsaw puzzle again just to occupy myself with something. That pastime didn't last long. So, after turning on every overhead light and every lamp downstairs, trying to lighten both the house and my mood, I found myself wishing that Mildred would need a driver again. She didn't, for Horace was now home and she was busy hovering. A new Lincoln Town Car waited in their four-car garage, but Horace refused to walk the few steps to go see it. Mildred couldn't understand his obstinacy.

"Because," she complained to me, "I haven't even sold the Boxster yet. It's still sitting right out there where it's always been, but I guess to him that Town Car is like the handwriting on the wall. He says if I sell his precious car, he just won't drive at all. Which, to look at it from the bright side, is one way to get him to follow doctor's orders."

"Oh, Mildred," I said, soothingly, "I hope it doesn't come to that. He's been through a lot these past few weeks. Maybe he needs to have something to look forward to, don't you think?"

"Not if it means he drives that tin can with rockets on it. He could kill himself, Julia, and somebody else, too. Because I'll tell you this, Horace's memory is just about shot. He asks me a dozen times a day where his Boxster is, and can't even remember after I've taken a picture of it sitting right out there in the garage."

"Well, I've heard of memory problems after having certain health issues. I expect it'll improve after a while."

"I certainly hope so," Mildred said. "I'm getting tired of telling him a dozen times a day that Ida Lee is not his sister."

Knowing Ida Lee as well as I did, I couldn't help but think that Horace should've been so lucky. But I also couldn't help but sympathize with him and with Mildred. He for having to put up with her, and her for vice versa.

After hearing the daily report on Horace's health and the general state of their marriage, I was even more thankful for Sam than I normally was.

But of course listening to Mildred's litany of complaints brought to mind a problem much closer to home. Not that I had a problem, but I feared that Sam did. Just the previous evening as we'd finished supper, Sam turned in his chair to get to his feet, and I saw a grimace of pain flash across his face.

"Are you all right?" I asked, immediately concerned.

"Just a twinge," he said. "I'm fine now." And, indeed, he seemed so, for he moved easily away from the table, thanked Lillian for the meal, then went on to the library with no other indication that his back was preparing to act up again.

Turning to follow him, I passed the telephone just as it rang, so I answered it.

"J.D. Pickens here," the caller announced. "I'm calling to thank you for steering Lloyd in the right direction."

As usual, his abrupt manner unnerved me, so it took a minute for me to respond. "He's spoken to you, then?"

"He has. Good move on your part. Tell Sam I'll pick him up about eight in the morning."

That was apparently all he had to say as he ended the call, leaving me to thank the Lord that I'd done something right. To please Mr. Pickens is a remarkable feat for anyone, especially me, and I went on into the library with a lighter step.

"That was your driver," I told Sam. "He'll

be by around eight in the morning." Mr. Pickens's plan was to rent a box truck, drive the two or so hours to Charlotte, load the truck with everything from the commode to the kitchen sink, then drive back — all in one day and at fire-sale savings.

"I wanted Lloyd to go with us," Mr. Pickens had told Sam, "to teach him the value of price shopping. But he's got school and the weekend's out for me. And we've got to get that house done. It's costing money."

So on that drizzling, foggy Friday, Mr. Pickens came by to pick up Sam, not at the early hour planned, but closer to noon. I declare, the man had good intentions but not much of a sense of timing. He should've gotten the rental truck the day before instead of waiting until the morning they planned to leave.

"I expect we'll be late getting back," Sam told me as I walked out on the porch to see them off. "That truck probably won't go over fifty. So don't worry about us. I'll call you when we're heading back."

"All right," I said, "but don't you be lifting or moving anything. You're just going to keep him company, not to throw your back out again."

He grinned and assured me that he'd be

fine. "Just company," he said. "Nothing else."

And off they went.

Later that afternoon, I stood at the living-room window watching rainwater drip from the eaves, trying to determine if I should call Dr. Crawford for a refill of Sam's prescription. Only as a precaution, you understand, because the weekend was upon us and I did not want to interfere with the doctor's time off. I could safely get a refill of that powerful medication to have on hand in case Sam had a relapse, yet easily be rid of it by donating it to the mission field if he did not. Win, win, I thought. If Sam didn't need it, it would go to someone far afield who did.

Turning away from the window, I wandered into the library, looked over the puzzle, then sat down to read the newspaper. That lasted just long enough to put me to sleep for a rainy afternoon nap. Finally waking, but still feeling groggy, I gravitated to the kitchen where Lillian sat at the table turning the pages of a movie magazine.

"You want some coffee?" she asked, preparing to rise.

"No, don't get up. I just want somebody to talk to." I sat at the table, too. "I'm glad

433

you're spending the night. I need the company. You're sure Latisha is being picked up?"

"Yes'm, she going home with the choir director's little girl. They say they gonna play Barbies all day an' all night, an' Miz Mabry say she bring her here after lunch tomorrow."

"Well, good. I just wish that Sam wasn't on the road in this weather, especially after getting such a late start. To say nothing," I continued with a sigh, "of worrying about the one he's going with."

"Oh, Mr. Pickens, he's all right. They be fine, Miss Julia, but I wouldn't look for 'em to be back till real late. In fact, I jus' been settin' here thinkin' 'bout what to fix for supper that'll still be good at 'leven or twelve o'clock tonight."

"Nothing, Lillian, don't fix anything. Let's just eat a sandwich or leftovers tonight. I'll scramble some eggs for Sam if he gets in that late."

When the phone rang, I motioned to Lillian to sit still. I was closer, so I answered it, listened, then pressed the phone closer to my ear. "What?" I said, responding to the voice whispering against a background of shouts and running feet. "Say that again."

So he did.

CHAPTER 48

"School just got out," Lloyd said, whispering hoarsely, "and I don't want anybody to hear me. I need to talk to you. Will you be home? It's important."

"Why, yes, of course. You want me to come get you — it's raining out there."

"No'm, I rode my bike today. I'll be there in a little while." And he hung up. Or punched off.

"What in the world?" I asked the world in general, but only Lillian replied.

"Who you talkin' to?" she asked, closing the magazine.

"That was Lloyd, calling to see if I'm home. He's never done that before. He just comes by when he wants to." I frowned, sat at the table again, and wondered what was so important that he had to whisper, then ride a bicycle in the rain to tell about it. "I hope he won't catch cold," I mumbled.

"He'll be hungry," Lillian said, getting to her feet to prepare an after-school snack.

"Thanks, Miss Lillian," Lloyd said, looking at the peanut butter and jelly sandwich, cut into little squares as Lillian always served it. "But I can't eat anything right now."

He sat at the table, after having shed his raincoat on the porch. His hair, still damp from the ride, glistened from the overhead lights.

"What's going on, Lloyd?" I asked, sitting at the table and leaning toward him.

"Well-l," he said and began contorting his face and canting his head toward Lillian. "Maybe . . . the library?"

"It's all right," I said, thinking that perhaps he'd heard some gossip at school about a certain married lady — a highly likely occurrence, given how fast rumors of misconduct flew around town. "Lillian knows."

"Whew," he said, "that's good. I need all the help I can get. Listen, it's like this. Word's out all over school that there's gonna be a party tonight — at the *happy house.* That's what they call it — the happy house. And I *know* it's the empty house we found, Miss Julia. It has to be."

"Oh, my goodness," I said, patting my chest. "Lloyd, are you sure? It could be

436

anybody's house, and a perfectly nice party."

"No'm," he said, shaking his head, "because I asked Leigh Swanson. She didn't want to tell me, 'cause if you're in, you just *know*. But I'm not, so I didn't. She finally told me it's off Staton Mill Road, out in the woods, and nobody lives there or anywhere around it. So, see, it has to be the one we found. She said it's safe because nobody knows about it, and I could go with her if I want to, but I don't. Except I don't know what else to do."

"Leigh Swanson," I said, turning the name around in my mind. "Wasn't she one of your dates to the dance?"

"Yes'm, and she's a nice girl, but she likes to be in on everything just to, you know, have a good time. So I'm thinking I ought to go and be sure she stays out of trouble."

"Uh-huh," Lillian said, "an' that's a good way for both of you to get *in* trouble."

"And anyway, Lloyd," I said, "you can't be sure it's the same house. There must be an untold number of abandoned houses out that way. But even if it is, what makes a house happy, anyway? Music? Dancing? Some boys bringing beer? Surely there'll be some adults there."

"Miss Julia," he said as if explaining to a child, "drugs. There'll be *drugs* there."

"Oh, my goodness," I said, drawing back. "Are you sure? How do they get drugs? Where do they come from?"

"I told you, remember? I told you about all the prescription bottles strewn around. Like the one I gave you."

"Yes, but where did they come from? How do they get there?"

"Well," Lloyd said, "I guess some of 'em come from medicine cabinets at home, and —"

"The one you gave me came from a drugstore in South Carolina. How'd it get up here?"

"Probably," he said, "because somebody had it to sell. I guess, 'cause I've never been to a party like that."

"And I hope," I said, "that you *never* go to one. The *idea,* selling drugs to children! Oh, I hope the sheriff's planning to put a stop to it."

"But, see, that's why I'm worried about Leigh. She just likes to be a part of everything. Anything exciting, I mean. She doesn't use drugs, but that won't mean anything if there's a raid. She'll be rounded up with the rest of 'em. And if she is, she'll never get in Chapel Hill."

"And neither will you," I said sharply, "if you're rounded up with her. No, Lloyd, you should stay away from that party. Anyway, how's Leigh going to get there? She's not old enough to drive, is she?"

"A bunch of girls're going together. Stacy O'Connor is a senior and she has a car. Leigh said if I had my license, I could drive 'em and be their security guard." Lloyd drew in his breath. "She laughed about that, but I wish I could, 'cause then I would drive around and get lost and not find that house till the party was over."

"Lloyd," Lillian said, as she put her hand on his arm, "some people jus' can't be helped. They won't let you."

"I know," he said miserably, "but Leigh's a smart girl and a good girl. She just doesn't have a lick of common sense."

"Well," I said, "this may help or it may not, but you know I turned that prescription bottle in at the sheriff's office. Coleman is out of town, but the desk sergeant assured me that they would take care of it. I told him where we'd found it, so he knows about the house. Now, whether they'll raid it tonight or not, I don't know. But the very possibility of it might help to discourage Leigh from going.

"And here's another thing. Everybody knows your father's in law enforcement, so if you tell the girls you've heard there might be a raid, they'll think you really know something. That may be enough to keep them away. Tell them they'd be better off going to a movie."

"I guess," Lloyd said, but he wasn't convinced. "I just wish I had my license. I wouldn't drive them, but I'd go out there and park somewhere out of sight. Then if there's trouble, I could get them out."

"You're a good friend, Lloyd," I said, appreciating his concern, "but if those girls won't listen to reason, there's not much you can do. Just be available, I guess, in case they come to their senses. They might still decide to go to a movie."

He gave me a smile, but it was a little wobbly. "Yes'm, maybe so. Anyway, Leigh said she'd call me if she needs anything. I think she thinks I'd get J.D. to help her out, and I would."

"No," I said, shaking my head, "not tonight, you wouldn't. He and Sam went to Charlotte and probably won't be back till midnight or later."

As it turned out, it was later. Sam called as Lillian and I finished a supper of pancakes and sausage — the perfect meal for a damp, chilly evening, although a little of that goes a long way. Especially when your stomach is already roiling with worry.

"Julia, honey," Sam had said, "looks like we're stuck here for the night. That truck Pickens rented blew a gasket on our way out of town. To make it worse, it's loaded to the gills with appliances, bathroom fixtures, and I-don't-know-what-all, so we have to wait till morning to get another truck. And to get some help moving everything from one to the other."

"You're not sleeping in the truck, are you?"

He laughed. "Not quite that bad. We were able to limp into a Quality Inn and have a place to park. I'll call you in the morning when we get moving again."

Briefly considering telling him my concern for Lloyd's friends, I decided that it would only make me feel better while distressing him. Time enough to lay it all out when he returned.

So I commiserated with him for having truck trouble, told him to be careful, and to hurry home because I missed him.

CHAPTER 49

Just saying that I missed him was an understatement of the first order. After hearing about Leigh Swanson and a number of other young girls — all from good families and friends of Lloyd — blithely putting themselves in harm's way, I longed for Sam's farsighted wisdom.

"I won't sleep a wink tonight," I told Lillian. "I can't get over the thought of those foolish girls, thinking that going to a drug party will be exciting and fun — when it's more likely to be their ruination."

"Maybe," she said, "it'll keep on rainin' an' they get stuck somewhere, an' won't none of 'em get to go."

"I'd call that a divine intervention, but I can't count on it. I'm just hoping that they'll heed Lloyd's warning of a possible raid. The thing about it, though, is that I don't know whether I should hope there *will* be a raid or that there won't. I certainly don't want any of Lloyd's friends to get arrested, but then again, I do want whoever's selling drugs not just to get arrested, but to be put away somewhere for good.

"And I'll tell you this, Lillian," I went on, "I don't know why in the world the sheriff hasn't cleared that place out already. I *told* them exactly what was going on and gave them explicit directions. They should've done something by now."

"If I had to guess," Lillian said solemnly, "I'd guess there won't be no raid tonight. Policemans don't like to get soaked to the skin any more than anybody else. I bet they'll wait for better weather."

"You may be right. And, meanwhile, kids — practically babies where good sense is concerned — will be taking that noxious stuff and getting addicted and ruining their lives. I'd like to get my hands on whoever's doing the selling."

"Miss Julia," Lillian said, "can't nobody sell 'less somebody wantin' to buy."

"Well, that's certainly the truth, so I guess I'd like to get my hands on those silly kids and shake some sense into them. In the meantime" — I stopped as a yawn overtook me — "we might as well go to bed. I'm just glad that Lloyd can't drive at night. We don't have to worry about him at least."

■ ■ ■ ■

My eyes popped open, and I lay there not knowing what had wakened me — until the phone rang again. Reaching for it in the dark, my mind darted from Sam to Lloyd to Mildred to who knows who else. As my hand scrambled for the phone, the bedside clock registered 1:33, and I thought, "A.M.? Who's calling in the middle of the night?"

"Miss Julia!" Lloyd whispered before I got hello out of my mouth. "Come let me in. I'm downstairs."

"What?"

"I'm at the back door. Come let me in."

Half befuddled, I threw off the covers, grabbed my robe, and ran barefooted out the door and down the stairs. Images of Hazel Marie and her babies in various states of mishap ran through my mind.

As soon as I released both locks on the door, Lloyd rushed in, shedding water as he came. "Leigh's in trouble, Miss Julia. She just called me. Can we go get her? I mean, I'd ask Mama, but we'd have to take my sisters and that wouldn't be good. Do you mind? Can we go get her?"

"Well, wait. Wait now, where is she?"

"She's at that house, and she doesn't have

a way home. The girl who drove them is out like a light, and she said everybody's acting crazy, and she's scared. She really is, Miss Julia, she started crying, and said she'd try to walk out but she's scared to do that, too. Please, can we go get her?"

Lloyd was shaking nervously so that the full raincoat he was wearing dribbled water on the floor. "Sorry," he said, "it's not raining bad. I just ran into a soaked boxwood in the dark."

Before I could answer, Lillian, wearing what looked like a flannel tent, burst in, asking, "What happened? Anybody hurt? Lloyd, you all right?"

So he started through it again, but, trying to decide what to do, I interrupted. "Was there a raid?"

"No'm. Leigh said she almost wished there was one. It'd be a good way to get home."

"I guess so," I said, right smartly, "with a stop at the jail on the way. But we have to go get her, I guess, unless . . . let me think. Deputies could get out there quicker than we can. If she's in real trouble, we ought to call them."

"No, Miss Julia, don't do that. She could've called them or her parents if she'd wanted to. She doesn't want anybody to know — she said her parents'll kill her. Let's us just go, okay? Can we?"

I looked at Lillian. "Lillian?"

"If it was Latisha," she said, "I'd want somebody to go."

"Let's get some clothes on, then." Halfway out of the room, I turned back. "What about your mother, Lloyd? Does she know what you're doing?"

"Ah, well, no'm. But I left a note on my pillow." He swallowed hard, then said, "We'll be back before she wakes up. I hope." Then holding up his phone, he went on. "Hurry, Miss Julia. I'm talking to Leigh, trying to keep her calm, but she's afraid somebody'll hear her. She's hiding in the bathroom now."

That filthy bathroom?

"Tell her," I said, "that we're on the way. And tell her to get out of there and start walking toward the highway — in the trees alongside the dirt lane."

By the time I got upstairs, I was shaking with nerves as badly as Lloyd had been. I couldn't decide how to dress — everything appropriate would take too long to put on — so I stuck my feet in a pair of rubber boots, slung Sam's long, heavy raincoat over my gown, and called to Lillian that I was ready to go.

She clattered down the stairs behind me, half dressed with a jacket over her gown. "Law," she said, "I hope don't nobody see us lookin' like this."

Snatching up my pocketbook from the counter, I rushed out behind Lloyd and Lillian to the car, where the two of them had a Keystone Kop moment about who would sit in the front seat. She insisted that he should and finally settled it by getting in the backseat and refusing to budge.

As soon as I cranked the car, Lloyd put his phone on speaker and, if I'd not been anxious before, I would've been then. Leigh's whispered voice came through, though almost drowned out by thumping music. "Hurry, Lloyd, please hurry. I don't know if I can get out without somebody seeing me, and from the way they're acting, I don't know what they'll do."

"Listen, Leigh," Lloyd said as calmly as a 911 operator, although I could see his hand shaking, "just walk out the back door like you know what you're doing. If anybody stops you, tell 'em you can't use that bathroom and you're going outside. Tell 'em you'll be back in a minute. Tell 'em anything, but get out. Then run to the trees and start walking. Just don't walk out in the open. You want to stay hidden in case somebody besides us comes driving in."

"But, Lloyd," she said, "how will I know if it's you? Are you in your car?"

"No, we're in a black sedan. It's a big one."

"Oh, me," she moaned, "there's a bunch of big, black sedans out here."

Lloyd looked at me as I sped down the empty street toward the turnoff to Staton Mill Road. "How will she know it's us?" he asked, and held the phone close to my face.

"Tell her," I said, "that once we turn in on the dirt lane, we'll stop every few yards and blink our lights."

Lloyd spoke into the phone. "Leigh? You hear that?"

"Yes, okay," Leigh said, with a slight hiccup. "Don't say anything else, Lloyd, till I get outside. Somebody might hear that I've got my phone on."

"That's good, Leigh," he said. "Turn it off and put it in your pocket. Then walk out with your head high. If anybody says anything to you, tell 'em you have a call of nature or something."

I heard Leigh giggle, but it had a nervous tinge to it. "I'll tell 'em," she said, "to fix me a drink, 'cause I'll have room for it when I get back."

"Yeah," Lloyd said, "that's good. Play

along with 'em. And talk to me once you're in the trees."

By this time, I'd turned onto Staton Mill Road and was heading along the familiar route toward The Safe Harbor. There was hardly any traffic, so I'd done a few moving stops at the stop signs on our way out of town — realizing that I wasn't setting a good example, but doing them anyway.

The highway looked slick, but it was moonlight shining on an already wet surface. Looking up, I glanced at the clouds drifting across the moon and hoped that they would keep drifting. A downpour was the last thing we needed. We tooled along at a good clip, finally passing The Safe Harbor looking lonely up there on its knoll with only the entrance and the office windows lit and a few security lights casting a yellow glow on the grounds.

"Slow down, Miss Julia," Lloyd said as he sat up to watch for the turnoff. "We ought to be pretty close."

I almost missed it, but the leaning mailbox caught my eye, so I braked hard and made the turn, bouncing from the highway onto the dirt lane. The first thing I noticed was the squishy surface of the lane from the heavy rains and the next thing was the deep ruts from recent traffic.

Guiding the car into the ruts and gripping the steering wheel tightly, I mentally shut my eyes to the possibility of getting stuck. Surely not, I told myself, not with this heavy car, unworn tire treads, and powerful engine. A few yards in, I stopped, opened our windows, and blinked the lights once. The three of us waited, watched, and listened, but all we heard was the wind swishing through the tops of the pine trees.

"Leigh?" Lloyd said into his phone. "Where are you? Can you hear me?" After a few seconds of silence, he said, "Go a little further in, Miss Julia. Maybe she still has her phone off."

"I just thought of something," I said. "You think our lights can be seen from the house?"

"I thought of that, too," Lillian said.

"Well, I have to have lights," I said, turning the beams to low as I eased the car along. "We might end up in the trees if I don't. Maybe they'll think we're latecomers to the party."

Lloyd grunted as he leaned out the window holding the phone to his ear. "Leigh? We're here. Watch for us. Leigh, where are you?"

Still stopping every few yards to look, listen, and blink the lights, we had driven well past the halfway point of the lane, and now we could see the glow of lights from the house and hear the beat of something called music, but wasn't.

"I'm afraid to get any closer," I said, slowing to a stop. "We'll be in the yard before long." I blinked the headlights once, then turned off all but the fog lamps.

We sat in silence — except for the low rumble of the motor, the sound of the windshield wipers, and the pattering of rain on the roof as we strained to see through the darkness around us.

"I don't know what to do," Lloyd said, an edge of panic in his voice. "Maybe I ought to get out —" He was cut off by a dark object flying out of the woods and thumping against the car.

"Lloyd! Lloyd, is it you?" A stringy-haired girl pulled herself along my side of the car, crying and mewling like a kitten. Both Lillian and I opened our doors, grabbed her, and shoved her and her mud-caked shoes into the backseat.

"Are you all right?" Lloyd demanded as he leaned over from the front seat. "Leigh, say something! Are you all right?"

"Yeah," she said, sitting up and brushing hair from her face. "I lost my phone, dropped it somewhere. My dad's gonna kill me."

"Shoo," Lloyd said, breathing out with relief, "you had us worried to death. Let's get outta here, Miss Julia."

Which created a brand-new problem — there was no easy way to get out of there. The lane was too narrow to turn around in, and I'd never backed up more than a few feet in my life, and each time had ended in disaster. Now there was at least a slippery quarter mile of muddy ruts between us and the highway, and I was faced with getting us there, back end first and in a night that was as black as pitch.

CHAPTER 50

"Let's go," Lloyd urged, peering through the windshield toward the lights of the house. "I don't like it here."

"Me, neither," Lillian said.

I didn't like it any better than they did, but I wasn't eager to begin driving a half mile backward, either. But I shifted into reverse and twisted around to look out the rear window. All I could see was a couple of feet of muddy ground, glowing red as I tapped the brakes. Everything behind us was in darkness for clouds had moved in, covering the moon. The glare from the raucous house reflected off the clouds, but that was in front of us, not behind.

"Watch for me, Lloyd," I said, as he leaned out his window. "If I can stay in the ruts, we'll be all right."

"Yes'm, keep going, keep going. Hold on, not too fast."

So I drove backward not by sight but by

feel, thankful for the deep ruts that kept the car in the middle of the lane. Lillian and Leigh huddled in the backseat, fearful, I supposed, that any talking would distract me from our slow and careful progress. Or, rather, our inch-by-inch regress.

"Whoa!" Lloyd yelped, ducking back into the car as the back end slid out of the rut and the car slewed to the right.

I overcorrected, making the back end swivel toward the ditch on the left. Lifting my foot from the accelerator, I tried to figure out which was the opposite way to turn to get us back in the ruts.

"You want to drive, Lloyd?" I asked, more than ready to yield the wheel. "You've had some practice in backing up."

"No'm," he said, shaking his head, "not that much."

"Lillian? What about you?"

"You doin' fine, Miss Julia," she said. "I jus' as soon you keep on."

Leigh leaned toward the front seat. "I prob'bly could. I've had driver's ed."

Nobody said anything, although several things occurred to me. I contented myself with a simple, "Thanks anyway, but I'll manage."

Then Lloyd sat straight up, stared through

the dark windshield, and whispered, "Listen!"

With all our windows down, the noise was unmistakable — shouts, yells, car doors opening and closing, loud laughter.

"That party's over," Lillian said. "They all goin' home, an' comin' this way."

Leigh moaned. "They're gonna think I reported them."

"Hold on," Lloyd said, opened his door, stepped out, and surveyed the back end. "Turn the wheel to the left, Miss Julia, just a tad. And ease up on the gas — just a little."

Although I was as blind as a bat, I did as he said, and felt the car slide back into the rut. Easing off before it swerved to the other side, I straightened the wheel and began a slow reverse again.

"Get back in, Lloyd," I called, fearing he would be hit if the car slid again.

"Keep going, keep going," he called back, then jumped the ditch and disappeared. In seconds — during which we might've gone a few feet — he was back in the car. "There's a clearing on the right," he said. "Maybe an old homeplace 'cause the ditch is covered over. It's rough, but let's back in there and wait 'em out."

"Are you sure?" I asked, as visions flashed through my mind of half the car sinking into a ditch or of scraping over stumps hidden in weeds.

"Pretty sure," he said, "but we're not gonna make the highway. Hear that?"

Engines were revving up, more car doors slammed shut, and louder voices echoed — all coming from the happy house.

Lloyd opened the door again and jumped out. "We've got to get off this road. Come on, Miss Julia, I'll guide you. Back on up, it's not far."

I began to back the car again, knowing that we had no choice, but praying, *Oh, Lord, don't let me hit him* and *Don't let us get stuck* over and over.

"Okay," Lloyd called from across the ditch. "Now turn to the right — not too sharp — and give it a little gas." I did until he yelled, "Straighten up, straighten up!" I did that, too, and felt the wheels bump over the rut and edge backward across the ditch, as the swish of weeds against the undercarriage told me we were moving off the road. Briars, small shrubs, and tree branches snapped and scraped against the car, and I wondered what a new paint job was going to cost.

"Okay," Lloyd said as he hopped back into the car. "Now go straight back real slow, and we'll be in the trees. There's an old chimney behind us, so we're in what was somebody's yard. Turn off the lights. All of 'em, and we'll wait 'em out."

Then, "Whup!" he said as I backed into something solid and came to an abrupt stop. "That's far enough."

I turned off the motor and the lights, and felt the night close in around us. The four of us sat in total darkness, watching the lane and hoping we were far enough in to be hidden from passing cars. Headlights began moving, casting beams through the trees, and soon we were watching a parade of cars heading for Staton Mill Road. Most were full of young people, going too fast for the lane conditions, as tires spun and slithered and spattered mud from one car to another.

Lloyd murmured, "It's already a sloppy mess — hope we can get out."

We sat listening as the eighth or maybe the ninth car — I'd lost count — passed us, then to the roar of engines as they gained the pavement of Staton Mill Road. Darkness and silence descended, and still we waited, none of us eager to commit to the lane again.

As the roar of one last car faded away, Lloyd said, "Maybe that's all of 'em. Hold on a minute." He opened his door, stepped out, and walked to the lane. Even though half blinded by the interior lights when the door opened, we were able to see his outline as he stood listening and looking in the direction of the house.

After a few minutes Lloyd returned to the car. Getting back in, he said, "I can't see even a glow of light from the house. I think they're gone. Let's get out of here."

"Lloyd," Leigh said as she pulled herself toward the front seat, "I don't think I saw Stacy's car, and I was watching for it. What if they left her?"

"Oh, good grief," he said. "Didn't a bunch of y'all come together? They wouldn't just leave her."

"I know, but . . . well, it got kinda crazy after a while, and, well, I guess they could've."

"In other words," I said with a sinking heart, "they might've."

Nobody said anything for many minutes, wondering as I was of whether to turn left toward the highway and home, or to turn right toward the house and who-knew-what we'd find.

"Miss Julia," Lillian said, using a certain tone that told me what I should do. I recognized it because I'd heard it many times before.

"All right," I said, cranking the car and

cringing at the noise it made in the quiet night. "We'll go see about Stacy. Fasten your seat belts. We're not out of the woods yet."

Truer words were never spoken, for I knew I'd have some explaining to do tomorrow when Sam saw my scratched and dented car. To say nothing of the clumps of mud tracked in on the spotless carpet, front and back, of the foot wells.

The lane was indeed a sloppy mess, as Lloyd had predicted, but a lot can be said for having a heavy car with wide tires and — I must admit — a by-now-experienced mud driver.

Our high beams swept the house and the heavily rutted yard as I pulled in and circled to park headed out. I let the motor idle and turned to Leigh in the backseat.

"No cars," I said with some relief, "so everybody's gone. Stacy is well on her way home. Okay, Leigh?"

"Um, I don't know," Leigh said, pulling herself toward the front seat. "She wasn't in any shape to drive when I left."

"Well," I said, almost at my wit's end, "wouldn't somebody else drive Stacy's car? With her in it?"

"Her sister, maybe. But they could've forgotten her. They were all pretty much wasted."

I wanted to bury my face in despair at the thought of what illicit drugs could do even to the natural bond of sisters. Sighing, I asked, "Where was she when you last saw her?"

"I'm not real sure," she said, then, "asleep in a corner somewhere, I think. But there're only four rooms, so . . ."

"Then we'd better go look," I said, dreading the thought. But as I started to get out, a mental light suddenly dawned. "I just realized something. This place has electricity, so it's not as abandoned as we thought. What if somebody sees the house lights come on again?"

"They already seen our car lights," Lillian pointed out, "if anybody's lookin'."

"Yeah," Lloyd said. "But we don't have to turn the house lights on. I mean we could use our phone lights, but that'll take longer — beams aren't that wide."

"I wish y'all would make up your mind," Lillian said. "I don't like it out here."

I scrambled to the bottom of my pocketbook, found my phone, and handed it back to Leigh.

"I don't know how to turn the light on, so you use it. But don't lose it." I opened my door and stepped out. "Lloyd, you and

Leigh come on. We'll go in, sweep the rooms, and get out."

"Well, I'm not stayin' out here by myself," Lillian said, opening the back door and lifting herself out.

I couldn't blame her, so the four of us walked up onto the porch, opened the front door, and crowded inside.

"Watch out!" Lloyd yelled, lunging to catch himself as something clattered on the floor. Phone lights danced wildly across the walls and ceiling.

"Oh, for goodness' sake," I said, knowing that we'd already been seen if anyone was looking. I swept my hand over the wall, feeling for a light switch. A dim yellow bulb, hanging from the ceiling, came on, revealing the remains of the kind of social to which no self-respecting Abbotsville lady would ever lend herself and her good name. Glass bottles, beer cans, pizza boxes, and an untold number of small amber vials were strewn across the floor, making every step hazardous.

"Pick your way through," I said to Lloyd, "and be careful. Switch on a light in each room, check it thoroughly, then switch off before going to the next. Leigh, I'll take my phone now. And," I went on as they turned for the next room, "don't forget to check the bathroom. If you find Stacy, call us and we'll get her out. Lillian, stay here with me. I don't want you tripping and falling on this stuff."

Leigh handed the phone to me as she and Lloyd left to survey the other rooms. I looked at the thing, fiddled with it for a few seconds, and wished I'd read the instructions.

"Gimme that," Lillian said, reaching for it. "What you tryin' to do? Call the sheriff?"

"No, I'm trying to figure out how to take pictures. The sheriff already knows about this place, and now I want to show him the proof."

"Well, that's easy enough. You jus' point an' click, like this." And Lillian began pointing and clicking away. "What all you want me to get?"

"Everything. Get some wide-angle shots of the room, then get close-ups of this stuff on the floor. The more and the closer the better."

Hearing Lloyd and Leigh move into a back room, I said, "Let's go to the kitchen." Moving carefully through the debris, we met them in the kitchen. I knew it was the kitchen because it had a rust-stained sink hanging from the wall and a rickety table in one corner — the only stick of furniture

462

except for old blankets and pallets that I'd seen in the place.

"Lloyd," I said as he and Leigh entered, "take close-up pictures of what's on that table." I pointed at a basket, some wadded papers, a couple of Corona beer bottles, and some amber vials. "I guess you didn't find Stacy?"

"No'm," he said, aiming his phone toward the rubble on the table. "Nobody's here but us."

Lillian was leaning over a corner of the kitchen, clicking away at a pile of rubbish. "I wish," she said, "*no*body was here, includin' us."

"Then let's go." I waited as they filed out of the kitchen, then switched off overhead lights as I followed them out onto the porch. Closing the door behind me, I huddled with them for a minute before we felt our way down the steps. The wind had gotten stronger, blowing rain with every gust, so we hurried to the car, locking the doors with one accord.

Lloyd's head snapped up as he fastened his seat belt. *"Listen!"* he whispered.

I had the key poised for insertion, but stopped as the deep, heavy rumble of a motor seemed to fill the desolate space around the cabin.

"Where's that comin' from?" Lillian whispered, as a chill crept down my back.

"From the back," Lloyd said. "Must be a back way in. Roll up the windows and let's go."

The heavy rumble was coming closer and getting louder. Leigh whimpered.

My hand was trembling, but I got the key inserted, then just as I turned the ignition, the whole world lit up with a blinding light. Beams from two large headlights, higher than normal, slashed through the rear window, hurting our eyes and putting us all on full display.

Covering her eyes, Lillian screamed and Lloyd said a bad word. Leigh flung herself to the floor.

"They seen us!" Lillian wailed.

"What is it?" Leigh moaned. "What is it?"

Lloyd, shielding his eyes, as he looked back at what was practically on top of us, said, "A pickup! A big one. Go, Miss Julia, *go*!"

I stomped on the gas pedal. The motor roared, working up to a high-pitched scream, but the car didn't move. I couldn't believe it.

"Put it in gear!" Lloyd yelled.

I did, and the car leaped like a jet taking off straight up. It was all I could do to tame the thing and aim for the lane. The chewed-up mud on the lane brought me back to earth, and I eased off the gas, but not before the heavy car slithered back and forth, slinging mud from both sides.

And still the bright beams of the pickup were right on top of us.

"Go slow, Miss Julia," Lloyd murmured. "Go slow. Don't want to end up in a ditch."

"Right, okay," I said, calmed by his easy tone. Concentrating on keeping the car on an even keel, I tried to ignore the blinding lights. It helped to twist the rearview mirror out of the glare.

"What's he trying to do, Lloyd?" I asked, glancing at him. "Run us off or run us down?"

"No telling." Lloyd's hand was gripping the armrest so hard that I could see his white knuckles.

Just as we reached what I figured was the halfway point of the lane, our front wheels suddenly dipped into a crevice. Giving it a little more gas, I felt the car pull out, spattering mud as it did. Mentally thanking German engineers much too soon, I felt and heard the rear wheels sink into the same fault, and stay there. I pushed gently on the gas and leaned forward to urge the car to pull itself out. The wheels spun, slinging mud all over the place, but the car didn't move.

"Oh, Lord!" Lillian cried. "We're stuck!"

"It's okay," I said, trembling. "We'll get out. Just give me a minute."

The fact of the matter was that I didn't know what to do but call a wrecker, and that was hardly feasible in the current circumstances. I tried rocking the car back and forth — from drive to reverse and back again — but all that did was dig us in deeper.

Then there was a jarring bump from behind, snapping our heads as the big truck made contact. Another bump and Leigh screamed, Lloyd turned to look back, and I just knew we were about to be crushed by the monster behind us.

I couldn't sit still for that, so with a spurt of high dudgeon, I shoved the gearshift into Park, unbuckled my seat belt, threw open the door, swiveled my rubber boot-clad feet out onto the muddy road, stood up, and almost slid into the ditch. Hanging on to the door was the only thing that saved me from an inglorious exit on my backside. It didn't matter. I'd had enough and intended to put a stop to such uncalled-for harassment.

"Get back in!" Lloyd yelled, trying to

466

unbuckle himself. "What're you doing?"

I barely heard him or Lillian, who was screaming as she tried to get out of the backseat. I pulled myself along by hanging on to the car, and then onto the hot hood of the truck. When I got to the driver's side window, I reached up and gave it an authoritative rap.

"Open this thing!" I yelled.

The window slid down, and a thin face with huge teeth, surrounded by stringy hair and a wispy beard, peered down at me. I reached up and grabbed his sideview mirror to keep from sliding under the truck.

"Young man, what do you think you're doing?" I yelled, having had as much as I could stand. "What's the matter with you?"

"Huh?"

"Stop ramming my car! You'll ruin it! And turn those lights down! You hear me? You're about to blind us."

"Uh, well, I 'uz jus' tryin' to he'p." But he dimmed his lights.

"Well, you're not helping, you're not helping one bit. You're a menace on the road, and I've had enough of it! Now get out of here and leave us alone!"

Having had my say, I turned to pull myself back to the car. He leaned out of the window and called, "Uh, ma'am, I got some burlap bags."

And that's how we got out of a hole in the road. Waymon placed the bags in front of the rear tires, I pressed the gas pedal, and the big car slid out as slick as you please. We learned that Waymon lived some way behind the cabin, and always checked it after a party for fear of fire.

"If them woods was to catch on far," he told us, as I strained to understand him, "we'uns wouldn't have a chance."

"True," I said, nodding soberly, but noting to myself that we'd had six straight days of heavy rain. But who was I to look a gift horse in the mouth?

CHAPTER 51

Lillian and I waited in the car while Lloyd walked Leigh to her front door. Every light in the house was on, and when we'd pulled to the curb, Leigh had moaned at the sight.

"They're gonna kill me," she said.

And well they should, I thought, for it was close to four o'clock, long past any reasonable homecoming for a teenager. Leigh's parents met them at the door, so I expected Lloyd to hurry back to the car. He didn't. The four of them stood in the doorway, talking and talking, along with a little arm waving, until finally the door closed and Lloyd trudged back to us.

"Now I know what it means," he said, slumping into the front seat and closing the car door.

"What?"

"No good deed goes unpunished," he said. "They thought I'd kept Leigh out this late."

469

"She didn't explain?" I asked, driving away.

He shook his head. "She just cried. But telling what really happened would've made it worse."

"They'll find out sooner or later," I said, reaching over to pat his knee. "You did a really good deed tonight, honey, and Leigh knows it."

"I guess," he said, as if resigned to the inevitable. "Lot of good it'll do, though, 'cause she's grounded till graduation. And," he went on, "she's a sophomore."

I couldn't help it — I started laughing and couldn't stop. Lillian joined in, and finally so did Lloyd. I was so giddy with fatigue and anxiety that it was all I could do to keep the car steady on a straight, paved, empty, and unmuddied street.

Even Lillian slept late that morning and so, I thought, had Lloyd. He'd spent what was left of the night with us, for fear of waking his mother if he'd gone home. But now, down the stairs he came just as I was pouring the first cup of coffee.

He stopped short when he saw me. "I didn't think you'd be up," he said.

"You, either. You want some toast? I'm letting Lillian sleep, so you'll have to have a make-do breakfast."

"No'm, I better get home. My note to Mama just said I was spending the night with you, but she'll be worried. What do you think I ought to I tell her?"

"Everything," I said. "Tell her everything — where and why we were tooling all over Abbot County in the wee hours of the night. She should know what a good friend you are. Besides," I went on, "pretty soon everybody's going to know what went on last night. Now," I went on, pushing my phone in front of him, "show me how to access all those pictures we took."

"What're you going to do?" He picked up the phone, punched a few buttons, then handed it to me. "Like this," he said. "You want the pictures on mine? We took a lot in the other rooms."

"Yes, I want them all, and what I'm going to do is take them to the sheriff this morning. I want something done about that place. And if the sheriff won't do it, I'll take them to the *Abbotsville Times*." Then, noting the concerned look on his face, I added, "So I want you to look through them and be sure there're no pictures of any of us. Or of anybody. And that reminds me — see if you can find out if Stacy got home all right."

He nodded. "Okay, I can do that."

"And," I went on, pointing to the phones, "see if you can isolate just the pictures of the evidence left behind — the bottles, the cans, and most of all, the prescription vials. There were too many of those little bottles to have come from home medicine cabinets. Somebody, Lloyd, somebody in this town with access to a lot of drugs is supplying them to your friends. I want to find out who that somebody is."

"Could be dangerous, Miss Julia." But he kept fiddling with both phones, lining up a series of undeniable proofs of wrongdoing.

"No more than it already is. Think of your friends being mixed up with whoever's doing it — if that's not dangerous, I don't know what is. I see it as my civic duty to put a stop to it. But I don't want you involved — not even a whisper that you know anything about it. So after you talk to your mother, go on about your business today — and by the way, what are you doing today?"

"Helping J.D. at the Rosewood house. No telling when he'll be back, though."

"About noon," I said. "Sam's already called and they were just leaving Charlotte. He said they have a full truck to unload when they get here, so run on home, talk to your mother, and try to get a nap."

"Yes'm, okay, and thanks, Miss Julia. Thanks a lot for last night."

"Anytime, sugar," I said. Then with a wry smile, added, "Though not anytime soon, I hope. Take a look at my poor car before you go."

Thirty minutes later, I sat at the kitchen table with a cup of cold coffee beside me. I had carefully studied the pictures that Lloyd had lined up on both phones, magnifying some of them to confirm what I was seeing.

I had gone back and forth about Dr. Don Crawford, swinging from admiration to distrust and back again ever since he'd been in town. I hadn't known what to make of him, but now I did.

One picture on my phone — I think Lillian had taken it — of an amber vial lying on a floor with several others told the tale. It was turned so that only half the label was visible, but that was enough to recognize it as the one that had held fifty-nine overprescribed oxycodone tablets when I'd dropped it in Dr. Crawford's basket for foreign missions.

Now, with Lloyd gone and Lillian still sleeping, the house had settled into a Saturday-morning silence, and I continued to sit alone, pondering, wondering, trying to decide the best way to proceed.

My first impulse was to dump both phones on the sheriff and demand action, then to come home and call everyone I knew to warn them. But the thought of Bob Hargrove, who'd devoted his life to the care of his patients, returning to a ruined reputation and a practice scattered to the winds stopped me.

As I imagined the resulting fallout from publicizing what I knew, a few other possibilities occurred to me. What, I kept asking myself, would cause the least damage to the innocent, yet still nab the guilty? And how could I be sure that I'd correctly identified the guilty from the innocent?

Hesitantly, though reasonably sure that I had, I went to the telephone, looked up a number, and punched it in. While waiting an inordinate length of time for an answer, Lillian pushed through the swinging door.

"Who you callin' this early?" she asked on her way to the coffee pot.

"Mrs. Crawford," I said. "Mrs. Dr. Crawford."

After a brief, unsatisfactory exchange on the phone, I clicked off, stood thinking for a second or two, then turned to Lillian.

"She didn't sound so good," I said, "and

now I'm worried about those children."

"What she say?"

"Not much of anything, to be honest. Just some hemming and hawing, and no clear answers at all. Actually, she sounded half asleep." I frowned, replaying Lauren's responses in my mind. "Maybe I woke her up. It's still early."

"Not that early," Lillian said, " 'specially with two little chil'ren in the house. I say we go over there an' see, Miss Julia. Maybe she take a sleepin' pill last night an' can't shake it off this mornin'."

O, Lord, a sleeping pill? And I had a slew of pictures of empty sleeping pill bottles.

"Get your pocketbook, Lillian," I said, "and let's go."

My car looked as if it'd been in a road race on a cross-country track and sounded like it, too. As we drove to the Hargrove house, dried clumps of mud loosened from the tire treads clunked against the undercarriage, then spattered along the street. We were a moving spectacle, but my usual reserve was no longer operating. I didn't care.

I turned onto the curved drive that led to the front of the meticulously kept Hargrove house, thinking again of how lovely it was, and I don't even like ranch-style homes.

Painted white with Charleston green shutters, adorned with gas-lighted lanterns by the door, boxwoods lining the foundation, and a magnificent magnolia in the yard, it was easily one of the town's showplaces.

But what it looked like no longer mattered, either. All I was concerned with was what we would find inside. And it took us long enough to get inside — no one answered the doorbell, although Lillian rang it over and over.

"I think I'm worried now," Lillian said. "You jus' talked to her, so she oughtta be here."

"Stay here in case she answers," I said, turning to leave. "I'll try the back."

Little Olivia opened the back door when I rapped on it. She and her brother, Jason, were playing on the kitchen floor among empty cereal bowls, spilled milk, and several wet stuffed animals. Both children were still in their nightclothes.

"Where's your mother, sweetheart?" I asked, stepping inside.

Olivia looked toward the front of the house as if she might see her mother through the walls. "On the sofa," she said.

"Come take my hand, then, and let's go find her. You, too, Jason. Let's go find your mama." Sidestepping the toys, shoes, and

Cheerios on the floor, I let the children walk me through the house, stopping at the front door to let Lillian in.

"Oh, you sweet little things," she said, immediately taken with the children. "Le's us go get some dry clothes on. I b'lieve somebody spilt something."

"Jason did," Olivia said. "He spilled his milk."

I nodded to Lillian, then turned to enter Sue Hargrove's spacious and lovely living room, where I'd spent many a pleasant hour sipping tea and eating finger sandwiches.

Lauren Crawford, still in a nightgown, sat on the sofa with a blanket wrapped around her. There was a dazed look on her face, and it took a few seconds for her head to turn in my direction.

"Lauren," I said, drawing a chair close, "what can I do to help?"

She just shook her head, but her eyes filled, then lowered as she seemed to sink into herself.

"Have you taken anything?" I asked, reaching for her hand. "Some pills? Medicine of any kind?"

She shook her head again, then whispered, "I don't know what to do. I didn't know . . . all of it."

"Where is he now?"

Her eyes closed and a look so bereft crossed her face that my heart went out to her. Until, with a sudden recall of the past night, I decided that I'd had enough of sympathetic pampering. "Where is he?" I demanded.

"Gone," she whispered. "He's gone."

CHAPTER 52

And good riddance, I thought, then thought
better of it. No way should he be free to
prey on the children of other towns. An all-
points bulletin would bring him back forthwith — not only to face the music, but also
to face a town of irate citizens of which I
was currently the most enraged.

Assured by now that Lauren was not
under the influence — I'd checked the
pupils of her eyes — and in no immediate
danger, I took matters in hand.

"Get up and get dressed, Lauren," I said,
standing over her.

"I don't . . ."

"What you do or don't doesn't matter.
What *does* matter are your children, Sue's
house that's in a mess, and the whereabouts
of your husband. You can sit here all day
grieving over something you should've done
something about long ago, but it's going to
get done now. Get dressed, then come to

the kitchen. I'll have coffee made, and you're going to tell me everything."

Trained, it seemed, to obedience, Lauren sat at the kitchen table, fully dressed in another shapeless outfit, her hair pulled tight in a ponytail, and her face bare of any enhancement whatsoever.

Leaning my arms on the small table, I stared at her, then demanded, "Who's he selling to?"

"I don't think —"

"Yes, he is. Or *some*body in the office is, but they've all worked for Bob Hargrove for years and the only one left is your husband. *He's* the one who was collecting drugs for the mission field — drugs he'd overprescribed to patients whose names are still on the labels. And those very drugs showed up at a party for teenagers. *Teenagers,* Lauren. Children of people I *know.*" I had to stop and take a deep breath to tamp down the rage that swept over me.

"Now," I went on when I recovered, "Don Crawford may not've sold them directly, but he supplied them to somebody who did. And I want to know who that somebody is."

She bowed her head, then said, "I really don't . . ." Then after a glance at my face, she said, "He keeps a little book with phone numbers. Not in his phone — he doesn't trust it."

"How long has he been selling drugs?"

"I don't know. I don't know what he does. We just keep moving, but I didn't know about the drugs, I really didn't." She swallowed hard, then reached over to put her hand on my arm. "And it really wasn't him. I mean, personally, it wasn't. He told me he always made sure they'd go somewhere else."

Listening to her disjointed defense of her husband, I nodded. "Smart," I said, "until he fouled his nest by selling locally. I have pictures, Lauren, of prescription drug vials with his name on them, the names of local pharmacies, as well as patients' names of people I know."

Lauren's eyes began to fill. "They weren't supposed to be sold in the same town. He promised me that, and he didn't know about it until sometime last night, early this morning. But I, I didn't know. I promise I didn't, not till he packed up and left." She covered her face with her hands, crying. "He was so angry, but I didn't know about the drugs. I really didn't, I promise I didn't." She wiped her face with a napkin, took a deep breath, and went on. "He couldn't wait for us." Tears began to flow again, enraging me even more. "I don't know what I'll do."

"Get a grip, Lauren," I said, thinking of what Lloyd had seen through a window. "You have plenty of options, and number one is putting him in jail and keeping yourself out."

That got her attention, and she cried, "But I didn't know what he was doing!"

I sat and looked at her — a grown woman, mother of two, wife of a physician, at least partially educated, and now claiming to be unaware of what had gone on not only in Abbotsville, but apparently in other towns. Shrinking violets who would not face ugly facts, but had no problem profiting from them, did not elicit pity from me.

I folded my arms, sat back in my chair, and softly but very firmly asked, "What *did* you know, Lauren?"

"Sam," I said, clasping his hand tightly, "I declare, I am just done in. Lauren told it as if it was the most natural thing in the world. But how he's gotten away with it is beyond me — how he could've even dared such a thing."

"Unbelieveable," Sam said, nodding. "Think of the nerve it took to pull it off, not just once, but over and over. It's enough to knock your socks off. And we didn't have a clue."

We were sitting in the library late that night while I recounted the events of the previous night and of the morning, tying them in with what he'd learned from the sheriff during the hours he and Mr. Pickens had spent at the jail. Don Crawford had had the nerve to call them both when he'd been brought back and booked. He'd wanted them to put up his bail, if you can believe that.

J.D. Pickens had pulled the U-Haul truck to the curb at the Rosewood house a little after noon that Saturday, both he and Sam worn to a frazzle. With the help of Lloyd, James, Nate Wheeler from next door, and a couple of dollies, they'd stacked boxes in the house, locked the door, returned the truck, and gone home to rest. But not for long, for that was when they'd been called to put up bond to free the detained Dr. Crawford. Do I need to say that they refused? Yet they'd gone to see him in his cell, and Sam had come home stunned at the man's audacity in asking, and not only at that, but at his assumption that his abilities were needed by the town.

"He acted like it was all a misunderstanding," Sam said, shaking his head in disbelief. "Even expressed concern for his patients." Then with a wry smile, he said, "I thought Pickens was going to deck him."

"Well, I'm glad that neither of you did," I said, "although he certainly deserves it. But, Sam," I went on, "why in the world did Bob Hargrove bring him in? And turn all of us over to somebody totally unqualified? Didn't he look into his background?"

"He did, honey," Sam said. "I know he did, because I had breakfast with him when he was looking through résumés from several applicants. Crawford had the best background and outstanding recommendations, and he made a good impression when Bob interviewed him. These things," Sam went on, stretching out his legs, "are usually handled through accredited agencies. Doctors who're willing to temporarily take on a practice register with an agency, and doctors who need help get a list of the applicants, and a match is made. If anyone's at fault, it's the agency, but even with more diligence, I'm not sure Crawford would've been found out. From what the sheriff learned, he'd taken on the identity of someone who is highly qualified, who'd had excellent training in Canada, and who now works on some kind of hospital ship off

Africa. I'd guess that's how Crawford was able to pull it off."

"But he'd been doing it for *years* — how does someone live that way? And Lauren, *she* knew, although she claims she knew nothing about the drugs. But she'd known all along that he wasn't a real doctor, and she put up with it — aided and abetted him, even. I don't understand it, Sam."

"Well, I'm not excusing her, but think back. She wasn't putting up with it all that well, was she? He seemed to be thriving, but she was fading to the point of considering doing herself in."

"But, see," I said, sitting upright, "that's what I'm talking about. How can anybody allow themselves to be so cowed and downbeaten that they'd even think of such a thing? Why didn't she put her foot down? Why didn't she take those children and get away from it all?"

"I don't know, honey, but some people — mostly wives, I guess — feel trapped, especially with children to be cared for. They get in so deep that they can't see a way out."

"Well," I said with a huff, "I'd like to see a man do that to me." Then I stopped, realizing that to a certain extent I had let a man do that to me. "Oh, me," I said, rubbing my forehead, "it's only too easy, isn't it, not to rock the boat. To go on day by day, knowing that things aren't right, but hoping they'll get better." I sat back and sighed, then recalled Lloyd's front-row seat on a rear window. "Maybe Lauren saw Nate Wheeler as a way out."

"She could do worse," Sam said, smiling.

"Worse?" I said. "Unfortunately, she already has." Then, as a wave of sadness washed over me, I asked, "What's going to happen to her, Sam?"

"Nothing, probably. Legally, I mean. She'll be seen as a victim, especially if she testifies against him."

"Well, I'm just glad they caught him, and so quickly, too. The way he knows how to turn himself into somebody else, it's a wonder that they did. But he didn't expect Lauren to give him away, especially as quickly as she did."

"No, and he didn't expect that certain vigilantes — who should've been home in bed — would come along and collect undeniable evidence."

"Well," I said with appropriate modesty, "we got lucky. But I'll tell you, Sam, I couldn't believe how fast the sheriff's department went into action. When they heard what Lauren had to say, then looked at the pictures Lloyd and Lillian took, they really hopped to."

Then with a surge of regret, I said, "Poor Waymon. He found himself in the same pickle as Lloyd — doing a good deed and getting blamed for it."

"Yeah," Sam said, "but after a few questions, it was plain that he wasn't the contact. I heard one of the deputies say nobody'd trust him to *sell* drugs. He'd take them himself."

"Well, bless his heart anyway," I said. "But I hope they find out who Don's contact is — whoever it was that bought drugs from him, then sold them to our children. And I hope they string him up when they do."

Sam nodded. "Crawford will tell. That kind always does when a little leniency is offered."

"That kind doesn't deserve any leniency. They ought to lock him up for life. But you know, Sam," I said, marveling at the thought, "*we* should've caught on that something was wrong. Remember how he didn't go to the emergency room to see Horace? And remember how he discouraged walk-ins? Probably because they were more likely to have acute problems. To say nothing of prescribing too many toxic drugs to too many patients. To tell the truth, I thought he was lazy, but, in fact, he was avoiding situations that would reveal how little he knew. But," I went on, "on the other hand, I can't forget how decent he was to Lloyd. He couldn't have been nicer."

Sam nodded. "He had it down to an art, all right, including how to avoid police reports and insurance investigations. Plenty of practice, I guess." Then he smiled at the unintended pun.

"I wonder, though," I said, musing over the possibilities, "just what Lauren will do — she'll have to stay around, for a while at least, to testify. Hazel Marie, bless her heart, has taken in her and the children, but that has to be temporary."

The telephone rang then and, since Sam answered it, I heard only one side of the conversation. He came back to the sofa, a pleased look on his face.

"That was Pickens," he said, sitting beside me. "He just got back from the sheriff's office and they're moving right along. The sheriff took it on himself to call Bob Hargrove in Sweden or somewhere and let him know that his practice is about to go to hell in a handbasket. Sorry, honey — I'm just quoting my source."

I laughed. "Oh, good. I'll be so glad to have our doctor back in town, especially since you helped move boxes today and I fully expect you to be laid up with back pain again." After Sam's strenuous day, I was worried that his back would flare up at any minute, so I'd been trying to distract him and myself from the fact that we were now without a physician, other than some nameless hospitalist. Which, come to think of it, would be better than the make-believe doctor we'd been trusting.

Sam raised his right hand. "I only supervised."

"Well, I'm sorry that Bob and Sue's vacation has to be cut short and that they'll be coming back to an absolute mess. But what a relief it'll be to have our real doctor back in town."

"He'll probably never take another vacation," Sam said with a wry twist of his mouth.

"I shouldn't be selfish about it, but I hope he won't." Then at a sudden thought, I sat up straight. "Oh, Sam, you know what? We need to get Sue's house cleaned up — I don't mean you, I mean me, Lillian, James, Hazel Marie, and, yes, Lauren. She can pack their things and move them out, and the rest of us can do the cleaning. Actually, it's not dirty, just disorderly — you can't walk without stepping on Cheerios."

"Have you thought of where Lauren can

move out to? Or has she?"

"I doubt it," I said. "I spoke with Hazel Marie right before you got home, and she said that Lauren still seems to be in a daze, doing what she's told, but otherwise just staring off into space." I stopped and thought a minute. "Maybe she needs to see a doctor."

"I wouldn't doubt that," Sam said, "but in the meantime, I have an idea. I'll be back in a minute — the phone number's upstairs."

He was gone longer than a minute, but when he came back he had another pleased look on his face. "Got us some more help," he said. "Nate Wheeler will help move Lauren and the children into Crawford's house on Rosewood. He says he's finished with it except for a few touch-ups, which he'll do tomorrow."

"Why, Sam," I said, surprised by what he seemed to be arranging. "Is that wise? She's in no state to . . . well, whatever."

"She needs a place to live, and that place is available. And it's hers, at least for the time being.

"Now," he said, sitting down and taking my hand, "let's talk about that car of yours. It's a mess, honey."

"Well, I told you we had to go get Leigh Swanson at that house, and —"

"But you didn't tell me you had to go through hell and high water to get there. It's not only caked with mud inside *and* out, it's scratched from one end to the other, and the back fender's bent, and no telling what else is wrong. You didn't let Lloyd drive, did you?"

"No," I said, drawing back at the thought, "absolutely not. I took the wheel, and I take full responsibility. Besides, it'll clean up. Won't it?"

"Well, if it won't," Sam said, giving me a sidewise teasing glance as he reached for my hand, "you can buy that little Boxster next door."

I laughed. "Oh, that would be just perfect for me. I can see it now — I'll have to have a pair of big shades and a long scarf to flap in the wind. And I'll need some driving gloves, maybe a leather jacket . . ."

"And," Sam said, "a couple of felt dice to dangle from the rearview mirror."

"Yes," I said, picturing it all, "and I'll need piles of high-end shopping bags in the back."

"And a good-looking man beside you."

"Oh, I have that," I said, leaning into him. "I already have that right here."

ABOUT THE AUTHOR

Ann B. Ross is the author of more than a dozen novels featuring the popular Southern heroine Miss Julia, as well as *Etta Mae's Worst Bad-Luck Day,* a novel about one of Abbotsville's other most outspoken residents: Etta Mae Wiggins. Ross holds a doctorate in English from the University of North Carolina at Chapel Hill, and has taught literature at the University of North Carolina at Asheville. She lives in Hendersonville, North Carolina.

The employees of Thorndike Press hope you have enjoyed this Large Print book. All our Thorndike, Wheeler, and Kennebec Large Print titles are designed for easy reading, and all our books are made to last. Other Thorndike Press Large Print books are available at your library, through selected bookstores, or directly from us.

For information about titles, please call:
(800) 223-1244

or visit our website at:
gale.com/thorndike

To share your comments, please write:
Publisher
Thorndike Press
10 Water St., Suite 310
Waterville, ME 04901

PLC

5/19

Bruton Memorial Library

3 1667 13792 9435